Praise for
THE RETRIEVAL ARTIST SERIES

One of the top ten greatest science fiction detectives of all time.

—*io9*

The SF thriller is alive and well, and today's leading practitioner is Kristine Kathryn Rusch.

—*Analog*

[Miles Flint is] one of 14 great sci-fi and fantasy detectives who out-Sherlock'd Holmes. [Flint] is a candidate for the title of greatest fictional detective of all time.

—*Blastr*

Part *CSI*, part *Blade Runner,* and part hard-boiled gumshoe, the retrieval artist of the series title, one Miles Flint, would be as at home on a foggy San Francisco street in the 1940s as he is in the domed lunar colony of Armstrong City.

—*The Edge Boston*

What links [Miles Flint] to his most memorable literary ancestors is his hard-won ability to perceive the complex nature of morality and live with the burden of his own inevitable failure.

—*Locus*

Readers of police procedurals as well as fans of SF should enjoy this mystery series.

—*Kliatt*

Instant addiction. You hear about it—maybe you even laugh it off—but you never think it could happen to you. Well, you just haven't run into Miles Flint and the other Retrieval Artists looking for The Disappeared. ...I am hopelessly hooked....

—Lisa DuMond
MEviews.com on *The Disappeared*

An inventive plot and complex, conflicted characters increases the appeal of Kristine Kathryn Rusch's *Extremes*. This futuristic tale breaks new ground as a space police procedural and should appeal to science fiction and mystery fans.

—*RT Book Reveiws* on *Extremes*

Part science fiction, part mystery, and pure enjoyment are the words to describe Kristine Kathryn Rusch's latest Retrieval Artist novel.... This is a strong murder mystery in an outer space storyline.

—*The Best Reviews* on *Consequences*

An exciting, intricately plotted, fast-paced novel. You'll find it difficult to put down.

—*SFRevu* on *Buried Deep*

A science fiction murder mystery by one of the genre's best.... A book with complex characters, an interesting and unpredictable plot, and timeless and universal things to say about the human condition.

—*The Panama News* on *Paloma*

Rusch continues her provocative interplanetary detective series with healthy doses of planet-hopping intrigue, heady legal dilemmas and well-drawn characters.

—*Publishers Weekly* on *Recovery Man*

…the mystery is unpredictable and absorbing and the characters are interesting and sympathetic.

—*Blastr* on *Duplicate Effort*

Anniversary Day is an edge-of-the-seat thriller that will keep you turning pages late into the night and it's also really good science fiction. What's not to like?

—*Analog* on *Anniversary Day*

Set in the not too distant future, the latest entry in Rusch's popular sf thriller series (*The Disappeared; Duplicate Effort*) combines fast-paced action, beautifully conflicted protagonists, and a distinctly "sf noir" feel to tell a complex and far-reaching mystery. VERDICT Compulsively readable with canny plot twists, this should appeal to series fans as well as action-suspense readers.

—*Library Journal* on *Anniversary Day*

Rusch offers up a well-told mystery with interesting characters and a complex, riveting storyline that includes a healthy dose of suspense, all building toward an ending that may not be what it appears.

—*RT Book Reviews* on *Blowback*

The latest Retrieval Artist science fiction thriller is an engaging investigative whodunit starring popular Miles Flint on a comeback mission. The suspenseful storyline is fast-paced and filled with twists as the hero comes out of retirement to confront his worst nightmare.

—*Midwest Book Review* on *Blowback*

We always like our intergalactic politics as truly alien, and Rusch delivers the goods. It's one thing to depict members of a Federation whining about treaties, quite another to depict motivations that are truly, well, alien.

—*Astroguyz* on *Blowback*

ANNIVERSARY DAY

A RETRIEVAL ARTIST NOVEL

KRISTINE KATHRYN RUSCH

*wmg*PUBLISHING

Anniversary Day

Book One of the Anniversary Day Saga

Published 2014 by WMG Publishing
www.wmgpublishing.com
First published in 2011 by WMG Publishing
Cover and Layout copyright © 2014 by WMG Publishing
Cover design by Allyson Longueira/WMG Publishing
Cover art copyright © Yvonne Less/Dreamstime, Philcold/Dreamstime
ISBN-13: 978-0-615-52179-4
ISBN-10: 0-615-52179-7

For the Fans.
Your enthusiasm for this series has kept it alive.
Thank you.

Acknowledgements

Thanks to my husband Dean Wesley Smith, who wrested the manuscript out of my hands when I got overwhelmed by the sheer vastness of this story. Many, many thanks to Annie Reed for her insightful comments. Thanks to the Sunday Lunch crew for helping me plan my moonscape. Thanks also to Colleen Kuehne for watching my back. Writers never work alone, and you folks helped me more than you know. All mistakes, however, are my own.

Author's Note

Dear Readers,

I never quite know what to expect when I write.

You have in your hands the first book of The Anniversary Day Saga. I had no idea this was the first book when I finished the book in 2011. Then I thought it was the first book of two, maybe the first of three.

What I didn't realize was how big this universe really was. And as the next book, Blowback, *unfolded, I caught a glimpse of the scope of the story that I'm telling.*

I did not intend for this saga to happen. It wasn't in my vague outline for the Retrieval Artist series.

When I first designed the Retrieval Artist Universe, I had two goals in mind. First, I wanted to do standalone mystery stories set in space. Each book would resolve the main issues, but the characters would learn and grow and become different.

I managed that through eight books, and I will go back to it when the saga is done.

Second, I wanted some books to focus on other characters besides Flint. This too is modeled on the mystery genre. I have always said that this series is my 87th Precinct. That's a reference to Ed McBain, who wrote dozens of books about the precinct, and rotated his characters in and out of the novels. Some books would focus on a few of the characters, others would focus on different characters.

I achieved that a little in some of the first eight books, but not as much as I wanted to. I planned side stories, and wrote some novellas in which Flint either doesn't appear (The Recovery Man's Bargain) *or in which he has a small role* (The Possession of Paavo Deshin).

Honestly, I see these books continuing as long as I'm alive to write them, in one form or another, covering one character or another. I'll bill the books with Flint as Retrieval Artist books and those that are set in the universe without Flint as Retrieval Artist Universe novels.

Which is a long way of telling you why I'm starting this book with a letter to the readers. Those of you who've read all of the first eight books know that Flint wanted to retire while he raised Talia. The next book in the series—number nine—was originally titled Talia's Revenge. *It starts after Talia gets out of school.*

I started writing that book, and realized that I was mostly writing back story—"and this happened in that year, and this happened in that year." Not only is that dull to read, but it skips over major things. I knew a lot of stuff happened. I also knew that Flint wasn't deeply involved.

I figured (dumb me) that I could write all of the important stuff in one book. As a writer, I often lie to myself like that when I start a novel. I wrote Anniversary Day *and realized it was the first third of a very big book. So I wrote* Blowback, *the second part.*

Then I started the third book—and I had to explain to myself what happened off-stage, outside of Armstrong. The first thing I wrote, a novella called A Murder of Clones, *which happens in the past, was 30,000 words long. Still, I thought, I could do it. I would just write a little more.*

Many, many, many words later, I finished the saga. WMG Publishing is releasing the six unpublished books in the saga in the first six months of 2015, so that readers can binge if they want to. Also, it's easier to read an entire story without years between "episodes."

I hope this works for you. And I promise, the next RA novel after this saga ends will stand alone—like the first eight did. (And no, I don't know when we'll get to Talia's Revenge. *I suspect there are one or two other novels that must come first. But I will finish it. Just not in 2015. I need a bit of a rest, after writing six Retrieval Artist novels in a row.)*

Here's the first book of the saga. I hope you enjoy the journey. I certainly enjoyed writing it.

—Kristine Kathryn Rusch
Lincoln City, Oregon
August 10, 2014

ANNIVERSARY DAY

A RETRIEVAL ARTIST NOVEL

THE BOMBING
(FOUR YEARS AGO)

1

BARTHOLOMEW NYQUIST PARKED HIS AIRCAR IN ONE OF THE HOVERLOTS at the end of the neighborhood. The dome was dark this morning, even though someone should have started the Dome Daylight program. Maybe they had, deciding that Armstrong was in for a "cloudy" day—terminology he never entirely understood, given that the Moon had no clouds and most people who lived here had been born on the Moon and had never seen a cloud in their entire lives.

He grabbed his laser pistol from the passenger seat. He always kept the pistol on the passenger seat when he was traveling, just in case something happened. He tucked the pistol in his shoulder holster, hidden under his already-rumpled suit coat, and got out of the car.

The neighborhood looked even darker than it should have, sprawled below him like something out of those Dickens Christmas plays his ex-wife loved so much. All it needed was some sooty smoke coming out of chimneys above each house to be authentically dreary.

Oh, his mood was bad. And for that, he could probably only blame himself. He should "buck up"—wasn't that what Chief of the First Detective Unit, Andrea Gumiela, had told him yesterday? *Buck up, Bartholomew. Everyone gets divorced. And yours was two years ago. The attitude was understandable last year. This year, it's becoming a problem.*

3

That after she made him watch the entire complaint vid his now-former partner had filed. Nyquist knew the complaints already, having heard them from previous partners and in his divorce proceeding: surly, impossible to work with, superior. Conversations filled with biting sarcasm— and that was on a good day. On a bad day, he didn't communicate at all.

And on this day, he didn't have to. Still on the force, still a homicide detective, and still without a new partner. He would have partner tryouts all week. The brass wanted to keep Nyquist. He had the best closing rate on the force. The problem was that regulations stated he needed a partner. He stated that he didn't. He worked better alone.

Gumiela knew that, but she followed the rules. Which was why she was his boss instead of the other way around.

Nyquist took the stairs to the sidewalk. He hated these cases in the outer districts of Armstrong. The row houses here rented for less than apartments downtown, but apartments were nicer. A lot of these houses had landlords who only owned one or two properties, and couldn't afford the upkeep. It showed in dingy walls that hadn't been upgraded in decades. Moon dust stains still clung to some of the siding, even though Moon dust had been cleared out of this area since the dome improvements two decades ago.

Not every part of the city was Moon-dust free, particularly Old Armstrong, which had stupid historic regulations that prevented certain kinds of upkeep. But Nyquist knew this neighborhood didn't have that kind of regulation, and so the lack of upkeep was either a financial or a business decision.

Not that he cared about the upkeep of houses as it pertained to regulations. He cared about it as it pertained to the kind of people living inside—people on the edge of hopelessness, people whose economic future wasn't quite bleak but could be with just one disaster, one horrible thing gone wrong.

When he reached the street, he peered around the corner, saw two squads, white-and-blue lights turning, crime scene lasers already up. He should've parked down here, but he'd needed the walk. Besides, on days

4

like this, he didn't want to be part of the squad. He liked being on his own, and parking his car away from the scene let him keep his autonomy.

He knew he would need it.

He sighed. He was supposed to contact Dispatch the moment he arrived in the neighborhood and he'd been putting it off. He knew what they would say. A tryout partner would be waiting for him at the scene. Gumiela had already done this to him once. A tryout partner on scene showed the brass whether or not Nyquist and the newbie worked well together.

It also prevented Nyquist from rejecting the new partner outright, based on clothes, appearance, or general lack of verbal defensive ability.

The question was which of those people loitering outside the crime scene was the one he'd be stuck with all day long.

Couldn't put it off any longer. He sent a ping to Dispatch through his links, hoping they'd only look at his location and not try to contact him.

Instead, a tiny image of this morning's dispatch—a woman with dark hair and matching dark circles under her eyes—appeared in the lower left corner of his vision. He hated that most of all. Couldn't they just use audio like everyone else on the Force?

"Detective Nyquist." It looked like she was speaking aloud as well as sending through the links. For the record? Probably. No one wanted to get in trouble because *he* got in trouble. "You'll be meeting your new partner at the scene. Her name is Ursula Palmette—"

Newly Minted Detective. I got it, he sent, deliberately not speaking out loud for any record.

"No, detective, not that newly minted at all. She has worked as a detective for five months."

What happened to her training partner? he sent. He stopped only a few meters from the house that seemed to be the center of attention. He didn't want to go any further while having this conversation.

"Early retirement," the dispatch said.

For some bad conduct? Nyquist sent.

"No, sir. Family troubles. His wife is dying and he didn't want to spend the last year of her life working."

5

That surprised him. He felt color touch his cheeks, something that didn't happen to him often. He was glad it happened before he met Palmette. He didn't want to step in it at the very beginning of their relationship.

All right, he sent, not acknowledging his discomfort or the slight reprimand the dispatch had given him. *Anything else I need to know?*

"Just that the officers on site say that they're ready for you, sir."

He was beginning to seriously dislike this dispatch. Who was she to subtly reprimand him like that?

Instead of challenging her, he just severed the link and walked the remaining few meters to the crime scene. Police line lasers gave the fake grass a reddish tint. An ambulance was parked sideways behind one of the squad cars, lights off.

He found that a curious detail. Either the ambulance wasn't needed and it could go off elsewhere, or it was needed and it had to stay, in which case its warning lights would be on low.

Two officers stood in front of the crime scene lasers. A tiny woman with a cap of brown hair leaned against one of the squads, holding a steaming cup of something—probably coffee—in her right hand.

As Nyquist approached, she stood.

"Detective Nyquist," she said. "I'm—"

"Ursula Palmette," he said, resisting the urge to add "newly minted detective." "I suppose you have documentation for me?"

She extended her hand. He hated chip-to-chip information transfer, but it was department policy these days. He grabbed her hand in a relatively loose grip, and felt the chip in the center of his palm warm, which was a signal that the information exchange was not only complete but accepted.

In the past, he'd go through a speech—*I'm the lead on this case. You shouldn't question my authority. I'll do all the talking*—but she already had had a training officer and she should know this crap. Besides, he'd been told by his previous two partners that his little opening speech was off-putting. He decided not to put Detective Ursula Palmette off. He simply did not have the energy for it.

"What do we know?" he asked.

"Well, sir," she said, then paused. "It is sir, right? Or do you prefer Detective? Or Bartholomew?"

"I prefer to know why the hell I'm here." He hated all the protocol with names. He certainly wasn't going to let her call him Bartholomew, which seemed to be what she was angling for. He didn't like casual relationships between partners. He preferred formality. She'd figure it out.

She nodded. She couldn't have been more than thirty, with that fresh-faced, straight-out-of-the-academy look. He preferred his partners to have worked their way to the detective squad, not get fast-tracked through so-called police education.

He didn't say that, which he would have had he met her in the precinct. Instead, he watched her peel the lid off her drink, which made it steam all the more, sending a smell of cinnamon and milk into the air, turning his stomach. She took a sip before saying anything else, as if the drink fortified her somehow.

"Um," she said, pressing the lid back on the cup. "We have a body —"

He resisted the urge to roll his eyes. Of course they had a body. They were *homicide* detectives. Someone had to die for the street cops to call him in.

"—in the front room of the house. The woman inside called it in. The responding officers say something is a little off in the entire thing."

"A little off?" Nyquist said.

Palmette shrugged. "Their words. You can talk to them. I was instructed not to do any investigating until you arrived."

Because he had the high closure rate, and one of his complaints about partners was that they made his job harder, not easier. They asked the wrong questions, contaminated crime scenes all by their little lonesome, and compromised witnesses.

"And yet you know about the body, and the scene being a little off," he said.

"Because Officer Saxe—," and she nodded at a young cop with curly red hair and copper skin standing near one of the squads, "—told me the minute I arrived. I told him we had to wait for you, and so he stopped. You want to talk to him now, sir?"

So she was going to stick with "sir." Fine.

"No," Nyquist said. "I want to see the interior. Got a suit?"

By that, he meant protective covering for her skin and clothes. Most rookie detectives had to make do with the full-body suits that the cops gave to civilians at crime scenes, but she tapped her arm.

"Already on, sir," she said.

That was when he noticed that her clothes were just a bit shiny. He took one of his protective suits out of the pocket of his coat. The suit was the size of his thumbnail, until he attached it to the button on his sleeve and tapped it.

Then the damn thing enveloped him. He hated that moment—it felt like walking into a gigantic spider web, which he had done once as a kid on vacation with his parents on Earth—and then the feeling went away.

"Okay," he said as he blocked the crime scene laser with his palm. Another chip on his palm made sure that none of the warning sirens went off. He stepped onto the fake grass and waited for Palmette to join him. "Let's see what we've got."

2

THE FRONT DOOR WAS OPEN, JUST LIKE IT WAS SUPPOSED TO BE, WITH one more officer stationed outside. He nodded at Nyquist as Nyquist went inside.

The interior was very dark, even though the lights were on. They didn't seem to have enough power to penetrate the house's gloom. The place smelled funky too—not just the smell of death, which, while Nyquist wasn't used to it, was at least something he expected at a crime scene.

No, this place smelled of greasy cooked food, coffee, and garbage. The front room was square and somewhat useless, standard in a row house like this one, where it seemed like the architect couldn't decide whether this room was an entry or a living area, so he decided to turn it into both.

Usually tenants turned the front room into one or the other. As Nyquist's eyes adjusted, he realized that the people who lived here had gone with the original architect's vision and kept it as both. Two faux-leather chairs leaned against the wall separating this room from the next (probably a kitchen). A table covered with dirty dishes, clothes, and some decorative rocks squeezed between the two chairs.

On the left side of the door was a mat for shoes, which were scattered haphazardly. Some kind of plastic runner made a trail between the door and the kitchen, leading him to a supposition.

Whoever lived here had lived on Earth. Or somewhere Earthlike, somewhere with weather that changed daily, got on the shoes, and had to be accommodated when a person came inside.

Soft voices murmured farther into the house. Palmette brushed up against him. He could feel her impatience. She wanted to get inside and look at the body.

She didn't realize that the body was the king of the chessboard—the reason for the investigation, but not the center of the investigation. Everything else was much more important, and if Nyquist didn't look at the details now, he would run the risk of missing even more in the future.

The walls were unadorned except for a series of coat hooks above the shoes, and a public access terminal on the wall beside the chairs. The terminal's screen was dark and covered with some kind of slime—probably that grease he was smelling—indicating that it hadn't been used in years.

Which meant that the people who lived in this house had their own way of connecting to the nets. They were probably linked, and unless there was a public viewing screen in another room, they seemed to prefer to entertain themselves rather than share entertainment.

Palmette stepped beside him, apparently trying to go in, but he blocked her with his arm.

"What are we doing?" she asked.

"Working," he said. If she couldn't figure it out, that was her problem. Hopefully, it wouldn't become his.

The body lay in a little nook beside the door, on the opposite side of the room from the shoes, and just in front of the chairs. That small section of wall had a window, which Nyquist knew from being outside, but the window wasn't just blocked off. It was covered with some kind of blackout material, so that no one could see in or out. So that it seemed like a part of the wall, instead of something that looked out upon the street.

Strange. He wondered if the other windows were blocked off. It would explain the smell. The house had its own air circulation system— all houses in Armstrong did—but they were enhanced by the circulation system in the dome. Open windows allowed an air exchange that kept everything fresher. Besides, the dome had stronger filters, so the air coming in was cleaner than the air going out.

He went a little farther in, staying on the runner. "Stand beside me," he said to Palmette. "Don't get on the carpet yet."

"Did we put this mat down?" she asked, revealing just how new she was.

"No," he said and crouched.

The body belonged to a man, folded in a near-fetal position. Blood pooled beneath the torso, and the face—aside from spatter—was undamaged. Hands and arms cradled around the abdomen. Impossible to tell how tall he was, but Nyquist got a sense of athletic solidity. The muscles in the legs, visible through the tailored pants, seemed pronounced. The hands had a muscularity to them as well, one that extended up the wrist. That, combined with broad shoulders, made Nyquist think that this man was probably tall as well.

Nyquist couldn't tell if the athletic ability was real or enhanced, and it probably didn't matter. What mattered was that this man appeared strong, and somehow someone had brought him down.

The man's hair was short with tight, black curls against his well-shaped skull. His eyes and mouth were open. He looked to be mid-thirties.

The corpse had a smell all its own. Loosened muscles usually meant loose bowels, but this stench was greater than that. Nyquist extended a hand, silently warning Palmette to stay back, then he stood and took two steps forward.

The carpet squished beneath his feet. More blood lost than what was obvious. Nyquist nodded to himself.

He went a little farther and crouched again. Hands clasped around the belly, not to cover a single laser wound, but to keep the insides from escaping. Something had gutted him—some kind of blade, probably— and had pierced his intestines in more than one place.

That explained the smell.

The man's hands were covered in black fluids. If this was his only wound, it had taken him some time to die. And he had been in agony.

Nyquist stood.

"Can I see now?" Palmette asked.

"If you want," he said, and squelched across the carpet to the front door. He scraped the lower part of his protective gear off, handed it to the officer to bag for a crime scene tech, and got out another suit for a second lower layer of protective gear.

Then he went back inside, ignoring Palmette, who crouched near the body, her feet exactly where his had been. He raised his eyebrows in surprise. At least she followed some rules. If she followed most, she might actually be a possible for a long-term partner.

He forgot all about her, though, as he stepped into the next room. It was a kitchen. The walls were legitimately grease-stained, like he expected from the smell. He had no idea how much work—or grease—it took to cover walls like that. Someone had to shut off the walls' self-cleaning feature or completely overwhelm it.

At the moment, he voted for overwhelm. Dishes stacked everywhere and all of them filthy. He had no idea how anyone could even live here, let alone cook here.

No one stood in the kitchen, not that there was a lot of room. It was more of a galley kitchen than a full kitchen. Someone—long ago—had changed this row house's standard design and cut the kitchen in half; an odd choice, he thought.

He stepped through the next door and found out why. A full formal dining room stood here and surprisingly, this room was clean. Stairs curved up the side of the room and disappeared into bedrooms above.

A woman sat at the head of the table, her eyes wide as she looked at him. He got a sense of nervous containment, as if she would jump toward him at any moment. Another woman—this one an officer— sat in a close chair, her hands wrapped around a coffee mug that was still full.

Smart woman. She hadn't had anything to drink from the mug, even though it had clearly been offered to her.

"I'm Bartholomew Nyquist," he said softly to the woman at the head of the table. "I'm the detective they sent over to talk to you."

Normally, he would have introduced himself as the detective in charge of the scene or the crime or the death, but he had a sense that would be the wrong thing to say here.

The woman, whose skin had an odd blotchiness, bit her lower lip.

"This is Alvina Ingelow," the officer said. "She lives here."

"Thank you, Officer," he said in his most gentle tone, not for her sake, but for the woman's. "Give us a few minutes alone, if you don't mind."

The officer nodded and stood. She looked like she wanted to say more, but she didn't.

Instead, he added, "If you don't mind waiting outside. I'll catch up with you in a few minutes."

Meaning he, not Palmette, would talk to her. He hoped the officer understood that. He didn't want her to talk to anyone other than him. She probably had some early arrival information that he couldn't get any other way, and he wanted to be the first to hear it.

He touched a chip on each hand, recording the conversation. But he didn't tell Alvina Ingelow he was doing that. He didn't want to scare her. He'd let her know in a while. He'd used this technique before, and while it was dicey legally, the information he got from these interviews usually remained part of the court case.

"I know you told the officer what happened," he said, and the woman nodded—a bit too eagerly, he thought. "But I want you to tell me. Take your time. I know this is hard."

She shot him a grateful look. The sympathy was calming her. Good, because he thought she was wrapped just a bit too tightly, even for someone who had just discovered a body in her home.

"I was coming home," she said. "I opened the door, and there he was."

Nyquist nodded, but didn't say anything. He had promised her time, so he wasn't going to derail her with questions. Not yet.

"I sent for help through the links, and then your people came. And the ambulance. They sent an ambulance." As if she were surprised by that. He would have to listen to the link contact. He wondered if she had said the man was injured.

Nyquist waited for a good minute, his gaze steady on hers. Her eyes were as odd as she was. The pupils seemed to vibrate ever so slightly. He wondered if that was a trick of the light, an enhancement of some kind that he wasn't familiar with, an effect of a link, or some kind of drug interaction.

But he didn't ask that either. He'd learned long ago to take investigations slowly, to absorb the information as it came to him, to study the people surrounding the deceased and to make suppositions, but not to assume they were facts.

When she didn't say anything more, he realized that was her story. Remarkable in its brevity and lack of emotion.

So he would have to ask questions after all. The trick now was to ask the right questions to draw out her story, not to direct it.

"You said you were coming home." He was careful to repeat her language. "From where?"

"Work," she said, folding her hands in front of him. The movement caught his eye. "I got the night shift."

Her hands were remarkably clean. They were probably the cleanest thing in this entire house, except for her dress, which was also clean, if a bit rumpled.

"Where do you work, exactly?" he asked.

She waved one of those very clean hands. "Near the port. I'm a cocktail waitress."

No business near the port employed actual cocktail waitresses. All of the bars there used robotic servers, especially late at night. Some places did employ women under the job description cocktail waitress, but they didn't wait on anyone and they certainly didn't serve cocktails.

She was either a stripper or a sex worker. Neither profession was illegal, but neither was that socially acceptable either. He wanted to lean back and look at her body, but he didn't. He hadn't gotten the sense that she was enhanced the way strippers usually were. If she was a professional sex worker, her enhancements might not be visible.

He tried not to shudder in distaste.

"When does your shift end?" He didn't ask where she was employed. He would circle back to that in a moment. He wanted her to focus on what happened here, not on her discomfort at her own job.

"Six," she whispered.

The whisper caught him by surprise. She said it almost as if it were forbidden information.

"And you came right home?"

She bit her lower lip again.

"Did you walk?" That was the only way to explain the time discrepancy. He had been told that uniforms arrived at eight. If she'd found the body and called, it couldn't have been any later than six-thirty if she had come directly home.

She shook her head once.

"Car," she said, almost as softly as that whisper.

He nodded. Something else to circle back to. "And when you came in, he was here."

"Yes," she said.

"And who is he?"

"He thinks he's my boyfriend," she said with so much venom that Nyquist resisted the urge to lean back. "But he's not."

Nyquist let out a small breath. So many directions to take here, and given her emotion, only one was a good direction.

He tried not to look at those really clean hands. He wanted her to stand, so that he could see the rest of her, but this wasn't the moment to ask.

Or was it?

"Did you make some fresh coffee for the officer?" he asked. "Because I would love a cup."

She smiled at him. The smile warmed her face, made her seem young—almost childlike—as if his request pleased her somehow.

"Sure," she said, and stood up.

She was taller than he expected. She smoothed her dress—which was more of a long shirt—over her legs. They were covered in black tights. She wore heels so high that she tottered as she went into that galley kitchen.

He didn't stand, but he did turn slightly in his chair so that his back wasn't to her. He slid the chair silently sideways so that he could see her move in the kitchen.

Her figure wasn't spectacular, the way a stripper's would be. So she was most likely a sex worker. He would have to ask, or have Palmette do it, very delicately. This woman was on an edge, one he didn't like.

I opened the door and there he was.

He thinks he's my boyfriend. But he's not.

Dishes rattled in the kitchen. Nyquist could see her moving plates around to find a mug. He allowed himself a shudder this time and hoped she wouldn't take it as an insult when he didn't actually drink the coffee he had asked for.

As he waited, he sent a silent message through his links to Dispatch: *Need to hear the emergency call for this residence ASAP. Through private links only, please. And need a timestamp.*

He got an automated acknowledgement. This kind of request was routine, although not something that usually happened while on the scene. Usually the detective got the auxiliary information back at the precinct.

"Here you go." She came back, carrying two mugs by the handle. They steamed. She set his mug down in front of him, then put one in front of her place. She smiled at him again, which struck him as really strange, considering there was still a dead man in her front room, a dead man she claimed she knew.

"Thank you," Nyquist said, and smiled back.

As she sat down, he looked at her shoes. Clean. He hadn't expected that. He had expected some dried blood on the bottom. Anyone who had gone near that corpse would have blood on their shoes.

"What's the name of the gentleman in the front room?" Nyquist asked.

"He's not a gentleman," she snapped.

Again the mood shift was sudden, the vehemence almost tangible.

16

"My mistake," Nyquist said calmly. "What's the name of the man you called us about?"

"Callum," she said as if she didn't want the word to pass through her lips.

"Callum what?"

Her eyes narrowed. "Why?"

Why? He'd never been asked that before at this stage of an investigation. "Just so that we can put the right name on the files."

"Sheel," she said as if it were top secret.

"And he's been bothering you," Nyquist said.

"You have no idea," she said.

"You want to tell me about it?" he asked.

"Boy, do I ever," she said, and began to talk.

3

THE WOMAN—ALVINA—HAD ONLY BEEN TALKING FOR TEN MINUTES, but it felt like two hours. Nyquist had wrapped his hands around the coffee mug and tried not to think about its slimy exterior. She had been going through a list of grievances against this Callum Sheel, and at this point, Nyquist wasn't sure if they were real grievances or imagined ones.

At this point, he wasn't sure it mattered.

Out of the corner of his eye, he saw Palmette move into the kitchen. He cursed silently, then sent her a message through his links.

Back off. She's talking.

I'll just listen and record from in here, Palmette sent back.

No, you won't, he sent. *Back off. That's an order.*

The woman stopped talking. He wasn't sure if that was because she heard Palmette in the kitchen or if his expression had changed, letting his irritation at Palmette show.

"You don't believe me," the woman said.

"Oh, I do," Nyquist said. "He stalked you."

"Yes! That's the word." Then she peered at the kitchen. "You hear that?"

Get out, he sent to Palmette, but she hadn't moved. Dammit.

"That," the woman said in the calmest voice. Then she stood. "He's in the kitchen."

Crap. It was exactly what Nyquist thought. She was delusional.

She moved quicker than he expected, crossed the distance between her chair and the kitchen door in five seconds, maybe less. He stood, but not fast enough. She had already gone inside, her hand finding a knife as big as her forearm, and it looked like it was covered with something.

She wielded it like a pro, and Palmette, surprised, didn't grab her weapon. Instead she raised her hands like a victim.

Nyquist grabbed his weapon, but kept the muzzle pointed downward. He didn't want the woman to see it if he could at all avoid it. He wanted to keep what little trust he had built up.

"Alvina," he said softly.

"I told you he'd be back," she said. "I *told* you. He's right there, and he's going to call for help. House! Off!"

And suddenly everything went dark. She had a smart house, despite the state of that public wall link. A smart house set to make sure she had the advantage, not anyone else.

Get out of the damn kitchen, he sent to Palmette. *Now!*

"Alvina," he said out loud. "I need just a little light here so that I can see him. I'll help you with him."

Faint light rose above Nyquist and the woman. The rest of the kitchen was in darkness, although even from this distance, he could see Palmette's shadowy form.

Alvina moved forward, slashing. He heard a crash, and a grunt. It didn't come from Alvina.

We need the ambulance team in here now, he sent, relationship with the crazy woman no longer a concern. *Right now.*

Door's closed and sealed, someone sent back to him.

Great, he thought. Then he sent, *Do what you must to get in here. I can't open it at the moment.*

Alvina had moved farther forward. He couldn't tell if the form he saw belonged to Alvina or to Palmette. He couldn't use the laser pistol. He stepped into the kitchen, his foot hitting fallen dishes, clattering them.

Someone—Alvina?—whirled. He raised his pistol—

And something banged.

But bang was too small a word for that sound. Something happened—a collision, an explosion—something so loud that he felt the concussion as if it had actually hit him.

He staggered sideways, and then staggered again, keeping a grip on his pistol. Someone screamed, and this time, the lights—all of the lights—went out.

He sent, *What the hell was that?* but no one answered.

Palmette? he sent.

Still no answer. His head felt different. It took a moment to realize that all of his links had been severed.

Had Alvina done that somehow? Was that the concussive feeling he'd had? If so, how the hell had she managed it? Only the highest end security systems had the ability to sever all links, including emergency links installed into emergency service personnel, like him.

"Alvina," he said, and then the building rocked again. Thudding or pounding or something so intense that he staggered into the counter, and the pistol fell from his hand.

He grabbed the edge of the counter—more slime, and it interfered with his grip, making him lose his balance.

He slipped in the fallen cups and plates, feet sliding out from underneath him, landing on shards of pottery and something else. It kept shifting beneath him, and then something fell on him, and more somethings fell and more, and a loud, booming crack resounded throughout the building, and that was when he realized it was all coming down on top of them.

Something had destabilized the building and it was collapsing. No matter how crazy Alvina was, she had nothing to do with that.

He crawled away from the kitchen and headed toward the table, keeping his head down, hoping nothing more would fall on him.

It was a vain hope. Bits of the ceiling had landed on him, pieces of wallboard. His hand gripped a chair leg and he let out a small sigh of relief. He found the table, and miraculously, there was nothing beneath it but carpet.

He crouched under there, listening to things fall. A wail had started from the direction of the kitchen, and beneath that, a voice. He thought maybe it was saying his name, but he couldn't tell.

His ears ached, and everything rocked, and he wondered how long it would be before he died.

4

THE SHAKING STOPPED, THE BUILDING STABILIZED, BUT THE KEENING continued. Something fell onto the mess beside him, but it was a solitary fall, like a water droplet in the sink, waiting for the last possible moment to let go of the faucet and plummet to the ground.

Dust rose around him, making him cough. The air smelled foul, worse than it had when he got in here, and his eyes watered. Something was burning, and he couldn't tell if it was in here or outside.

He reached into his pocket, removed a small face mask to cover his mouth and nose, wishing he had thought of it earlier. It wouldn't keep out the stench, but it would keep out the particles. Then he reached into his other pocket and found the emergency light he'd bought years ago, and transferred every time he changed suits. He'd never needed it before. Indeed, one of his partners (and he couldn't remember which one) always teased him for having so many supplies on his person.

But he never knew when he was going to need them. So he carried them.

And now he needed this one.

He clicked it on. Dust, dirt, and shards of broken mugs had slid under the table. He moved the small light to look out from under the table. Chairs had fallen, and bits of the ceiling or the wall (he couldn't tell) had fallen on them. Some areas were mounded. Others weren't.

Dust rose everywhere, filling the air with particles, which told him that the circulation system had either collapsed or shut down. Or both.

The moaning continued, along with some rustling as someone tried to move.

He reached for his pistol, but he had lost it in the chaos. He tried his links again. The silence that greeted him was disconcerting. It made him think of childhood when he was alone in his head, before they had installed links, before he went to school. He could have a thought and even try to force it out of his brain as a send, but it felt as if the thought bounced off the interior of his skull, trapping it inside.

He pulled himself out. The whimpering got louder and, it seemed to him, had a tinge of fear.

He wasn't sure who he should call for. Palmette or Alvina? Palmette was his partner, but Alvina was dangerously unstable.

"Hey," he said, deciding to call on neither of them. "Anyone's links working?"

The rustling got louder, then something toppled, falling in a tinkle of glass.

His hands were covered in grit. He looked at them, saw shards of glass embedded in the protective covering he wore for the crime scene. He was probably covered in glass and who knew what else. If he crawled, he'd get even more on him. Eventually the sharp things would break the protective layer, and he would get injured.

Still, he couldn't exactly stand on the pile of debris, not with it shifting underneath him.

He moved some debris and found the floor. It looked uneven to him, but he wasn't sure if that was his own perception. He stood, and used the light.

It hadn't been his perception. The floor was canted. One of the walls had collapsed toward him, resting on the table and other bits of furniture. The ceiling had fallen there as well, revealing part of the next floor. That's what some of this debris was—stuff from the second floor.

He turned his light forward, and his breath caught.

Alvina was moving, and she had the knife clutched in her fist like she was about to bring it down.

She was close to Palmette's last position.

And the whimpering had stopped.

"Alvina!" he shouted. "I need you! Callum is over here!"

She turned, her eyes wild, her hair, face, everything, covered in dust.

"Where?" she asked, the edge in her voice terrifying all by itself.

"Here!" he said, keeping the light in her eyes so that she couldn't see anything. "Behind me."

She staggered toward him, tripping on the debris, extending her hands to catch herself. For a moment, he thought—prayed, really—that she had dropped the knife, but she hadn't.

She waded through the debris as if it were knee-deep water, lifting her legs, moving forward with an intense momentum.

He didn't have the pistol, and he was no match for that knife, but he had his cuffs. He pulled them out of his belt and held them loosely in his left hand.

"Where?" she asked, so close to him now that he could smell her, the sharp odor of sweat combined with the rusty scent of blood.

"He just dove under the table," Nyquist said.

Her eyes narrowed. "I'll get him," she said as if they were conspirators. "You stay here."

She bent down, and he shoved her forward, half wishing she would impale herself on that damn knife. Instead, she squealed and turned slightly, up toward him, still clutching that stupid knife.

But he was too quick for her. Years of practice subduing everyone from the wiriest to the biggest attacker. He shoved his knee into the middle of her back, then put all his weight on her, not caring if he broke something.

He grabbed her knife hand first. She tried to wrench it away from him—and she was strong, one of the strongest he'd ever fought. The crazy ones always were. His training partner had told him that, and damn if the man hadn't been right.

24

She kept struggling, using her other hand to try to get purchase on that canted floor, so that she could turn around and use the knife.

He slammed her knife hand against the ground over and over again. Just when he thought she would never let go, he heard something snap. Finger, knuckle, he didn't care. The knife clattered, and he yanked her arm backwards, grabbing for the other at the same time.

He got them both and shoved them into the cuffs, setting them on high. He didn't care if they shut off her circulation. He didn't care if they ended up cutting off her hands and killing her—not that they could. There were fail safes for that, fail safes he didn't know how to override.

She started kicking as the cuffs tightened, and then she started bucking. He almost fell off her. He reached for his other set of cuffs, but they were gone.

This woman was going to be the death of him. Or of Palmette.

He grabbed something out of the debris pile. He wasn't sure what it was because he had dropped his light as he fought with the woman, but whatever he grabbed was jagged and big and filled his hand. He brought the thing down on the top of her head with such force that her head bounced against the floor, not once, but twice.

And she stopped moving.

He didn't see if the blow had killed her. He didn't care. He tossed the jagged thing far from the table. If she was badly injured or dead, he would come back here and find something jagged that sort of fit, press it against the wound, and then drop it near her.

No one would notice.

No one would care.

Not after what she did to Palmette.

Or what he thought she did to Palmette.

He wasn't sure.

All he knew was that Palmette was terrifyingly quiet.

And that wasn't good.

5

NYQUIST FOUND PALMETTE. SHE WAS HALF BURIED IN DEBRIS, HER EYES closed. He touched her shoulder and his hand came away wet with blood.

He cursed. He'd picked up his light after knocking Alvina unconscious, and he used it now to see if he could figure out what was going on with Palmette.

What was going on was that she was losing a lot of blood. More than he wanted to think about.

He felt in his pockets for some kind of emergency kit, something to help, but he couldn't find anything at all. He would have to make do in this mess somehow. He needed to see the wounds, see which was bleeding the worst, and figure out how to stop it.

For good measure, he tried to send for help on his emergency links, but got no response. Maybe he could send, but he couldn't get any message in return. He had no idea, after all, and no way of knowing, so he set the emergency link on automatic, having it ping the system every thirty seconds, requesting an ambulance, backup, and help for the crew outside.

Then he went cold.

How long had he been in here since the crisis started? Five minutes? Ten? Thirty?

The exact time didn't really matter. What mattered was that none of the group outside had tried to come in.

The thought made his pulse race. Something was seriously wrong, something that was way beyond this house or even this set of row houses. His people should have broken in by now.

He made himself take a deep breath to calm down, then immediately regretted it because the air tasted of dust. He shone his light around, saw piles of junk and no cloth.

But there was a tablecloth in the other room and if he remembered correctly, it was relatively clean.

He picked his way back in there, as quickly and as carefully as he could, shining the light on Alvina first to make sure she hadn't moved. Then he grabbed the cloth which was still on the table. Some of the cloth wouldn't come—it was trapped under the fallen bit of ceiling. But he tugged as hard as he could and the cloth ripped free.

Then he carried it back into the kitchen.

He shone the light on Palmette. Her hands were on top of the debris and they were covered in defensive wounds. Blood oozed from those. A bad slash on the top of her arm, but it avoided the arteries on the underside, at least so far as he could tell.

The bulk of the wounds, though, were on her torso, and he wasn't sure how to stop them from bleeding.

He could tie off her arms, but he couldn't tie off her chest.

He wished for the damn links. Somewhere on there, someone or some stupid FAQ file could tell him what to do to tie off wounds, help him be creative with what he had.

But he was on his own here.

He put the light between his teeth and slung the cloth over his shoulder. Then he dug the debris away from her. Her stomach had been slashed, and another slash ran along her thigh.

The thigh wound was bleeding the most. Solution to that one was obvious. He had to tie it off. He ripped some of the cloth, and tied it around her leg (thank God she was thin) and pulled as tight as he could.

He wished he could research her to see if she had signed up for an emergency healing service, something that would close up small wounds with a simple command. She probably didn't or she would have ordered it the moment the wound happened.

Still, she might not have been thinking clearly—most people didn't when attacked—or she might have passed out too soon.

Although he doubted she had. She had been the one who was moaning.

He tied off her arms too, and then peered at that stomach wound. It was bad. She'd bleed out, just like that poor man in the living room had.

Nyquist needed supplies and he wasn't going to get them in here.

He pressed the remaining cloth against her stomach, put something flat, heavy, and unidentifiable over it to hold it in place, hoping that would at least staunch some of this.

Then he wiped his hands on his pants. "I'm going to get help—"

He was going to say her first name to comfort her—people liked hearing their names in moments of crisis—but he couldn't remember it. He didn't think calling her Palmette was right.

"I'm going to get help," he repeated softly. Then he shone his light on that opening into the front room. Part of the ceiling had come down there as well, and blocked the door. But nothing had fallen on the body, oddly enough, and that window seemed remarkably untouched.

So if whatever had blacked out the window wasn't made of an unbreakable material, he might be able to smash his way out of here.

He had to try.

6

IT FELT LIKE CLIMBING A DAMN MOUNTAIN TO GET TO THE WINDOW. A TRIP that had taken Nyquist only seconds an hour ago now took him at least ten minutes. Ten minutes, he—or more properly, Palmette—didn't have.

Along the way, he'd found two heavy cylindrical items he could use as cudgels. He had long ago given up trying to figure out what something was. In the dark and the dirt and the chaos, everything familiar seemed like something alien.

And the body, sprawled on the floor beside him, seemed vastly unimportant. Nyquist just had to be careful to stay out of the sticky and congealing puddle of blood.

The blackout material over the window was some kind of nanofiber. Unbreakable, untearable, without proper authorization, and he doubted, given Alvina's level of paranoia, that she would have left the protective authorization for emergency services. He didn't even try, because he was inside, and the theory was that someone inside was there by invitation.

He should be able to get the blackout material to lift on its own.

His effort was almost anti-climactic. He rolled up the bottom of the screen, and it continued to roll the rest of the way. He'd volunteer to do a commercial for the manufacturer when this crisis was over. The only part of the house still functioning was the nanofiber blackout curtain.

The window itself was so covered with filth—on the inside—that Nyquist couldn't see out of it. He doubted anyone had opened the damn thing in a decade.

One benefit of not having a conventional smart house was this window actually had handles so that someone could open it. He set one of the cudgels down, tucked the other underneath his left arm, and grabbed the window handle, wincing at the slimy feel. Then he braced himself and lifted upwards.

For a moment, he thought the window was stuck. Then it slid up and open, sending in light and air and noise—sirens and shouts and moans—and a stench so sharp he thought of closing the window again.

It took him a moment to recognize the smell. Burning chemicals. His eyes watered and he had trouble catching his breath.

What the hell had happened?

He didn't have time to think about it. He squeezed out of the window into the noise and smell, and eased himself to the ground.

The ground wasn't ground, not really. It was debris, just like in the house. In fact, much of it might have fallen from the house. He surveyed the neighborhood—saw more collapsed or canted buildings. Parked vehicles had moved, and the air had a sludgy oily feel.

A brown haze covered everything, and there was something wrong with the dome.

He squinted at it. The dome looked closer, and he didn't believe it was a trick of the light.

He tried his links before he even had a chance to think about it, trying to see if the dome had some kind of addition here, but got nothing.

His links were still down.

He couldn't think about. He had to get help for Palmette.

Two men—he thought maybe they were medical personnel from the ambulance—crouched over the male officer by the door. No other officers appeared in Nyquist's line of sight. The crime scene lasers had fallen away from their moorings, sending their thin red lights into the air. That alone had added to the cacophony—warning sirens went off when light from crime scene lasers got broken.

No one had fixed that, not in the last hour.

His heart was pounding.

The medical workers looked like they were working on the male officer. Nyquist didn't interrupt them. Instead, he headed to the ambulance. If nothing else, he would get a wound repair kit himself.

Inside, he found two other people on stretchers and one harried looking medico supervising them.

"Your links working?" Nyquist asked.

"I need your help here," the woman said. "I need someone to monitor their vitals—"

"I have an injured woman in the house back there who needs immediate attention," Nyquist said. "Are your links working?"

"No," the woman snapped. "No one's are."

"What the hell happened here?" he asked.

"What the hell happened everywhere?" she asked. "I'm not in charge, nothing's working and I have no damn idea. Now help me out."

"If I do, Palmette will die." For all he knew, she might already be dead. "She's bleeding out."

The woman looked at him with compassion. "If you stay here, I'll get her."

Nyquist shook his head. "You'll never find her on your own. Just give me something and some instructions on how to use it. I'll try to get her to you."

The woman gave him a strange look, as if she didn't believe he could do that, then she shrugged.

"Bleeding out from what?" she asked.

"Stab wounds," he said.

The woman paled. "You stabbed her?"

"Hell, no. I'm a detective with the Armstrong PD." Although he probably looked a lot more disreputable than that right now. "My partner and I were called here to investigate a death, and the killer attacked her."

The woman cursed, then grabbed a kit. "Some AutoBandages here," she said. "They should last long enough to get your partner out here. But I don't have anything to replace the lost blood."

He couldn't worry about that now. He had to deal with one thing at a time. First thing, stop the bleeding. Second, get Palmette out of that house. Third, deal with the blood loss.

Maybe by the time he got her out here, links would work again and someone could help them.

But he doubted that would be the case.

This wasn't a simple little disaster, covering one block. From what he could see—which was damn little—the entire neighborhood had been affected.

He was on his own with Palmette and Alvina—and he had no idea how long that situation would last.

7

NYQUIST DIDN'T WANT TO GO BACK IN THAT HOUSE. THE WHOLE THING looked unstable, not like a block of row houses at all. They had toppled inward against each other, roofs caved, walls leaning precariously against each other—or against nothing at all.

He recognized Alvina's only by the emergency workers still working on the officer in front of the door.

Not that he could go in that way anyhow. Debris had fallen in front of that door, and it opened inward.

He was going to have to crawl through that window and over that body one more time.

He crossed the yard quickly, and stopped in front of the window, feeling a bit stunned. It was higher than he expected. He didn't remember such a far drop to the ground, but he had to have made it.

He placed his hand on the sill and levered himself upward, balancing precariously. Then he hoisted himself over the edge, careful to step down as near to the wall as he could to avoid the drying blood.

The wall felt wobbly. He wondered if it truly was wobbly or if that was his imagination working extra hard now that he knew what condition this place was actually in.

He paused long enough to listen to see if he heard anything. A moan, a rustle, anything. He hoped to hear a moan from Palmette, and he didn't want to hear anything else. He didn't want Alvina to have gotten loose from her cuffs and come after him.

He heard voices from outside, over the sirens, but nothing from inside, at least that he could tell. He stepped back over the debris pile, then made his way to the kitchen.

He glanced at Palmette. She hadn't moved, which was a bad thing. He wanted her squirming, maybe trying to get to the door. But she hadn't done anything.

Still, he had to go past her to check on Alvina first.

Alvina was still splayed face down near the table. She didn't look like she had moved either, and he wasn't sure if the splotch of blackness he saw on the floor near her head was a growing puddle of blood, or something else entirely.

He didn't go near her to check. The last thing he wanted was to get close enough to have her grab at him, pull him down, or use some hidden shard of glass as a weapon.

Instead, he went back into the kitchen and crouched near Palmette.

She was still breathing. Her skin was clammy and she was even paler than she had been before. Despite his efforts, she was losing blood.

She was dying.

He grabbed the kit, slid health gloves over the protective material he already wore on his hands, and then grabbed the AutoBandages. Only one was big enough for that stomach wound.

He pulled up her shirt and hesitated for just a moment: remove the cloth he had stuck in the wound or leave it there? He had no idea which would be better or worse. He wanted to download the information through his links, but he didn't have it.

He was alone on this.

Finally, he gave it a bit of a tug, figuring if it was loose, he would pull it out, and if it wasn't, he would leave it.

It was loose.

He pulled it out. It was barely recognizable as cloth, and it dripped as he cast it aside. The kitchen already smelled so bad he couldn't tell if the stink around him came from the bandage, the wound, or the garbage in the room.

So he just ignored it all. He opened the AutoBandage, held it over the wound like he had done a dozen times before for other officers down in the line of duty, and then pressed.

AutoBandages attacked the skin and the wound, binding to it almost immediately, becoming part of the injured person's body. He had no idea how doctors got the damn things off or if they just managed to reverse the process somehow, and he didn't care.

All that he cared about was that it staunched the blood flow.

He used the rest of the bandages on the rest of her wounds, and hoped he got everything in the dark and the dust.

Then he took a deep breath, pulled off the gloves, and tossed them into the pile that was the kitchen. He pushed a path to the door, knowing that taking a few minutes now might save him a lot of grief while he carried Palmette. The last thing he wanted to do was fall on her, or drop her on something sharp. That would only make matters worse.

He shoved debris away from the door, then he went back for Palmette.

She still hadn't moved, but she didn't look worse—so far as he could tell, anyway. He apologized to her as he scooped her in his arms. He had to be hurting her. He hoped she couldn't feel it.

He would have draped her over his shoulder in a fireman's carry, but he was afraid of making that stomach wound worse. He hoped this would work.

She was heavier than she appeared, and her clothes were sticky with blood. Her head tilted back, her arms trailed down the side, and her legs hung free. He staggered a bit, trying to get his balance—he was tired, which surprised him—and then managed to move forward along that path he had carved.

Sometimes her feet grazed the debris. Once he bumped her head against something and he apologized again.

But she didn't move, and if it weren't for her shallow breathing, he would have thought he had already failed, that she was already dead.

As he picked his way across the dirt, he found himself mentally apologizing for all the bad thoughts he had had about her ever since he heard he would have yet another new partner, all the bad expectations, all the horrible plans he had for dumping her as quickly as possible.

He hadn't been fair to her, and it hadn't been her fault. She had done the best she could following his instructions—better than any other new partner—and she had waited as long as she could before seeing if she could get involved in the investigation, following department protocols.

It wasn't her fault that she got injured. It was his. He should have been watching out for her, instead of trying to keep her away.

He made it to the door. He juggled her form, bracing it against one side of him as he reached for the latch. He managed to pull it open, startling the emergency workers outside.

The officer on the ground was covered in bandages as well. It looked like they were operating on him on the spot.

"Can one of you guys help with this?" Nyquist asked.

He must have looked a fright, covered in dirt and dust and blood.

But one of the emergency workers stood and took Palmette from him.

"We have an ambulance," the emergency worker said, "but right now the streets are blocked. The dome sectioned, and we're trapped here. There's no hospital in this section."

It took Nyquist a moment to understand what "the dome sectioned" meant. It meant that the dome's protective walls came down, here at least, and maybe all over the city.

"There's been a breach?" Nyquist asked. That was the only thing that he knew of which would cause a dome's protective walls to come down.

Although he had heard, after that Moon Marathon disaster, that the city itself could order parts of the dome partitioned off from other parts.

"We don't know," the worker said. "Our links are down. Nothing's working. We assume so, though, given the smell."

The burning chemical smell. Nyquist hadn't gotten used to it, but he had started to ignore it.

"You sure that's not happening in this section?" he asked.

36

"We're not sure," the worker said. "But it hasn't gotten worse in the last hour, and that's a positive at least."

A positive. They were searching for positives. Which made Nyquist even more worried than he already was.

"Well," he said, "Do what you can for her. I have a prisoner in the back that I have to get into some kind of custody."

"A prisoner?" the other worker asked.

"The reason we all came here in the first place," Nyquist said. "The woman inside that house murdered a man in the front room."

He didn't add that she might have murdered his partner as well.

"I think she's better off in there," the worker said.

Nyquist shook his head. "Too many possible weapons," he said. "Besides, she's our responsibility if the building collapses."

The back of the squad could be modified into its own tiny jail cell. He was going to use that.

Provided she didn't kill him first.

"Wish me luck," Nyquist said, and went back inside.

8

ALVINA WAS STILL UNCONSCIOUS WHEN NYQUIST GOT TO HER. SHE HADN'T moved at all, and he didn't think anyone could be that motionless for that long if they were faking. To be safe though, he checked her hands. They held nothing, the wrists still tight in the cuffs.

He took a deep breath. He was lightheaded—probably from that smell—and his eyes still burned. No air was on in this place, so nothing got scrubbed. He wasn't used to toxins in the air at all. The dome usually protected everyone from things like that.

As he crouched, his clothes stuck to him. He was covered in all kinds of stuff, most likely Palmette's blood.

He didn't want to think about that. Instead he considered his options.

No one would blame him if he left Alvina and she died. She had killed the man in the next room. She had attacked Palmette. If Alvina didn't make it out alive, not even a murmur would follow him.

But he could see her breathe. And as long as Alvina was alive, she was a danger. If someone else came back in here—rescue crew, other officers—and Alvina attacked that someone, injuring or even killing them, then Nyquist would get blamed.

His third option, which no one would blame him for, was simple:

He could kill her.

He watched her back rise and fall. She was crazy; she was dangerous; and keeping her in custody would be hard—especially right now, with everything falling apart around him.

The logical choice, the smart choice, was to slam her head until she stopped breathing. No one would look at the head injury. The coroner would think she died in the collapse of the house.

No one would think twice about it.

Except him.

He let out a small breath. This stupid woman's death would haunt him for the rest of his life. He would think about her and think about the moment he decided to kill her and he would remember the action, he would remember how it felt to bring that weapon—whatever he chose— down on her head repeatedly.

And he would feel like a damn hypocrite, arresting others for killing. Or he would have to drop off the force because he couldn't do his job, and then what would he become? A Tracker, finding Disappeareds for money? Some kind of private detective, beholden to the corporations? He already had only a fragment of a soul left. He really didn't want to lose the last of it.

He swore, then checked her again, saw no weapons within grab-bing distance. He couldn't bind her feet, not without taking off his suit coat and using that, and he wasn't about to. Even though the damn thing was sticking to him, it felt like armor. He knew that was irra-tional, but he deserved at least one private irrational moment on this totally irrational day.

He wasn't going to pick Alvina up, not like he picked up Palmette. That left him too vulnerable. If Alvina woke up, she would start kicking and pounding him, and he wasn't sure he was up to the onslaught.

So he grabbed her feet and pulled her away from the table. Then, when he could get around her, he dropped her feet, went to the side, and grabbed her bound hands.

He yanked them over her head, and pulled her in a circle, turning her around so that he could drag her to the door.

She didn't wake up. Her head lolled. Blood dripped down the side of her skull into her eyes and alongside her mouth.

He'd really hurt her. He probably gave her a serious head injury, one that he was now compounding. But he didn't care. He was getting her out of this house, where she would become someone else's problem.

When he got to the door, he pulled it open with one hand. The emergency workers were still there. The second one had come back. He looked at Nyquist.

"You want me to take her?" the emergency worker asked.

Nyquist shook his head. "She can't go in the ambulance."

"She clearly needs to," the worker said.

"She's dangerous."

"We'll strap her down. We have one more bed left."

"Save it for this guy," Nyquist said, nodding at the officer.

The other worker stood, pulling off his gloves. "There's no point." He looked tired. There were tubes and multicolored AutoBandages all over the officer's skin, but none of that seemed to make a difference. His features were lax, his eyes fixed.

Nyquist knew what that meant. He'd seen dead people too many times not to recognize another one.

"We'll take her," the first emergency worker said.

"She'll try to kill you if she wakes up," Nyquist said.

"Yeah, we got that," the worker said.

"Keep her away from Palmette," Nyquist said.

"We'll put this one on the street," the worker said. "If they ever find us here, we'll send her on the second ambulance."

"Thanks."

The second emergency worker gently took Alvina's hands from Nyquist. Then the worker eased her to the ground to examine her wounds before he moved her again.

Nyquist staggered away from them, and went to sit on the fake yard, with the crime scene lasers pointing at the sky. The dome above him was black, not because it was Dome Night, but because of some substance coating the inside. Whatever that substance was, he had been breathing it.

He wiped his face, then wished he hadn't because of the goo on his hands. He looked around. The dome had sectioned, and clearly the problem wasn't near here.

He wondered if he could walk out.

He wondered if he had enough energy for it.

Then his links whispered, and crackled, and suddenly the emergency channels were back online, filled with panicked talk and shouting and messages and warnings.

A bomb had exploded inside the dome, damaging a section. A fire was sweeping through that section, but the emergency protocols had worked; the other sections were protected.

People should sit tight: if they needed help someone would reach them. If they were emergency personnel and they were all right, they needed to use their own personal codes to report the situation in their areas.

Dispatch would triage.

Nyquist listened to the noise in his head, never thinking he would be grateful for it. He didn't send his personal code. He figured the ambulance workers would do that—and sure enough, just as he had that thought, he heard the codes for this section go through clearly, with mention of life-threatening injuries. Needed to get the ambulance through a protected section of the dome to a hospital. One of the workers swore about the fact that there was no hospital in this section.

Nyquist listened even though he normally would have tuned out. Then he mustered the last of his strength, stood, and headed to the ambulance. If they let him, he would go with Palmette, make sure she got the right kind of care in this situation, before he cleaned up and went back into this mess.

He would also keep Alvina away from her.

He should go with the prisoner, he knew, but he wasn't going to. They would strap her down. She was cuffed. The hospital would figure it out.

He reached the ambulance door. Palmette had some color in her face. The attendant had wiped off the blood.

Nyquist sat on the bumper, not talking to anyone, and listened to the sound of his city, coming back to life.

ANNIVERSARY DAY
(NOW)

9

FIFTH POLITICAL FUNDRAISER OF THE WEEK AND IT WAS ONLY WEDNESDAY.
It was also Anniversary Day, a day Mayor Arek Soseki hated.

Of course, he couldn't let anyone know he hated Anniversary Day.
On Anniversary Day, everyone got together to celebrate the fact that the
City of Armstrong had survived a bomb large enough to destroy a sec-
tion of the dome.

The dome had worked properly—it immediately isolated the section,
leaving that part of the dome exposed to the vacuum that surrounded
the Moon, while the rest of the dome managed to survive.

Damaged, but it survived.

Soseki dwelt on the survival when he gave his Anniversary Day
speeches. The strength of Armstrong, the quick response of the authorities, the resiliency of its people. He had given these speeches for three
years now, and he could recite them in his sleep.

He practically was asleep. He stood in front of the podium in the
backroom of O'Malley's Diner. O'Malley's wasn't a diner and its owner
was not named O'Malley. O'Malley's Diner was one of the more upscale
restaurants near the port, and its location, rather than its food, had made
it a place for politicians to hold quick-and-dirty fundraisers. Easy access,
not to mention some rather hidden back routes from the port itself, kept
some of the fundraisers secret—or at least, some of the attendees.

Soseki had lost count of how many times he'd given a speech here. He almost felt like he should carve his initials into the real wood podium. The entire backroom was paneled in real wood of a type he wasn't familiar with. Not that the mayor of Armstrong needed to be familiar with wood. Wood was one of those things the rich indulged in that Soseki didn't understand.

He scanned the crowd. Two hundred super donors. Of the two hundred men and women in front of him, only about twenty represented their own interests. The rest belonged to some corporation or another, here for the express purpose of dumping funds into Armstrong's city council elections through legal means.

Fortunately it was election season, because that made his Anniversary Day speech just a little more interesting—at least to him. He had to combine two canned speeches into one.

Not that he was so fond of election season any longer. Something he never thought he'd admit to anyone, particularly himself. He used to love running for office, the glad-handing, talking to the voters. Hell, he even liked manipulating the media while they manipulated him right back.

But he'd been mayor for six years now, and it looked the job was his for life if he wanted it, thanks to the political machine he'd installed throughout Armstrong. That meant elections weren't that much of a challenge any more. Even the fundraisers had become pro forma—the mayor shows up, the mayor asks for money, people donate money, the mayor passes the money to the proper candidate, and the proper candidate wins. End of story.

He used to love the challenge of politics, but politics would not be a challenge again unless he ran for Governor-General of the Moon—and that particular title held less actual power than his position did. He could have more of an impact as mayor of Armstrong on everything from Moon politics to Earth Alliance regulations because he controlled the largest port on the Moon, not to mention the largest city here, the most cosmopolitan city outside of Earth.

Eventually, everyone came through Armstrong—usually on their way somewhere else, but they came through. And stopped. And spent money. And got a little taste of the city.

His city.

And the first thing they saw when they left the arrival terminal in the port? A floating sign with his image, saying that Mayor Arek Soseki welcomed them.

People remembered that.

They remembered him.

And he hoped they didn't remember that he had been mayor during the bombing. He saw Anniversary Day as the anniversary of the greatest failure in his career. To date, no one had caught the bomber.

The Chief of Security for the Moon, Noelle DeRicci, thought that a suicide bomber had set off that bomb. Even if DeRicci, who had gotten her job as a result of her performance during and after that bombing, was right, it made no difference. While the officials of the City of Armstrong thought they knew who was behind the bombing, they weren't certain.

And certainty mattered, particularly in cases of terrorist attacks.

Soseki shook off the thought, made himself focus on the crowd, which watched him with rapt attention. How could they be interested when he didn't give a damn? He had become very good at faking enthusiasm, which also disturbed him. A part of him was still idealistic enough to believe that he should care about all aspects of his job, even the distasteful ones.

Like fundraising.

He was helping corporations buy his councilors, and he didn't care so long as those same corporations dumped money into the city. Not as much money as some of the cities on the moons of Jupiter—cities owned outright by Aleyd or Fortion or other corporations—but enough to keep Armstrong in the black for a decade or two.

As long as he was mayor, he wanted Armstrong to remain one of the greatest cities in the solar system. Hell, if he had his way, it would become *the* greatest city. Maybe it didn't have the history of Paris, Dubai, or New York, but history wasn't everything.

Commerce was.

And that was the theme of this speech.

The theme of every speech this week, really. Every speech this year.

He really didn't remember half the things he said here, but the crowd was clapping, people were buttonholing him, and he was posing for vids and pictures, glad-handing, like he had done since he ran for head of his neighborhood association at the ripe old age of sixteen.

And finally, it was done. His invaluable assistant, the dapper Hans Londran, put his small frame between Soseki and the last of his admirers, saying some nonsense about the mayor being tired.

Soseki wasn't tired, at least not physically. He was just tired of the constant talk about nothing.

He let Londran and the security guards flank him as they headed out of the back room into the restaurant proper. This was on Soseki's orders. Most politicians snuck in and out of venues like common criminals. Soseki went through the restaurant, grinned at the patrons, shook a hand or two, and then waved as he headed out the front to the limo, paid for by the city, and always at his disposal.

He ran a finger over his palms, making sure his chips were protected and the SkinSoft covering he wore wasn't bunched up. People wanted to think they were shaking his actual hand, not touching some kind of pseudoskin covering that protected him from everything from germs to rapid-acting, touch-sensitive poison.

The door opened, he smiled, and patrons at white-cloth-covered tables started shouting his name.

This part of his job never got old. He shook hands, grinned, greeted a handful of people he knew, and bustled out the door in a blaze of lights. The limo had touched down on the sidewalk—the only non-emergency vehicle in Armstrong that could—and one of his guards opened the door for him.

He was almost there when a hand brushed his sleeve.

"Mr. Mayor?"

He turned but didn't see anyone except Londran and the guards, all frowning at him.

"Mr. Mayor?"

That wasn't a stranger's voice. That was Londran's and he looked concerned. Why would anyone look concerned, especially after the meeting had gone well, the money donated was within expectations?

"Mr. Mayor?"

Then he realized what was going on. He hadn't moved from the entrance to the restaurant even though he thought he was walking across the sidewalk. He should have been to the limo by now. He should have slid inside. He should be careening through Armstrong's streets, heading to the next meeting, working on the next crisis.

But he wasn't.

And he wasn't even sure if Londran was repeating himself or if the phrase had been caught in a loop in his own mind. He should have answered by now. He should have asked, "What?"

He usually asked "What?" when Londran used that tone. But Soseki couldn't move his mouth or his legs. And his arm ached.

No. It didn't ache. It was cold. He was cold. Chilled, like he hadn't been since that conference of Earth Alliance mayors held in, of all places, Alaska in the winter.

The chill was moving from his arm, down his chest, reaching for his heart. And, for the first time that day, for the first time in weeks—no, years— he actually felt afraid.

That chill didn't dare reach his heart.

Because when it did, his heart would shatter. He would shatter.

And everything would stop.

10

MILES FLINT PULLED HIS AIRCAR INTO THE PROTECTED UNDERGROUND parking facility beside the Armstrong Wing of the Aristotle Academy. His daughter Talia sat beside him, arms crossed, staring out the window as if she was seeing something new.

Of course she wasn't. They drove into this parking structure every single morning. It was the protected part of the Academy's parking, for VIPs and others who wanted the highest level of security for their children.

Flint's car had the six different kinds of identification the Academy required, and he still had to stop one floor down from ground level to show the palm of his hand, letting one of the identification devices read the chips embedded in his skin and his DNA. Talia also had to stick her hand out of her window and let the system examine her.

She hated it, but she had done it.

Which led Flint to believe she wanted to go to school this morning more than she was admitting.

Even though they were already an hour late. Talia claimed illness at first, and then when Flint threatened to run a diagnostic, she backed off her claim. Just said she didn't feel up to it.

When he pushed, she stopped talking to him altogether, something she hadn't done in a while. When he first brought Talia to Armstrong, she had resisted school more than anything else.

It turned out that her mother had enrolled her in an accelerated school in Valhalla Basin. Talia had found the public schools in Armstrong easy. She hadn't been challenged, and Talia needed to be challenged.

So Flint enrolled her in Aristotle Academy, the best school on the Moon, and certainly the best system of schools in the Earth Alliance. Out of the more than two hundred Aristotle Academies scattered throughout the system, the Armstrong Wing had been consistently rated in the top five, and often held first place. After a few weeks, Talia's complaints about going to school vanished.

Until this morning.

"It's just stupid," Talia said as Flint pulled the car to the parking area near the underground entrance.

Those were the first words she had spoken since he told her she was going to school no matter what. She had flounced around, gathering her things, glaring at him, and stomped to the car.

He had done a lot of research on raising a teenager since Talia came into his life, but he was still surprised when that research was right. Sometimes Talia was just plain difficult, for no reason that he could see.

"What's stupid?" Flint asked.

"Anniversary Day," Talia said. "They're going to make us listen to dumb speeches, and then everyone's going to talk about what they did on Anniversary Day, and how they cried or how they knew someone who got hurt or how they were scared when the dome sections came down. It's stupid."

Flint did his best not to nod or mutter *ahhhh*, although he was tempted. So that was what bothered his daughter about school. Four years ago, she had been living happily with her mother, believing the lies her mother had told her.

Four years ago, Talia had been a normal (if unbelievably bright) child, living with her divorced mother, in the house she had grown up in. Now Talia's mother was dead, and the day she vanished, Talia learned that not only had her mother lied to her about almost everything, Talia wasn't who she thought she was either.

She was a clone of the child that her mother had had with Flint. And Flint hadn't abandoned them like her mother had told Talia. He hadn't even known about Talia.

Clones had no respect in the Earth Alliance. They weren't even considered human without proper legislation. When Flint found Talia, he had gone through all the procedures to make her his child under the law—his *human* child.

Still, neither he nor Talia told anyone she was a clone, and they almost never told anyone about her past.

"Are you supposed to participate?" Flint asked.

Talia still stared out the window, but she nodded.

Flint had hunch she didn't want him to see the emotion on her face. She hated seeming weak to anyone, which he would have said was something she got from him, except that he hadn't been around her in her formative years.

He waited for her to tell him more and when she didn't, he let out a small sigh. The problem was exactly what he thought it was: she didn't want to talk about her past. Not just because she didn't want her classmates to know about it, but because she was still ambivalent about the memories it brought up.

She really didn't know if she should acknowledge how much she missed that life, considering it was based on a lie. And she didn't want to acknowledge how much she loved her mother, considering what a horrible person her mother had turned out to be.

"Just tell them about Valhalla Basin," Flint said. "Be brief and don't talk about much more than school there."

"I don't want to," Talia said with great venom.

"Then pass," Flint said. "Don't participate."

"If I do that, I'll fail. It'll have a huge impact on my grade."

So it was easier to be sick. He wished he had known that before checking her in. She had taken a smart way out.

"Then fail," Flint said, a little reluctantly. He wanted her to do well at school, but not at the expense of her own identity.

She looked at him. Her eyelashes were wet and stuck together, but that was the only evidence of tears on her face.

"But Daddy," she said, and his heart lifted. She almost never called him that. "It'll ruin my grade."

"I know," he said. "That's okay."

She looked at him, then frowned, clearly working over the angles in her mind. "Can you give me something that says you don't want me to participate?"

"No," he said, almost without thinking about it. "This has to be your decision."

"Why?" Her voice went up slightly.

"You're going to spend your whole life choosing when to tell people who you are and when to keep that information to yourself. You're supposed to learn things in school. This seems to me like a valuable lesson."

"You take all the fun out of things," she said

He shrugged a shoulder and let himself smile. "That's my job."

She leaned over, kissed his cheek, and got out of the car. "Thanks, Dad," she said as she slammed the door shut.

Then she ran in front of the vehicle to the side door. She put her palm on the entrance, and the doors slid open. She stepped into the school and the doors closed behind her.

He sat there for a minute, feeling a little stunned. Of course, he always felt a little stunned at this parenting stuff. It seemed so easy from the outside and from the inside, it was fraught with tiny but important decisions.

On this day, he made his daughter happy and he got her to school. He supposed it couldn't get better than that.

He sighed and headed out of the parking area. He wasn't sure what he'd do today either. He hated Anniversary Day as well, but for different reasons. He wasn't a celebration kinda guy. Not that this was a celebration, exactly. It was more of an acknowledgement.

But still, it wasn't a day he enjoyed.

He would just have to get through it.

Like everyone else.

11

"HE'S WHAT?" NOELLE DERICCI, CHIEF OF SECURITY FOR THE UNITED Domes of the Moon, sank into the chair behind her desk. The chair, designed to accommodate her form no matter how she was sitting, shifted slightly and she wanted to growl at it.

She wanted to growl at everything.

Even her beautifully designed office, with its floor-to-ceiling windows, its comfortable chairs, its green plants at strategic places, failed to calm her.

Or maybe she expected too much, particularly, when her assistant, Rudra Popova, stood next to the desk, threading her fingers together as if she could pull them out of their sockets.

"Mayor Soseki's dead, sir." Popova swallowed hard. Her normally impassive features were drawn. Her long black hair, usually as smooth as water, was mussed, and her eyes were red.

She'd known Arek Soseki. They both had.

DeRicci had known him better. She had countless meetings with him since, as mayor, he was the head of Armstrong Dome. He'd often butted heads with the governor-general of the United Domes. He believed the mayors should have more power regulating DeRicci, even though she worked for the United Domes.

DeRicci couldn't quite wrap her mind around the word "dead" combined with "Soseki."

Arek was a dynamic man, not the kind who keeled over in early middle age.

"What happened?" DeRicci asked softly. She'd had her external links off, leaving only the emergency links and the contact information for people who worked with her directly.

Popova wiped the bottom of her left eye. A tear. Even the great Popova—the calmest woman on the Moon—had emotions.

DeRicci felt faintly surprised at that.

"They don't know," Popova said. "He seemed fine, and then he froze and collapsed. His last physical came out fine. He had no health problems, nothing that would have caused this. They're wondering if it was murder."

"Wondering," DeRicci repeated. "It would be nice to know."

Because if it was murder, she had an entire set of protocols she had to follow. If it was just a death (*just* a death; what a thought), she had another.

She had to be able to function right now. She didn't have the luxury of tears.

"I'll find out if he died of natural causes, sir," Popova said, wiping at the other eye as if it annoyed her.

DeRicci wondered why Popova was so broken up about the mayor. She'd been through other high-profile deaths before.

"Who is investigating this thing?" DeRicci asked.

"I don't know, sir," Popova said.

"I want some answers, Rudra, right now. I want the place where he died blocked off immediately—the wider the perimeter the better. I want one of our investigators down there—the best one we have—and I want someone from the police department, someone good, there as well."

"Detective Nyquist?" Popova asked.

DeRicci stiffened. Everyone knew she and Nyquist were involved, but she tried to keep that part of her life personal.

"I don't tell the police department how to run their business," she said. "Except for this. They better have the best investigator in charge of this thing, and by best, I mean someone who can close cases *and* someone considered incorruptible. If this is murder, then we have to plan not just for an arrest, but for a conviction."

"And if it's not murder?" Popova asked softly.

"That's not a concern at the moment," DeRicci said, knowing she sounded cold. "We're going to proceed as if it is. Get some medical examiner down there too. We need answers as fast as we can."

"Already done, sir," Popova said.

DeRicci didn't doubt that. Popova had a great ability to multitask. She had probably been sending messages through her links as DeRicci spoke. Back when DeRicci first got this job and she discovered that Popova was going to be her assistant, it irritated her that Popova could do more than one thing at a time. DeRicci didn't entirely believe it; she felt like people who multitasked the way Popova did were less competent.

But Popova was more competent because of her work method, and DeRicci now relied on it, even if she didn't understand it.

"I assume there's some kind of audio or visual footage," DeRicci said. "I want that immediately. I want eyes and ears on this case right now."

Popova nodded, then hovered. Popova never hovered. That was odd, too.

"Thank you, Rudra," DeRicci said. "Now give me a minute."

"Yes, sir," Popova said, and walked out of the room. Just from her tone, DeRicci could tell Popova thought DeRicci was going to take a private moment to mourn.

But she wasn't. As shocked as she was, she was also calm. She hadn't really liked Soseki, although she worked with him. She never felt like she knew the man, just the politician.

She sighed, got up, and walked to the floor-to-ceiling windows that overlooked Armstrong, and curving in the distance, the dome. From this vantage, nothing looked different. But on the ground, she knew, everything was about to change.

She knew how things changed in an instant. She'd been through it more than once. The worst time was four years ago today, when an unknown suicide bomber tried to destroy the dome. The resulting blast ruined an entire section of the dome and demolished a whole neighborhood.

She had been the chief investigator on that bombing. She had learned most of what happened—what kind of bomb it was, why it did the kind of damage it had, what it had destroyed. What she hadn't learned—no one had—was who the bomber was, and why that person had tried to destroy the dome.

Usually this view reminded her that not everything had an answer—and even without answers, the city went on. The people continued, life moved forward, and everyone could recover from catastrophic events.

She had no idea if Soseki's death was a catastrophic event.

She would find out—and if it was, she would minimize the damage, just like she was paid to do.

12

BARTHOLOMEW NYQUIST AT HIS DESK IN FIRST UNIT OF THE ARMSTRONG Police Department's Detective Division. Somehow he had managed to keep his office through all of his recent ups and downs. People still treated him as if he was fragile—hell, the *brass* still treated him as if he was fragile—and he'd been back on full duty for months now.

He felt different. Who wouldn't, after being sliced to pieces and nearly killed by a Bixian assassin? Although he had no one to compare the experience with. He was one of the few people to ever survive a Bixian attack, and that, he believed, was because the assassins, who work in pairs, went after the man he was with first.

Not that that detail mattered. The survival mattered—survival because Nyquist fought back and won, not because he was rescued at the right moment. People should treat him like a victor. Instead, they treated him as if he were still in his hospital bed, about to die at any moment.

He sipped the completely stale coffee he'd set on the side of his desk. At least he wasn't on limited duty anymore. He'd been working cases ever since he got back, and he no longer felt rusty. He felt useful, and embarrassingly grateful to be alive and working.

He had opted against all but the most basic enhancements after the attack. He had gotten rid of the worst of the scars, but he had left a few, not because he was anti-enhancement, as a few folks had accused him of, but because he wanted a visual reminder every time he looked in the mirror, a reminder that he felt different because he was different.

He was calmer now, less prone to anger, a bit more resigned. And willing to deal with his own death, where he never had been before.

The door to his office was only partly open. He had a shade over the window, even though he usually kept the shades up. It was Anniversary Day, and people were giving speeches, holding tributes, and having ceremonies all over the city.

He was supposed to get some plaque or medal or something in the neighborhood where he'd rescued Ursula Palmette, but he had declined. He'd gone the first year and felt horribly embarrassed; he'd just spent the previous day giving depositions in the Alvina Ingelow case, and they had gone badly. She'd had a good attorney. That case dragged on for another year, and Ingelow got lifetime detention in a cushy mental health facility instead of solitary confinement in one of the Moon's harshest prisons like she deserved.

Part of the reason was him: he hadn't collected evidence properly for the first (and only) time in his life. Of course he had an excuse, but the excuse didn't trump hard evidence, which was then contaminated by the bombing. The jury "couldn't be sure" that Ingelow murdered Sheel. Nor could a different jury "be sure" that Ingelow had caused Palmette's injuries, although Nyquist knew she had.

He hadn't witnessed the attack. He had just heard it. And when the building collapsed around them, Ingelow's attorney argued, things in that horrible kitchen could have caused Palmette's injuries.

Yeah, things in the kitchen could have caused the injuries—in a universe filled with magic, not science. But the juries wanted certainty—and they usually got it. They rarely had cases where things went so badly awry as they had here.

Besides, Ingelow was clearly nuts. At least the juries had believed, on some level, that she was homicidally nuts, which was why she was detained at all.

Nyquist leaned back in his chair and rubbed his hand over his face. He was staying in his office, finishing the details on half a dozen cases instead of working a new one, because he wanted to avoid Anniversary Day. Yet he was thinking about the damn bombing anyway.

There was no way to escape it. It was as if the entire city had some kind of post-traumatic stress syndrome. Or, as Noelle DeRicci had said to him a few days ago, it was as if the city decided it had been unjustly hurt and wanted to play the victim.

He liked that about DeRicci: She had no more patience with victimhood than he did. He liked survivors, people who overcame their problems, not people who returned to those problems and blamed them each and every day for the tough things that life threw at them.

Which actually brought him back to Palmette. She had filed suit against the department because she couldn't go back to detective work. She kept failing the psych evaluations.

Nyquist knew how tough those evaluations were; he had gone through them himself not too many months ago. As invasive as the evaluations felt, he understood the need for them. This job was tough, not just in the things a person saw, but in the choices he sometimes had to make. Choices that weren't really right, but were what passed for justice in this strange town.

He hated some of the things he had to do for his job, but he did them. Because if he didn't do those things, what good he did manage to do would get wiped away.

Compromise. It used to make him feel dirty. Now he understood how important it was.

Palmette hadn't had time to learn that. Then she nearly died, and when she recovered, she had to go through two separate trials against the woman who nearly killed her. Palmette hadn't had time to heal.

Plus, the rules mandated that anyone who failed three psych evaluations in a row had to wait a year to reapply for the job. So she had gotten some desk job that pretended to be investigative at Traffic. The nice thing about the job was that it paid as much as detective work. The tough thing was that it was a desk job.

Nyquist knew that as well because he had looked into those jobs when he was still healing. For months after the attack, it hurt to move, and he wasn't sure he would ever be limber enough to get back onto the street.

But the doctors kept assuring him that his muscles would be repaired properly and that, with the enhancements, he would feel like a new man.

He did feel physically stronger, but he didn't feel like a new man. He felt like the guy who had been sliced and diced, the guy who had nearly died, and who had come out of it all with a lot of scars and a new perspective.

A guy who still hated Anniversary Day.

Nyquist got up, grabbed his mug, and went to the small area off the hallway that passed for a kitchen. He poured out the coffee, then started a whole new batch.

It wouldn't taste any better, but it would be fresher. Besides, it was something to do, something that might refocus him, something that would get him thinking about the future instead of the past.

The past had hurt him and left him scarred. The future still held possibilities.

If only he could figure out what they were.

13

DETECTIVE SAVITA ROMEY CROUCHED NEXT TO MAYOR SOSEKI'S CORPSE. How anyone could have mistaken this death for a natural one was beyond her. She knew that his aides didn't want to cause a panic, but their caution had already slowed down an important part of the investigation.

The man was gray. Steel metal gray, the kind you could see in the Museum of the City of Armstrong on the old ships originally flown to the Moon hundreds of years ago. Uneven gray—darker on his left side, and getting lighter across his face, until there was no gray at all on his right side.

None.

She had no idea what this was, but she'd bet her entire career on the fact that it was intentional.

"I need vids," she said to one of the on-scene officers. "And we need to canvas. I want to interview everyone who was in the area when this happened."

"Everyone?" the officer said, with some surprise.

She looked up at him. Young, so innocent that he didn't even have frown lines around his mouth. He probably hadn't been on the job longer than a year.

"Everyone," she said.

"What do you consider to be the vicinity?" he asked. Which was a really good question. She had no idea. One block? Five? Ten? It didn't entirely matter. She had taken so long to get here—the system had taken so long to contact her—that if anyone wanted to get away from the crime scene they could.

"Five-block radius," she said, just because it sounded good. "Up and down. See if anyone saw anything from windows and aircars, too."

He nodded crisply. She had a hunch he'd get this done efficiently, which would make her life easier.

She should have gotten his name, and by the time she had that realization, he was already gone, doing what she needed.

The mayor's aides were fluttering around her, trying not to ask her questions, looking nervous. She should feel nervous as well, but she didn't. Even though this was the biggest case of her career.

The mistakes had already been made. One hour from death to a detective on site. That was the biggest error, and it wasn't hers. She'd make note of it in her report as a cover-her-ass moment. Not that she needed it.

This investigation would be gone over, detail by detail, by the law enforcement branch, by the press, and by the hundreds of conspiracy theorists who seemed to thrive in the Moon dust.

She couldn't think about them. She needed to think about doing this properly.

She had full control of this investigation. The chief of police had hand-picked her due to her closing record and her ability to handle high-profile cases. He gave her carte blanche. She could pick her team, and she could conduct the investigation as she saw fit.

She saw a lot of fit. Crime scene lasers in the wrong place, too many people close to the corpse, too many ways into and out of the scene, from the door to the restaurant to the open limo door to the sidewalk, up and around.

She sent a message to Dispatch on her links. *I needed crime scene techs an hour ago. And how come there's no coroner yet?*

Ethan Brodeur wanted to make sure his lab was in order before he brought in such an important corpse, the dispatch sent. She didn't just send audio but added an icon, a sketch of herself rolling her eyes, which was more of a commentary than Romey had ever seen from anyone on Dispatch.

Not that anyone liked Brodeur. He was marginally competent at best, and he'd screwed up more cases than he had resolved. Romey had a hunch he was a political appointee—or he knew where all the bodies were buried, and he used that knowledge to keep his job.

Send that new coroner—the one with the stupid name—?

Jacobs? Dispatch sent.

Yeah, her. What's her first name?

Marigold, Dispatch sent.

This time it was Romey's turn to roll her eyes. How could she forget a name like that? But she had.

Send her, Romey sent, *and get Bartholomew Nyquist here ASAP. I need someone competent, and right now, I'm surrounded by politicos and street cops.*

Anyone else? Dispatch sent.

Not at the moment, Romey sent, even though she should have reminded Dispatch that she was supposed to have a supervisor/advisor of sorts from Moon Security.

That was the only part of this case that really bothered her. She didn't have a true buffer between her investigation and the United Domes of the Moon. When she knew anything, she was supposed to contact Security Chief DeRicci.

Romey supposed she should contact her now. But she was going to wait a few minutes. She half-thought she'd let Nyquist do it, but that wouldn't work. The stupid man had some kind of relationship with DeRicci, and that alone might complicate the case.

It certainly explained why Romey had lead here, and not Nyquist. Since he'd got back from sick leave, he'd gone back to his old ways—closing more cases than anyone and alienating partners.

He'd asked her to partner with him twice, and she'd said no, not because they'd be a bad team but because they'd be a damn good one.

He was the first man she'd met in years who intrigued her. Who more than intrigued her.

Who fascinated her.
And that didn't make for a good working relationship.
Except when she needed him.
Like right now.

14

THE SIRENS MADE A SHIVER RUN DOWN NYQUIST'S BACK.

He got up and went to the window of his office, tugging on the shade with his bare hand. The shade slid up, reminding him of that moment four years ago, when he had celebrated the rise of another shade, one that he worried would trap him in that horrible building forever.

Four years. He was in the same office, but in a different place mentally. And this window was clean. It opened onto the outside—as outside as things got in the dome. He could see the street below, a street filled with people going about their daily routines.

Vehicles with sirens blaring had left this building an hour ago, and more were leaving now. Normally that didn't bother him. Normally, it didn't catch his attention at all.

Sirens blared all the time around here—enough that some detectives had taken to listening to music on their ear chips to block out the sound. Orders had come down from headquarters—no music in the office—and the detectives had filed complaints.

So the windows got some soundproofing. Not enough to block the sound completely, but enough to make the sirens less abrasive.

Not that they had ever bothered Nyquist.

Until today.

And probably, if he was honest with himself, last year on Anniversary Day as well. He didn't remember going to the window to see what caused the sirens, but he probably had.

Or had he still been recuperating from the Bixian attack?

He didn't want to look at the calendar to remember.

The second set of sirens had an immediate sound to them. Not that one set of sirens could be more urgent than another. But it seemed that way to him. Or maybe it was the number of response vehicles.

Or maybe it was the Day.

He left the shade up as he went back to his desk. He would get this work done even if he had to stay here until midnight.

As he eased himself into his chair, his link chirruped: Dispatch, also urgent.

His heart rate increased. He could feel it. He really was on edge.

This day's dispatch was an older woman, with frown lines on both sides of her mouth. Either she'd had enhancements so long ago they'd stopped working or she was as contrary as he was, refusing to use artificial means to hide aging.

"Detective," she said, using audio, which was just as unusual as using an image. Right at the moment, her image ran across his left eye only, making her seem like her tiny image was floating a meter above his desk. "Your presence is requested at O'Malley's."

He sighed. He'd kept up on Anniversary Day activities. "What kind of trouble did the mayor get himself into this time?"

"This is not a secure link," the dispatch said. "I will transfer."

She winked out, and Nyquist frowned. What the hell? Why would Soseki want to summon him, and why would that take a secure link?

Then the dispatch winked back in, floating in front of his right eye this time. He didn't know if that was because this link was secure or if she just felt like playing with his mind. Probably the latter. He had a hunch personnel put all the budding sadists into Dispatch.

"This information has not yet been released publicly," the dispatch said with such great formality that Nyquist realized she was recording everything more than once to cover her own ass. "The mayor is dead."

"What? How?"

"No one is certain. Detective Savita Romey is the primary detective on this case and she has requested your presence to assist."

Romey was primary on such a major case? Before his injury, he would have been primary on something like this.

"Has anyone informed the Security Office of United Domes?" he asked, not wanting to be the one to tell DeRicci.

"They're sending personnel as well," the dispatch said.

"Is this related to the Anniversary Day celebrations?" Nyquist asked.

"We have no information as of yet, Detective," the dispatch said. "The scene is locked down, and teams are heading there now."

Nyquist frowned, brought up the timestamp at the base of his links, then said, "Wasn't the mayor supposed to be giving an Anniversary Day speech across town about now? Why was he still at O'Malley's?"

Dispatch sighed. "Please direct your questions to the primary detective and do so on scene. We need you there immediately. A squad is waiting below."

"If you want this to remain quiet, then stop sending so many squads out with their sirens on," Nyquist said.

"We've have a number of emergencies today," the dispatch said. "Anniversary Day is becoming one of the worst for troubles throughout the city."

Then she winked out.

Everyone hated Anniversary Day. He hadn't realized that before.

And now they would hate it worse, with the mayor dead.

The day of the bombing, everyone believed the terrorist attack was only the beginning of the attacks on Armstrong. People expected another attack that day, and when it didn't happen, they expected one that week, then that month, then that year.

For four years, all of Armstrong had lived in anticipation of yet another attack—and the attack hadn't come.

Nyquist took a deep breath, then let it out slowly. He hoped to hell Soseki was dead from natural causes. Nyquist had never wished anyone had a massive heart attack or a surprise brain aneurysm before, but he hoped for that now.

Because if someone had killed Soseki, today of all days, the entire city would go insane.

15

SAVITA ROMEY FELT OVERWORKED, MAYBE BECAUSE SHE *WAS* OVERWORKED. She had twice as much to do now, because Soseki's aides dithered more than she would have had she arrived an hour earlier.

She had done what she could outside: she had protected the body. But even that had taken some effort. The street cops who arrived when the aides made the call had done some of that, but not in the way an experienced homicide detective would have. They made the perimeter too wide, and didn't ask who had walked close to the body.

The other problem with coming in late was that there were too many people milling around aimlessly. Someone had ordered the remaining people to stay on scene, so some of the patrons of the restaurant still sat at their tables, the remains of their meals scattered before them. Waiters, recognizable only because they wore uniforms, sat at empty tables. Chefs remained in the kitchen, and the owner hovered near the reception desk.

The back room still had people who had come for Soseki's speech. Some of those people were important—rich business owners, a few politicians, a couple of bigwigs from off-Moon. Soseki's aides wanted her to deal with them first.

She had to figure out a way to deal with the aides. They were irritating her, and getting in the way of the investigation. But they had been in charge of the scene from the moment Soseki died, and she wasn't quite sure how to deal with them, without alienating them, without getting the information they didn't even know they had.

For all she knew, one of them had killed Soseki.

The interior of the restaurant smelled of garlic and baking bread. Her stomach growled as she worked. She needed a command center, she needed a place to put the witnesses, she needed staff to interview those witnesses, and she needed the crime scene techs to get here before the entire scene got contaminated.

The coroner's van showed up first.

Romey left the restaurant, stepped around the crime scene lasers she had placed around Soseki's body, and watched as the back of the van opened. She worried that Brodeur The Incompetent had overruled her and had come instead of Jacobs.

But Romey shouldn't have worried. Brodeur hated extra work, and important cases were always extra work.

Jacobs stepped out of the back, her kit in hand.

Jacobs was tiny, muscular, and no-nonsense. She had bright yellow hair, which couldn't have been natural. If it was natural, then her parents deserved to be chastised for naming her Marigold, because her hair was precisely that color.

Jacobs had an angular face, intelligent eyes, and a calm manner. Her husky voice seemed genderless over audio links. She nodded at Romey, then set to work, without having to be told what to do.

Romey let out a small sigh. At least one thing had gone right this morning.

One of the street cops approached her from her left. He was careful to avoid the crime scene lasers as well.

"Detective," he said, "there's someone here from the Security Chief's office?"

His tone made it clear that he didn't believe the outsider was from the security chief's office, which made her realize the young cop hadn't even asked for identification.

"Thanks," she said as she headed toward the man the cop indicated. "And next time, officer, make sure you check credentials before you get me."

The cop started, then flushed, making her wonder just how new he was. That thought flitted across her brain and left it as she walked down the sidewalk, past two businesses that she had ordered closed. Their employees and patrons waited inside for interviews, the very thought of which overwhelmed her.

She was so far behind, and she had just started.

The man the cop had indicated stood near a dark government-issue car. The man was tall and broad-shouldered, clearly uncomfortable in a suit. It tapered along his muscular body. His features were so chiseled, he looked like a model rather than a security agent. Only the muscles in his shoulders and arms gave him away. No model would let himself get so enhanced that he couldn't squeeze properly into a suit.

"Credentials," she said as she approached.

He held up a hand. A badge appeared on his palm. That wasn't enough for her. She extended her hand, and touched his.

Banyon Kilzahn, Security Office of the United Domes of the Moon. Fifteen years' experience in dome government security, three years with the United Domes. In other words, he had worked security for the various governments on the Moon before the United Domes had become the dominant entity, certainly before the Security Office for the United Domes of the Moon had been created.

He watched her as the identification ran. Her palm warmed as the credentials and his DNA got approved through Armstrong Police Department's database.

"You're an observer only," she said. "You're here on my sufferance. You make any mistakes, interfere in any way with my investigation, and I'll have you out of here so fast, you won't know what hit you."

He smiled. The smile was warm and made him even more handsome. "It's nice to meet you too," he said.

She glared at him. "You may mock me all you want, Director, but this is no laughing matter. When the news about the mayor gets out, this entire city is going to be in an uproar, especially considering this is Anniversary Day."

His smile faded. "I wasn't mocking you, Detective. I've just never met anyone who didn't go through the niceties before."

"I don't have time for the niceties," she said, "and neither do you. You have a choice. You can stand where I tell you to, or you can get briefings from one of my assistant detectives. Which do you prefer?"

"I'll stick with you, if you don't mind," he said.

"I didn't say stick with me," she snapped. "I said you can stand where I tell you to."

He nodded, his smile so far gone that it almost seemed like his face didn't bend that way. "My mistake, Detective."

"Don't make another one," she said. "And come with me."

She turned her back on him without seeing if he was going to follow that order. She was being unduly harsh with him, but she wanted him to know who was in charge. And she wanted to keep a close eye on him. Observers like Kilzahn often reported the wrong things back to their superiors, making investigations worse.

She stepped around the crime scene lasers and went back into the restaurant. Then she checked to see if he was following her.

He was, as if he was guarding her.

"You will stand right here," she said, placing him next to the reception desk. "You will not speak to anyone without my authorization. Nor will you report to your boss without clearing that report through me. Is that clear?'

"I'm sorry, Detective," he said. "But I don't work for you."

"I run the crime scene. That means I control the information which leaves this crime scene. If you want to be in my crime scene, you will do as I tell you. Or I will send you back to the Security Office and ask Chief DeRicci to send me a liaison who knows his place. Do you understand me?"

A hint of a smile returned to his face. "Yes," he said.

"What am I doing that's amusing you so?" she asked.

73

He shrugged one of those massive shoulders. "I have never met such a fierce detective before."

"You haven't seen fierce yet," she said. "You interfere with my crime scene in any way—and that means releasing the wrong information to your boss at the wrong time—and you will see fierce."

He nodded once, crossed his arms, and started to lean against the desk.

"You touch anything without authorization, you're interfering with my crime scene," she said. "The techs haven't been here yet."

Then she reached into her pocket and removed a small disk that held a protective suit, the kind she usually gave to civilians.

"Here," she said. "Put this on."

He took the disk and attached it to one of the buttons on his suit. The protective gear covered him, making him look like a flash of unfiltered sunlight hit him. Then the image vanished.

"That suit does not mean you can touch anything without my permission. It's just that I don't trust you. I hope we're clear," she said.

"Perfectly," he said. "May I at least tell my office I'm here and that you have the investigation underway?"

"You may tell them that you're here," she said. "That's all."

Then she left him, feeling her irritation rise. He was just a symbol of all that could go wrong on this case. An hour-long delay, an untrained observer, a dead mayor on the wrong day of the year—not that there was a right day. Romey wondered how she ended up being the lucky one this morning.

She also wondered where Nyquist was.

She should have told Kilzahn to go home and make Nyquist liaison. Although that would have been a waste of a lot of investigative talent.

She wondered where the hell he was.

She wondered where the hell the crime scene techs were.

She wondered where the hell the murder weapon was.

She wondered a lot of things, and she doubted she'd get the answers she wanted.

16

NELIA BYLER LEANED AGAINST THE WALL IN THE STUFFY MEETING ROOM, her hand shielding her face, one eye closed. She needed to concentrate, and it was hard, with the invasive sound system. She had to actively de-couple the sound from her links, and she couldn't do that, not since she was supposed to be monitoring the governor-general's speech.

But Byler had heard the speech a hundred times, or maybe a hun-dred and one. Besides, she had helped write it. She was supposed to monitor it so that she could tell the governor-general if she had done a good job or not, but right now, Byler didn't care about a good job.

She cared about the message Rudra Popova was trying to send her.

No one in the room watched Byler, no one except a slender blond man who stood only a few meters away from her. He was young, maybe twenty-five if he didn't have enhancements, too young to be this interested in a routine political speech given on the anniversary of the bombing.

He was probably related to one of the victims, although Byler didn't remember any light-skinned victims who had such pale blond hair. Byler had only met a handful of people with those looks, one of them a Retrieval Artist who was a friend of the security chief. The Retrieval Artist was aggressively blond, with curly hair and arresting blue eyes.

This kid was pale, as if someone or something had leeched him of color. He seemed bland as well, vanishing against the real oak paneling, despite his blue clothing and the anxious tick of his right hand.

He was probably waiting for someone.

He kept glancing at Byler as if she made him nervous. She probably did.

She was trying to focus on Popova, but this really wasn't the place. Dignitaries from all over the Moon were here, along with some minor ambassadors from even more minor countries scattered throughout the Earth Alliance. A few victims' families, some victims' advocacy groups, and a few political organizations representing tolerance and anti-violence campaigns also filled the room.

This would be the perfect media opportunity, but the governor-general hadn't wanted the media here. She actually wanted to make a policy statement, and kick off a tolerance campaign.

The Moon is the place to start this, she had said to Byler a month ago, back when this idea had first come up. *We're the crossroads of the universe. Everyone wants to go to Earth, and they have to go through us to get there.*

Or everyone wants to leave Earth, Byler almost said, *and we're the doorway out.*

But she didn't contribute. She'd been in politics long enough to know that when a politician got an "original" idea, no one should point out that the idea was impossible, had been tried before, or was just plain ridiculous. The City of Armstrong was already one of the most tolerant places in the Earth Alliance. It had to be, for precisely the reasons the governor-general named. It was the rest of the Moon that was xenophobic, and in most cases, it didn't matter. Armstrong had the only big port, and the most aliens. It also had the largest transient population in the solar system.

Rudra, Byler sent through her links, *can't this wait? The governor-general is giving a policy speech that I'm supposed to pay attention to.*

You need to pay attention to me! Popova sounded agitated. Popova was never agitated.

76

Byler leaned over farther. She noted a visual marker in the corner of her link to Popova and activated it.

Rudra Popova didn't look like herself. Her eyes were red, her skin blotchy. Her lower lip trembled, and tears glistened on her eyelashes.

Byler's heart skipped. She had known Popova for a decade, since they were in school together. She had gotten Popova her job in the Security Chief's office.

She had never seen Popova look like this.

What the hell, Rudra? Byler sent.

Arek is dead. A twitch appeared in Popova's left cheek. She wasn't speaking this. She was sending this message without saying a word, which also indicated how upset she was.

Soseki? What happened? Byler glanced at the governor-general. She was so tiny that the raised podium didn't make her look taller; it made her look like she was floating. Her black hair was pulled away from her face, accenting her large black eyes. Byler thought of that as her "sincere" mask, although she would never, ever, tell the governor-general that.

No one knows how he died yet, Popova sent. *But it's not looking good.*

Byler frowned and brought her hand up to shield all of her face from the crowd.

I'm not supposed to let anyone know, Popova sent, *but I had to tell someone, and I figured it should be you, just in case...*

Byler went cold. She caught the implication. Just in case the death wasn't natural. Just in case it was an assassination. That meant everyone in Armstrong would get mobilized.

She glanced at the security detail hovering near the governor-general. They looked solid and alert, but somewhat detached, like they always did when she gave a speech.

They hadn't gotten the word yet.

I'm so sorry, Rudra, Byler sent. *Are you heading over there?*

Even though she didn't know where "there" was. Soseki was giving speeches all day just like the governor-general. In fact, he was in greater demand on Anniversary Day because it had been his city, his dome, that had gotten hit. His response had been measured and calming.

There'd even been talk that he would run for governor-general in the next election cycle, until he quelled it. He didn't want the honor, he had said, but what he had meant was he didn't want to lose his power base. The United Domes had no real power. All of the power remained with the cities. They were, as the governor-general often said, little city-states, and each, given the right chance, wanted to take over the Moon.

I can't, Popova sent, and her expression made the words seem desperate, even though they had no sound. *No one here knows.*

Byler let out a small sigh. Of course no one knew. She had initially advised Popova to keep the relationship quiet until the relationship looked permanent. Popova and Soseki had been seeing each other for six months, and Popova had fallen in love.

It had seemed permanent to Byler. Maybe Popova hadn't thought so.

Not that it mattered anymore.

Applause started all around them. Byler cursed silently.

I'll meet you later, Byler sent. *After all the events end today. Unless you need the governor-general to do something...?*

Popova shook her head. *You might want to let her know. Keep quiet to everyone else though. And tell her security detail. Just in case.*

People were standing, crowding forward, wanting to talk to the governor-general, to let her know what they thought of her proposals.

Byler had to get in there and pay attention so that she could offer advice.

I'm so sorry, Rudra, she sent, *but I have to go.*

It's okay, Popova sent and signed off.

Byler sighed and went around the chairs, trying to find a way to get to the podium. The slender boy was gone, probably ducked out the back way.

Then Byler saw him, near the front of the crowd, as if he wanted to talk to the governor-general. He probably was one of the children of the victims or maybe he was an anomaly, like she had been, one of those kids who actually found politics fascinating, and dreamed of a career in it.

She sent a message to the governor-general's security detail as she walked toward the front: *Go to high alert status.*

She didn't have to justify it, nor did she have to explain it. It was probably a false alarm anyway. Arek Soseki was one of those men who seemed healthy, but he ate all the wrong foods and participated in a lot of risky behaviors. He probably had some kind of medical condition that the stress of the day brought out.

The security detail moved closer to the governor-general. She was smiling at the young man.

Suddenly, one of the security detail grabbed the governor-general and hoisted her away from the crowd. He carried her toward the back. An urgent message filled Byler's emergency links, along with an encoded message.

Situation 8564

Her breath caught. Medical protocol for the governor-general, because the governor-general couldn't activate it herself.

Byler sent the correct codes into the governor-general's links, hoping that would help. The governor-general had all of the latest medical tech, including medical nanobots that theoretically blocked any foreign agent in her system.

Clear the room! Byler sent to the remaining security team. *Make sure everyone is detained! Get an emergency team here now!*

She ran the rest of the way to the front. The security detail had already disappeared through the designated escape route.

She ran to catch up, swearing at herself the whole way.

She should have acted sooner. She should have sent some kind of warning through the entire system.

She should have, she should have, she should have.

But she didn't.

And now the governor-general would pay.

17

SOMETIMES FLINT WONDERED WHY HE CAME TO HIS OFFICE. HE DIDN'T take clients anymore. He had retired as a Retrieval Artist, at least until Talia had made it through school.

He had put her in danger too many times.

Flint's office was in an unprepossessing building in Old Armstrong. The dome was ancient here, and the filters didn't work very well. Outside, Moon dust covered everything.

Inside his office, the Moon dust was no longer a factor. He had bought a state-of-the-art filter and upgraded it continually. His environmental systems here were as close to perfect as such systems could get on the Moon itself. They were almost as good as the ones in his space yacht.

He was rebuilding his entire computer system from scratch. As a young man, he had gotten his start in computers. When he had married Rhonda, Talia's mother, his programming skills were legendary, and he combined them with hardware skills.

If his daughter Emmeline hadn't died, he probably would have stayed in computers and never gone on to work for the City of Armstrong Police Department or branched out on his own as a Retrieval Artist.

Of course, that's what he always assumed. Since Rhonda died and Talia came into his life, he wondered if his assumptions were wrong.

Rhonda had planned her escape from their marriage years before Flint had even known there was a problem.

Still, he found it hard to get past years of assumptions with what he actually knew had happened. Particularly when what had happened was so very inexplicable. And Rhonda was dead, so he couldn't ask her about her motives.

He desperately wanted to ask her about her motives.

Computer parts sat all around him. He had disassembled his entire front desk. Only one screen still worked. It was a floating holoscreen and he had it on random, so sometimes it was in his line of sight and sometimes it wasn't.

He had it on a live feed that mixed entertainment news with sports and a few current events. Normally he had regular news or history programming on while he did this kind of work, but today he knew all that he would get was Anniversary Day programming. Either he'd hear all of the stupid speeches live or he would listen to the history programming droning on about what had happened.

Suddenly the screen stopped floating, and flew with great deliberation to the space just in front of his eyes. The entire screen glowed red.

Breaking news. Something important.

He sighed. He didn't even want to look. It was Anniversary Day. Either the news would be something stupid or it would be something awful.

He expected stupid. Some politician said something idiotic in a speech or a bystander accidentally dropped a knife.

He glanced up and concentrated on the female anchor standing in a sea of images. He didn't recognize this woman. He hadn't paid attention to reporters since Ki Bowles died, probably because he still felt a bit guilty about that.

"...shortly after giving his speech, Mayor Arek Soseki collapsed outside O'Malley's. Aides say Soseki died of natural causes, but add that the authorities must always investigate a sudden death...."

Flint frowned. Authorities didn't have to investigate a sudden death.

He tapped the screen and opened it to all the Soseki news. Each media service had the same story. Then he glanced at his own computer system in pieces around him. His most powerful system was down.

But that didn't stop him from using the little screen in front of him. He tapped it because he never used voice commands in his office—voice commands were too easy to compromise—and he searched for information that he knew had to be publicly available.

All of the Moon's senior public officials had to put their latest health records into a public database. DeRicci had complained about this, because not every dome had ratified that law, which was a United Domes of the Moon law. But Armstrong had.

So Soseki's health information should have been readily available.

Flint found the file quickly enough. But his screen told him that he couldn't access that material because the system was overloaded.

He shook his head slightly. The system never got overloaded, not for a simple information search.

That little excuse was something that officials used when they took down information they didn't want the public to see.

The hair rose on the back of Flint's neck. He didn't like this.

No reporter had ever flagged Soseki's health. In fact, the reporters always expressed surprise at how very healthy Soseki was. Flint moved away from the public file and went back to the old news files.

There they were: all the reports on Soseki's good health.

He leaned back, frowning. Why take down Soseki's public health records if Soseki had been in perfect health?

Why would anyone cover that up?

Unless Soseki hadn't died of natural causes.

Flint pushed the screen away, and it returned to its random float. He was being too paranoid. He always thought in terms of things going wrong.

Only something *had* gone wrong here.

Soseki had died on Anniversary Day, and now someone—for whatever reason—had decided to blame Soseki's death on natural causes. But that same someone hid the health records which would have backed up that claim.

Flint didn't like this. Right now, the news was calm, reporting the death of the mayor exactly way that the authorities wanted it reported. But eventually a dogged reporter, like Ki Bowles had been, would discover that something was odd.

All it took was one bad news story on a day like this, and the entire city would panic.

He stood and wiped off his hands. He didn't want Talia to be alone if panic broke out.

Not that she would be alone, not at Aristotle Academy. The place was a fortress.

But she wouldn't have him there.

If something went wrong, Talia would need him.

And maybe, if he was being honest with himself, he would need her.

18

DeRicci had put the visual with Savita Romey on the big screen in her office. The screen was in the middle of her office floor, and it rose up like a live thing, covering the floor-to-ceiling windows, and extending from her favorite comfy chair to some green plant-thing whose name she always forgot.

She wished she hadn't made the screen so big when Popova let her know that Romey wanted a visual link. DeRicci thought it would be nice to cover the windows, so she wouldn't be focusing on the city itself. But the oversized visual hadn't blocked the city from her mind.

Instead, it had made her concern worse.

Romey was talking to her from the crime scene itself, and it was a crime scene, no doubt about that. Soseki's corpse didn't even look human. DeRicci had seen a few aliens that color, but never a human being, and not in those gradations. Human skin wasn't the same color all over, but it was usually within some kind of range unless the person purposely changed the colors.

She knew Arek Soseki. He would not want people to see him in shades of gray.

She winced at the mental pun, then wondered if that was intentional. It couldn't have been, could it?

She wondered if she should mention it to Romey, then decided against it, at least on a link everyone on the Moon could hack into if they really wanted to.

"I've already asked for a different coroner," Romey was saying.

"Let me guess. You had Brodeur first."

Romey nodded. "And I've asked the crime scene techs to double-time it here. But we lost an hour to some dithering about the cause of death—"

Meaning that the aides' unwillingness to call it a murder had put the detectives behind.

"—and I think we've lost maybe half a dozen witnesses, maybe permanently—"

Meaning the suspects had probably escaped.

"—so we're already behind in this investigation—"

Meaning if the killer never got caught, it wasn't Romey's fault.

"—I also wanted to let you know I've requested Detective Nyquist. I think he's one of the best investigators on the force."

DeRicci kept her expression impassive. Popova had suggested Nyquist and DeRicci had decided not to ask for him, to keep any taint of politics out of this investigation. But if something controversial came up, she could hear the reporters and talking heads now: they'd blame her for having her boyfriend investigate the crime scene.

At least she could now point to the record, which showed her not making a specific request. The actual request had come from Romey.

"You're right," DeRicci said. "There aren't many detectives better than Detective Nyquist."

The words hung between them for a moment. Then Romey said, "Your man, Kilzahn, is here. He has no investigative skills. I'm not sure what you would like him to do."

And that was when DeRicci realized Savita Romey was ever so much better at diplomacy than DeRicci had ever been, particularly when De-Ricci had been with the force.

Romey had just requested that Nyquist be the liaison between Moon Security and the Armstrong Police Department.

DeRicci was going to let her own reputation for a lack of subtlety speak for her. She pretended to misunderstand.

"Just keep Banyon informed," she said. "I deliberately sent someone not trained in homicide, so he wouldn't be active in that part of the investigation. But he has clearance on issues that never make it to the local level and that might be important."

Meaning this case might be bigger than Armstrong, although De-Ricci sincerely hoped not.

"And keep me apprised too, Detective," DeRicci said. "Unlike the members of my team, I do have experience in homicide, so I might see a few things that echo from my new job into my old one. I'll have my assistant send you a list of banned substances that might cause the skin tone gradations, and I'll send a few other things."

Things that she couldn't mention on a public link, like information on groups that specialized in such substances, groups that were not allowed in Armstrong, or in the Earth Alliance itself, for that matter.

"Anything else, Detective?" DeRicci asked.

"Not at the moment, Chief," Romey said. "Thank you."

DeRicci nodded as she severed the connection, wondering what the heck Romey had to thank her for. DeRicci used to hate it when the brass or another department got involved in her investigations. She suspected Romey did as well.

The screen pinged her links, asking if she had further use of it. She didn't like it when inanimate objects talked to her, and she used to refuse to answer. But now she just sent a simple no, and let the screen slowly and majestically descend into its little cage or cubby or whatever the hell it was stored in.

She sighed and leaned back in her chair. She wasn't going to do the next part by visual link. That would simply be too irritating. Because now she had to inform the governor-general they had a situation, and then the governor-general would probably tell her to inform some other group, and DeRicci would spend the rest of her day talking about ways to "handle the crisis" instead of handling the crisis herself.

She'd already handled a bit of it, by having Popova send a message to the governor-general's office that DeRicci was well aware of the death and was investigating to see if it was a United Domes matter.

Now that she knew it was, she was going to have to go into full crisis management mode.

Sir? Popova sent via the office internal link. *We have another situation.*

What? DeRicci sent.

"Better to show you." Popova had opened the door. Apparently she had been walking toward it as she contacted DeRicci—or the news had been so severe that she had leaped out of her chair and sprinted to the door.

She didn't even wait for DeRicci to tell her to go ahead. Instead, she raised that damn screen back up and it was already running.

Eight different 2-D images ran along the edges. A small holoimage dominated the middle.

They all showed Keir Julian, mayor of Moscow Dome, being hustled inside a building by his security people. He was stumbling and looked wild, but DeRicci couldn't tell, through the cacophony of voices, what actually happened.

So she muted everything except the holoimage in the middle.

The redheaded reporter looked like she was standing above the floor. She also was so tiny that it seemed like DeRicci could pick her up and throw her through a window as easily as she could throw a coffee cup.

"…attempt on his life," the reporter was saying. "Moscovitius University Hospital reports that his condition is stable at this time…"

Hospitals were always supposed to say that about heads of state.

DeRicci muted the redhead too, although her image continued to hover as the redhead pointed to various images behind her desk. Images within images within images. If DeRicci wasn't careful, they would give her a headache—as if that, and not the day itself, would cause the headache.

"What have we got?" DeRicci asked.

"Nothing," Popova said, her voice a little shaky. She still hadn't recovered from the Soseki announcement. "No one from Moscow Dome has contacted us."

"Get them to," DeRicci said.

"Sir, Moscow Dome is as far from here as you can get—"

"I know," DeRicci growled. She was familiar with the Moon's geography. And she understood the implications. "Get busy, Rudra. We need investigators there too. Send one now, maybe with an advisor from Armstrong PD."

"Any suggestions, sir?"

DeRicci was tempted to recommend Nyquist just to get him out of her hair. But she didn't. She wanted him here.

"No," she said. "That's not my job. Someone good. Now get busy."

"Yes, sir," Popova said and left the room, with one hand pressed against the side of her face as if she could talk through the chips on her palm.

DeRicci might have to replace Popova for the day. The woman was too shaken to do a good job, and she usually took on the job of half a dozen people without a blink.

But DeRicci didn't have the time to think about that at the moment. She issued an emergency warning to all heads of state here on the Moon, informing them of the dual attack and cautioning that they might be in danger. Then she wiped the screen in front of her clean of imagery and requested a visual conference with the governor-general.

Some low-level assistant appeared in a cramped low-level office.

"I need the governor-general, *now*," DeRicci said.

"Yes, sir, I'm sorry, sir," the assistant said. He looked like he was about twelve. "I can't get her for you, sir."

"You will, or you will find me someone who can," DeRicci snapped.

"I'm sorry, sir, it's not that I won't. It's that I can't. She's just been taken to Deep Craters Hospital, and I'm not sure she's going to survive."

19

NYQUIST TOOK HIS OWN CAR AND DIDN'T USE THE SIREN FUNCTION AT ALL. Still, as he drove to O'Malley's, he heard six different sirens. Dispatch hadn't been kidding when she said Anniversary Day had more than its share of trouble.

He parked a block away from O'Malley's—after showing identification to get into the perimeter. Emergency vehicles were everywhere, along with vehicles left by the patrons who couldn't leave the stores and restaurants in the area.

O'Malley's wasn't in the best section of Armstrong. The restaurant bordered the port, which made it a great place for political meetings. People—diplomats, money managers— could come in secretly, take one of the back routes into O'Malley's, have a meeting, and leave without anyone, especially the press, being any wiser. Soseki loved O'Malley's, which always made Soseki a bit suspicious to Nyquist.

Not that Nyquist loved politicians. Or rather, not that he loved people who went into politics voluntarily.

More and more, Noelle DeRicci's job had become about politics, and he had strong feelings for her.

He let out a small sigh as he got out of his car. He couldn't even use the "love" word inside his own head. Strong feelings was accurate. Love—well, he didn't really know what that was. He assumed what he felt was love.

The neighborhood had a dingy feel. The buildings weren't dirty like they were in outlying areas of Armstrong, but they were old, and for the most part, not kept up. A neighborhood revival had started, although it was haphazard—a few stores next to O'Malley's that catered to the slummy rich, a couple of coffee places for people who needed legal stimulants, and that was about it. The rest of the neighborhood had the usual sex shops, which were legal but frowned upon; the Hookah Place, which catered more to the Gdetry, an alien group that had fallen in love with smoking opium; and storefronts whose businesses changed almost daily. He'd made more than his share of arrests down here, usually in the storefronts, which often sold everything from illegal weapons to aliens to human children.

The formal crime scene was set up around O'Malley's front entrance. He wondered if they had established a scene around the back as well, then remembered that Romey was in charge. Of course they had established a matching scene around back, and probably around the lesser known exits as well.

A crowd of people had gathered around the crime scene lasers. All of the people looked official—uniforms mixed with crime scene techs mixed with lower level detectives. A few uniforms stood outside nearby buildings, arms crossed, apparently keeping customers inside.

He removed one of the protective suits from the pocket of his coat, attached the disk to a button, and tapped it. The damn thing enveloped him, making him feel momentarily sticky. No matter how many times he did that, he still hated it.

As he pushed his way through, touching his hand to every single identification post floating around the scene, he noted the coroner's van parked right next to the scene. As he got closer, he saw well-shod feet extended along the sidewalk, attached to legs whose socks had fallen slightly, revealing unnaturally colored skin.

Soseki?

Nyquist braced himself, then put his hand into the nearest laser beam. The crime scene laser sent him a message: *Crime scene under investigation.*

Please watch for markers, Detective Nyquist. Make certain you walk only in the prescribed areas.

As if he didn't know that. As if he hadn't been the one to argue for more markers on a scene after many of his former partners trampled the areas around the corpses, ruining them.

But there was no talking back to automated messages, no matter how much he wanted to.

The markers were spread around the feet which were, as he suspected, attached to Arek Soseki's body. Only Soseki didn't look like himself. He looked like an artist's cast for a statue made out of pure silver. Although what mayor would want to be cast in a prone position, a look of puzzlement on his great stone face?

Nyquist had never really liked Soseki, but no one deserved to end up like this. Nyquist sighed and stepped on the prescribed marker. He recognized the coroner from her hair. An orangy gold which was, someone had told him, the color of the flower marigold. He was always a bit startled by it. Except for her hair, Marigold Jacobs was a very serious woman. He was glad she was here instead of Ethan Brodeur or anyone else from his office. The coroners in this city ranged from brilliant (Jacobs) to venal (Brodeur), with matching degrees of experience.

"Hey, Marigold," Nyquist said softly. "Finding anything useful yet?"

He didn't ask if she had found anything interesting. He suspected she found the corpse very interesting. Nyquist certainly did. He couldn't remember ever seeing a human turn that particular color.

"No, I haven't," Jacobs said, "and you'd think I'd've found something by now."

"How long have you been here?"

"Fifteen minutes, tops," she said. "But whatever hit him hit him fast. He was shaking hands one minute and dead the next. And before you ask, he had SkinSoft on, and he was wearing it properly. Nothing that we're familiar with should have gotten through his hands."

"You're thinking he was poisoned," Nyquist said.

"I'm thinking something altered his body chemistry. We tend to call that a poisoning, although I don't know if the term is accurate at the moment." She sighed. "I'm going to have to take him back and do everything from toxicology to a full autopsy."

"You're going to cut him open?" Nyquist asked. Almost no one did that kind of autopsy anymore. With bots and cameras and nanoprobes, it usually wasn't necessary.

"I'm thinking about it," she said. "Mostly because I'm not sure what I'll find. His skin on the dark gray side is so hard it doesn't feel like skin anymore."

"May I?" Nyquist asked and crouched.

She put out a hand, stopping him from touching anything. "Have you suited up?"

Having her ask the question didn't irritate him. It pleased him. If more coroners were that cautious, he would have closed a few more cases that his former partners had screwed up.

"Yes, I'm suited up," he said.

She moved her hand. He touched the arm of Soseki's coat. Even though Jacobs had told him what to expect, Nyquist was still startled by how firm the arm felt. Less like an arm and more like that statue cast he had thought of when he first looked at the body.

"If I were to slam my fist against his arm," Nyquist said, "would it shatter?"

"Don't do that," she said, not looking at him. The entire time they talked, she was taking samples, making notes, moving bits of fabric.

"You know me better than that, Marigold," he said.

"Sorry. Caution. No one but you seems to know proper crime scene procedure." She moved some bags of samples into the case she always carried with her. "And I suspect the corpse would shatter, at least on the left side. That's something else I'll test when I get him back to the morgue. We are going to have to treat this body carefully."

"I take it you've ruled out a contagion?" Nyquist asked.

"I haven't ruled out anything," she said. "But considering that no one else is showing symptoms and this crime scene has existed for hours, I'm guessing there isn't one. If there is, it's slow moving."

"Shouldn't we take precautions just in case?" he asked.

"Sure," she said, and rocked back against her heels. Now she did look at him. Her eyes were a light brown, which he suspected matched her actual hair color, not that awful yellow she always sported. "Of course we should have taken precautions. The minute he keeled over. Someone should have roped off the area, called in the Hazmat team, sealed off everything, and kept people in quarantine. But no one did that. No one reported the damn thing for nearly an hour. So if it is a contagion, we'd better hope the dome filters take care of it, because it had plenty of time to get ahead of us."

Nyquist smiled at her, unperturbed by her tone. "You don't think it is a contagion or you would have taken action anyway."

Her eyes twinkled just for a moment. Anyone who didn't know her would not have seen that.

"You know me too well, Bartholomew," she said quietly. "I wish you were leading this case."

"Savita Romey is a good woman," he said.

"Not as experienced as you," Jacobs said.

"But just as thorough."

Jacobs shrugged one shoulder, a noncommittal response.

"She's the one who asked for you." Nyquist didn't know that for certain, but he had a hunch. He would have made sure that he had Marigold Jacobs on a case this politically sensitive. There was no room for error here, especially since some earlier errors were made.

"That's very kind of her," Jacobs said, then bent back over the corpse.

"You're not blaming her for the delay, are you?" Nyquist asked.

"This crime scene was chaos when I got here," Jacobs said, the disapproval clear in her tone.

"I checked the logs as I drove. She was brought in long after the first report. I doubt she'd been here more than fifteen minutes before you," Nyquist said.

Jacobs didn't answer that. She had made up her mind, and he knew from long experience that Jacobs' mind could snap shut in an instant.

"Besides," Nyquist added, "she asked for me too. She's trying to do this right."

"I don't think there is any right, Bartholomew." Jacobs spoke softly.

She looked at him sideways. What he had taken for disapproval was something else. Worry? Fear? He couldn't quite identify it, but he knew that Jacobs was unsettled.

She beckoned him with one finger. He leaned in and shut off his recording links for just a moment. Then he sent her notification that he wasn't recording anything.

She nodded, then said softly, so softly that even someone standing nearby couldn't have heard her, "It shouldn't have been this easy to kill the mayor. Especially on Anniversary Day. Especially Soseki. He took precautions, like the SkinSoft. He knew attacks could come at any moment."

Nyquist knew that too. "You think this was planned," he said.

"I know it was planned," she said. "It's the only explanation. Nothing that we have here on Armstrong could have caused him to die like this. Nothing. Whatever it is had to have come in from the outside. And to bring it into this port took planning. The question you have to answer is how many people are involved. Are there aliens involved too? And why would they target Arek Soseki today of all days?"

Nyquist sighed. "I'd already thought about the second two questions," he said. "I guess I'll also have to focus on the first."

You can turn your recordings back on, she sent him.

He nodded.

"I'll let you know when I have something," she said. "But don't hold your breath. I suspect it'll take a while."

He suspected the same thing. And the thought didn't please him. In fact, it worried him more than he could say.

20

DE RICCI PACED AROUND HER OFFICE, STUDYING THE CARPET AS SHE WALKED. She had long ago given up on that big screen. It made her nervous, and she couldn't be nervous. She needed to concentrate, and she needed to remain calm as she held conversations along her links.

She had probably done fifteen circuits of her office already, and she had a lot more to do. She was handling a lot of information, and doing most of it in her head, which would piss off Popova.

Too bad. DeRicci didn't have time to worry about niceties or legalities. She had to deal with a lot of people, and a lot of problems.

This was the first time in years that she had dealt with a Moonwide emergency. Last time, the bureaucratic system she was a part of got in her way. Now it was crumbling around her.

The governor-general did not have a replacement. Regulations stated that the Elected Council of the United Domes of the Moon would pick a replacement should one be needed. And one would be needed in case the governor-general died or became incapacitated.

Which she was now. DeRicci had just finished talking to the head of Deep Craters Hospital, a man used to handling delicate inquiries. Deep Craters was the best, most expensive private hospital on the Moon, and it had the best facilities off Earth—some claimed better than those on Earth. Everyone who was anyone and had health issues went to Deep Craters.

Even Nyquist, after he was attacked by a Bixian assassin more than a year ago, ended up there. But he ended up there because DeRicci's old partner, Miles Flint, had picked up the tab, not because Nyquist's government health insurance allowed it. Someone had made the decision that the governor-general needed the best possible care, not the care that her government health plan dictated.

That worried DeRicci more than anything.

Most of the heads of the domes had checked in, all except for the mayor of Glenn Station. He liked to shut off his links, including his emergency links, just like DeRicci used to when she was a cop, so she had to press upon his staff that this was urgent and life-threatening and he had to contact her immediately.

She was aware that the deep sense of frustration she felt after that encounter was ironic. She finally understood why everyone else in the Armstrong Police Department had been irritated with her all those years ago.

She also reached every single councilor for the United Domes. None of them had been attacked—yet, she stressed—and she encouraged vigilance.

Against what, she wasn't sure.

But she didn't like this. She knew this was some kind of coordinated attack, much more subtle than the kind they'd seen four years ago when Armstrong Dome got bombed. More akin to the biological agent that Frieda Tey had tried to unleash inside the dome five years ago.

The domes were always under attack by some crazy: Dome life was delicate, and people knew that. But most attacks were vast plots against the domes themselves, which made the attacks easier to deflect or defeat.

Someone with a brain realized that they could accomplish a sophisticated terror attack by targeting leaders. Communities went into lockdown, panicked, froze, when their leaders got attacked.

When their leaders died.

And things were worse here. Even though Soseki's deputy mayor, Diane Limón, had already issued a live don't-worry message to the city, that wasn't the same as having a healthy living mayor.

No one had reported yet that Soseki's death was anything other than natural causes, so on that front, the mayor's staff's decision to hesitate about the cause of death had been a good thing. But it had hampered the investigators.

And time was of the essence in figuring out who the killer was and what group or groups he was affiliated with.

Because these coordinated attacks were not an accident.

And it wasn't long before other people—regular people, *media* people—figured that out.

21

NORMALLY THE RESTAURANT WOULD BE A FULL-BLOWN CRIME SCENE, but it had been compromised from the moment the crime happened. Romey made certain that crime scene techs had gone over the table nearest the manager's office first, gathering what evidence they could. She recorded it all, then when they were done, piled her own information on top of it.

That table became her on-scene command center. She set her own flat screen on top of the table, and expanded the image size. Then she pressed information from one side to another, including the list DeRicci had sent her concerning the banned substances in the City of Armstrong.

Romey had just assigned that to one of the crime scene techs— as in, *check for any of these*—when she got another, coded message from DeRicci.

And the message was enough to make her knees buckle.

The governor-general unconscious at Deep Craters. Mayor of Moscow Dome nearly dead of similar attack. Mayor of Glenn Station unavailable, maybe off links, maybe injured. Critical that we have information about your investigation as soon as you have it. You'll share that info with your counterpart in Moscow Dome. Might be coordinated attack. Need to stop it now.

Might be a coordinated attack? Was DeRicci insane? Did she miss the clues? Or was she trying to be discreet because she sent the message across the links? If so, she wasn't discreet enough.

"You okay, Savita?" The voice was new, not one Romey had been hearing all day.

She looked up. Bartholomew Nyquist stood on the other side of the table.

She had never been so relieved to see his slightly mismatched face. He had no scars, but in the right light, he looked like he hadn't been assembled properly. His rumpled clothes didn't help. Nor did his slouch. He was one of the few people she knew who didn't care at all about how he looked, no matter where he was or what he was doing.

And she found that oddly comforting right now.

"I'm glad you're here." She sounded a bit too relieved. But she felt very alone on this and she knew whose hide this entire mess would come out of if her investigation failed.

With Nyquist on board, it wouldn't fail.

She had to believe that.

He gave her a small smile—an appropriate smile, given the circumstances they found themselves in, rueful and acknowledging and gentle.

"You need to see this," she said, and forwarded DeRicci's message to him.

His eyes widened, then his gaze met hers. He was too much of a professional to comment out loud, but he sent back: *Crap.*

Her sentiments exactly.

He bent over the screen. "What have you got?" he asked.

"Nothing yet," she said. "Not even a preliminary coroner's report. People are gathered everywhere and right now, I have uniforms interviewing them."

He was staring at the list DeRicci had sent over. "And this is?"

"The substances that could have caused the death. Have you seen the body?"

He nodded. He still wasn't looking up. That list seemed to fascinate him.

"What are you seeing?" she asked.

"Nothing yet," he said. "But something's close."

99

"We have to move fast," she said. "I'm not used to that kind of investigation. I want the time to talk to everyone, to put all the information together—"

"We can do that," he said, "but our first priority is to find out what, exactly, is going on. We know a few things already. Whoever planned this is not a suicide attacker."

She looked at him, then let out a small sigh. She was letting herself get overwhelmed with what hadn't been done, instead of what she could do. She nodded, encouraging him to continue.

"And," he said, "we know that whoever did this could blend in, which unfortunately, is a strength. We also know that he, she, it, whatever the hell it is, has access to some pretty exotic substances."

She looked at him, still stuck at *blend in*. O'Malley's was a human enclave. The people who came here were known for their love of politics. They also wanted to keep Armstrong's city government as alien-free as possible—and by aliens, they didn't mean humans from other places. They meant nonhumans. They wanted to keep nonhumans off the council and out of the mayor's office.

"We're looking for a human being," she said slowly.

"Most likely," Nyquist said, "although I'd want to find out who did food prep first. Whoever touched that food or any beverages that Soseki had might have a way in."

"Or the hands he shook," Romey said.

"We need to track his last movements," Nyquist said.

"I already have someone on that," she said. "And the crime scene techs are looking at everything he consumed. I'll have that expedited."

"And everything he touched," Nyquist said. "Not with his hands. Jacobs tells me he was wearing SkinSoft and he had it on properly."

"You talked to Jacobs?" Romey felt a twinge of discomfort. Jacobs should have talked to her before anyone else.

"Just before I came in," he said. "She doesn't know anything yet, which is why she hasn't reported to you."

Romey gave him a sharp look. He had noted her twinge and realized the cause of it. He was good, better than she could ever hope to be. The

Chief of Police had made a mistake; Nyquist should have been in charge of this investigation, not Romey.

"The only thing she does know," he said slowly, as if he was giving her time to process all of this, "is that whatever killed him isn't something that is familiar to the Armstrong coroner's office."

Romey noted how he phrased that. He didn't say it was unusual for Armstrong. He didn't even say that it was unusual. Just that it wasn't known in the Armstrong coroner's office, which was an entirely different thing.

She let out a small sigh of relief. She hadn't realized how deep she'd been inside her head until he arrived. "It's nice to have someone to talk to."

"Someone smart," he said, more to himself than to her. She heard the echo of every failed partnership in that sentence. She'd had a few failed ones herself, but not as many as Nyquist. Some of his failed partnerships were legendary in the department.

"Yes," she said, "someone smart. Someone who understands investigation."

"And urgency." He finally looked up. "You want to coordinate, since you're in charge, or you want to help me on the substances here?"

"You're going to track them?"

"I think that's our best lead," he said.

"Go," she said. "I'll find out how whatever it was got into his system, and who had access."

"Think you can cover that in an hour?"

He was turning this into a competition, so that they wouldn't concentrate on the emergency, just on getting the knowledge. And that was brilliant. It took the emotions out of the investigation.

"I'm sure I can," she said.

His smile was sadder than the previous one. "You're on."

And he was right: she was on.

She was the one in charge, the one the spotlight focused on. She was on. Not him, not anyone else. Just her.

And this was one investigation she had better get absolutely right.

22

DMITRI TSEPEN WAS DRUNK, AGAIN. ADRIANA CLIEF RESISTED THE URGE to slap his sagging face. The entire office smelled of beer, which meant he had spilled somewhere and the bots hadn't found it yet. Or he had shut off the cleaning bots. He did that often, claiming they made too much noise.

Since they were programmed to be noiseless, she quite naturally didn't believe him. But Dmitri Tsepen had excuses for everything, even though the excuses often didn't make sense. If she were just a little more naïve, she would wonder how he ever became mayor of Glenn Station.

But she knew.

It was because of her.

She tucked a loose strand of hair behind her ear and studied him. His face was flushed, his head tilted back, his mouth open. He wasn't quite snoring, but he would be soon. His reddish-blond hair was thinning and he hadn't opted to enhance it, despite her nags. All his other enhancements were failing as well. The capillaries in his nose had broken, and if his eyes were open, they'd be red and rheumy.

The drink was overcoming everything, including the artificial means she had urged him to get to make sure no one else knew about his problem.

He was fifty years old, still young by any standard, and passed out like he was, he looked at least thirty years older.

She sighed. She could give him the stimulant booster, which would clear his head. She could then give him a special cleansing wash that would clear the beer stink from his mouth and pores. She could get him to wash his face, and put some whitener on his teeth, and she could remind him to smile.

But it wouldn't do a lot of good.

Oh, he'd show up at the Anniversary Day luncheon speech he was already ten minutes late for, and he would give a rousing, inspiring rendition of his classic "No one can touch us! We're the best people in the system!" speech, and everyone would cheer and applaud and he would wave to them, and for a moment, she would be buoyed, thinking he had finally heard them, finally understood how much his constituents loved him.

Then he would step out of the room, get into his limo, and look at her. He would say with a resigned sigh, *They'll applaud for any old crap, won't they?* and she would feel disappointed all over again.

Once upon a time, she had been a true believer. Once upon a time, she thought the right person in the right place could save the universe. Once upon a time, she had thought Dmitri Tsepen was the right person. She had believed in him so much she had given up a career-track job in public relations to manage him.

And he had been good back then. She had to believe that or she would think she had given up her life for nothing. She had gotten him elected, convinced him that he might want to run for governor-general the next time the job opened up, or maybe take a diplomatic post inside the Earth Alliance.

He had nodded at her, told her to plan it, told her *she* was the brains of the operation, told her he would listen to anything she presented.

And true to his word, he had listened.

He just hadn't acted.

She sighed, staring at him. The room—his beloved inner sanctum— was dark, a book collection all around him. Expensive old books from Earth itself, rare and unusual and very valuable. Once he had told her he could spend the rest of his life in the dark, one light on his desk, a book beneath the light, a beer in his hand. Nothing more. Just a room, a desk, a light, a book, and a beer.

She had laughed, not realizing he was telling the truth.

She could wake him. It would be so simple. She could wake him and clean him up and send him to that damn speech.

Or she could let him sleep.

He would fail for the first time. He would probably fire her. He certainly wouldn't listen to her entreaties to clean himself up, to go into a program, get a genetic manipulation, have one of those rehab enhancements that removed all cravings.

He *liked* his beer, or so he told her. And he really didn't care about politics any more.

She did.

But she didn't care about him.

Odd that she would realize it on a quiet day in the middle of the year. Nothing had tipped her over the edge, nothing had provoked her. She had just cleaned up his messes too many times.

She left his office, pulling the door closed behind her. Her office was across the hall in the City Building, and her office had windows, lots of light, and no old-fashioned collectibles at all. Her office smelled of flowers. Instead of pictures on the wall, she had screens, tuned to every news feed, constantly scanning for mentions of Tsepen or Glenn Station.

How long had she been the unofficial mayor?

Forever, it seemed. Maybe from the beginning. Certainly from the first time he looked at her, befuddled, asking her what he should do, asking if she could explain what the council meant, asking if she knew how to handle a situation.

She walked into her office, feeling shaken. Soon someone would contact her, wondering where he was. She wasn't sure what she would say. That he was drunk? That he had passed out? That he had decided to blow off the speech?

Or maybe she would do what he always did, shut off her links and let events happen around her.

She sank into the comfortable chair behind her desk.

Then she looked up at the screens. They were all showing variations of the same image.

Something had happened in Armstrong. Again. On Anniversary Day.

She leaned forward and ordered the sound up on the nearest screen. Mayor Soseki was dead. The deputy mayor was assuring the city that everything was fine.

Clief felt cold.

Whenever Clief assured people that things were fine, they weren't. They were worse than they had ever been. She was certain that Armstrong's deputy mayor was doing the same.

Clief glanced at the closed door across the hall.

She should wake him and tell him the news.

She should.

But she wasn't about to.

No matter what happened, she was done. She was completely, absolutely, and utterly done.

23

He knew he was being overprotective.

Miles Flint walked through the gates of the Aristotle Academy. He had parked in a different lot, one that he could access quicker if he needed to. But that meant he had to enter the school through the main entrance.

The grounds were quiet—no students in the various playgrounds, no teams practicing esoteric sports. The main entrance, which opened onto a broad lawn covered with real flowers, trees, and plants. The Academy held ceremonies here and often paid the dome to change the lighting to something appropriate for the ceremony.

That was how much money Aristotle Academy had, which didn't surprise him, considering he spent more for his daughter Talia's tuition each semester than he had spent for his top-of-the-line space yacht.

He had come in on this side because the younger children were housed in this part of the building. Aristotle Academy, for all its pomp and circumstance, thought homemade art in the windows—rotating digital portraits, tiny handmade stuffed animals—was much more welcoming than the huge gabled building itself.

Modeled after some of the most prestigious schools on Earth, Aristotle Academy looked dark and forbidding, even with the brightly colored art scrolling across the windows. When Flint had first brought Talia here after her disastrous weeks in public school, she had balked.

She thought the school looked like a prison, even though she had never seen one. Flint had seen prisons, and knew she was wrong. Aristotle Academy looked like the prisons in the ancient Earth books he'd had to read for his Classics of the First World class in college, not like the prison starbases he had visited. Those looked sterile and scary because they had no stimulation at all.

He shuddered, thinking it was the day that brought up these thoughts. He hadn't been in Armstrong during the bombing, so he didn't quite understand the obsession with it. Although he had seen the aftermath and helped work on clean-up, which was more than Talia had done.

She was smarter than anyone he had ever met, but that didn't preclude her from getting scared when something out of the ordinary happened. She could handle herself, but the emotional toll was great. He'd seen that after a case he worked on over a year ago, a case Talia had participated in. That case had made Flint decide to take a leave of absence from his Retrieval Artist business, at least until Talia was grown up and out of the house.

He knew the decision was the right one—he had too many cases that put his life or the life of someone he loved in danger. Better to let the work go for a while and concentrate on Talia. He didn't need the money.

But what he found was that he had a lot of time on his hands, time he didn't know what to do with. He volunteered with a few charities, acted as a behind-the-scenes advisor for some Disappearance Services, and consulted on some cases that he couldn't avoid. Mostly, however, he managed the money he had acquired when he quit the police force. The money took a lot of his time— he hadn't really paid attention to it before—but it wasn't his favorite occupation.

He spent most days keeping up with the current news and taking apart the latest computer systems.

Flint let himself into the school. It smelled faintly of sweat and dirty feet. No matter how hard the air filtration system worked, it couldn't get rid of those kid odors. Flint always found that oddly comforting whenever he came in here. School was school was school.

The hallways were empty. All of the classes were in session, which also made him feel good. He didn't see anyone heading toward the auditorium in the middle of the building nor did he see open classroom doors.

He checked a few as he went past, peering in the windows cut into brightly colored doors. Kids sat in circles or on the floor or in neat rows, heads down as they worked, or hands up as they all struggled to answer the teacher's question. Only a handful of different races were here. The bulk of the students were human, not because of any overt discrimination, but because many of the other cultures didn't like the old Earth teaching methods used here, thinking them too human centric.

Perhaps they were. But that didn't hinder Aristotle Academy's reputation as the place that the brightest students in Armstrong attended. Flint had always heard that. What actually impressed him, however, was the Academy managed to keep Talia interested. Her brain was so powerful that she usually blew through the standard lesson plan for gifted kids. Then she would get distracted, and she would lose all respect for anyone who tried to help her, from the teachers to the school itself.

So far, that hadn't happened at the Academy.

Flint hoped it never would.

He walked past a series of potted plants, all of them set up near the cafeteria, mostly to create oxygen that would clear up food odors. He then turned to his right and headed to the administrative section of the building. In addition to housing the financial part of the Academy and an incredibly elaborate internal system of computers, this section also housed the office of the headmistress.

Flint had known Selah Rutledge for years. Three months ago, she had coaxed him out of his leave of absence to help her with a case involving Luc Deshin, one Armstrong's better known criminals, the kind of man everyone knew ran illegal activities, but no one could prove.

Deshin's son attended the Academy and nearly got kidnapped on its grounds. That, more than anything, encouraged Flint to help with the case. He wanted to make sure the Academy was the safest place he could send Talia. When he found out how security had been breached, he was a lot calmer. It had been a fluke occurrence, something he helped Rutledge plan for in the future.

She owed him. Hell, Deshin owed him, although the man didn't know it. Still, Flint kept it in mind. One day he would collect upon a debt.

The entrance to the headmistress's office looked like any other in this section of the school. A solid door with no window, and a small sign at eye level identifying the room's purpose. This sign simply said, *Office of the Headmistress*, without even identifying who she was.

That was something else Flint liked about Selah Rutledge. Even though she had risen to the top of her profession, she had no real ego about it. As if Headmistress of the Armstrong Wing of the Aristotle Academy was as unimportant a position as, say, a uniformed officer in the Armstrong Police Department.

He knocked on the door, then grabbed the knob, turned it, and let himself in. The school was old-fashioned down to its doors, although that door knob had more sensors in it than the door knob outside the office for his Retrieval Artist business. The networks here in Aristotle Academy just confirmed who he was, what connection he had to the school, and what the physical indicators of his mood were. That last was an addition he had made to the network, so that distraught people (and students) had a tougher time getting into important parts of the school.

The Office of the Headmistress was a comfortable place—for adults, anyway. Large plants, interspersed with three desks, made the room seem smaller than it was. Chairs sat in nooks and crannies around the room, so that kids sent here for punishment or to finalize some kind of appointment didn't have to sit next to each other. They didn't even have to look at each other if they didn't want to.

Rutledge didn't have human secretaries or receptionists. She let the doorknob tell her who had arrived in her office. She did have a security detail, but it wasn't visible. Otherwise, anyone who came to the Headmistress's Office had complete privacy.

Flint was alone here at the moment. He stood among the desks and plants, wondering if Rutledge was even in. He threaded his fingers together, feeling nervous.

That was a relatively new emotion for him as well—nervousness. Or maybe it was an old emotion. He had felt it when Emmeline was a baby, the constant worry that he was doing something wrong. He'd had to remind himself that inexperienced humans had been taking care of babies since the beginning of the race.

But when Emmeline had died, he had lost some of the jittery emotions. He had stopped caring about himself. Sure, he got nervous, but not this kind of impatient nervousness, the kind that made him want to do something immediately, even if doing that thing was counterproductive.

Then the door to the back office opened and Selah Rutledge came out. She was wearing her trademark cape, which made her seem as Old Earth as the gables on her school building. Her dark hair was pulled back into a bun, accenting the lines on her face. She looked tired.

"Sorry, Miles," she said. "I didn't mean to keep you waiting. It's a busy day."

"I know." He made himself sound calmer than he felt. "I trust you heard about the mayor."

She nodded. "That's part of the busy-ness. I had to bundle two dozen children out of here before they heard the news, because their parents wanted to deal with it. The entire city government is in an uproar."

Then she frowned.

"Should I have contacted you as well? I didn't realize that Talia knew Mayor Soseki."

"I do," Flint said, "but I don't think she ever met him."

Rutledge's expression didn't change. Flint liked that about her. She remained calm even when she was surprised. And he had surprised her, even though she hadn't said so. He could tell from her slight shift in posture.

"But she is emotionally fragile," he said, "and if the school goes into crisis mode, I'm afraid it'll hit her harder than she's willing to admit."

His cheeks were growing warm. When he said this out loud, it sounded silly.

"I'm probably out of line here," he said. "I just wanted to be at the school if you declared a crisis."

Rutledge gave him a soft smile. "I don't think you're out of line, Miles. I'm very familiar with Talia's file. As tough as she pretends to be, she'd gone through more than most people experience in a lifetime. Traumatic events are bound to echo, and whether she admits it or not, you're her anchor. So I think having you here is just fine."

"You haven't declared an emergency, have you?" he said, realizing he hadn't asked.

"Not yet," she said. "And no offense to the mayor, but if his death turns out to be natural like they say, I won't declare one. We had to lock down the campus during the bombing, and that was traumatic enough. I really don't want to go through it again."

He nodded. He hadn't realized that. He usually refrained from asking people what they had been doing during the bombing; the memories were still raw.

"If she finds out I'm here, and there was no actual reason for it, she'll be furious at me."

"Well, then," Rutledge said. "We'll wait for the next announcements on the mayor, and if there's nothing to worry about, you can go home. Talia need not be the wiser."

It was his turn to smile at Rutledge. "So, I'm one of those annoyingly overinvolved parents."

Rutledge grinned at him. "Does it matter, Miles? You're trying to do what's best for your daughter."

His smile faded as the truth of her words sank in. Particularly the word "trying." He was trying. He just wasn't sure what to do.

"Thanks for understanding, Selah," he said.

"Oh, I have a vested interest in keeping you here, Miles," she said. "Should something go wrong, it's always better to have a computer expert on hand, particularly one who knows all the tricks."

Her smile was gone too. He felt cold. "You think something is going to go wrong, don't you?"

She shrugged one shoulder. "I don't like it. It's Anniversary Day and the mayor's dead. That could be a coincidence, bad luck, or bad timing."

"Or it could be deliberate," Flint said.

She stared at him, then sighed. "I just have an awful feeling about this," she said.

And as she spoke, he realized he did too. That was why he was here. Because everything about this day, about the mayor's death, about the anniversary itself, felt wrong.

24

ROMEY CROWDED NEAR THE FAR WALL OF THE RESTAURANT, SILENTLY thanking every single god she'd ever heard of that she had put someone good on the visuals. Emmanuel Tyr should have retired decades ago, but he loved solving things. In particular, he loved processing the visual information that came filtered through a case.

Tyr had muscled his way onto the scene carrying his specialized equipment. Romey had learned long ago to let him set up wherever he needed to. His equipment was finer, more refined, than any other she had seen. She had argued with him on their very first case together. It was one of the few times in her life that she was happy she lost.

Tyr had scouted the entire restaurant, stepping around the crime scene techs as they cleared him. He finally settled on the area near Romey's make-shift headquarters. He bullied the techs into finishing that area first, then he set up five screens. He attached them to a network only Tyr touched (Romey had learned that the hard way as well) and then got to work.

He also worked faster than anyone Romey knew, as if he were part computer.

She was glad for it on this case, because this case had more visuals than any case she had ever worked.

Almost everyone who had attended Soseki's speech had recorded it for personal use. O'Malley's itself had made four recordings of the speech from different parts of the room. Then there were the security cameras, the kitchen cameras, the back hallway cameras, and once Soseki had entered the restaurant proper, more visuals from more onlookers who were determined to have a bit of Soseki to take with them.

Why the man had decided to go through the crowded restaurant instead of disappearing out the back like most politicos baffled Romey. But she wasn't here to understand him, not yet, at least. She was here to look for something, someone, suspicious.

Within fifteen minutes of setting up, Tyr claimed he found something. He made Romey stand near the far wall, and she brought some of her lieutenants. Banyon Kilzahn wanted to watch as well, but she wouldn't let him.

She wanted to know what Tyr had before she let Kilzahn report to DeRicci.

For all his enthusiasm, Tyr could occasionally see connections that no one else could. That didn't mean those connections weren't there. It usually meant that Romey had to send him back to work so that he could communicate with "the little people." She never told him she often found his attitudes offensive.

She figured that was part of the price she paid for working with Emmanuel Tyr.

As Tyr's audience gathered, he offered them a variety of viewing options. Tyr's five screens had holo capability, so that the watchers could feel like part of the scene if they were so inclined.

Romey wasn't so inclined.

She told him so. Then she told him to get straight to the report, doubting he would be able to. Emmanuel Tyr loved convincing other people of his own brilliance.

That was the only downside of working with him. He had a tendency to over-explain, and Romey had a tendency to tune out. She didn't dare on this one, although she'd missed a lot of the explanation already.

"I had the choice of tens of thousands of images per nanosecond," Tyr was saying. He was a short square man with a full head of black hair.

The black hair had to be an enhancement, some kind of holdover from his youth. It looked out of place against his leathery skin, something he'd obviously decided not to enhance, thinking—or so he had once told her—that aged skin gave a person an air of authority.

"I have a program that selects for the best image based on customized details. I set up six different versions of this program, searching for suspicious behavior, someone manipulating our guy's food or his drink or touching him inappropriately, stalking him—you get the idea."

Yes, she got the idea, but she knew better than to push Tyr. She didn't add anything, because he'd hear the addition as a question, then he'd answer it, and she'd lose even more time.

"When you set up a stalking program for a politician," he said, musing aloud, "You have to be careful to exclude bodyguards and majordomos. You still get a lot of false positives, but that's where we got our best hit. Watch this."

She leaned toward the screens.

Tyr pointed to the center one.

"See that guy?" he asked, finger brushing against the image of a thin blond with floppy hair and an arresting face. "Watch him."

She was still staring at the blonde's appearance. Blonds were rare anywhere, but they were particularly rare on the Moon. This one was young, maybe twenty-five, unless he had enhancements to make him seem young.

But she didn't think so. He moved like a very young man, and he had that thinness that most men outgrew by the time they were thirty. Even if they used enhancements to stay thin, they never had that stick-like appearance again.

The blond stood in the back, arms crossed, expression neutral as he watched Soseki give his speech. Fortunately, Tyr had the sound turned off. Romey had heard most of Soseki's speeches, and no offense to the newly deceased mayor, but they had a certain sameness to them, one she didn't need to experience again.

115

Then the mayor finished, all two hundred plus people in the room applauded—except the blond—and then most moved en masse toward the podium for a moment or two with Soseki.

He posed for pictures, shook more hands than she ever wanted to consider, and chatted happily with a number of people he clearly didn't know. All the while, his bodyguards and his aides stood nearby, looking impatient.

She already knew that the substance which killed him hadn't come through his hands. He wore SkinSoft and except for the epidermals from all the various hands he touched, his SkinSoft had nothing on it.

He was, she had learned this day, a cautious man, one who never ate at these events, who brought his own liquids, who in fact never ever did anything that would allow people to harm him—at least using known methods.

Soseki had lived through the dome bombing. He'd been brash back then, but the bombing taught him caution. He'd also received an inordinate number of death threats, particularly as the press reported on the political machine he'd built inside the city. He could have been, according to more than one person she'd spoken to this afternoon, mayor for life. And, she had thought a bit unkindly, he had been.

She would have been pursuing the mayor-for-life angle if the governor-general and the mayor of Moscow Dome hadn't been attacked as well. This was not a vendetta against a particular person. She doubted this attack had much to do with Soseki at all. It had to do with his being mayor of the City of Armstrong.

It was symbolic—and Soseki would have hated that.

Tyr continued to point out the blond man. Each time Soseki moved, the blond man moved as well. But the blond man was good. He didn't hover, nor did he stalk. He didn't even seem obvious.

At one point, he simply looked like a man who wanted to get out of the restaurant, and when one of the bodyguards blocked him, he looked annoyed.

Finally, the blond man made his way to the door. He stepped outside just before Soseki finished glad-handing. If someone had been watching the blond man—and Romey wasn't sure anyone had—they would have seen a man impatient to get out of a crowd, and then once out, a man who needed to catch his breath before he went on.

Romey wagered that when she showed this to the bodyguards— who wouldn't remember the man until they saw him—they'd say that he claimed to be uncomfortable in crowds. If she hadn't seen him in the room where Soseki was making the speech, leaning comfortably against the wall, unconcerned when people brushed past him, she would have believed he had some kind of phobia against crowded places.

Poor Soseki. His bodyguards weren't as good as they should have been. They should have noted the difference in the blond guy's behavior inside the back room and then in the corridors.

On the visuals, Soseki's bodyguards came out of the door, with Soseki in the middle. Romey frowned. She hadn't realized just how obviously a bodyguard's stance told an attacker exactly where the potential victim was.

The blond guy moved just a little to the side—not much—adjusting his own position so that he could get close to Soseki.

Then all the blond guy did was brush casually against Soseki's arm.

Soseki didn't notice. Neither did the bodyguards.

The blond guy scurried away, as if he were afraid the crowd would catch up to him, and as he did, Soseki froze in place.

"What the hell happened?" Romey asked.

Tyr was prepared for the question. He let the wide image dim, and focused on that moment when the blond guy brushed against Soseki. Tyr magnified the image until all that was visible were the sides of both men's sleeves.

The fabrics touched so lightly that they didn't even indent. Soseki wouldn't have felt anything at all. But as those two bits of fabric touched, a small needle-like object emerged from the weave in the blond guy's sleeve.

"That needle thing," Tyr said as they watched, "is so tiny that the naked eye can't see it. I've had to magnify this…"

But Romey stopped listening after "naked eye." She watched the needle thing slide into Soseki's sleeve. Then the needle thing disintegrated, and the sleeves separated.

"Will we find trace elements of that thing on Soseki's sleeve?" she asked.

"How would I know?" Tyr asked. "I don't think so, but I don't specialize in that kind of thing. I've gone over this a few times, and even at an even greater level of magnification, I don't see anything left on the mayor's sleeve. But that doesn't mean it's not there."

"Right." She knew it would matter when they had the blond guy in custody. When they prosecuted him. But it didn't matter at the moment, unless that trace amount of whatever told her what exactly caused Soseki's death.

Although it was pretty obvious. Tyr zoomed back out. A second or less after the needle went in, Soseki froze in place. Then the gray color started spreading over him.

"That's enough," Romey said. "I don't need to see that again. I need some good images of this blond man, holo images as well as 2-D."

"Already got it," Tyr said and sent it to her via her links. She let the flat images whiz past her left eye, and did not even look at the holoimages because she knew what they would show. They'd show the blond guy in motion, so that the officers would see his gait, his height, his gestures. The officers would know exactly how this guy moved and got around. They might even be able to track him just from the image.

She forwarded all of the images to the entire Armstrong PD with a notice that this was the guy they wanted—"for questioning," of course. She did want him for questioning. She wanted to know what the hell was going on.

Romey also sent it to DeRicci. And then, because Romey promised, she also sent it to the investigators in Moscow Dome.

Immediately, she got a scrambled text response from Moscow Dome: *You're kidding, right?*

She moved away from her team, and answered on the same encrypted link. *No. You recognize this guy?*

Hell, yeah. We're looking for the same guy.

Romey frowned. *I thought the attacks happened at the same time.*

They did. The liaison from Moscow Dome sent her a series of images. It looked like the same guy, only he was getting close to Moscow Dome's mayor.

Romey cursed. *Clones?* she asked. *They're using clones?*

What else would it be? The liaison sent back.

It made no sense. Clones were obvious. They got noticed. They were easy to track, particularly if—like most clones on the Moon—they were registered.

Anyone claimed responsibility for yours yet? she sent.

DeRicci was the one who responded. Clearly she'd been monitoring the communication. *No one's claiming responsibility for any of it,* she sent. *But, clearly from these images, it's only a matter of time.*

25

DEEP CRATERS HOSPITAL SMELLED LIKE PUKE. AT LEAST, THIS WING DID. In some room, not too far from the waiting area, someone kept retching over and over again. The sound alone was enough to make Nelia Byler's stomach churn, and the smell didn't help. Apparently the air filters here, along with the hospital's state-of-the-art cleaning bots, weren't enough to get rid of the odor instantly.

Or maybe the fact that the smell lingered had more to do with her own acid reflux, which was staying ahead of her medical programming, which was the same programming the governor-general had. When the governor-general wanted to upgrade her medical protocols to the latest model, she asked if Byler would be her guinea pig.

Try it first, Nelia, and see if it works, the governor-general had said. Then she had added, with a bit of a sheepish smile, *If you don't mind, that is*.

Fortunately, Nelia hadn't thought of herself as squeamish. She thought of herself as a courageous person who always took one for the team. Whatever Celia Alfreda asked for, Celia Alfreda would get—at least as long as Nelia Byler worked for her. Nelia thought it a privilege to work in the governor-general's office, at the governor-general's side, doing the governor-general's bidding.

Now all of that might be over.

She wouldn't let herself think about that.

She wrapped her arms around her torso and paced. The waiting area was nice, homey, with comfortable couches that reminded her of those in the house she grew up in. Every table top had a screen with entertainment programming so powerful it could block out everything else, and make the viewer lose track of time. One specially set up screen would order from every single restaurant in the city.

She could live here if she wanted to. Apparently, people did.

But not today. On this day, she had the waiting room to herself. Except for the champion vomiter down the hall, this wing was empty. They would bring Celia here if she survived the surgery—or whatever the hell they were doing to her.

Byler's eyes filled with tears, and she blinked hard to keep them back. No one knew what exactly was wrong with the governor-general. They only knew that she was dying by centimeters, that every part of her body was solidifying.

Celia's state-of-the-art medical protocols had slowed everything down, but they couldn't overwhelm whatever it was—at least that was what Byler heard in the last update. Not that the person who had updated her—and it had been a person, not an automatic message through her links, not an avatar, not some kind of bot—had known exactly what was going on.

The people who specialized in Celia's condition—as much as people could specialize in her condition, given that no one knew exactly what was wrong with her—were working desperately on Celia, trying to save her life.

But Byler had gotten the distinct impression that saving her was next to impossible.

Byler had her arms wrapped so tightly around herself that she could barely breathe. She really needed to loosen her fingers; they dug deep into her ribcage, sending an ache through her entire body.

But she was reluctant to let go. The pain made her feel alive. Or maybe it was a tiny punishment for her inability to stop this attack.

No one even knew how it happened. The governor-general's security detail had secured the scene. Last Byler heard, they were waiting for someone from Armstrong's Police Department to officially handle the investigation.

The rest of the team had gone back to the governor-general's office. Because this was Anniversary Day, only a skeleton staff remained there. Most everyone who was anyone was either making a speech, cutting a ceremonial ribbon, doing some kind of publicity, *something* to make the day seem less ominous than it actually was.

Byler hated celebrating—if that was the word—a disaster. Marking a disaster, then. She had hated it before Celia fell ill. Now Byler wondered if they hadn't brought this entire crisis on themselves simply by marking the anniversary in such a public manner.

It was an invitation to all the nutcases in the universe to do something spectacular and have it mean even more than it should.

Those tears threatened again. She stopped pacing and looked out the window at the city, going about its business. A few cars flew past, their passengers looking away from the shaded hospital windows. She could see out, but she knew from experience that no one could see in.

People, looking like nanocreatures themselves, walked on the sidewalks below. People or aliens or something two-legged and mobile. Of course, she wasn't even sure of the two-legged part.

Her fingernails found a way through the fabric of her shirt. The last thing anyone needed was the attacker to be something other than human. Then the entire Earth Alliance would get involved, and it would become an Alliance-wide incident, not just a Moon incident, which was bad enough.

She really should have gone back to the office. She should have coordinated all of the publicity, she should have prepared the press releases, she should have been doing interviews.

But she wanted someone here in case Celia woke up, someone Celia trusted, someone Celia knew actually cared for her.

At least, Byler hoped Celia knew. She probably didn't. She probably thought Byler was as opportunistic as everyone else. And maybe Byler was, on some level. But she couldn't imagine working for another politician. No one would be like Celia, an innovator as well as an organizer, someone who knew how to get others to do her bidding, even when what she wanted was desperately unpopular.

Byler let out a shaky breath. What if this attack was related to Celia's policies—to *Byler's* policies. Because Byler had written half the damn agenda. Byler decided which things should get the most attention. Celia had just signed off on them.

Byler abruptly sat on the couch. They didn't prepare you for this kind of emergency, not even when you majored in foreign relations and diplomacy, government and Earth Alliance politics. No matter how many internships you did, how many campaigns you apprenticed on, nothing prepared you for this moment, when the person you worked for, the person you *believed* in, was a hair's breath away from death, a moment away from a true assassination, not just an assassination attempt.

Something blared across her links. She put her hands to her ears, even though the sound was internal not external. A red light flashed across her eyes, and tears did fall for a moment, tears of pain.

She wiped at them, frowned, and then remembered that everything except her emergency links got shut off from the moment she stepped into the hospital.

She stood, took a deep breath, and answered.

What?

She had no idea who she sent that to, and she was surprised to see Noelle DeRicci's face pop up in front of her.

In all of this, Byler had forgotten about Soseki. Her stomach clenched, and she thought sympathetically (for the first time) of the vomiter in the nearby room.

This was part of a pattern. She had forgotten.

You had your links off, DeRicci sent.

I'm in Deep Craters waiting room, Byler sent back. *I didn't shut them off on purpose.*

DeRicci nodded, then asked for an update. Byler told her all that she knew, which wasn't much.

You didn't contact me for that, though, did you? Byler asked. DeRicci could have gotten the update from anyone on the governor-general's staff. Even though Byler was a bit fuzzy-headed, she had been thinking clearly enough to keep her own people apprised of the governor-general's condition.

You're right, DeRicci sent. *I didn't contact you for that. I wanted to know if you've seen this man.*

She sent an image and then a vid of a man crossing a room. Byler's breath caught. The man looked completely familiar. She had been watching him when Rudra Popova contacted her about Soseki's death.

Yeah, Byler sent. *He was at the governor-general's speech.*

Did he touch her? DeRicci asked.

Byler shrugged, then realized DeRicci couldn't see her. *I don't know.*

But? DeRicci asked.

But something was on the edge of Byler's brain, something she couldn't quite recall. He had vanished—or she had looked away—and then when she looked back...

He talked to her, Byler said. *I think he was talking to her when she fell ill.*

Her heart pounded. Was that true? She wasn't sure of anything anymore.

You'd have to check with security, though, Byler continued, covering her ass because as a politician's assistant, it was a damn reflex. *I was in the back of the room, and he had moved to the front. I remember looking at him just before I got the medical protocol message.*

The what? DeRicci asked.

I'm hooked into the governor-general's private medical program, Byler said. *Me and a few others, including security. The program kicked in right at that moment, and we all jumped into action.*

Or, rather, security had. She had been too far away.

She added, *I think that's the only thing that saved the governor-general's life.*

If, indeed, she was going to live.

Do you have any idea who that man was? DeRicci asked.

No, Byler sent. *But he had to be cleared. We have strict security procedures since the Mars crisis. No one comes close to the governor-general without about six layers of specialized clearance.*

DeRicci cursed. *I suppose I have to go to her security team for that as well.*

Yes, sir, Byler sent. *I'm sorry I'm not much use to you at the moment. I felt someone should monitor her condition.*

Well, she's not dead yet, DeRicci sent, with characteristic bluntness. *That's a good thing. Soseki died within seconds.*

You think this is the same thing? Byler asked.

You described her symptoms, DeRicci sent. *They sound like an extremely mild version of what killed Arek.*

Byler swallowed hard. *Do you think she'll survive this?*

I don't know, DeRicci sent. *I sure as hell hope so. But until we know what they did, we may not be able to do much more than hold off the inevitable.*

They? Byler sent.

Clones, DeRicci sent. *The image I sent you was of Mayor Julian's attacker. The vid is of the man who attacked Arek.*

Byler's breath caught. *Why would they make clones?*

Why indeed? DeRicci asked. *I've got people trying to figure that out. In the meantime, the governor-general hasn't made some anti-clone statements I need to know about, has she?*

Last summer, she spoke to a gathering of families who have adopted clones, Byler sent. *She told them she supports a change in the Earth Alliance policy that has regulated clones to second-class status. But it has no teeth. She can't do anything more than a private citizen can. She just has an opinion. She has no power over the Alliance.*

As you well know, she thought, but didn't add. A burst of anger ran through her at DeRicci. *She* was head of security for the entire damn Moon. How come she hadn't seen this coming?

That shouldn't anger them, DeRicci sent. *Thanks, Nelia. Let me know the moment she wakes up.*

If she wakes up, Byler sent, but DeRicci had already broken the connection. Which was lucky. Byler didn't want to seem that pessimistic, not on a semi-open link.

She rubbed a hand over her face. Somewhere along the way, she had stopped hugging herself.

A clone. A series of attacks. Planned, of course, for Anniversary Day.

If Celia were awake and able to listen, she would hear a bunch of I-told-you-sos from Byler. But Byler couldn't say that to her, not now, maybe not ever.

She leaned her head back and closed her eyes, and wished, wished hard, for this day to come to an end.

26

ADRIANA CLIEF SAT AT HER DESK, HER HAND COVERING HER MOUTH, HER heart pounding. Her links were cluttered with messages from all sorts of people, wondering why Dmitri Tsepen hadn't shown up for his speech yet. On the various screens in front of her, reporters repeated the news of Mayor Arek Soseki's death, although no one knew what of.

Her head ached. She had just decided not to do anything to help Tsepen anymore, but she hadn't expected to get inundated in contacts. People still expected her to be the competent one, even though she had decided not to be.

Besides, they couldn't reach Tsepen—which was normal—so they were in the habit of contacting her.

She got up and watered a few of the flowering plants. Then she picked off a few dead buds. Deadheading. That was what it was called, and that was what she was doing, not just to the plants, but to Dmitri. She was deadheading him, picking him off because he had become useless.

She looked down the hall at his closed door. He was probably still passed out, not that he would be useful anyway. If she sent him to the speech, she would have to find something that would clear up his drunkenness, and most of the remedies, except the rather stringent nanobot cleaning, left him muzzy-headed or didn't work at all.

He really had become a fall-down drunk, and like any codependent person, she hadn't noticed.

A red line flashed across her right eye, followed by an urgent message.

Then the image of Noelle DeRicci, Head of Security for the United Domes, rose in Clief's vision, making her headache worse.

"Let me put you on visual," she said, trying to take the message out of her vision.

"No," DeRicci said. "This is a coded transmission. Anything visual would break the code."

Clief sighed, and moved away from the plants. She plopped down behind her desk again and wished she could close her eyes and lean her head back, ignoring everything.

"I suppose they're all contacting you because he hasn't shown up at his stupid speech," she said. "I'm sorry for that. It won't happen again."

"What?" DeRicci said, and Clief swore she heard a tinge of panic in DeRicci's tone. "Tsepen's missing?"

"In a manner of speaking," Clief said. "He's passed out drunk in his office."

DeRicci let out a sigh, and it seemed like a sigh of relief, which also surprised Clief.

"Look," DeRicci said, "what I'm about to tell you is classified. You cannot tell anyone. Are we clear?"

"Clear," Clief said, wondering what the hell was going on.

"A group of clones have targeted the leaders of various Moon communities. There's been an attack on the governor-general and on Mayor Julian in Moscow Dome. I'm trying to reach the other mayors now."

"And Arek Soseki?" Clief asked, her heart suddenly racing.

"Yes. They killed him." DeRicci's tone was flat. "And we're not sure the governor-general is going to make it either. So it's good that Dmitri didn't make it to his speech."

Clief shook her head. "He lives a charmed life."

DeRicci frowned. "People are complaining that he's not there?"

"Yes," Clief said.

"So they're still waiting for him?"

"Yes," Clief said.

"Excellent. Close the hall where he's supposed to speak. Don't let anyone in or out. I'll coordinate with law enforcement in Glenn Station. We're going to search for one of those bastards."

Clief shook her head again. If they caught one of those bastards, Tsepen was going to look like a prescient saint instead of a drunken screw-up.

"Can you work with me on this, Adriana?" DeRicci asked.

"I'd be happy to, sir," Clief said. So much for her vow of non-involvement.

"All right," DeRicci said. "Here's what we're going to do."

27

Nyquist commandeered a table near the back of the main part of the restaurant by the hallway that led to the room where Soseki made his final speech. Unbeknownst to Romey, Nyquist had done a quiet walk-through of the place, just to see if there was anything anyone had missed.

He couldn't tell if there was. The large meeting room looked abandoned, as if the meeting had just ended. Garbage littered the floor, some glasses covered a nearby table, a half-empty bottle of water stood on the stage near the podium. He did send a message to the crime scene techs to make sure they picked up all the bottled water, labeled it properly, and then tested it, although he was pretty certain that the water hadn't killed Soseki.

Nyquist had seen that needle that Tyr had isolated off the vids. There was, in Nyquist's opinion, no defending against something like that. It went to something he always said to DeRicci when he was trying to calm her down: *Something will get through. A determined terrorist can get past all barriers. Your job is to make sure those barriers are sound, and what does get through is a fluke.*

He wasn't sure this was a fluke, but he did know that these people were determined.

He had watched a few minutes of the rest of the vid Tyr had prepared, the clone waiting for his moment to get close to Soseki. The fact that there were more of them made Nyquist extremely nervous. Something—some*one*—big had planned this attack for a long time.

After he had that realization, he commandeered his table. He set up a small command, a networked screen, a bit of crumpled up napkin so that it looked as if the table was in constant use.

Then he left again, slipping out front so that he could find out how Jacobs was doing.

She still crouched near Soseki's body, a laser knife in her hand. A ring of uniforms stood around her, facing the street. Another group of uniforms was moving from building to building, as if they were searching for someone. Someone who had seen the clone?

He didn't know, and at the moment, he didn't care. The clone was Romey's problem. Nyquist's problem was pretty simple and extremely complex at the same time.

He tried to get to Jacobs, but one of the uniforms held him back. So Nyquist sent her a message. She nodded, then squinted, the way some people did when they were using their links.

Clearly she hadn't sent a message to him. The message was going to the uniforms, telling them that Nyquist had clearance.

He slipped past and stopped near Jacobs.

"Come closer, Bartholomew," she said, "and take a look at this."

She beckoned him to crouch beside her. She had opened a tiny section of Soseki's deltoid muscle. Or what should have been Soseki's deltoid muscle.

Instead, it looked like she had carved into the sidewalk.

"Is that as thick as it looks?" Nyquist asked.

She handed him a small screen that magnified the image from the tip of the laser. He didn't see muscle or skin or blood vessels. He saw only grayness so solid that it looked like part of a tube.

"I couldn't cut into it with a regular knife," she said. "I had to use the laser. This is his right side. The attack happened on his left. It's even more solid over there."

"What is this?" Nyquist asked.

"I have no idea," Jacobs said. "But it's both fast-acting and terrifying. I say we don't ever let the cause of death out. I say we just tell people he was poisoned and leave it at that."

"I'd love to order that," Nyquist said, "but I'm not in charge of this investigation."

She pursed her lips. She had already made her opinion known on that.

"So let me make sure I'm understanding this," Nyquist said. "It turned his insides to sludge."

She shook her head. "More like it filled in his skin with this new substance, destroying everything else it came into contact with. And I'm not even sure there's any skin here either. This may just be the substance, using his body as some kind of mold, and working through it."

Despite himself, Nyquist shuddered. It really had turned Soseki into some kind of statue.

"I can give you the chemical compound," Jacobs said, "but this is post-reaction. I don't know if the compound is the same before it comes in contact with the skin."

Nyquist nodded.

She handed him a small disk, which surprised him.

"You could send this through my links," he said.

She shook her head. "I'm telling you, Bartholomew, this stuff scares me. It's quick, lethal, and effective. I don't want any part of it out there. I don't want anyone to know what it really is."

He closed his fist around the disk. "Someone already knows what it is, Marigold," he said softly. "And worse, they know how to use it."

She bit her lower lip, then teared up.

"Sometimes I hate this job," she said.

"I know," Nyquist said. "Believe me. I know."

28

DeRicci paced around her office. She hadn't felt this alone in years. Alone and terrified. The news was awful. So far she was keeping it under wraps, but she wasn't sure how long she would be able to do that. It was a miracle she had managed so far.

In some ways, the fact that Soseki's aides had dithered about reporting his death to the authorities helped. It made Soseki's death seem like less of a crisis, more like a death from natural causes.

Except for one or two people, no one had been in the room when the governor-general collapsed, and even then, fewer saw it. Deep Craters Hospital was good at keeping secrets, something that usually irritated DeRicci, but made her feel better at the moment.

She clasped her hands behind her back. She had asked Popova for coffee half an hour ago and hadn't gotten it. Coffee and some food from somewhere. Neither had arrived.

DeRicci had learned, no matter how serious the crisis, she had to eat. She wouldn't be getting enough sleep, so eating was extremely important.

She knew Popova was upset—abnormally upset—and figured that was just a sign of things to come. Assassinations coupled with Anniversary Day would be tougher than the heartiest soul could handle.

DeRicci wished she could contact Nyquist. But she didn't dare, not since Romey had put him on the case. DeRicci didn't want to be seen as influencing the Armstrong Police Department, particularly not where Nyquist was concerned.

It was strange to be thinking of the future right now, but she had to. She had to think about the current investigation, about preventing more attacks, about stopping whoever the hell this was, and about the way that journalists, historians, and conspiracy nuts would look at everything once the case ended.

Conspiracy nuts.

Clearly, they wouldn't be nuts in this case. And that was the most disturbing thing of all.

She sent a curt message to Popova. *Coffee and food? Important for all of us.*

And she didn't wait for a response. Instead, she turned toward the gigantic screen that still dominated her office. The screen she had been trying to ignore. The screen she really, really, really didn't want to think about.

Her stomach churned. Coffee and food wouldn't make it better, but it would keep her going. And she doubted she'd have a calm stomach for months after this.

The vid from Moscow Dome was in. The *edited* vid. They had asked if she wanted the unedited vid, and she had said no. She wanted to see this attempted murder in action.

Images moved all over the screen. Reporters, talking about Mayor Soseki. One network already had a retrospective that anyone could order, complete with holorecordings of Mayor Soseki's speeches, a virtual recreation of his acceptance speeches on his election nights, starting with the first mayoral acceptance, and an examination of his home life.

She immediately sent a note of that to Romey. The network might have had a special like that ready for a bunch of celebrities, but it was unusual to have something this fast, no matter what. Maybe they'd had warning.

She made herself sit down to watch the vid. Pacing was driving her nuts. Sitting probably would as well, but at least she would be doing something different.

The tech from Moscow Dome had given her the option of watching everything in holographic mode, but she chose not to. Already this entire thing was much too vivid in her mind. She didn't need to superficially live through it.

She faded the other images into the background, however, and used the entire screen to watch the images the tech had spliced together from a thousand different images.

DeRicci hadn't been to Moscow Dome in years. She had no idea where this was taking place. She supposed she could touch part of the screen and get an exact map of the city—and she would if she were the primary investigator, to see if there were other patterns at work here—but she didn't. She sank into her chair and let the events unfold in front of her.

Everything began on the street outside the venue—whatever the hell it was. It took her a moment to realize that what she thought was a street was really an alley. When she had been there, Moscow Dome had a lot of old streets, alleys that went nowhere, buildings that needed to be torn down. Apparently that hadn't changed.

The assassin (she didn't know what else to call him) looked impossibly young here, younger than the one at Soscki's speech. She did a capture of the image and sent it to Romey, with a note about this shooter's age. Maybe this clone was created later. Maybe they all weren't part of a batch.

DeRicci didn't want to think about how they were created at the moment. She just wanted to observe.

He wore the same clothing, and his hair was cut exactly the same way as the others. He moved a little differently. He was jittery. He kept glancing over his shoulder as if he expected someone to come after him.

The vid itself was a bit jittery, since it seemed to take images off different cameras at random moments. So for five seconds, she watched the assassin from the front, then suddenly she was looking at the top of his head, then at his right side.

But that did give her a perspective of the alley. It had a number of doors and a surprising amount of garbage. Apparently Moscow Dome didn't have the garbage collection regulations that Armstrong had either.

135

She made a note of that as well and set it for a future date. If the governor-general lived through this, DeRicci would discuss garbage collection with her, because that could be a health issue for the entire Moon, something that should come under the purview of her office.

She stopped the vid and made herself take a deep breath. She was in some kind of denial, thinking that Celia would live through this. Everything had changed this afternoon, just like everything had changed four years ago, during the bombing.

DeRicci rubbed a hand over her forehead, then started the vid back up again. She thought she saw a shadow at the mouth of the alley but she wasn't sure. Maybe it was just the camera angle, maybe it was because the assassin kept looking over his shoulder.

She clasped her hands over her stomach. The assassin pulled open a door and slipped through it.

Then the perspective changed. Suddenly, she watched him coming into the building, through a back entrance that should have been guarded but wasn't. The corridor was dark, which she thought very strange.

He slipped into a side room—a storage room—with the lights off. The cameras in there only caught a bit of him as he hunched underneath some shelving.

That was when she realized that he was waiting. He had arrived so early that the lights inside the building were off. She wished now that she had watched the extended footage; she would know exactly what time this took place.

She made herself take another deep breath. She wasn't focusing. She wasn't running that kind of investigation. This was something Romey had to watch, Romey needed to figure out how all of the assassinations or the attempted assassinations went down. DeRicci didn't have time for it. That was why she had to watch the shortened version, why she had to concentrate, not on the hows, but on the common elements with the other attacks.

And the uncommon elements.

She was pretty sure that the assassin in the Soseki case just walked into the restaurant like the other patrons. And the assassin in the governor-general's case had a ticket to the event.

So not everything was the same. Some details differed.

Which meant that the clones weren't acting on some kind of script, but on specific targets in specific locations.

Which meant the clones had some kind of autonomy.

The lighting changed in that room. The assassin slipped out, adjusted his clothes, took some kind of badge from his pocket, and walked down the corridor.

The corridor's lights were on as well. And there were people inside, people who nodded at him, people who stopped him and checked his badge. More than one security member frowned at it, but he spoke to them—DeRicci didn't have sound on this, so she didn't know what was said—and when he spoke to them, things changed. They nodded, although more than one security person looked at him with suspicion.

He was one of the last people inside the room where Keir Julian, the mayor of Moscow Dome, was supposed to give his Anniversary Day address. This wasn't a standard auditorium or even a politico's room with a podium and a lot of people.

This was some kind of studio. Apparently Julian's speech was supposed to be broadcast on Moscow Dome's various networks. She suspected every Anniversary Day speech of import was on the nets, and probably being anthologized, so that people could buy the various collections—although she never understood why people would buy speeches, just like she never understood why people would voluntarily listen to them.

The studio seemed small, seating maybe a hundred people. The tech who compiled the vid felt it important to show the room without the assassin in it.

Then the image focused on Julian. He was laughing as he sat in a chair on the small stage. The stage held only one other chair, and a table between them, more of an end table than a coffee table, something to set beverages on.

Julian looked pleased with himself. He wore an expensive black suit, made of a material so fine that it shined with silver highlights in the bright studio lighting. He had rings on all of his fingers and some kind of studded buckle on his shoes.

He seemed to be talking and joking with everyone in the room, and like most people around a politician, the others smiled and joked in return, although their smiles didn't seem as genuine. DeRicci wondered just how lame his jokes were, how biting his humor seemed to the people around him.

The imagery changed to an area behind the stage. The assassin walked past it, grabbed something—a bit of make-up? a drink of water? DeRicci couldn't quite tell—and walked out on stage.

One of the security guards who had frowned at the assassin's badge hurried after him. The assassin clearly said Julian's name. Julian looked up, extended his hand, and the security guard got close enough to block the touch. But, as he turned around, the assassin brushed against Julian.

Two other security guards had already rushed the stage, and someone was shouting. Julian looked surprised. More and more people flooded forward, some looking both determined and competent.

DeRicci could no longer see Julian, and she figured that was no accident. His staff was blocking all of the cameras. The studio itself had devolved into chaos. The doors had clearly been locked—no one could get out—and judging by the way half the audience put their hands to their ears, the links had been severed as well. Maybe even the emergency links, since DeRicci hadn't seen much news coverage from Moscow Dome either. Just that Mayor Julian's speech had been canceled.

The guards rushed Julian out of the studio, but DeRicci couldn't see more than his hands, dangling. And she wasn't sure if they were grayish or if she was imagining that. He was alive at that point—he was still alive, or so she had been told.

He looked like he was in as serious condition as the governor-general.

The vid wasn't over yet. The chaos caused by people rushing the stage, by the security guards taking care of Julian, by the links getting shut down and the doors being slammed, gave the assassin an opportunity to slip into that corridor again.

DeRicci couldn't quite tell, but it looked like he had rigged the backstage door to let him into that corridor even though someone had locked the studio down. He ran through the corridor, unimpeded, and went back into the alley. He turned left on the outside street and then the cameras lost him.

He had effectively disappeared.

She cursed. The one man they had needed to hang on to and they had lost him.

How hard could it be to find four men who looked exactly alike?

She pushed herself out of her chair, and started pacing again.

Food, Popova, she sent. *Now.* Because otherwise, DeRicci would leave this office herself and dive into one of the investigations. She wanted to be back on the street for this, getting messy, looking for suspects, taking information.

She wanted to be in charge—not in charge of the entire Moon's security—but in charge of the case.

For the first time in years, she wanted to be a detective again.

Maybe because this was a case she could believe in.

She wanted to catch these bastards, and she wanted to do it fast.

29

LILLIAN MIYAKI STOOD AT THE ENTRANCE TO THE BOHEMIAN THEATER and clasped her hands behind her back. She had always thought the theater the most stunning building in Glenn Station.

The theater stood in the very center of town. The building itself had five theaters, but everyone only discussed the biggest. It seated about five hundred people—small, as city theaters went—and the seats ran at an incline toward the stage. At first glance, nothing about the stage seemed unusual. The theater's style dated back to old Earth. The proscenium arch allowed the local theater company to perform ancient works by Sophocles and Shakespeare, as well as modern works from all over the Earth Alliance. The theater was also a great place for the annual pre-election debates.

Miyaki preferred attending concerts here because the best thing about the theater wasn't its proscenium arch or its comfortable seats, but its ceiling, which actually opened onto the dome. Sometimes it felt like the entire universe watched as the Glenn Station Symphony Orchestra played works by Litaafaa and Tarming.

But that wasn't what was supposed to happen here today. Today, Mayor Dmitri Tsepen was supposed to give his annual Anniversary Day talk, combined with his State of the City report. And he was half an hour late, which wasn't that unusual.

In fact, if Miyaki hadn't just received a message from Adriana Clief with a coded warning from Security Chief Noelle DeRicci, Miyaki would have thought that Mayor Tsepen had finally blown off a speech because he was too drunk to talk.

Instead, there was some kind of weird threat tied to the sudden and somewhat mysterious death of Armstrong's Mayor Arek Soseki.

Miyaki had already ordered the theater to be locked down. She had briefed her staff and sent them an image of the man everyone suspected of planning an attempt on Mayor Tsepen's life. She had guards stationed at every exit, and even more down the streets. She also had mass transit routes from the city blocked, and air traffic routes monitored, just in case this potential perpetrator had seen the unusual activity and bolted.

She sighed, almost inclined not to believe in anything that got Mayor Tsepen off the hook. He had moved to this location last year only because, she had thought uncharitably, no one could smell the stink of alcohol on him on a stage so far removed from his audience.

Adriana Clief had not done him or the city any favors covering his back as long as she had.

If Miyaki were less capable of doing her job, she would have told Tsepen to come anyway, and promised to protect him. He was a popular mayor despite (or because of?) his drinking problem, and she worried that he would get re-elected yet again. If he had come and gotten hurt in the assassination attempt...

She sighed as she contemplated that idea. He would probably have been re-elected anyway.

In a landslide.

She used her security network, set up only for her security team, to signal them to begin the search. First the Glenn Station police were using some kind of state-of-the-art visual software to go over each face in the audience. Then she would get notified of where the suspect sat.

She planned to go to his chair and arrest him with little fanfare, then let the Glenn Station police department handle the exit interviews for everyone else in the theater.

Nothing, the police sent her less than five minutes after the facial recognition search started.

Do it again, she sent.

We did, sent her contact. *We've run the search four times. Do you want us to use a fifth?*

She squinted, tempted to bring the house lights up even farther than they already were. Instead, she used a combination of a heat sensor built into her visual security program and a map of the theater itself.

Two empty seats. One in the very far back left hand corner, and one square in the center of the room.

She sent images of those to the police using the facial recognition program. *Were there people in these seats earlier?*

The affirmative came less than thirty seconds after she sent.

Check the restrooms, other theaters, back stage, and concessions, she sent. *Someone knew we were coming.*

It's illegal to use facial recognition in the restrooms, sent the police.

I don't care, she sent. *We have a credible threat, and besides, I'm informed that the suspect is a clone. He's not subject to the same rights as real humans. Run the scan. We'll worry about the law later.*

She slipped out the door into the corridor between theaters. She kept her heat vision on, and flipped on a light night-vision program as well. That way she didn't have to order the lights in the corridor to turn up. The doors to the other theaters were locked—or so the building's environmental program told her.

Still, she saw the echo of a heat signature near the door of the children's theater.

It was the smallest theater. It got its name not because children's plays were performed there, but because Glenn Station's school children used it for their own private performances, some run without any adult supervision at all.

Which meant that the theater itself had extra monitoring equipment plus high-level safety protocols, the kind that kids' restaurants and playgrounds had.

Link me into the building's protective systems, she sent to her own network. Suddenly a flood of information flowed through her links. She shut it all down, focusing only on the Children's Theater.

One small heat signature, fading slowly.

She didn't like the fade.

Emergency medical programs on! She sent into the building's systems.

Lights went on along the Children's Theater's door, along with silent alarms. She heard the automated verbal command for an ambulance, as well as one for any medical personnel to attend the Children's Theater. The Theater also informed her that the medical avatars had started work, but had no idea if they could save the patient because they "were not programmed for an emergency of this type."

"Crap," she said, and ordered the door to the Children's Theater unlocked. She slipped inside, saw the floor had turned into something she called medical mush as the emergency programs turned on. The mush—a whitish foam kind of soft thing which she had never heard the name for—turned the entire theater into a kind of protective bubble, so that whomever was hurt would be stabilized while waiting for the emergency personnel to arrive.

The avatar floated above the center of the floor. The avatar surprised her. It was a busty cartoonish doctor with a classic beauty and a look of complete stupidity in its eyes.

This was what the patient ordered? Or was this the standard avatar for the Children's Theater?

Miyaki didn't have time to guess. She strode through the mush to the middle of the floor, prepared to help.

But when she saw the patient, she stopped.

It was a man—and he might have been the man in the images that Chief DeRicci had sent her. But Miyaki couldn't tell for sure. His face was dark gray, metal gray, his eyes closed, his posture rigid. He was sinking through the mush as if he was too heavy for it.

She knew the mush wouldn't suffocate him—if, indeed, he was breathing at all.

But she also didn't want to touch him.

She wasn't sure if what happened to him was contagious.

If it was, she didn't want to contract this horrible thing.

If she hadn't already.

Lock down the entire area, she sent. *We might have a pathogen.*

Nothing registers, her second in command sent back to her. *We'd get some kind of reading.*

I'm none too trusting of technology right now, she sent, deciding not to add that he wouldn't trust technology either if he saw the man-thing she was looking at, and the avatar trying desperately to treat him. *Just do as I say.*

Yes, sir, her second sent back.

She backed out of the theater, letting the door close behind her. She stopped in the corridor, her heart pounding.

She had seen a lot of things during her career. Memorable things. Horrible things. But this one was bad. It was the stuff of nightmares. She wouldn't be able to sleep for weeks.

If she lived another few weeks.

She shoved off the thought and went to the front of the building to wait for the emergency squad. As she walked, she checked for other heat signatures.

Did you find anything? she sent to the police scanners.

No, sir, they sent. *The rest of the theater is empty.*

Or the occupants in the other parts of the building are already dead. But she didn't send that either. She took a deep breath, wondered if the air was tainted, and then decided she didn't care. She couldn't do any more than she had already done.

She could only hope she would make it just a little bit longer.

Long enough to figure out what was going on, at any rate.

Long enough to figure out what, exactly, had gone wrong.

30

Sixteen years on the force, and Isti Piaja had never been involved in an investigation like this one. Covering six square city blocks, dozens of businesses, hundreds of apartments, and he—like everyone else in the Armstrong Police Department—believed that they had already let their man get away.

Searching was make-work, but it was make-work they had to do.

Several squads got brought in on this case. Each squad got assigned a different area: interviewing witnesses, looking for escape routes, and the most important one—looking for the suspect.

Piaja lucked out: his squad was looking for the suspect. He hated interviewing witnesses, because the lead detective would always complain about the shoddy job the street cop did. The lead detective would see the witness after the witness had time to think about his story. The lead detective would actually know what questions to ask.

The street cop was just poking around in the dark, trying to find one useful piece of information in a lot of junk that always started with, *I dunno. I was just sitting there, and then everyone rushed forward, and I heard he was dead...*

Looking for escape routes was just as useless. They'd figure out the escape route when they caught the bad guy, not before. And the bad guy would have done something creative to get out, or someone on some squad really and truly was stupid, missing all the clues or just letting the bad guy walk past.

Searching for the suspect, though. Searching for the suspect was organized, and no one blamed you if you didn't find him. Only one guy could find the suspect and that guy would get all the glory.

But if Piaja wanted glory, he wouldn't have stayed on the street. He actually liked it here, talking to citizens, stopping petty crime, every day different. He used to think he had seen everything, and then he saw even more.

Now his job was mostly as referee. He had to deal with humans and aliens, people who belonged, people who didn't, people who didn't understand Earth Alliance laws, and people who didn't want to. He understood all of it—he'd actually thought of becoming a lawyer once—but he didn't have to do much more than the frontline work.

He wasn't the guy who sent some kid off to pay for her mom's crime because the idiot mother violated the law of some species that insisted on punishing the firstborn. He wasn't the guy who had to explain to some refugee that he had to be sent back to his place of origin because of some new Earth Alliance treaty.

Piaja got to find these people, and then he got to pass them off to the various departments, and if he was really lucky, he never had to think of them again.

About two years into the work on his law degree, he realized his street job was the best of all worlds. If he got the law degree, those people really would haunt him, no matter what side of the law he decided to live on.

Piaja was working a grid set up by his squad leader. Each squad got a different section of the six-block radius. Some brilliant squad leader decided to expand the radius, so an additional block was added on either side, on the theory that the bad guy would sit just outside the radius and watch the bumbling cops try to find him.

But the crime scene lasers marked off an entire neighborhood—no one in or out—which the businesses were already complaining about. They worried about the business they were losing, instead of the business they'd gained because their customers were trapped inside.

Piaja was at the eastern edge of the crime scene, four blocks over and two blocks up. No one had come this far. He and his partner Julie Hu got this block to themselves. Twelve buildings, none smaller than eight stories, and all with various tenants, businesses and offices.

This part of the search radius was a bit more upscale than the other parts. The neighborhood was gentrifying. Buildings he remembered as rundown, now had new facades or clean walls or a fresh coat of paint. Expensive cars actually filled the parking lots, which had real attendants and some high-end security systems.

No high-end jewelry or clothing stores here however. Just mid-level restaurants, a few trendy bars, a dance club that was beginning to get some notice, and some mid-range offices for business that had just started branching out.

He and Julie stayed together because that was regulation on a suspect search. Too many cops got killed confronting someone. Better to have backup on hand—real live human back up, not some bot, not some emergency computer program.

Julie Hu didn't look like much, but she was the toughest partner he'd ever had. She was tiny, barely reaching his shoulder, and probably weighed no more than a ten-year-old kid. She had dark hair and even darker eyes, a killer smile that she only used with the people she liked, and a wicked tongue.

She had taken martial arts training to an advanced level, and more often felled a suspect with her bare hands. She rarely used her weapon, and when she did, it was often under orders.

She was under orders today to use that weapon. No one was supposed to touch this guy. For all anyone knew every single part of him could kill them if they so much as brushed against him.

That was the only part of searching for the suspect that Piaja hated. The surprise factor. And these kinds of searches always had a surprise.

The store Piaja had just left was a store specializing in custom-made baby clothes. The clothes didn't just fit the baby perfectly, they also acted like a tiny environmental suit, controlling his temperature, taking readouts of all of the bodily fluids, and even seeing if the kid was hungry. A few of the clothes could be tied into people's links.

It was illegal to link up children before they were teenagers, so Piaja sent a note about the place to the net squad. They could see if these clothes were legal. He couldn't do it. He was searching for a suspect.

But it was amazing the crap he was finding as he did so.

Julie stood outside the door, waiting for him. He had had to train himself to call her by her first name, but she insisted. There were dozens of Hus in the department, and she was the only Julie. Using the first name minimized confusion.

As he stepped beside her, she caught his arm. "The coffee shop's empty," she said softly.

He hadn't even realized there was a coffee shop. Apparently it was the storefront in the next building he was supposed to investigate.

"So?" he said, just as softly.

"I've been here before," she said. "There should be staff."

Some coffee shops had only serving trays and automated drink preparation. Piaja moved just a little closer, saw the sign, and the advertising that flared through his links. This place advertised its personal touch. The ads claimed that coffee made by machine wasn't the same as coffee made with human hands.

Human hands. There were code and law violations all over this street. No one could limit employment in the City of Armstrong to humans only.

He made another note, then squinted. "Is it closed?"

She shook her head.

"Then we approach this one cautiously," he said.

Normally he would have let her go first. She was smaller, easier to overlook. But he didn't. He stepped around her and peered into the clear windows.

And realized that Julie was wrong.

There was someone in the coffee shop. Sitting alone at a table toward the rear of the store, his back to the wall. He had a steaming mug of something in front of him, and he was watching the windows as if he expected a guest.

It was the suspect.

"We found him," Piaja said to Julie. "Send for back-up. Tell them to be quiet."

"Are we going in?" she asked.

"We're supposed to secure the scene," he said. "I don't want to spook him. We'll move slow."

"He'll get spooked when he sees the activity around here," she said.

Piaja nodded. "We'll wait to the last possible moment," he said. "And then we'll talk him out."

If there was any talking to this guy. If there was anything they could do at all.

31

MARIGOLD JACOBS' PARANOIA HAD INFECTED NYQUIST. HE TOOK THE CHIP Jacobs had given him back to his makeshift office in the middle of the restaurant. He didn't want to touch anything, suddenly afraid he would die as quickly and horribly as Arek Soseki.

Nyquist had nearly died during that Bixian assassins' attack. That attack had probably taken minutes at the most, but it had seemed to last forever. And it had seemed to take even longer for someone to find him, although given what he knew about human anatomy, they had found him in record time. It only took minutes to bleed out, and he had been on his way.

But if you had asked him, from his own perspective, how long all of that had taken, he would have said it had taken hours, maybe days, maybe weeks, maybe even years. He still had nightmares about it, waking up in a cold sweat, slashing at the damn things. And those nightmares would trigger memories, yet another detail he had noticed and had somehow forgotten in the trauma.

It made him realize how much the human brain resembled Tyr's cameras—catching everything, but understanding nothing.

So the very thought that Soseki's death which—according to Tyr's cameras—had taken seconds might have seemed like a lifetime to Soseki. A slow and painful lifetime, in which he gradually realized that he had no hope of survival.

Nyquist shook off the thought. That had been his own experience, lying on the floor of that apartment, slowly (or not so slowly) bleeding to death. No hope of survival. He really had thought he was going to die. He had even started to make lists of the people he wished he had talked to, things he had wished he had done.

The ironic thing was that he hadn't done any of that when he recovered, and the thought of some of it made him cringe.

He leaned back in the chair—a chair he had swabbed with some cleanser guaranteed to get rid of everything hazardous. The cleanser itself was probably hazardous, and he didn't want to think about that.

He had had enough presence of mind to double-check that the crime scene techs had gone over this area— he didn't want to destroy anything with high-level cleanser —and when he got the okay, he cleaned up and sat down.

Then stared at the little chip Jacobs had given him.

The screen Nyquist had here was networked to the Armstrong Police Department, the very department that Jacobs didn't want to have the information on the stuff that had killed Soseki.

So Nyquist had to jury-rig a way for that chip to connect to his private links, and then he had to separate the information on that chip from everything else. Initially, Nyquist had hoped the chip would have a simple formula on it, but the chemical compound Nyquist was dealing with wasn't simple at all.

And he was no scientist. He had no idea how to memorize the information on that chip. Comparing it to other compounds without the help of a computer or some kind of fast-moving network would be difficult as well. It would probably take him hours, which he didn't have.

The investigation seemed to be going on apace. He had pretty much lost track. Groups of people came in and out of the restaurant, talking to Tyr, talking to Romey. Romey often excused herself, went toward the kitchen as if that area gave her privacy, and put a hand next to her ear, like so many people did when they spoke privately on their links.

Nyquist rarely did it. He wasn't sure what caused the impulse except maybe that so many linked messages came through as audio files.

It seemed like someone was talking next to the person receiving, when really the information was going directly to the person's brain, activating synapses instead of vibrating through the ear drum.

He didn't understand the science of it—he didn't understand the science of most things—but he had been curious enough about it all to learn why people put their hands to their ears, making what should have been a private conversation just a little bit more public.

Jacobs had left quite a while ago. He'd been working at his makeshift desk since he spoke to her. For a man who didn't understand a lot about science, he did understand one thing: He knew that the solution to this case wasn't to get one of the suspects in custody—people rarely broke, except at the hands of a very skilled interrogator, and then they only broke when the interrogator got lucky.

No. This case would break when the unusual weapon got traced to its source, whatever that source was. An unusual weapon was the break in this case—the only break so far. Not the matching killers, nor the ostentatious attacks.

Whoever had planned these coordinated attacks had planned for an investigation of the killers and had planned for an investigation of the public nature of the crimes.

However, the person—or persons or creatures (God, he hoped it wasn't a nonhuman attacker; that would have diplomatic consequences he didn't ever want to think about)—who planned this attack probably hadn't thought of the weapon as a way to trace the crime. The weapon was a means to an end, something that could get smuggled into a public place, something that would act quickly. It was, most likely, an afterthought.

For everyone except Nyquist.

He put the chemical compound aside and went through the list of possible substances that Romey had given him, looking at the symptoms caused when those substances made contact with a human. If he found anything that matched, he would then compare it chemically to the compound that Jacobs had given him.

If he couldn't do that work quickly or easily, he would have Jacobs do it. He knew for a fact that her lab was not accessible to everyone in the department. She had to approve anyone who wanted contact with her network, which kept it pretty inviolate.

If this was a regular investigation, he would let Jacobs do all of this. But it wasn't a regular investigation. The faster he worked, the faster they caught the mastermind. And if they caught the mastermind, they would stop this—or at least be on the road to stopping this.

Because Nyquist believed this was just the opening volley in a war he didn't yet understand.

Romey's list wasn't short, but it was easy to sort through. Somewhere in the middle of doing so, he realized the list had come directly from DeRicci's office, which was why everything was in such neat order. He could sort by symptom, but that turned out to be more complicated than he thought. Each symptom seemed like one of those if-then problems he had hated so much when he was in school.

If the temperature was below freezing, then the first symptom to appear would be...

He finally sorted by rapidity of symptom onset, and that was where he hit his jackpot.

Only one substance worked as quickly as the thing that got Soseki, moved from point of impact across a victim's body, and turned the victim various shades of gray. Banned by the Earth Alliance as one of the most toxic substances ever developed, the substance's scientific name was so hard to pronounce Nyquist didn't even try. Instead, he used the substance's nickname: zoodeh.

A long-defunct corporation named Giitel developed zoodeh as a quick drying, sturdy building material for colonists and travelers planning to build temporary housing in new places. Soon Giitel realized that zoodeh wasn't stable enough to work with. Researchers got ill and died within a few minutes of touching the material. At times, the deaths seemed inexplicable because the researcher had used all proper precautions—gloves, suits, masks. Finally, someone realized that all it took was a single touch against skin before zoodeh entered the human body and completely transformed it, destroying the interior, using the skin and bones as a foundation, and then solidifying as if the human being was actually a wall of a house.

Research on zoodeh stopped until Giitel got sold, its patents sold with it. Someone found zoodeh and realized it would be a fantastic weapon. The Earth Alliance banned the substance after assassins used it to target heads of state (that sounded familiar, Nyquist noted), and the zoodeh moved to some of the unaffiliated countries and planets at the edge of the known universe. Because zoodeh was hard to transport and easy to detect, it hadn't come back into the Alliance.

Until now.

The question was: how did zoodeh get so deep into the Earth Alliance? How did it end up all over the Moon? Zoodeh should have been flagged as it came into any port.

Nyquist slipped into Space Traffic's database, looking to see how recently ships got flagged for carrying zoodeh.

He found nothing recent—not within this year, last, or even the past ten. Half a dozen ships had come in carrying zoodeh in trace amounts, but all of those ships had come in thirty, forty, fifty years before.

And gotten quarantined.

Quarantined. He tapped a finger against his lips, thinking. He had dealt with quarantined ships on more than one investigation. Quarantined vessels usually went to Terminal 81 where the Traffic Squad Quarantine Unit or robotic units dealt with the ships. Most of the ships got destroyed.

Then he stopped tapping his lips and moved his finger sideways, touching his too-smooth cheek. In the investigation that nearly killed him, he learned about ships that were quarantined which had never made it to Terminal 81. Some of the ships' owners paid off port authorities. Sometimes the ships landed and then the toxic substances were discovered.

Sometimes the quarantine was a ruse to keep the owner from the ship itself.

Nyquist had revealed this to DeRicci and she had been appalled. The responsibility for the quarantined ships had initially resided with Space

Traffic Control. It still did for the ships that went to Terminal 81. Every once in a while, Space Traffic contacted DeRicci's Security Office to have the office deal with whatever had tried to come into the City of Armstrong.

But the ships that had made it to Armstrong's port but did not land in Terminal 81 now fell under the United Domes of the Moon Security Department.

And a special administrator had gotten hired to take care of the ships one by one. To investigate them, to determine the reason for the quarantine, and then to either make the ship go away, destroy it, or to release it from quarantine.

Nyquist looked up the name of the administrator, and then smiled. He had gotten his second break in this case. He wouldn't have to go through piles of rules and regulations to talk to some bureaucrat. He knew the bureaucrat.

He had saved her life once.

It was Ursula Palmette.

32

THE MESSAGE MADE A WEIGHT LIFT OFF HER SHOULDERS. *THEY FOUND the assassin*. Romey paused for just a moment, hand on the table in front of her, and let the message sink in.

Crime scene techs continued to work in the back room. Bots moved through, carrying all kinds of material out of the kitchen. Tyr continued to monitor the vids, looking for even more information. Squad leaders constantly buzzed her links, giving her updates.

She let it all wash over her, felt the relief as it went past. Deep down, she'd been afraid they would never catch this guy, they would never know what was really behind it all.

Maybe that was the effect of Anniversary Day itself, the reminder that some cases were unsolvable, that some things would remain forever unknown.

That and the fact that word had just come in that the attacker in Glenn Station had suicided. Or they believed he had suicided. She had seen the images of the dead man. His corpse looked like Soseki's: dark gray, rigid. The computers said that his features matched the features of the men they were looking for.

She had to take the computer's word for it. With the distortion, the man looked like anyone—and she was glad she didn't have his death on her conscience. She already had a poor chance of closing this case properly, due to the scope and the political nature of it all. She didn't want a dead attacker to complicate things as well.

An attacker dead by suicide. The way that everyone believed the bomber four years ago had died, although no one knew for certain. It was just the most popular theory.

She let out a breath. This day already seemed eighty years long. The news that her people had the attacker in sight felt like she had reached the mid-point of a lifelong investigation, instead of a few hours into her afternoon.

She glanced at Kilzahn. He had been watching her, and there was an odd expression on his face. True to his word, he hadn't interfered with her investigation. He had done his best to blend into the wall, to observe and not participate.

She wondered if he knew about the dead man in Glenn Station as well, or if he had heard through a different source that Soseki's attacker was about to go into custody.

"You," she said to him, "you're coming with me."

She didn't want to get in trouble with DeRicci after all. Better to keep this guy in the loop than try to work around him.

Then she glanced over at Nyquist. He had left his post once to talk with Jacobs. Then he had come back and mentioned to Romey that Jacobs was reluctant to share the information on this case via links, and that Romey needed to talk to the coroner directly.

Romey would have asked him why he was talking to Jacobs instead of her, but she didn't. She had discovered how good Jacobs was through Nyquist, asking his advice after a particularly maddening episode with Brodeur a few months back. Nyquist's relationship with Jacobs was long-standing. Even though Romey had asked for Jacobs on this case, she didn't have Jacobs' loyalty yet, and she knew it.

Yet another reason to have Nyquist on this case.

Romey stopped at his table. He was so intent, comparing information on his screen with something that made him tap the palm of his hand, that he hadn't even seen her coming.

"Bartholomew," she said softly.

He started as he looked up at her. If he were a suspect, she would have thought he was hiding something.

"We've located the attacker. Would you like to be in on the arrest?"

He gave her a distracted smile. "It's your case, Savita," he said. "You get the glory."

Something in his tone made her frown. "You don't think this is glory, do you?"

He looked down, paused, a frown creasing his forehead. Then he sighed, as if he had come to some private conclusion.

"This case is complicated," he said. "I think we haven't found out how complicated yet."

She nodded. His words touched on a feeling she hadn't quite let herself acknowledge. She was deeply unsettled by all of this. Maybe that was why she was so pessimistic about her own ability to solve this case. Maybe, deep down, she felt there was no resolution.

After all, she rarely went into an investigative situation doubting her own ability to handle it.

"You've found something," she said softly, hoping Kilzahn hadn't heard.

Nyquist shook his head. "Not really."

She noted that he hadn't said no. He had just given the kind of denial that she used to give her bosses when she had no evidence. Just a hunch.

"I hope your hunch pans out," she said, making him look surprised for the second time in the past five minutes.

"Me, too," he said softly. "Me too."

33

"I CAN SEE YOU," THE SUSPECT SAID.

Piaja didn't so much hear him as read the man's lips.

No matter how cautious Piaja and Julie had been as they moved outside the window, they caught the man's attention. His hand was wrapped around that steaming mug. Then he smiled. A servo-tray brought him a thick pastry, covered in white frosting.

He took the plate off the tray and set the plate on his table next to the mug. Then he looked away, glancing out the side windows, and then over his shoulder, as if trying to determine if someone had come in the back.

The other squads would arrive soon. They were only minutes away, maybe seconds.

The suspect took a bite of that pastry, licked his lips as if the pastry was the best thing he'd ever tasted, and then he set the pastry down. He wiped his fingers on the leg of his pants.

Piaja watched each movement closely. He hadn't moved—neither had Julie—but the suspect knew they were there.

The suspect looked at Piaja at that moment, and that was when he spoke.

Piaja felt a shiver run down his spine. He wanted to say, *So you see me? Well, good for you*, but he didn't.

"Are you afraid of me?" the man asked. Then he said something that Piaja couldn't read.

What was that? Piaja sent to Julie.

He said, "Don't you want to know why I did it?"

Piaja still hadn't moved. In fact, he hadn't taken his gaze off the suspect. Julie hadn't either. So far as the man could tell, they were motionless, watching him, keeping track and doing nothing else.

He wants us to come inside, Piaja sent.

I know, Julie said. *Our instructions are clear.*

As if Piaja was ready to go in. As if he was going to make a mistake. As if he didn't know they needed this suspect alive.

"I'm only going to talk to you," the suspect said, his eyes meeting Piaja's. "If someone else shows up, I'm not going to talk at all."

The man's eyes were a clear blue, pale blue, the kind that looked odd against darker skin, but against skin this fair, they looked even creepier, as if the color had just leached out of him.

Why does he want us to come inside? Piaja sent, not because he felt that Julie knew, but because he had to discuss this. It was making him nervous, just like the suspect wanted it to. Piaja didn't want the suspect to know that he was getting through.

I don't know, Julie sent back. *Maybe to take us out?*

Piaja had that suspicion as well. But the suspect could have taken them out through the window, even before they knew he was inside. So that didn't make sense.

See if you can get someone to access the coffee shop's systems, Piaja sent. *I want to know what happened to the employees.*

You don't know any were on duty today, Julie sent.

I do know, he sent. *Haven't you been looking at the ads?*

A slight movement of her mouth told him that she hadn't. She had been focused entirely on the suspect.

"I know someone else is coming," the suspect said. "I know our time is running out."

At least that was what Piaja thought he was saying.

I'm going to have them check to see if there's a bomb inside, Julie sent. *Maybe that's why he wants us in there.*

Piaja doubted he had a bomb. But he understood the thought, particularly on Anniversary Day. Besides, he couldn't quite tell why he discounted the bomb idea. Maybe because bombers liked to take out as many innocents as possible.

The suspect would want the entire squad here when the bomb detonated. He wouldn't want it to go off before they arrived.

I'm sure there's security vid from his arrival, Piaja sent. Which begged the question, how come none of the computer systems saw this? They should have been tracking security vid throughout the city, trying to catch this guy. They had an image of him after all. How come that didn't work?

No one flagged it, Julie sent.

Doesn't mean it doesn't exist, Piaja sent. *Let's find out what's going on.*

She moved her head slightly, almost a nod, before she caught herself. But the suspect saw it, and he smiled.

He was smarter than Piaja expected him to be. When Piaja had heard he was a clone, he was expecting something designed for this one job, something programmed, the way you would program a servo-tray.

He hadn't expected someone to think and to challenge him and to be, if Piaja was honest with himself, someone who could take charge of this situation just with a few simple movements.

He's aware of us, Piaja sent to the entire department. That was for the suspect, if the suspect had somehow hacked into the operations link. Then on an encoded link, something that no one could hack into—at least that Piaja had ever heard of—he sent this to Romey and the other team leaders: *I need to know the moment you approach the block. He's unpredictable, and he's planning something.*

Don't engage, Romey immediately sent back.

Too late, Piaja sent. *He's already engaged us.*

There was a moment of silence, which Piaja knew hid a curse. Then Romey. *We need him alive. Have you got a protective suit?*

Just the kind that'll protect a crime scene, Piaja sent.

I'm not sure that's strong enough, Romey sent. *You can't lay a finger on him. Don't get close enough to let him so much as brush against you.*

Piaja almost frowned. He could feel the movement begin and he hoped he caught it soon enough. *You think he can kill that easily?*

I know he can, Romey sent.

Great. Piaja suppressed a sigh. Just great. They couldn't arrest this guy, but he had already engaged them. So this situation was moving quickly, whether Piaja wanted it to or not.

"You can't stall any longer," the suspect said. "At least, not and listen to what I have to say."

The coffee shop has a pretty high end security system, Julie sent. *Everyone is reviewing the vid now, but they've looked at the building itself, and they're not getting any readings that would indicate a bomb. However, they do caution that he might have something we don't recognize.*

"You have one minute," the suspect said. "One minute before I shut up forever."

That clinched it.

Piaja was going in.

34

MOVING THE ESSENTIAL PERSONNEL WAS LIKE MOVING AN ARMY. ROMEY had never been in charge of an operation this big. Someone—and she wasn't sure who—wanted to take a vehicle to the suspect's location.

She didn't. If she had been on her own, she would have run there. But she couldn't do that either.

So she glanced at her own map of the area, saw that even with a vehicle, they would have had to park two blocks away, and on top of some kind of structure. The real-time map showed vehicles everywhere, trapped because of the lockdown of the entire area.

She couldn't run. She needed to keep Kilzahn beside her and he didn't seem like the running type. She also had some squad leaders and lead detectives, who needed to move along as well.

As they hurried through the streets—or whatever this group did that approximated a hurry—she felt increasing pressure.

The suspect was in a coffee shop. The image the on-site officer had sent showed him eating a pastry and drinking something, probably coffee. He looked calm.

Romey hated that.

She also hated the fact that he had found the most upscale part of this little part of Armstrong. He wasn't waiting in some dive—and there were plenty. She was passing them in her fast walk.

He was waiting in a nice coffee shop, with a pastry that looked edible (and was probably made of real flour, not Moon flour), a mug of something steaming hot, and a chair that had molded to his slight frame. He was comfortable.

He sat beside two banks of windows.

He wanted to get caught.

Or at least get noticed.

This entire plan was about getting noticed. The clones, the attacks in public places, Anniversary Day.

And then she got the on-site street cop's queries to various agencies, about security vids, about bombs, and she realized something was happening there, something important. She had been about to contact the lead officer on site when he contacted her.

She told him not to engage—and he told her it was too late.

Which meant she had already lost control of the scene.

If she ever had it.

"We're going to pick up the pace," she said to her group.

And then she started to run.

35

PIAJA PULLED HIS LASER PISTOL AND STEPPED FORWARD. JULIE CAUGHT his arm.

"Don't," she said.

It took him a moment to realize she spoke instead of sending him the message.

He moved his eyes so that he could see the suspect through the window of the coffee shop. The suspect was smiling.

The bastard.

Piaja was damned if he did anything; damned if he didn't.

If Piaja didn't go in, and the guy died or set off a bomb or killed himself, then everyone would ask why Piaja didn't take the opportunity to talk to him. Same if the guy shut up and never spoke again.

But if Piaja did go in, and the guy suicided or set off a bomb or injured or killed Piaja, then Piaja would get blamed for inciting the guy.

There was less risk if Piaja went in right now. The others hadn't arrived yet. If a bomb went off, it would only harm Piaja and the suspect. If the suspect killed himself, Piaja would have to live with that. If the suspect killed Piaja, then it would be news and little more. Unlike Julie, Piaja didn't have family. No one would mourn him. His colleagues might miss him, but no one else.

He took another step forward.

"Isti, please. Don't," Julie said, her grip on his arm tightening.

"Make sure people leave the building in case there's a bomb," he said to her. Then he shook off her arm and pushed open the door.

The interior smelled of coffee, mixed bread and fresh baked goods. Piaja had expected to smell blood and vomit. He had expected dead employees, probably behind that counter. But it didn't smell like anyone had died in here, and no one was moaning in pain.

Piaja kept his gaze on the damn suspect.

The suspect's smile grew. Piaja's stomach churned. He hated doing what the creeps wanted. But here he was.

"So," he said, as he stood inside the door, "where are the employees?"

The suspect raised his eyebrows. "I've just seen a servo-tray."

His voice was deeper than Piaja expected, richer, almost musical. Piaja had thought the voice would be nasal and harsh, not something liquid and mellifluous.

"Lie to me and I leave," Piaja said.

The suspect's smile faded. He didn't like losing control. He nodded toward the counter. Exactly what Piaja thought. The only place he couldn't see from the window, except for the bathrooms.

Piaja sent, *You guys getting this? How come you didn't let me know about the employees?*

We're not getting any readings of anyone in that coffee shop except you and the suspect, someone from headquarters sent back.

Piaja's stomach clenched harder. He stood on his toes, peered, saw one gray arm leaning against the wall, hand up and open, defenseless. No readings because the employees had died just like Soseki had.

Piaja looked at the suspect. His smile was back. And in the seconds it took Piaja to look at the employees, the suspect had pulled a laser pistol.

Piaja started to back through the door, but the suspect shot beside him, the laser bouncing off the clear window and barely missing Piaja. Piaja's heart was racing.

"I thought you were going to talk to me," he said as he groped for the door.

"You do realize I'm going to kill you, too," the suspect said.

A confession. Confessions were always nice. They made cases easier. But they made moments like this harder.

"So that's why you brought me here?" Piaja asked, pleased that his voice didn't shake. "To tell me that you're going to kill me?"

The suspect shrugged.

"Then there's no point in continuing this discussion, is there?" Piaja asked and pushed on the door. It didn't budge. Something had sealed it.

What the hell's with the door? he sent.

The suspect has control of part of the system, headquarters sent.

He's in your system?

There was no answer, probably because the shop's security had given the suspect a backdoor into police headquarters.

The suspect laughed softly. Then he shot at Piaja again, deliberately missing on the other side. The laser skittered along the floor, burning Piaja's right shoe.

Piaja brought up his own weapon. "Stop this," he said.

"We both know you're not going to shoot me," the suspect said.

"You might know that," Piaja said. "I don't."

"You want to talk to me," the suspect said. "You want my information."

"Not so much anymore," Piaja said. "You lied twice already in this conversation."

"Not really," the suspect said. "I told you that all I've seen is a servo-tray. That's true for the last hour or so."

"You said you had something to tell me," Piaja said.

"So I do," the suspect said. "And the nice thing about it is that I can tell you and then I can kill you and I get the best of both worlds. Because your people are watching this."

Piaja's mouth was dry. His grip on his laser pistol tightened, but he kept the weapon low. If he raised it just a bit, he could hit the bastard in the leg, and then the threat to Piaja would be gone.

"So tell me," Piaja said.

The suspect raised his eyebrows, paused, and said, "These killings today. They're just the beginning."

"What do you mean?" Piaja asked.

But the suspect didn't answer. Instead, he shot at Piaja and this time he hit Piaja's right foot square on. The pain seared through Piaja's system, and before he could think, he raised his own pistol, and took the shot he had planned.

The shot hit the suspect in the knee, but the laser didn't flare red the way it was supposed to. Instead it expanded, moving up along the suspect's body, spread out along the suspect's stomach and then localized at his heart.

Piaja could see the man's heart for just a second, and then it burst—the way a heart did when hit with a too-strong laser blast. But Piaja's weapon was designed to injure, not kill. He'd never seen the use for a kill shot.

Yet the suspect tumbled backwards, his chest smoking, his blood everywhere.

"No," Piaja said. He figured the guy might suicide. He figured he could stop it. He'd figured on a bomb, even. But he hadn't planned for this.

He lifted his right foot, the pain so tremendous that his eyes had filled with tears. Behind him the door opened.

Too late, of course. It had all happened too late.

36

ROMEY ARRIVED AFTER THE BACK-UPS, AFTER THE OTHER SQUADS, AFTER the ambulance, for crap's sake.

After the deed was done.

The entire street was full of people, most of them in uniform. They all crowded around the damn coffee shop as if they could do something, as if they could make some kind of difference.

She shoved her way through them, saw some civilians in the mix, wondered if they'd been tested for any kind of residue or one of those sneaky needles that killed Soseki. Probably not.

She avoided the civilians, and got to the door, already knowing what she would find. She would find Piaja all apologetic, his partner a bit belligerent, and a dead suspect, whom she wanted alive.

But before she got close, ads assaulted her. Ads for marvelous coffee, all made by hand. She had to shut off the commercial part of her links, figuring someone else could deal with the ads, the untended commercialization, the strange surreal nature of an active business that had just become an historically notorious crime scene.

Ahead of her, the street cops formed a small cone around the door. And standing near that was a broad-shouldered uniformed officer, one foot raised. The air stank of blood and burned flesh.

"Step aside," she said as she pushed her way through. She reached the front of the cone, and her gaze met the uniformed officer's. That had to be Piaja.

She'd checked his file as she hurried toward the scene. Sixteen years as a street cop, turned down all promotions that might include a desk or might get him off the street. He was one of those lifers who preferred the hazardous day-to-day work in some of the most crime-infested areas of Armstrong.

Like so many long-time street cops, he was probably an adrenaline junkie, the kind of man who preferred that moment of terror when he opened the wrong door or stumbled on a crime in progress.

That probably explained why he went inside, risking getting blown up, risking death, certainly getting injured in the process.

She thought it ironic that a street cop—once called foot patrolmen on Earth way back when—had gotten shot in the foot.

But she didn't mention that. She also didn't mention medical attention. She figured he knew he needed it.

She also figured he was waiting for her.

"You disobeyed my orders," she said as she approached.

He was leaning against the door. The lean was subtle, almost unnoticeable, just a brush of his spine against the door jam, enough to give support but not enough to collapse into it.

"Beg pardon, sir," he said, "but I didn't."

"I told you I wanted him alive."

"I know, sir," he said. "I don't think that would have happened no matter what I did."

"You don't deny that you killed him?'

"Why should I?" he said. "Everyone was watching through security feeds and links. But I will say this: I didn't kill him intentionally."

"If you had stayed out—"

"If I had stayed out," he said, "we wouldn't have gotten him talking. He didn't say much, but he said enough."

"And he still would have died." This from the woman next to Piaja.

Romey recognized her from one of the cop gyms that Romey sometimes frequented. She was one of the many Hus on the squad, one of those who preferred her first name—Janet, Janeen, Julie. That was it. Julie. She actually encouraged people to call her Officer Julie.

She was tiny, barely coming up to her partner's shoulder, but she had muscles upon muscles visible on her arms and along her torso. Romey knew, because she'd seen Julie Hu naked inside that locker room, that those muscles were the real thing, not enhancements.

"You're convinced he would have died, Officer?" Romey asked, unwilling to break protocol by using a first name even though it was what the officer wanted.

"I am." She kept one hand on her partner's arm. "I was watching him. You can look too. He had a hand on that laser pistol the whole time."

"Which means nothing," Romey said.

"He was going to kill himself," she said. "Watch how he died. He didn't have to bring the pistol up at all. He could have shot himself in the foot and whatever the hell he was wearing would have guided the shot to his heart."

Romey looked at Piaja. His head was down. He wasn't confirming or denying, but she recognized the posture. Whether or not the partner was right, Piaja blamed himself—and always would.

"What did you learn, Officer Piaja, when you went inside?"

He looked over at her, a momentary look of surprise on his face. He expected her to chastise him further, and she just might after she reviewed the events. But she didn't have time now. Right now, there were still other clones to find, more work to do, and a large task to finish.

The presence of the clones themselves told her that these men weren't the ones in charge of the operation. Someone else was.

"What did I learn?" he asked. "Obviously you don't mean that as a personal question."

He said that last bit softly, as if he was speaking more to himself. And that single sentence confirmed her hunch, that he would continue to blame himself for the rest of his career.

"I learned that he was a cold bastard," Piaja said. "He didn't care that he had killed three people in the space of an afternoon."

"Three?" Romey asked.

"There are two employees behind the serving counter," Piaja said. "Unless I miss my guess, they died the same way that the mayor did."

She nodded. "What else?"

"He wanted me inside," Piaja said. "He wanted me to kill him."

"That's obvious," she said.

"Maybe it seems that way now," Piaja said, "but he seemed more eager to talk than he was to die."

"So he had a message," she said. "What was it?"

"That this was just the beginning," Piaja said. "This was, in his opinion, something small to get our attention. Something larger is going to happen."

Romey caught her breath. What could be larger than killing all of the leaders on the Moon? Killing all of the leaders of the Earth Alliance?

"You can listen to him, of course," Piaja said, "but his exact words were, 'These killings today. They're just the beginning.'"

"He said killings?" she asked. "You're sure?"

"Yes, sir. 'These killings.'"

She sighed, not liking it at all. So the suspect—the killer—wanted them to know about the others, wanted them to know everything was linked, and wanted them to worry.

About what? Just a general fear? Or something worse?

She couldn't thank Piaja. She still wasn't sure if he had done the right thing. But she had a hunch he made a good call.

She nodded at him, then turned to the other officers. "I don't need you all standing around here. There's more work to be done. Let the crime scene unit in here, get this man to an ambulance, and get back to work."

Surprisingly, they all moved away from her, almost as if they had been waiting for her to give them permission to leave.

She walked up to the door of the coffee shop and peered inside. The suspect's face was blood-spattered but intact. A servo-tray hovered, as if it wondered why no one was putting the empty plate on it so that it could clean up.

She put on a protective suit and went inside. She didn't peer over the counter—she didn't need to see innocents, horribly dead—but she did look at her dead suspect.

Then she double-checked her gloves, put on another pair, and another. Still her hands trembled as she reached for his neck, hoping that nothing on his skin would puncture through all the layers she wore.

Nothing did. Or at least, she didn't feel anything. She wondered if Soseki had felt something.

There was, of course, no way to know.

She bent the suspect's head forward, prepared to move the hair away from the back of his skull to look for his clone mark.

But she didn't have to move the hair. The hair near the mark—a mark most clones struggled to keep hidden—had been shaved off.

She stared at the number for the longest moment, feeling numb.

Fifteen.

He was the fifteenth clone off the same embryo.

She knew about three.

There were twelve more.

37

THE MORE INFORMATION DERICCI GOT, THE MORE IT UPSET HER. SHE watched the security vid from the coffee shop, listened to the "suspect," as the police were calling him, confess to the crime, taunt the officer, and then die.

The "suspect" was smart and articulate, clearly not someone programmed to kill.

And DeRicci wasn't sure whether she was relieved or not.

She felt alone in her office, as if she was operating a command center all by herself. Essentially she was. After a lot of nagging, she had gotten Popova to bring in food, food that had been tested first, because everyone was feeling paranoid.

In fact, outside the building, an entire group of security guards looked for the clone that was after DeRicci. There was no proof, of course, that any clone was after her or that she was considered a large enough target to warrant an attack. But she had to operate on the assumption that she was.

Popova had brought four different kinds of coffee, and two dozen sweets on top of an entire meal, which DeRicci polished off in spite of her private vow not to. Popova hadn't joined her at all, like she often did when DeRicci had food brought in.

Popova hadn't done much at all.

DeRicci paced the inside of her office, which she'd been doing since this disaster started. She was amazed that there wasn't a gigantic track worn into her rug by now.

Outside her windows, the city had emptied out. Word of Soseki's death made some places close early. Others hadn't been open at all because of Anniversary Day. In deference to the mayor, all public events were canceled.

The press had finally figured out that something was up, but DeRicci's press liaison was actually making headway, warning of a catastrophic result if people knew their leaders were being targeted.

More than once, DeRicci had spoken to the head of a media conglomerate, asking that person to wait to report on the attacks on the governor-general and the other mayors. Everyone agreed to wait to use the word "attack," but a number of outlets were reporting "stepped-up security" on the leaders of the Moon, along with canceled events and "scares" that were leading to "rumors" of injury.

That was the best DeRicci could do.

She privately thanked the Earth Alliance's rather draconian secrets law—which she had opposed as a young detective. The secrets law made it illegal for any media outlet to report state secrets should that news result in a large "adverse" reaction as a direct response to the news.

Riots caused by the murder and attempted murders of mayors on the Moon counted.

And she had threatened to invoke the secrets law twice this afternoon alone.

But she wasn't sure how much longer she could do that, particularly after Romey's news about the bastard who had killed Soseki. A clone mark of fifteen meant that there were at least fourteen others just like him, and at least five of them had already been active in murders or attempted murders on this day.

They weren't fast-grow clones, which she had suspected at first. Fast-grow clones didn't grow in a day or two. It took a few years for them to reach their adult height and weight, but emotionally, they were little more than children.

If these were fast-grow, they wouldn't have been able to carry out such a complex maneuver. The attacks would have had to have been simpler, something straightforward, like the firing of a laser pistol or the hurling of a bomb.

But these were complicated attacks, attacks that took timing, thought, and a bit of guile. No one with a child's intellectual and emotional development could pull such a thing off.

Nor would a fast-grow clone have been able to converse the way that the "suspect" had. The fast-grow clone would have known a few choice phrases and little more.

Which led to an even creepier thought. These men, these clones, were either recruited for this task (which DeRicci hoped was the case) or they were grown specifically for this, and the attack had been in the planning for decades.

The whole clone angle bothered DeRicci. While Romey and the other detectives were working to catch the perpetrators of today's crimes, DeRicci wanted to know who was behind it all. And the only way to find that person was to find out where these clones had come from or if they had been recruited.

She wanted Popova to start that research, but once again, Popova wasn't responding to anything on her links.

DeRicci finally sighed and decided to do things the hard way. She went through the door into Popova's office.

Popova was sitting at her desk, head bent, long black hair masking her face. Her shoulders were shaking.

It took DeRicci a moment to realize that Popova was sobbing. DeRicci's strong, unflappable assistant, who had helped her through emergencies even more dire than this, had dissolved into tears.

"Rudra," DeRicci said.

Popova took a deep breath, raised her head, but didn't move her hair.

"Is there something you want to tell me?" DeRicci asked.

"I'm all right," Popova said, her voice thick with tears.

"You're not, and I need to know why. What is it about Arek?" DeRicci deliberately used Soseki's first name, because she had a hunch.

"I didn't mean to," Popova said, her voice rising. "It's just he was so wonderful and we liked each other so much and it wasn't like he was married or I was but we had our jobs, and we weren't sure if there was a conflict of interest and…."

She strangled on another sob. DeRicci, who prided herself on her own detecting abilities, felt stupid for not noticing this one. Popova's willingness to be the liaison with the City of Armstrong. Popova's ability to find a way to have business take her near the city offices around eight p.m. Popova's mood. It had been lighter of late.

"I'm sorry," DeRicci said. "I'm so sorry."

"I'll be all right," Popova said, face still covered by her long hair.

"No, you won't," DeRicci said. "I'm going to have to send you home."

"*No*, please," Popova said, and this time, she turned toward DeRicci. Popova's perfect skin was blotchy and her eyes were swollen. "I'll do what I can."

DeRicci sighed. She knew that Popova wouldn't perform to one tenth her normal standards. But she also knew Popova was probably better off here. Like so many in DeRicci's high-powered staff, Popova lived alone, and she didn't need to be on her own right now.

Besides, Popova loved information, and sending her home would cut her off from information on the greatest crisis of her life.

"You stay then," DeRicci said, "but I need someone to act as my assistant. Someone who can process a lot of information quickly and already has access to some of the higher levels."

"Yes, sir," Popova said. "I should have thought of that. I'm sorry."

She should have thought of a lot of things, but she wouldn't, not when she was in this condition. Which was why DeRicci couldn't use her as her main assistant.

"I need this person now," DeRicci said. Then she sighed, knowing how harsh she sounded. "I really am sorry, Rudra."

"I know," Popova said, then put a hand to her ear, shades of the old Popova, and set about getting DeRicci a new assistant.

As DeRicci went back into her own office, an urgent message came across her links. Two more failed attacks—one in Gagarin Dome, one in

Tycho Crater. The failure was due to the warnings she had sent. Images came with the message, and DeRicci accessed those on the large screen.

Two more clones. Exactly the same, from looks to clothing. Authorities in Tycho Crater were zeroing in on theirs now. They'd have more information in a few minutes.

Maybe by then, they'd have actual answers.

38

NYQUIST FOUND IT SURPRISINGLY EASY TO GET TO THE PORT OF ARMSTRONG, considering the police presence around the city. Security at the port was high, but people and aliens and goods still flowed in and out. He wondered if he should say something to DeRicci, then decided against it, at least for the moment. He needed to focus on Ursula Palmette.

The port was a windy twisty building that had several wings. Really it was several buildings all attached to one hub, but the city preferred to consider the port as one unit. Rather odd, considering that it might be easier to shut down a section of the port if it were considered a different building than it would be to shut down the entire port.

Still, he wasn't in charge, and he was glad of it. He would have hated to run the port, much more than he would have hated to have DeRicci's job. DeRicci took care of the entire Moon, but she thought of it the way he thought of his city, as a unit. And she was working security, not running the Moon itself.

No one was running the Moon itself. Not yet anyway. Although he was seeing the government centralize more and more. He wouldn't doubt if the office of governor-general and the United Domes council became more important during his lifetime, rather than less.

Particularly after a crisis like this. Leaders down, and only DeRicci's office with the authority to handle the Moon-wide emergency.

He watched security let through two slender blond men without giving them any greater check than anyone else. Nyquist hurried toward them, and caught one of them by the arm, taking an image of the man's face and comparing it to the suspect's image via his inks.

"Sorry," Nyquist said. "Thought you were someone else."

"It's okay," the man said and headed into nearby restaurant. The other man had disappeared into the crowd and was long gone.

That decided Nyquist. He sent a message to DeRicci via the emergency links. *I'm at the port following a lead. Security is lax here. You might already have lost the suspect. Better double-check your security order for here.*

He got an audio message back with an audible curse embedded in it. That curse made him smile. Apparently that curse was just for him.

Thanks, Bartholomew, DeRicci sent. *Am having trouble with Popova. Apparently she forgot to send the revised message through. Will take care of it now, and hope for the best.*

Problems with Popova? That was really unusual. The woman was scarily efficient. Had this emergency finally taxed her to the limits? If so, even that would surprise Nyquist. He hadn't thought Popova had limits.

He headed back the way he had come when he'd been pursuing the blond men. His stomach growled as he passed another restaurant, this one smelling of frying meat. He stopped at a nearby stand and bought an apple, one of the few things he knew would be fresh at the port.

Then he went through the police door. Even the security for that was still on the low-end. All he had to do was open his palm so that the door could read his badge number. The system should have done a retinal scan and a living tissue scan at this point in the crisis.

But he wasn't going to bother DeRicci again. He had done what he could. Now he had to find Palmette.

The back corridors in the port were narrower than the main corridors. They were unadorned, and didn't have the floating ads that the public areas had. Nor did they have pop-up directories with maps or port behavior rules.

He had to remember the layout himself or call up a detailed map, the kind only available to authorities who worked the port.

He let himself into Space Traffic Control. This was the heart of the port, with more people, doorways, and corridors than any other part. There was a security section, an operations section, a decontamination section, and dozens of others. Nyquist hadn't been inside most of them, although he had been inside the decontamination area on one memorable evening.

He never wanted to go in there again.

Now that he was inside Space Traffic, he had to find Palmette's section, and he couldn't do that on his own. So he called up the directory via his links and asked it to locate Palmette's desk.

Her name didn't even register, which bothered him. Instead, the system asked for a job title and/or a job description.

He sent back Special Administrator for Quarantined Ships, and hoped he had the title right. Otherwise, he would have to go into Space Traffic's reception, which he hated to do.

Murray, the guy who ran it most days, was a genial sort, and that made him a talker. They had a friend in common—Miles Flint, the Retrieval Artist who, long ago, used to work as a cop in Space Traffic. Murray liked Flint and thought he could do no wrong. Nyquist always felt uneasy around Flint, and worried that Flint was masking illegal behavior under the guise of cooperation.

Nyquist didn't want to tell that to Murray, and so always tried to avoid conversations with him.

Fortunately the map displayed a path to Palmette's desk, through a twist of warrenlike corridors, near the back of Space Traffic. Nyquist frowned. He had thought her job important, yet she had been shuttled to the very back of the building, away from everyone else.

Maybe that was the nature of dealing with quarantined vessels. Maybe there was a reason she was isolated.

He hoped not. He remembered talking to her a year after she had recovered from her injuries. She was going through psych evaluations, and failing them.

Nyquist had had to go through those as well before he got his shield back. He wasn't allowed to work anything but a desk job until he passed each evaluation. And the desk job was a courtesy, given to him because of his rank and years on the force. He really didn't do much work during that time, because no one wanted him on major cases.

He had hated that time of his life, sometimes wondering why he had survived the attacks at all, wondering why his service record and his closure rate made no difference. Later he understood: he'd seen others break down from post-traumatic stress or sheer terror based on an attack they survived.

Not everyone was designed to return to a job that had nearly killed them.

Apparently Palmette was one of those people. She had appealed to Nyquist, asking him for a recommendation to the board, trying to reinstate herself in the Armstrong Police Department. He hadn't known her well, and was reluctant to do so, but he did talk to the Chief of Detectives Andrea Gumiela about it. His argument was essentially that Palmette, injured in the line of duty, should be allowed to prove herself as an investigator while she went through these evaluations. At least give her a desk job, which Gumiela had. Palmette had contacted him, thanking him for the good words.

Not that it lasted. She never passed the psych evals and was told that if she wanted to remain in law enforcement, she had to take the desk version of an investigative job. That was when the Special Administrator came up, and she had taken that, hoping it would lead to something better.

Apparently it hadn't.

He had to go through a rabbit warren of narrow corridors to reach the back of this building—or section, as it was called. He expected to find an office, with Palmette's name on the door. Instead, he found a desk crammed into a cubby filled with other desks. Her desk was walled off from the others by a kind of clear material that could be opaqued. She couldn't even have true privacy.

For such an independent woman, this must have been hell.

He sighed. She wasn't at her desk. In fact, her desk looked like it hadn't been used all day. The chair was pushed in, the screen was off, and there were no personal items—no glass of water, no forgotten mug of coffee. There wasn't even anything in the nearby garbage can—not even a stain or two.

Now that could be attributed to a zealous cleaning bot, but he didn't think so. The desk felt unused.

There were no other employees nearby at the moment. Those desks, however, looked like they were being used, the chairs askew, jackets or sweaters on the backs of them, a purse still remaining on the floor.

No one to ask about Palmette however. So he did the next best thing: He used his link to ping her. Because she was Space Traffic and he was police, he should also be able to get her location.

The ping bounced back: *Ursula Palmette is in the middle of an important assignment. She will return your message when she has a moment. If this is an emergency, use the emergency link system.*

He was surprised. No cop should ever get that message from someone else in the department.

So he looked at her location, and started in surprise.

She was, according to the computer system, sitting at her desk. Working hard, in fact, because he got the same message warning him away. A message that told him how hard she was working.

He delved deeper into Space Traffic's system, requesting her arrival time that morning, and her movements throughout the day.

She had arrived at 9 a.m, and except for a short lunch break, remained at her desk all day. The system was useless.

Or it had been rigged.

Which made him nervous, given Palmette's job.

Something quarantined had made it into Armstrong, and now the one person who was in charge of quarantine ships had false information on her job report. Someone had tampered with it.

His heart raced.

Ursula Palmette was in trouble—again.

39

SOMEONE WAS GOING TO HAVE TO COORDINATE THE INVESTIGATIONS, AND it couldn't be Armstrong PD because the attacks were Moonwide. De-Ricci stared at the giant screen in her office, which had, in effect, become the investigations board. An attack in Gagarin Dome, another in Tycho Crater, two in Armstrong, one in Moscow Dome, and a lot of clones unaccounted for. The governor-general was incapacitated, maybe dying, the council had to vote on her successor, and the other leaders of the Moon were already in hiding.

DeRicci was—once again—the only one in a position to do anything.

She peeked out her office door. Popova was standing beside her desk, listlessly moving her arm as she described the layout of the office. Clearly, the young man standing in front of her was the new assistant.

He looked twelve. Maybe thirteen. Certainly not old enough to grow a beard. He had copper hair and dark skin, eyes so green that they looked like they were backlit, and a strong chin. His face shone with intelligence, which was a good thing.

DeRicci stepped into Popova's office.

"Rudra?" DeRicci said.

Popova turned. DeRicci had never seen anyone look like the life had been sucked out of them before. Whatever made Popova Popova had vanished, leaving a shell of a person with haunted eyes.

"This is our new assistant," Popova said, her voice hollow. "Ephraim Hänsel. He's been running network security, linking the various domes, or trying to. Most places don't want their private networks linked to a main network. He's got the highest clearance I could find on such short notice."

DeRicci was familiar with the work that Hänsel did. She just hadn't been aware of the man in charge of it. He was good at his job, which didn't mean he would be good at this one.

"Rudra misspoke a moment ago," DeRicci said. "You'll be assisting me. She will aid you in figuring out how to go about some of these tasks, but for the most part, you'll have to act and act quickly. Do you think you can do that?"

"Yes, sir," he said, but his voice wobbled. She made him nervous. Of course, she was getting to the point in her life where she made everyone nervous.

Or maybe it was the job.

"Have you ever worked in a detective unit?" she asked.

"No, sir," he said.

"Any type of investigation?"

"No, sir."

She wanted to curse, but she didn't. He wasn't what she needed, but then even Popova, if she had been functional, would have had trouble with what DeRicci needed too.

"All right," DeRicci said, already mentally dismissing him from 90% of the work she had wanted him for. "I need you to do two things. I need you to draft a statement to every government in the Earth Alliance, telling them that the Moon has found itself under attack, and warning them to keep an eye on their own leaders. Step up security, that sort of thing."

"A draft, sir?" he said.

"I'm going to approve this. If I find out you sent it out of this office without my input, you will be in more trouble than you have ever been in your entire life. Do you understand?'

"Yes, sir."

"Secondly," she said, "I need you to set up a meeting with all of the security chiefs or their equivalent in the Earth Alliance governments. Work with my counterpart in the Alliance. See if she wants to include represen-tatives from each government. I'll need this meeting within the hour."

"Yes, sir," he said. Then he swallowed hard. "Um, which job takes priority, sir?"

She stared at him, then gave Popova a disapproving look. Two spots of color appeared on Popova's cheeks. Even in her depleted state, she knew that this man would never do. She had also already explained him. He was the best they had available.

"They're of equal importance," DeRicci said. "I need both, and I needed them an hour ago. Get busy."

"Yes, sir," he said. "May I bring in help, sir?"

He was competent enough to know that he was about to become incompetent. That, at least, was a plus.

But DeRicci didn't want a bunch of new and inexperienced people in her office. She couldn't deal with them and the crisis at the same time.

"No," she said.

"I'll make sure it gets done," Popova said.

And DeRicci gave her another hard look. Had Popova deliberately brought in someone unqualified so she would have to stay? She wasn't usually that manipulative, but she was frightened and not herself.

"Thank you, Rudra," DeRicci said, then went back into her office.

For the first time ever, she felt the urge to lock the door. She knew better than to ask herself if this day could get any worse.

She knew from personal experience that it could.

And that was the last thing she wanted.

40

NYQUIST SPRINTED DOWN THE CORRIDORS LEADING TO THE MAIN OFFICE OF Space Traffic Control. He had already sent a message to Murray Atherton, the man in charge. In fact, much as Nyquist tried to avoid Murray on a good day, on *this* day Nyquist was relieved Murray was on duty because Murray was sensible—and would go off the books if need be, but knew when the rules had to be followed to the letter.

Nyquist suspected this was one of those off-the-books situations.

He was almost there when his emergency link chirruped, then opened. A see-through image of DeRicci stood before him, and it was so real that he stopped rather than run into her.

"Bartholomew," she said through a clearly scrambled channel, "I really need you. Can you get to the Security Building as soon as possible?"

He hadn't seen her look this frightened and frazzled since he woke up from surgery after the Bixian assassination attempt. And it broke his heart to answer her. Although he couldn't do so verbally because there were cameras everywhere in these corridors. He had to send his response on the link.

I'm sorry, Noelle, he sent. *I'm on an important lead. I'll need back-up here before I leave. I can be there in an hour or two.*

She shook her head. "That's too late. Thanks, I'll come up with another solution."

And then she was gone. He stood in the corridor for a moment, feeling really unsettled. DeRicci didn't get upset by much—at least not the asking-for-help type of upset.

If he didn't believe that Palmette was in trouble, he would go immediately. But Palmette had control over a lot of quarantined vessels—the kind that weren't well monitored—and if this attack was just the beginning the way Soseki's assassin said, then subsequent attacks could come from those vessels as well.

Nyquist didn't dare lose track of this part of the investigation.

But he had no idea what could make DeRicci so frazzled.

He sent a ping to her links, telling her he'd be there anyway. Then he hurried down the corridor.

After a moment, she sent a message back. *I have an organizational issue, Bartholomew, nothing more. I just need someone competent since Rudra is overburdened. I thought of you. I'll find someone. You take care of what you need there, and when you're done, let me know. I'll tell you if I still need you.*

And that was it. The message ended right there.

It was a typical sent message, without inflection, and yet it seemed curt, dismissive, and filled with hurt. Maybe he was just imagining that.

Everything with DeRicci had been dicey lately, and most of that was his fault. He was defensive and difficult—always had been, if truth be told—and he wasn't sure how much longer he wanted to be in this relationship.

But she had cared for him, and she had helped him get back on his feet.

And now that she had finally come to him with something that made him feel as if she respected him again, he had to turn her down. As he ran down the corridor, he wondered if he had refused her so quickly because he was angry at her.

Then he ruled that out. He had to track down Palmette.

And he had to do it soon.

41

SHE HADN'T EXPECTED NYQUIST TO SAY NO.

DeRicci stood in the center of her office, her back to that gigantic screen. She felt like she had been punched in the stomach. Her brain knew it wasn't Nyquist's fault. She was the one who had insisted he stay off the case; Romey was the one who hired him and put him on whatever it was he was pursuing.

He was acting in good faith, like the tremendous cop that he was. He had to finish whatever it was, because he and Romey were working the case on the street. Even with Soseki's assassin dead, there was still another—the one who tried to get the governor-general. And there was probably someone else as well. These men didn't get into Armstrong with all of that specialized equipment on their own.

They had help. And Nyquist's link put him at the port.

When DeRicci realized that, she realized that Nyquist was probably right: whatever he was working on took priority. She was trying to organize a large investigation; he was already in the middle of one.

The problem was twofold: She needed an experienced investigator, someone who could find out information quickly and organize that information just as quickly.

She also needed someone she trusted.

She knew there were a lot more experienced investigators in Armstrong than there were people she trusted. By factors of a thousand.

She gripped the back of the chair tightly, her fingers digging into the soft material. She could contact Andrea Gumiela, the Chief of Detectives, and ask for someone to come to her office. But DeRicci and Gumiela hated each other. They had a truce—they had both realized how effective the other one was—but they didn't trust each other. And even in an investigation this important, DeRicci couldn't trust Gumiela to get the best person for the job that DeRicci needed.

Gumiela would send the best person for the job that Gumiela needed, whatever that was. If their needs met, then DeRicci would get a good assistant. If they didn't meet, then DeRicci would end up with a mole from the Armstrong PD, and a lost afternoon.

Her other choice? She could bring Kilzahn back. He had been observing Romey all day long. He wouldn't have to come up to speed on the investigation. He would know the entire Soseki part of it.

But Kilzahn wasn't an investigator. He was a top notch security man, able to find holes in the tightest security system. He was detail-oriented, and he saw through people. That was why DeRicci sent him in the first place, because he *saw* things.

But that wasn't enough.

She needed help. Real help. Someone whose skills were equal to hers. Someone whose intelligence was as quick as hers. Someone who understood how she worked, and could survive her quick temper.

There was only one person left to contact. She rubbed a hand over her mouth. If something went wrong, she would never live this down. But half a dozen things had already gone wrong today.

If she screwed this up—if she failed within the next twelve to twenty-four hours—there might not be any governments on the Moon at all. She couldn't worry about future recriminations.

She had to think about surviving the day.

And to do that, she needed someone brilliant, someone she could trust to work without supervision.

She needed Miles Flint.

42

Fifty paid security personnel had just arrived at Aristotle Academy. They set up all along the gate leading into the Academy as well as on school grounds itself.

It felt like Flint was suddenly trapped inside an armed state. He was unnerved, even though he had known the security personnel were coming.

Selah Rutledge, the headmistress, was having Flint monitor the computer firewalls, looking for security breaches, not just inside the compound that was the Academy, but also in the computer networks themselves.

So far, Flint hadn't found anything. He doubted he would. He had developed this system himself and kept it up to date with the latest technological changes that he found in his various cases. He had a vested interest in keeping this school safe, since Talia spent so much of her time here.

She still didn't know he was on the grounds. He hadn't gone near her classroom. The students didn't know that the security team was here either, although they'd get a clue when they saw the weapons.

Selah was going to handle an announcement soon; she just wasn't sure what to say. Both she and Flint tried to parse the information coming through the various news feeds. Nothing was clear, which Flint knew from his own experiences as an Armstrong Police Detective, meant that something was seriously wrong. He just wasn't sure what.

He had checked the systems in the computer section, and then had come back to Selah's office. He wanted to stay at the center of everything, just in case something went seriously awry. He had the network protocols set up so that he would get contacted the minute something went even the slightest bit off.

He had also set up a monitoring system on one of the empty desks in Selah's office, just so that he had a home base here, so that he wouldn't be running back and forth between sections.

Selah was monitoring all the news feeds. So far, they said the same thing (which was also suspicious): that Soseki was dead; that cause of death was undetermined, but was initially thought to be of natural causes; there had been two attacks made on Anniversary Day speeches in Gagarin Dome and in Tycho Crater; the governor-general could not be reached for comment at this time; Chief of Security for the United Domes of the Moon, Noelle DeRicci, said her office is monitoring the situation, but at this time, she had no idea if the attacks were something the population might have come to expect from disgruntled elements on Anniversary Day; the immigrant and alien communities were calm; some events had been canceled due to the targeting; and there was no comment so far from the Earth Alliance, not that anyone wanted them to say anything.

The security forces were the thing that made Flint the most nervous. Four different groups of private security had contacted Selah within fifteen minutes, just before the announcements of the Anniversary Day attacks. All four groups claimed their orders had come from different parents, all of whom were leaders in government.

When Luc Deshin contacted Selah, that's when she decided to bring in her own security team. Luc Deshin was the closest thing Armstrong had to a master criminal. He was impossible to catch—or so Flint was told—because he had set himself up as a "legitimate" businessman. Whatever he was, he loved his strange little son Paavo, and wanted the boy protected.

Deshin was going to send in his own security team, which Selah decidedly did not want. So she told him that security was on the way, and called the firm that handled all of Aristotle Academy's security. She ordered a maximum number of trained marksmen on site within fifteen minutes.

The security team arrived in ten. From that moment on, she had been dealing with concerned parents and employees of concerned-but-couldn't-be-bothered-with-details parents, letting them know that the security system was well in hand.

All of this told Flint that the Anniversary Day attacks were related, Soseki was more than likely assassinated, the governor-general was either targeted, hurt, or dead, and something had gone very, very wrong.

When Selah mentioned that she might close the school for the day, Flint argued against it. If indeed something had gone wrong around Anniversary Day, then dispersing the students of the rich and powerful around Armstrong was the worst thing she could do. The best thing was to make sure they would be protected—and he promised to help.

He wasn't sure that was the best idea either because the school made one gigantic, tempting target, but he had a hunch it would be easier to defend than dozens and dozens of high-end houses throughout the city.

Why he felt that such a defense was necessary, he didn't quite know. But he had learned to go with his gut a long time ago.

He was checking the security system for the tenth time when Noelle DeRicci suddenly appeared in the vision of his left eye. She looked exhausted, her clothing rumpled as if she had been tugging on it, her curly hair even messier than usual. The area around her lips was chapped. She'd been rubbing her hands over her mouth again, one of her more serious nervous habits.

His pulse rose at the sight of her. DeRicci had been his partner years ago. She was hard-nosed and efficient, compassionate as well, and the kind of woman who strong-armed her way through any situation. He would never have chosen her for a job that required political finesse, but she had done tremendously well. She turned out to be suited for the work. She thought fast, she took action even when no one told her to (especially when no one told her to), and she had great instincts.

The fact that she looked exhausted and alarmed at the same time meant that something was seriously wrong.

You alone? She sent.

He didn't move, nor did he look around. He continued to stare at the screen so that no one would realize he was on his links. *No.*

I need to talk to you. Can you get somewhere now?

Yes. He stood.

Selah was making notes for the speech she was going to give the students in a few minutes while she kept watching the various news feeds hoping to learn something new.

"I'm going to double-check something," he said to her. "I'll be right back."

"Is everything all right?" she asked.

"Just a small bobble. Probably a burp in the system. Not anything to worry about."

Yet she looked worried. Sometimes lack of information was more frightening than the information itself.

"I'll let you know if something is wrong," he said and let himself out of the office.

He went a few meters down the hall to a blind spot in the security coverage, a blind spot he'd been meaning to fix.

What's up, Noelle? he sent. He wasn't going to talk through this just in case someone came by.

Where are you? she sent back. Unlike most people, Flint had disabled all of the tracking software inside his links. No one could find him unless he wanted them to.

Aristotle Academy.

I need you here, DeRicci sent. *Can you get down here immediately?*

He took a breath. He didn't want to leave Talia. He was getting more and more uneasy.

What exactly do you need, Noelle? he sent back. *I'd like to stay with Talia if I can.*

I need an investigator, Miles. Someone I can trust. Someone who will work his ass off.

What about Nyquist?

Already on a different part of this investigation.

I'm going to get you in trouble, Noelle.

If I don't bring someone good in, there'll be no one left to get in trouble with, she sent back.

A surge of fear ran through him. DeRicci didn't make statements like that—at least not to outsiders. And whatever their history was, that didn't change the fact that Flint was now an outsider.

Can I work here? he sent.

No, she sent back. *I need someone on site. Bring Talia. She's as good with information systems as you are. Maybe better. And she'll be safer here than anywhere else in the city.*

Safe from what, Noelle? he sent.

If I knew the answer to that, Miles, I wouldn't need you. Her mouth formed a thin line. It looked like she wanted to say something out loud, but she didn't. Not after that first contact. *I'll send someone for you.*

No, he sent. *I'll get there quicker on my own. You just make sure the building allows both of us to come to your office.*

You got it, DeRicci sent. *I appreciate this.*

Wait until the work is done before you send any thanks, Noelle, he sent. But she had already signed off.

He was alone in the corridor, with nothing flowing along his links except the usual chatter. DeRicci had called on Flint before in a few instances, but generally with things that had to happen off the books. The fact that she was bringing him into the office itself meant that something had gone seriously wrong. And worse than that, she didn't expect any repercussions from bringing in a Retrieval Artist, a man who sometimes worked on the wrong side of the law.

She figured she wouldn't get in trouble for it. Or that she could defend it.

Or that everything was so far gone that it didn't matter who worked with her, so long as the work got done.

He took a deep breath, then headed back to the office to tell Selah about his change of plans.

43

Nyquist let himself into Space Traffic headquarters. It wasn't much: a large room with a desk, and chairs for the handful of visitors that came into Space Traffic every year. A mural on the wall always caught his eye because he thought it so strange and out of character with the government drab the rest of the Administration Center had as its design. The mural showed the history of spaceships from the very first capsule-like thing to some of the high end models of ten years before. Someone needed to update the damn thing.

Someone needed to update the entire area.

Except the space behind Murray Atherton's desk. The equipment there was truly the headquarters of Space Traffic Control. Not the Control systems that actually handled the Armstrong's space, but the command systems for every single Space Traffic officer, as well as the ships, the squads, and the entire port itself.

There were redundant systems elsewhere, but if you needed information about the port and needed it quickly, the person who could get it for you was Murray Atherton.

Murray himself looked eighty, but had to be in his mid-fifties. Sometimes Nyquist wondered if the guy had gotten reverse enhancements, the kind that made a person look old, just so that he would have gravitas. He would have had to have done that years ago, and Nyquist used to wonder if Murray regretted it. Now that Nyquist had chosen not to get enhancements on his own, he understood: Sometimes not looking perfect gave a person a lot more power than looking like a shiny new model straight off the shelf.

Murray saw Nyquist and beckoned him to the crowded area behind the desk. Screens showed all kinds of numbers and dots and things Nyquist didn't understand. Murray did—he could translate that into actual information quicker than anyone else could. It also prevented people from glancing at the screens and getting information quickly.

Nyquist knew from experience that there was a simple hand command that would turn the screens to information the average man could use, but he didn't know the command. He didn't usually have a lot of dealings with Space Traffic. Not of this kind, anyway.

"I just found her," Murray said, "not two seconds before you came in the door. She really cocked things up."

Nyquist slid into the tiny space behind Murray. Some of the screens still showed blips and dots, which Nyquist thought—but wasn't sure—were ships. But Murray wasn't working off those screens. He was working off two in the center. One showed Palmette's desk—still empty—and the other showed a dim area around what seemed to be a ship.

"I thought you could track all employees," Nyquist said.

"I'm supposed to be able to," Murray said with some annoyance. "I'm supposed to be able to track *everyone* in this damn port at any time that I want to. Apparently, I haven't been tracking her for months."

That sentence sent a chill through Nyquist. "What do you mean?"

"Ever since you contacted me, I've been scanning the visual logs while I've been trying to undo her mess." Murray sounded annoyed. Maybe more than annoyed. Angry? Nyquist wasn't sure he had ever seen Murray angry. "And I don't see her anywhere she's supposed to be. If her link says she was in the cafeteria, then I look at the visual and I don't see her. She hasn't been where she's supposed to be for months."

Nyquist clenched his right fist, then made himself unclench it. "Is she even around?"

"I have no idea," Murray said. "Her personnel file says she lives alone, so no one would report her missing. She works by herself on that quarantine stuff, so no one's really supervising her except your girlfriend."

DeRicci. Nyquist repressed the urge to correct Murray about DeRicci. She was so much more than his girlfriend—if she could even be called that.

"It's my understanding that Palmette has an administrative position," Nyquist said. "I didn't think you guys were supervised."

Murray grunted, which Nyquist took for an assent. Murray was peering at one of the screens, the one with the very dim ship. He expanded the image tenfold. There was a woman in front of the ship, and it looked like Palmette.

But Murray, cautious man that he was, compared her image to one on file. Or maybe something in the floor or the air could do a DNA scan. Nyquist didn't know, and he wasn't sure he cared. He just wanted to find out what was going on.

"Is that her?" Nyquist asked.

"According to everything I have here," Murray said, but he sounded unconvinced.

"You don't trust this?"

"She fooled it for months," Murray said.

"Or someone did," Nyquist said.

Murray looked at him, frowning.

Nyquist shrugged. "When I met her, she didn't have the skills to defeat a system like this. She was a detective, same as me."

But not the same. A new detective. Six months on the job, with a new partner and unachieved goals.

"Her file says she just has minimal computer skills," Murray said, glancing at yet another screen. Nyquist didn't see the file, but then, he didn't see much on those screens.

"Have you checked an old version of the file?" Nyquist asked.

Murray looked over his shoulder at Nyquist. "You think someone tampered with her personnel file too?"

Nyquist shrugged. "They tampered with her location files."

Murray nodded. He touched a screen, put a hand to his ear, and his frown deepened. "I don't like any of this," he muttered.

Nyquist got the sense Murray was not talking to him. "The old file says something different?"

"No," Murray said. "And these are backups no one can tamper with. She doesn't have the skills anywhere. She'd have to have worked developing computer systems to have the skills to mess with our system. I only know a handful of people who could do it, and none of them know her."

That Murray was aware of, but Nyquist didn't say that either. He just kept his mouth shut and watched.

"We'll figure out how she did this later. I need to talk to her now."

"If that's her, you ain't talking to her," Murray said.

It was Nyquist's turn to frown. "Why not?"

"Because that's Terminal 81, and you don't have clearance."

"What?" Nyquist asked. Terminal 81 was the place where they parked the bulk of the quarantined vessels until they got destroyed or sent back to where they came from. "What's she doing in there?"

"I don't like this," Murray said again, and this time, Nyquist realized he wasn't talking about Palmette's computer skills.

"Murray, *what's she doing?*"

Murray looked up at him, expression tight, as if he didn't want to show his true emotions. "She's going through a web of protection."

Nyquist's breath caught. Webs of protection were put around extremely dangerous items, from tiny bombs to large ships. Webs of protection were designed so that no one, not even anyone authorized, could get into a ship without moving slowly and cautiously. All the way along, the webs asked if the person wanted to go farther, and sent out all kinds of warnings.

Only Murray should have been notified of those warnings. Apparently he hadn't been.

"You're sure?" Nyquist asked.

"My system ain't lying to me about this," Murray said.

"But it didn't notify you."

"It didn't, did it." Murray didn't sound surprised. "She's not wearing hazmat gear."

Nyquist let out a small breath. "Should she be?"

"If she don't want to die," Murray said.

"What the hell's in that ship?" Nyquist asked.

"I don't know," Murray said. "The file's tampered with."

"Someone's been planning this," Nyquist said.

"No kidding. I'm going to the old file." He worked.

"I need to get in there," Nyquist said.

"You don't have the training," Murray said. "I'm sending in the Quarantine Squad."

"They'll spook her," Nyquist said. "I can talk to her."

Although he wasn't really sure he could.

"This woman don't look like she's in the mood to talk," Murray said.

"You don't know that," Nyquist said. "She might be taking action to protect someone else. She might be coerced."

"She'd tell you that?"

Nyquist shrugged. "Me as much as anyone."

He wasn't going to mention that he saved her life once. He would if Murray didn't authorize him.

"You got exactly ten minutes to get to Terminal 81 and gear up," Murray said. "That's how long it'll take the squad to get there."

Nyquist's heart pounded. He'd won, but he wasn't sure that was a good thing. "Thanks."

"Don't thank me," Murray said. "At the moment, I got no idea what's on that ship. For all I know, it could kill anyone wearing a hazmat suit. So you're risking your life."

"I risk my life every day," Nyquist said. "It's the job."

"Maybe on the street that's the job. Dealing with this kind of mess, that's not your job."

"I'm not dealing with the mess," Nyquist said. "I'm dealing with one woman, who might or might not need help."

"Don't you touch nothing," Murray said. "Let the squad do that. You talk to her. Nothing more."

"Got it," Nyquist said. Then, because he truly didn't know, he asked, "Where do I meet them?"

"In front of Terminal 81. I'll send you the guidelines as to what ship she's messing with." Murray wasn't looking at him. Murray was working at least two screens, maybe more.

"Thanks," Nyquist said as he headed toward the back exit.

"Don't thank me," Murray said. "I hate it when people thank me for doing something that could get them killed."

"My decision, Murray," Nyquist said, and headed into the corridor. He had less than ten minutes now to find a hazmat suit that fit and meet the squad at Terminal 81. Maybe by then, Murray would know what Palmette was doing.

Maybe by then, they would all have some answers.

44

THEY'D CLEARED OUT THE TOP OF THE DOME EXCEPT FOR THE HOSTAGES in the circular restaurant. Captain Polly Keptra hated this place. She had warned people for years about it, but no one listened to her. She even went before the licensing board here in Tycho Crater to get them to rescind or at least fail to renew Top of the Dome's business license. But that hadn't happened either.

She had expected something to happen, but she hadn't expected it to reach the upper levels of Tycho Crater's government. The mayor was safe—squirreled out of the Sky Auditorium by his protective detail the moment the image of the assassin came through everyone's links.

But the damn assassin had realized he'd been made, ran out of the auditorium brandishing, of all things, a laser rifle, and reached the circular restaurant before anyone could catch him.

She stood outside the restaurant's main doors now, along with three members of her team. The doors were closed and bolted shut from the inside, but she already had confirmed that the department had an override code.

She would get in. The question was what she would find once she was inside.

Half the lunch crowd escaped. The rest were inside with a madman who, the United Domes of the Moon Security Office told her, would commit suicide before he'd get caught.

Keptra wanted to turn to Josiah Strom, her second in command, and ask him to remind her again why she had taken the Assistant Chief's job. But he would just give her a sideways look that would say everything: she hated the way the department was run; she felt that someone who actually knew how to do the work should be in a position of power; and she had no family, so she could show up day or night if there was an emergency.

Like this one. Which somehow managed to happen in the middle of a very long day.

She had a tactical team of twenty officers with her. She'd been drilling them in hostage rescue and dome security for six months now, but this was their very first actual test. Tycho Crater was at the end of nowhere, even though it tried to set itself up as a tourist destination. That's why the dome government had been unwilling to get rid of the Top of the Dome—because it was the only hotel/resort of its kind, and it was Tycho Crater's biggest draw.

And its biggest potential disaster.

Built literally in the circle at the very top of the dome, with "sky elevators" leading to it, the Top of the Dome had been part of Tycho Crater since the dome was built. Initially it had provided housing for the workers who did the intricate work on the dome layers. Then someone got the bright idea to attach the free-floating platform, and turn it into a restaurant. The restaurant became a hotel, the hotel became a resort (with a terrific view), and the Top of the Dome was born.

Of course, no one cared that the thing—because of all the continual jury-rigging that the engineers did—was unstable and could fall onto the population of the city. Nor did anyone care that the damn thing blocked the view of thousands of residents who lived below the Top of the Dome.

Eventually, the city attached the Top of the Dome to the dome itself, so as the light changed on the dome, it also changed underneath the Top of the Dome. But that also made the Top of the Dome even more vulnerable. If someone took over the resort, they had access to all of the dome's major systems and that, Keptra maintained, was a risk the city should never, ever take.

Of course, the city had taken that risk against her advice.

And now some wannabe assassin with a laser rifle held dozens of people hostage in the restaurant. The assassin was part of a group of assassins who had targeted (with some success) the other leaders of the other cities on the Moon. No one knew if the assassins on the ground had help or if they worked alone.

So Keptra had no idea if the man she was going after had someone to help him—people to turn out the lights on the dome, people who could open the dome without warning, people who could wreak all kinds of havoc in the city without doing much more than lift a finger.

She had to believe that the assassin worked alone. She had to believe that if he had that kind of assistance, he would have used it by now. Because if she believed anything else, she would be paralyzed.

She had sent guards to the various systems throughout the dome, and asked city officials to have their best specialists on hand to override any problems, but that didn't mean that the problems wouldn't happen anyway.

No one had attacked Tycho Crater before. Not the city itself. Not once in its long history.

Now it was happening on her watch.

If she survived this, she owed a hundred people a thousand I-told-you-sos.

At least her team had practiced rescues at the Top of the Dome. She had always believed it was the most tempting target in the city. It certainly had attracted its share of suicides in its long existence, until someone figured out how to put a clear protective barrier around the resort itself.

The rescues had gone well, and so had the tactical assault practices. But now her team had to do it for real: they had to get into that damn circular restaurant with its 360-degree view of the city, the crater, and the dome itself, and somehow rescue all of the hostages without anyone getting hurt—not even the damn potential assassin.

She glanced at Strom. He looked as nervous as she felt. In the first two drills her people had gotten so distracted by the views that they had lost focus on the mission. In the more recent one, they'd seen too many reflections in the clear walls and actually "shot" each other. She had "lost" five team members that day, and had let everyone know about her great displeasure.

She hoped the rest of the team was remembering those mistakes. She wanted them to be at the best of their abilities, not their worst.

This time, they wouldn't get another chance.

Through her link, the dispatch gave her an estimate: fourteen hostages, including some family members of the VIPs who had gone to the mayor's speech. The family members included children too young to sit in an auditorium for an Anniversary Day celebration.

Great. Children as well. Her mouth was dry. In some ways, she was no more experienced than her team. She had no idea how they were going to pull this off—and she was the one who had to have an idea.

Need security footage, she sent back to Dispatch.

It's been disabled, Dispatch sent.

A shot of fear went through Keptra. Maybe that assistant she had been worrying about actually existed. *How'd he do that?*

He didn't, Dispatch sent back. *It went down months ago, and no one fixed it.*

And Keptra had never checked the restaurant's footage on her practice drills because she had footage of her own. Her stomach clenched.

They were going in blind.

Anyone inside have visuals they can send? she sent.

We haven't received any contact from inside, Dispatch sent.

Which could have meant anything. The group inside might be too young to have links (God forbid). They might be too inexperienced to realize they could help the police. Or the assassin somehow used a device to disable links—which meant he had even more technological sophistication than she expected.

All right then, Keptra sent back. *Let me know if anything changes.*

Then she nodded at Strom.

Everyone in place? she sent to her team on their private link.

She got affirmatives from all the unit leaders.

She had the largest team, with four, because they were going in the main doors.

All right then, she sent. *Let's go!*

45

NYQUIST WAS BREATHING HARD. HE HAD MANAGED TO GET A HAZMAT SUIT and arrive in front of Terminal 81 in less than the ten minutes that Murray had allowed him. Putting the damn suit on, however, was proving a problem.

Fortunately, the Traffic Quarantine Squad that Murray assigned to this job was willing to wait for him. Besides, they had to figure out how, exactly, to get to Palmette.

Apparently, she was deep inside Terminal 81, near an old ship without a lot of data attached to it. The old ship records were sketchy at best. Most of those ships were supposed to leave Terminal 81 when their owners or some government reclaimed them.

But not all ships got reclaimed. And some had remained in port for decades.

Like this one, apparently.

The squad was trying to figure out the best way to get to the ship, a way that took them through the fewest webs of protection, and away from the most dangerous quarantines.

Nyquist wondered if Palmette had thought about any of that.

Probably not, since she wasn't wearing a hazmat suit. Or, if she had been coerced, she probably figured it didn't matter: She was dead no matter what she did.

That thought sent a little twinge through him. Wouldn't she have insisted on a hazmat suit? And if not, if she knew the result of cooperating with whomever was trying to coerce her was her own death, then what was the point of cooperating?

The corridor here was narrow and dark. When he had arrived, he noted how forbidding it was, compared with the corridors leading to the other terminals. It was as if someone wanted anyone who entered here to feel uncomfortable, to know that they had gone to the wrong place.

Most of the squad had arrived ahead of him, and they had already started a discussion about entering Terminal 81. It wasn't a matter of hitting a palm on the identification pad. It took access codes from four different people, authorization codes from higher ups, and the ability to go through fifteen different webs of protection just to get to the standard identification pad at the front of the door.

It took Nyquist a minute to put on his helmet. He hated hazmat suits. They made him think of the worst investigations he had participated in, the ones that ended badly, the ones that had led him to question his job.

Nyquist pulled on the suit's helmet. He had asked for a face-hugging helmet even though it meant that he wasn't as protected as he would have been in a larger one. He wanted Palmette to see him.

The helmet made him even more aware of the suit.

Oddly, the cases where he had needed a hazmat suit and hadn't had one—the day he saved Palmette's life came to mind—had given him a kind of inner strength that he hadn't had before. On the afternoon of the bombing, as he waited for the dome section to open, he thought about the murder, about Alvina, about Palmette—about his terrible life—and he had had a realization.

Instead of making him want to quit his job, that dark day had made him realize how much he loved his work—and how frightened he was of losing it. He had been afraid that everything would change after that, and many things did. But not his job, not investigation, not police work in general.

And he had changed. He knew he was strong enough to face all kinds of terrible odds—which helped him later when he found himself alone with Bixian assassins. It helped him now, because he knew the city would get through this.

But he wasn't sure how many people would die in the meantime. And every second it took the squad to open a web of protection made extra loss of life even more probable.

He wanted to tell the squad to hurry, but he knew better. They didn't dare avoid protocol. If any of those webs of protection were tainted, it would cause Terminal 81 to get sealed off. If the damage in Terminal 81— or the threat in the terminal—was too bad, then someone (probably De-Ricci) would have to decide whether or not to destroy the entire area.

After evacuations, of course. After the dome protections had fallen, so that any explosion would be contained.

If there was an explosion. This terminal had also been designed to open directly into the vastness of space, the nothingness that was the Moon itself. If the threat was chemical, then the chemical would disperse in the lack of atmosphere. If there was a fire or an explosion caused by something lethal, then the lack of oxygen would shut that all down.

Any contagion would disperse as well.

So theoretically, Terminal 81 was the safest place to have a crisis in all of Armstrong.

But that didn't explain why Nyquist's heart was pounding, why he was having so much trouble regulating his own breathing.

He was nervous, maybe even a little frightened. And as much as he told himself that such feelings were normal in a situation like this, he didn't really want to believe it.

He couldn't believe it, and be effective.

He had to stay calm.

He had to do this right.

46

THEY BROKE THROUGH THE DOOR WITH RELATIVE EASE. TO KEPTRA'S surprise, the interior of the restaurant was light. All of her training had told her that a perpetrator would keep it dark.

But he hadn't.

The assassin stood in the center of the circular restaurant, at the maître d's station. It was surreal. Her people stood in all the doorways, which were placed around the restaurant at regular intervals. Between them, booths lined up against the windows. At every third booth, hostages—most of them families with small children. The windows next them showed the crater walls. Below, the lights of the city beckoned, and above them, the dome. Just barely visible through it, the lights of the solar system itself against the blackness of space.

Usually that view held the attention of everyone, but no one looked at it now. Not even the assassin.

He had the maître d's station on slow rotate, so his back wasn't to anyone for very long. He clutched the laser rifle, and as he rotated, Keptra noted that he had a laser pistol tucked into the waistband of his pants.

None of the hostages sat at the tables scattered through the middle of the room. There were no employees either, and the kitchen door was barricaded. The employees, apparently, had made their escape.

Leaving families, a handful of single adults, and way too many children under five.

Just like Keptra had feared.

She cursed, then sent to her team, *Remember, no one shoot until we get the hostages out of here.*

The last thing she wanted was a malfunction, not of her people's weaponry, but of that weird technical stuff the other assassin—the one in Armstrong—had worn, the stuff that had taken a knee shot and brought it all the way to his heart. If the technical stuff had malfunctioned, it might ricochet any shot around the room, randomly killing people.

Randomly killing children.

She took one small step forward.

"I'm Captain Polly Keptra," she said. "I'd like to talk with you."

The assassin stopped the maître d's station from rotating, then he turned to face her. As he did, she saw a reflection around him. Something on that station was set up to mirror imagery, so that he could mask where he was really standing.

Or maybe it had a more innocuous purpose: maybe it had just been there so that the maître d' could see anyone new who came into the restaurant, no matter what door they used.

"So talk," the assassin said.

He had no discernable accent; she had expected an accent. She *wanted* an accent. She *needed* an accent. She needed him to be something *other*, more than being a clone.

She didn't want him to seem rational and human and oh, so reasonable.

It didn't help that he was thin and young and relatively attractive, with his unusual blond coloring and his pale eyes.

"It would be easier to talk if you let the hostages go," she said.

He tilted his head, as if her request amused him. Then he nodded, ever so slightly, and said, "It would, wouldn't it?"

It took her a moment to process the words. She hadn't expected them.

"I tell you what," he said, ever so reasonably. "I will let them go, if you let me keep this one."

With his left hand, he lifted a man from the floor behind the maître d' station. Given the man's powder blue tuxedo dotted with stars, he had to be the maître d' himself.

The man looked almost catatonic.

"How about you take me instead?" Keptra asked.

"How about everyone stay?" the assassin said, in that very reasonable tone.

"All right." She had no idea if she was agreeing too fast, but she didn't care. That was for the review board to decide, days from now, when this entire ordeal was over. "We'll get the hostages out of here."

"Actually," the assassin said, "they're not hurt. They can leave under their own power."

Her heart was pounding. This had better go well.

"You heard him," she said to the hostages. "Please leave slowly and carefully through the nearest door."

They scrambled out of the booths, the single adults nearly knocking over children in their haste to escape. The adults who were responsible for the children grabbed them, picking some of them up and carrying them, dragging the others out by their hands.

It was a relatively quiet evacuation, and quick. They cleared the restaurant in less than two minutes flat.

If hostage situations were judged by how many hostages survived, then Keptra had just negotiated a successful deal.

Somehow, she suspected that this wasn't about hostages.

"I'm still willing to trade myself for your remaining hostage," Keptra said.

The assassin shrugged. "But I'm not willing to make the trade. In fact, I think I should get rid of him, don't you?"

He brushed a hand over the man's face. Keptra, remembering the images of the dead Armstrong mayor, tensed.

"I don't think anyone should be gotten rid of," she said.

I have a shot from the back, one of her team sent.

That's just what he wants, she sent back.

212

She had to be willing to let that poor maître d' die. How often had she told her people that occasionally sacrifices needed to be made? It was so easy to say, so hard to do.

"I can kill him with a touch," the assassin said.

"I know you can," she said. "But you're not going to."

"Why not?" he asked.

"Because you still have something to say to me." She was just guessing, but that assassin in Armstrong waited to talk to the cops before he died.

This assassin looked surprised at her words. "How did you know that?"

She shrugged, trying to seem nonchalant. "Because you people are running someone else's game, and in the instructions, you're supposed to tell me something before you force me to kill you."

His mouth opened slightly. He was surprised. He hadn't expected her to say anything like that.

He looked like he wanted to ask questions, but he didn't. Instead, he flung the maître away from him, raised that laser rifle, aimed it at her, and paused, as if he was waiting for someone to shoot him.

"We're just the beginning," he said.

"I know that," she said. "Your friends said the same thing. The beginning of what?"

He looked panicked for the first time. Then he moved the laser rifle slightly and shot. The bolt was brighter than any she had ever seen. It shattered the window next to her—the supposedly unbreakable window—and before she realized what was happening, he sprinted toward her.

She ran for him, but she hesitated before touching him. She didn't want to die like Armstrong's mayor and she couldn't get that image out of her head.

Other members of her team were swarming around her, but somehow the assassin eluded all of them. He launched himself through that window and into the emptiness at the top of the dome.

His scream faded as he fell, then cut off abruptly.

"Son of a bitch," Strom said beside her. "Son of a bitch."

47

Flint had Selah Rutledge summon Talia to the headmistress's office. Both Flint and Selah had talked about it, and they determined it was best not to interrupt class nor have Flint show up at the classroom door. Too many strange things had already happened today, and since the school had—so far—elected not to go into lockdown and not to send the children home early, Selah thought it was best to keep things as normal as possible.

As normal as they could be with guards everywhere and other children—children of "important" people—already leaving.

Flint waited outside the headmistress's office. He shifted from foot to foot, ready to leave. DeRicci had made him nervous with both her secrecy and her willingness to use him at the Security Office. He would have understood if she wanted him to do some work in his own office. But she didn't. She wanted him to work in a government building, doing something her staff couldn't do.

He heard a rustling down the hall, and then Talia appeared. Her height always struck him first. She had grown tremendously since he had brought her to the Moon two and a half years ago. Her curly blond hair tumbled around her face, and her copper skin accented her blue eyes, making them seem exceptionally bright.

His daughter was beautiful, and he knew it, and it worried him more than he could say. He didn't want to tell her how worried he was—she thought he worried too much already (and maybe he did)—but a girl that beautiful got into trouble easily because men found her so attractive.

Of course, Talia was one of the most brilliant students the Armstrong Branch of the Aristotle Academy had ever had, and she had street smarts as well. Flint knew that of all the beautiful girls in this school, Talia was probably the one to worry about the least.

But she was here, and she was his, and he did worry. More than he could say.

When she saw him, she rolled her eyes.

"No one's coming after me, Dad," she said. Leave it to Talia to have already sussed out the situation.

"I didn't say they were." He sounded defensive and knew it. So he decided to move past that. "I just got notice from Noelle DeRicci. She wants me in the Security Office to help with something, and she told me to bring you as well."

She hadn't exactly requested Talia, but Talia didn't need to know that.

Talia's expression changed from a gently tolerant one to one that was suddenly both serious and frightened. He had worried about that. His daughter, for all her brilliance and street smarts, was very fragile emotionally.

"It's really bad then?" Talia asked.

"I don't know," Flint said. "But it is unusual."

She didn't ask why he was at the school and he didn't tell her. He didn't really want her to know how long he had been there. He put his hand on her back and led her to the parking area.

He always parked near one of the exits— a long-standing habit that had saved his life more than once. He was more or less retired right now, but that didn't stop him from maintaining his old habits.

"This is serious, isn't it, Dad?" Talia asked as they left the building, passing three guards who stared at them with an intensity that Flint didn't like.

"This is very serious, Talia," Flint said. "I have a hunch we're about to find out just how bad it is."

48

UNLIKE THE REST OF HER TEAM, KEPTRA DIDN'T LOOK OUT THAT BROKEN window to see what had happened to the assassin. She knew what had happened. He had leapt through the window in the circular restaurant, fell, and hit the clear ledge the engineers eventually built to keep suicides from falling all the way down to the city below and killing someone on the ground.

The ledge was far enough down that the suicides would get hurt, not too far that they would die (unless something went terribly wrong). The idea was to give them some second thoughts the next time they decided to try to kill themselves in a public place.

She scurried to an interior door that led to a service staircase. She probably could have taken an elevator, but she didn't think it would save any time. She still had to go into the service hallways.

Her team was discussing the assassin on the links:

...didn't expect him to land so close...

...he didn't either...

...didn't take anyone with him...

She was grateful for all of those things as well, but she didn't participate in the discussion. Instead, she reached the landing that led to the area around the ledge.

Unlike the public parts of the Top of the Dome, the service parts didn't have great views. There were no clear windows, only solid gray walls. Not because the builders felt that employees didn't deserve a spectacular view; she had no idea how the builders felt about employees. No. It was because someone outside—even, apparently, someone who had just tried to commit suicide—didn't need to look inside and see the unsightly service sections of the building.

She used her police identification to unlock the door. Then she stepped onto the ledge.

It wasn't really a ledge. It was more like a balcony. It was open several meters up, but it ended on this floor. A clear wall blocked the exterior side, so that the possible suicide couldn't drag himself to the edge and then fall again. He was trapped here until someone got him out.

She had already sent for back-up—both from her team, and medical back-up as well. If this guy hadn't landed wrong and died, then he would be hurt. But it would be just their luck that he had landed wrong—hit his head, cut an artery, something that would kill him, even though he wasn't supposed to die.

Or he would figure out what happened and use that weird poison on himself.

She pushed open the door, her heart pounding. That weird poison really did scare her more than anything. She didn't want it near her.

She peered out, saw legs twisted in the wrong direction, suggesting breaks in the bones or at worst, a shattered spine. She eased out, making certain she stayed out of reach.

His left arm was outstretched, his right tucked against his face as if he had just fallen to sleep. His eyes were closed, his skin even whiter than it had been before.

She didn't want to touch him to see if he was still alive. She didn't want to get close to him at all.

But she was supposed to be the tough one, the strong one, the one who ran the team. So she grabbed a protect suit from her gear, pinched the small button, and the suit enveloped her. Then she put on extra gloves for good measure.

She willed herself to be calm as she stepped forward.

His chest wasn't rising or falling, that she could see anyway. She had no idea if he was alive.

She crouched next to him, and put a finger on his neck. The chip inside her fingertip recorded his heart rate at 51 beats per minute, his blood pressure as low and falling, and his respiration too slow. He was probably bleeding internally. She didn't have a sophisticated enough chip to tell her that.

But he was alive.

He was alive.

He was the first of the assassins to be caught alive.

She forgot all about her hesitation at touching him. She cuffed him with hands away from his body so that he couldn't poison himself if he came to, then she sent for back-up all over again, reminding them that they had to do everything to keep this one breathing.

She took his weapon, which had fallen a meter away, and then she leaned against the gray interior wall.

Her first hostage situation and everything had gone right. The hostages were free and uninjured (except maybe for that maître d'), the potential assassin didn't assassinate anyone (not even himself), and none of her people were injured.

Those thoughts didn't calm her any, but they did make her smile for the first time since she'd arrived at the Top of the Dome.

She had done it. She had given not just Tycho Crater a break in their case, but United Domes Security a break in all the cases.

She hoped the break turned into some very real lead. Because she knew from all the chatter that they needed a lead right now.

Particularly with the assassin's warning.

Since this was just the beginning, after all.

49

THE INTERIOR OF TERMINAL 81 LOOKED VERY DIFFERENT FROM THE INTERIOR of all the other terminals. There were no floating signs to point to important sections of the terminal, no announcements drifting along the bottom of one eye offering an audio tour, no colored lights leading to a particular ship.

Instead, warnings assaulted Nyquist from the moment he stepped inside: *Make sure your hazmat suit is sealed; Do not approach any ship without authorization; Touch nothing with your bare hands.*

And on and on and on.

If he hadn't been here before, he would have been frightened. Most cops let the Traffic Quarantine Squad handle problems inside Terminal 81. Most cops could not bear to go in here more than once.

Nyquist had been here seven times. Seven times in which he had to don the damn suit and sneak around these ships that were carrying potentially lethal cargo, ships that could kill—like Soseki's assassin—with a single touch.

Still, he didn't like the visible webs around the ships, the rust and age that many of the ships displayed. That looked dangerous all by itself.

But he said nothing. He let the squad lead, following them as they hurried along the suggested path, their weapons already drawn.

If he had been completely in charge—and he wasn't—he would have argued against the drawn weapons. But he couldn't argue. He had the authority to deal with Palmette and nothing more. If the squad leader believed that Palmette was a threat to the squad, to the terminal or to the port itself, he would kill her.

Nyquist didn't know what she was—threat or threatened—and he wanted to find out. This day had already seen more than enough death.

Besides, he didn't want this woman to die. He had saved her life; he didn't want to think he had done that for nothing.

He kept behind the team, struggling to stay on the path in the dimness. They were used to operating in full hazmat gear. He wore the equipment rarely, and almost never did he have to move as quickly as they were moving now.

Still, part of him wanted to run ahead of them, to find Palmette on his own.

She had to have known what was coming, what rules she was breaking. She was the Special Administrator for the Quarantined Ships. She had to know what happened to people who tried to break into them without authorization.

Any unauthorized person inside Terminal 81, disabling webs of protection without permission, was automatically considered a danger to the city and could be shot on sight.

Palmette had permission to come inside because of her job. But she had to follow procedure: she had to wear her own hazmat suit, and she had to have back-up ready in case something went wrong.

Maybe she thought she had the ability to come and go as she pleased. Or maybe someone else thought she had that ability, someone who was forcing her to disable the webs of protection right now.

But she did not have permission to undo webs of protection. Only the squad could do that. That order provided another layer of protection for the ships and the terminal and the city.

If Palmette—or anyone else—needed to examine the interior of a ship, she was supposed to do so remotely while one of the experts went inside and investigated.

The squad turned down a narrow path between ships so large that Nyquist couldn't see around them. The webs of protection brushed against his suit, warning him that he was too close. The paths got narrower and narrower the older the ships were. Old ships were slated for destruction, but the port had gotten behind. Mostly because no one knew exactly how to dispose of these ships. Launching them derelict into space was no longer an option, and destroying hazardous material—even outside the protection of the dome—had been banned by most of the Moon's domes, except outside of a 100-kilometer radius. The problem was that so many companies had applied for extensions of that radius, that 99% of the Moon's surface was in a protected zone.

Finally, the squad turned a corner, into a pile of haphazardly parked old ships. The system from 100 years ago was much less organized than the system now. And the ships were bulkier, less sleek, more dangerous, their webs of protection larger.

The tiny map in the corner of Nyquist's right eye lit up. They had arrived at the ship.

He sent a non-verbal order, reminding the squad that he got to go first. Then he pushed his way to the front of the group.

Palmette stood in front of an active web. It flashed red, sending warning notices to anyone within range. Three other webs glowed green in front of her, and one—the exterior web—actually collapsed. It didn't light up at all and the actual physical part of the web—a microfiber that would brush against a suit warning the wearer of the danger—was black and shriveled.

She had cut the first web, and somehow not managed to sound the alarms. Probably because of her high clearance level.

She wasn't wearing a suit. She stood, hands out, looking like a child caught breaking into a cookie jar. Still tiny, she still wore her brown hair in a cap around her face. But her face was very different.

No longer young, no longer eager. Even though she had had enhancements to smooth her skin, her eyes looked old. She had seen too much. She would never again be the woman he had met on that long ago morning.

"Ursula," he said softly. "It's Bartholomew Nyquist."

She held up a small penlike device in her right hand. At first he thought it was something she used to open the webs. Then he realized it was some kind of lighter.

The head of the squad sent Nyquist a private message: *If she goes into that ship and lights the cargo, the explosion will blow open the port and send toxic gas into the city.*

Nyquist knew that. He had known what was in the ship since he discovered she was trying to get inside. It wasn't zoodeh. It was a different substance, much more volatile. When Murray told Nyquist what was in that ship, neither of them had known why she was trying to get in. Nyquist had hoped she was looking for some kind of clue.

Standing orders, the leader sent. *We shoot to kill if she goes any farther.*

You'll wait for my order, Nyquist sent. And before the leader could argue, he added, *And I'll take the heat if things go wrong.*

Not that he would live through it.

He couldn't think about that.

He couldn't think about anything right now—except Palmette.

50

ONCE THEY REACHED THE SECURITY OFFICE, FLINT MADE TALIA TAKE the stairs. Flint always took the stairs, particularly in crisis situations. Elevators, floating stairways, moving ramps, were all too dangerous and could be diverted.

Even a building this secure, with guards on every level, might be at risk in the middle of a crisis.

Which he assumed this was, given the nature of DeRicci's request.

The building was huge, but Flint had been here before. The main floor had no windows at all, so that no one could see in and, unfortunately, no one could see out.

DeRicci called the entry the "basement" even though it was above ground. She also called it the crypt, the cavern, and that mess.

Flint understood the design, although he would have been even more cautious. He would have scattered the security personnel for the United Domes of the Moon all over Armstrong, maybe from city to city, just so that no one could take out one building, and kill most of the United Domes' security.

He had mentioned this to DeRicci, who had given him an exasperated look. She knew about the problem.

"The money was spent before I got hired, Miles," she said and left it at that.

Flint had no trouble crossing the lobby and heading to the side stairway, but Talia did. Her identification, showing that she had a day of creation instead of a birthday caused consternation throughout the system. It didn't matter that he had adopted her or that she had acquired, through him, full human status.

The fact remained that she was a clone, and clones had fewer rights on the Moon than almost anyone.

Flint had just gotten exasperated enough to contact DeRicci when the security system let Talia pass. He took her hand, led her to the back staircase, and for the first time in months, she didn't complain about the climb.

Instead, she looked nervous and frightened. She clutched his hand tightly as they climbed. He knew if he pointed it out, she would let go and deny that she was upset. So he didn't point anything out, just set the pace as they went to the top floors which held DeRicci's offices.

The offices were plush, too fancy for a security chief, in his opinion. DeRicci had actually toned down the look of wealth, getting comfortable furniture and getting rid of the high-end art. She had only two indulgences—her budget for expensive (often Earth-made) food and the live plants in her personal office, plants that someone else maintained.

The staircase opened into another small reception area. This time, no one stopped Talia. Flint went inside, then found the short staircase to the upper level where DeRicci's offices actually were.

That staircase spiraled into the outer reception area, presided over by DeRicci's assistant, Rudra Popova. Popova was both the most efficient and the most humorless woman Flint had ever met. He didn't like her—and the feeling was mutual—but she was efficient. And DeRicci had said from the first that efficient was better than friendly any day.

He led Talia into Popova's office and stopped in surprise. A young man sat at Popova's desk. His cheeks were red, his lips chapped because he was biting them even now. His hands flew across the desk screen and he was clearly monitoring something on his links.

He didn't even notice Flint or Talia.

Neither did Popova. She was looking at her fingernails as if they were the most fascinating things she had ever seen. Her skin was blotchy, her eyes red and swollen.

If Flint didn't know better, he would have thought she had been crying.

"Rudra?" he said.

"Oh, Miles," she said, and she sounded relieved. "Chief DeRicci will be glad you're here."

No snide comment, no jealous look. Just a quick and honest statement.

The young man at the desk raised his head, surprised.

"Who's this again?" he asked.

"I'm Miles Flint," Flint said stepping forward, his hand out. This was actually a test. Security wasn't supposed to shake hands upon first meet. Too many people downloaded information from someone else's palm chips.

"Ephraim Hänsel," the young man said, passing the test. "I'm helping out."

Then he glanced at Popova as if he had said too much.

"I take it this is Talia?" he said when Popova didn't rebuke him.

"Yes," Talia said somewhat curtly. She did not like being ignored.

"I'll let the chief know you're here," Hänsel said, putting a hand to his ear. Someone needed to break him of that habit too.

Popova was watching Flint. "You know about Arek?" she asked, and something in her tone caught him. Her tone and her use of the mayor's first name.

"Yes," he said gently. He didn't say *terrible tragedy* or any of those things people said to fill the silence. He wasn't sure exactly what he could say without being a hypocrite. He wasn't sad Soseki was dead, but he was upset that Soseki was murdered.

"You knew him?" Talia asked, unwittingly helping Flint along. She had caught the strangeness in Popova's tone as well.

Popova nodded, her gaze still on Flint's face. "Maybe too well."

And then he understood. She had been in love with Soseki. Rudra Popova, the ice maiden, actually loved someone—Armstrong's uptight mayor for life.

Flint wouldn't have put them together, but then he wouldn't have put either of them with anyone. And he hadn't liked either of them much. So maybe they suited each other.

"I'm sorry," Flint said, and this time he meant it. Not that Soseki was dead or even that Soseki was murdered, but sorry that Popova was grieving.

Maybe that was why DeRicci wanted Flint up here.

As if she heard that thought, DeRicci flung open the door to her office.

"Miles," she said. "Thank God. Please come in."

And so he did.

51

THE SHIP WAS LARGE, OLD, AND NEARLY HIDDEN BEHIND THE WEBS OF protection. Terminal 81 was dim, although the squad leader had ordered the lights raised when the group had finally found Palmette.

Palmette faced Nyquist, a slim lighter in her hand. She didn't look relieved to see him. If she was in trouble, shouldn't she have looked relieved?

Nyquist stepped close enough so that he didn't have to raise his voice. The squad could hear him through the links, of course, but he wanted this conversation to seem private, even though it wasn't.

He was going on instinct here, and it made him nervous. Especially considering the stakes.

Whatever was in that ship did not mix well with fire. The ship would explode first. The squad could shut down the atmosphere in Terminal 81 (killing Palmette, who wasn't wearing a suit), but they couldn't control the atmosphere inside that ship, not unless they got inside. And they wouldn't, with Palmette in the way.

It was all a matter of timing.

Exquisite and somewhat alarming timing.

Nyquist forced himself to be calm. He had to think only of Palmette, not of the consequences if he failed.

"Ursula," he said quietly, "what's going on?"

Her lips thinned. She gripped that lighter so tightly her knuckles turned white.

"You think you're so important," she snapped. "You work for the city and you believe in law and justice. Have you ever looked at what you do in the name of law and justice?"

Her words surprised him. He wasn't sure what he expected from her. Maybe a calm and somewhat quiet request for help. Maybe a coded request, something that sounded like a non sequitor.

Not this angry rant. In all of his interaction with her—which, granted, wasn't much—she hadn't been the angry-rant type.

"Have you?" she said, just a bit louder. "Have you looked at what you do in the name of law and justice?"

She wanted him to engage her. Was this the code? He'd do his best to play along—without making the squad too nervous. He hoped they knew that as long as she was talking, she wasn't going to harm the ship or the port or the city.

But justice and his role in it wasn't a topic he usually discussed. He didn't like a lot of the laws he enforced. Which was why he was primarily a detective, not a street cop. He often went in after the crimes had been committed, so that he could find the perpetrator. He didn't have to make quick judgments at the scene; he could decide how to handle a case at his leisure.

"I look at what I do all the time," he said.

"And you can accept what you do?" Her hand was shaking.

He didn't know where the trigger was on that lighter. He also didn't know what would happen if she set one of the webs of protection on fire.

"I can't always accept it," he said truthfully. "But I have good days. I saved you on a good day."

Her back straightened. She clearly didn't want him to talk about the bombing or to talk about what had happened between them.

"That bombing was not a good day," she said.

"You're right," he said. "Terrible things happened, all because someone wanted to make a statement. A statement that got lost in the aftermath. No one has ever really understood what happened."

"Our statement won't get lost."

His heart sank. She really was involved. She wasn't speaking in code. She believed this stuff. Somehow she had gone from eager rookie detective to a bitter violent woman about to set off her own explosion inside the city.

He wasn't a psychiatrist. He didn't know how to handle her. He did know if he pushed her wrong, she would try to destroy everything—and the squad would have no choice but to kill her.

Nyquist swallowed hard. "If you go inside this ship, you'll set off a bomb just like that person did four years ago. You'll kill and maim and ruin countless innocent people."

"I don't care," she said just a little too fast. So she had thought of it, and she was trying not to.

"Why don't you care?" he asked. "You know what it feels like to be the innocent victim of someone else's political statement."

Her lower lip trembled. She raised that lighter and shook it at him.

"We're worthless," she said. "We're worthless to the city, we're worthless to the corporations, we're worthless to the Earth Alliance."

"You're not worthless to me," he said softly.

She gave him a bitter smile. "You're just saying that so I won't go into the ship."

He shook his head ever so slightly. "I didn't have to go back for you that day. I could have left you to bleed out. I may have treated you badly that morning, but I valued you. I still do."

She stared at him, and he thought he had her.

Then she whirled and grabbed the next web. Around Nyquist, laser rifles rose.

That's what she wants, he sent to the squad. *Don't do it.*

He didn't ask her if the group she was working for valued her. He knew how such organizations worked, even if he didn't know which one she was affiliated with. They took a disaffected person and made her believe she had value. And she did, just not the value she thought she had. Her real value was in her access, of course. Her real value was in her ability to create the most mayhem for the least amount of effort on the organization's part.

Of course, the organization wouldn't say that. Instead, they would soothe a bruised ego, making her feel important for the first time in a long time.

Some organization had done that to Palmette. He had no idea who. But he did know—through all of his experience as a detective—that they had already hooked her emotionally.

He couldn't undo that with a few simple sentences.

She opened the fourth web. There was only one more before she got access to the ship.

"I'm going to let the squad go," he said to her. "I'm going to stay here with you. I'm not going to live through another bombing."

"They won't leave," she said. "They have orders."

She was counting on them to kill her.

"They'll leave," he said, hoping he was right.

Stand down, he sent. *If I tell you to leave, please go.*

She can't be allowed to get on that ship, the leader said.

She won't be, Nyquist sent. Or, he privately corrected, she wouldn't be allowed to ignite the cargo. He would stop her no matter what. He hoped she didn't realize that.

The laser rifles went down.

She looked at Nyquist in surprise. "What are you doing?" she asked.

"Keeping my promise to you," he said.

"You promised they'd leave."

Nyquist swallowed hard. He looked at the leader. The leader didn't move for a long moment. Then the squad turned around and walked away. Nyquist had no idea how far away they went, but he did know that he couldn't see them any longer—and if he couldn't, she couldn't either.

"Don't go through with this," he said to Palmette.

"Why not?" she asked. "I've already come this far."

"You have," he said. "Don't you think that's far enough?"

He wasn't good at this. His heart was pounding. Hard. He was working off instinct, and his instinct with people wasn't the best.

She didn't move.

"Logically," she said after a moment, "it's better if I die."

He didn't ask why. On some level, she was right. She had helped in at least one murder, and would be an accessory in at least two others.

"Are you saying I shouldn't have saved you?" he asked, deliberately misunderstanding her.

"No," she said quickly. "It's just different now."

"Why?" he asked.

She shook her head. "They took me off detective detail. They put me here."

"At one of the most important jobs in the city," he said. "That's what you've been doing, right? Finding the holes in the quarantines? Seeing how terrorists could exploit them? You've made your point, Ursula. Now it's time to tell the city what you've found."

She turned around slowly. He had given her a way out. Hell, he had given her a legal argument. He would wager there was little to disprove it.

Except, of course, Soseki's death.

But he was gambling that she wasn't thinking clearly.

"You believe that?" she asked.

"I know how eager you were to solve crimes," he said. "Sometimes that leads to some risks. I know that. I've taken a few bad risks myself."

She bit her lower lip.

Then she stepped forward.

One step. Two. Past the green webs, to the cable.

He was shaking, but he still managed to meet her. He took the lighter from her.

"I have to cuff you," he said. "It'll keep the squad from attacking you."

She nodded. She knew that was a lie, and she didn't care. She was smart; she probably knew everything he said was a lie, and she didn't care about that either. She just hadn't seen a way out, and he had given her a tiny one.

Not that her life would be any better. It would be worse.

Her bitterness from the bombing, from the loss of her dreams, had brought her here, blaming the city instead of blaming the terrorist who bombed the dome.

He gently took her hands and cuffed them behind her back. Then he sent a message to the squad as well as Murray Atherton.

Got her.

52

SHE KNEW SHE SHOULDN'T HAVE BEEN SO RELIEVED, BUT SHE WAS. Noelle DeRicci led Miles Flint into her office. His daughter, Talia, followed him uncertainly, and DeRicci realized she hadn't given Talia explicit permission to join them.

DeRicci gave the girl a tentative smile, and Talia smiled back, then lowered her head, as if that big a display of emotion was too much for her.

They hadn't had a great deal of interaction—Talia and DeRicci. Usually when DeRicci needed to talk to Flint, Talia excused herself and left the room, or was at school. DeRicci did know that Talia was as gifted at computers as her father—maybe more gifted—and she was scary brilliant.

She was also beautiful in an exotic way, that blond hair on top of copper skin. Most women had to use enhancements to achieve the same effect, and they often forgot to change the color of their eyebrows. But Talia's looks were completely natural. Smart, beautiful, and athletic—or so Flint said. Talia had never applied herself to sports before, but she was now. She had been too gangly before to be very coordinated.

That wasn't a problem now.

Talia moved with the smooth grace of a dancer.

In short, she was growing into the kind of woman who made DeRicci both nervous and self-conscious.

Both Flint and Talia stood next to the big screen in the center of the room. DeRicci had frozen all of the images when she realized that Flint had arrived. She didn't want him to watch the crisis unfold. She wanted to tell him about it herself.

"You saw the mess out there in my office, right?" DeRicci asked Flint.

He nodded. "Popova and Soseki were involved?"

Flint sounded both skeptical and appalled—probably because he had never really liked Popova.

"It was news to me too," DeRicci said, "but she's devastated, and she begged me to let her stay. She can't work, and the assistant we brought in—well, it'll take him weeks to get up to snuff. I need someone who can coordinate information for me, and help with a Moonwide investigation."

"What's Nyquist doing?" Flint asked. He clearly knew how things worked. He knew that DeRicci wouldn't have brought him in if she had other alternatives.

"He's following a very important lead, or so he says. He couldn't be here as quickly as I wanted."

Of course, Flint hadn't arrived in record time either. It had taken nearly thirty minutes for him to make it to the office. Had DeRicci known it was going to take that long, she would have stressed the urgency even more.

"Do you want me to wait out front?" Talia asked, her voice so soft DeRicci almost didn't hear her.

"No," DeRicci said. "I need people with excellent computer skills. However, you have to swear to me that you won't say anything about this investigation. It's confidential, and if you tell one unauthorized person, you'll put the entire Moon in danger."

Talia's back straightened just enough to make DeRicci realize how tall she was—taller than DeRicci, certainly.

"It seems to me," Talia said stiffly, "that the Moon is already in danger."

"Talia," Flint said.

"I mean it," she said. "There's all kinds of rumors everywhere. Kids were being pulled out of classes because they're killing all the important people. I heard people died as far away as Moscow Dome."

DeRicci looked at her in surprise. Not so much at the mishmash of information, but that she had put together the nature of the threat from all the leaks.

DeRicci was going to have to make some kind of statement, and do it soon.

"Talia." Flint put his hand on his daughter's arm. "This isn't the place—"

"Actually, it is the place," DeRicci said. "Talia's right. We're in trouble here, and it might extend throughout the entire Earth Alliance. Something is going very wrong. I don't have the resources to investigate it properly. Governments not used to handling this kind of thing are scrambling to respond. My people are spread throughout Armstrong. The police department is working on two separate cases—"

"Two cases?" Flint asked.

She had forgotten. No one knew about the governor-general.

"I don't think Celia's going to make it," she said softly.

He cursed.

Talia looked at him in concern. "That's the governor-general, right? Someone tried to kill the governor-general?"

DeRicci looked directly at the girl. She needed Talia to remain calm, but she probably couldn't in the face of this information. Better to give it at once.

"You never answered me. Can you keep everything we discuss in this room confidential?"

"Of course I can," Talia snapped.

"Talia," Flint said, but it sounded like a reflex. Then he looked at DeRicci, as if he knew he had to step into this. Poor man, he was out of his depth. With no wife to steer him through the difficulties of raising a teenage girl.

DeRicci would have smiled in a different circumstance. She remembered being the same kind of girl Talia was—smart, defensive, shy, and insecure. It made for a volatile combination, particularly with all the hormones added in.

"Talia's great at keeping secrets. She knows how important some of them can be." Flint gave his daughter a sideways look, almost a cautionary look, and for the first time, DeRicci wondered what kind of secrets Flint was keeping.

Then she shook off the thought. She didn't have time to mistrust him. Besides, he had proven himself trustworthy repeatedly over the years. She needed to believe in that.

"All right then," DeRicci said. "Let me tell you what's going on and exactly what kind of help I need."

53

NYQUIST'S HELMET SAT BESIDE HIM ON THE BENCH. HE HAD HIS HAZMAT suit half off, and soon he would have to go through decontamination. He was in the exit room—a place no one got to unless they had been inside Terminal 81.

The exit room was like a giant locker room, the kind that existed in schools and around athletic stadiums. There were lockers and showers and decontamination units. The only difference here was that people didn't come here regularly—or at least *most* people didn't come here regularly. The various members of the Quarantine Squads did and, for all he knew, they had regular changes of clothing here. But most people did not.

Fortunately for Nyquist, he didn't have to go through major decontamination. He just had to remove his suit and go through standard decontamination, the kind he would have to go through if he had traveled here on a sanctioned space liner from Earth.

Still, he was shaking. The squad leader had put a hand on Nyquist's shoulder, felt the shaking, and grinned. "Adrenaline," he'd said.

But Nyquist had felt adrenaline before. He'd felt it the day he saved Palmette's life. This didn't feel like an adrenaline reaction.

This was something else entirely, something he didn't want to examine too closely.

He ran a hand over his face. Palmette was in custody. The Traffic Squad Quarantine Unit had taken her through major decontamination. They would run her through a dozen procedures before Nyquist saw her again.

He almost felt sympathy for her. He'd gone through major decontamination before. It was invasive and difficult, as personal as sexual assault, just not as violent. He doubted Palmette was in a frame of mind to handle it well.

He removed the lower half of the hazmat suit, then tossed it in the decontamination bag. He adjusted his own clothing and stepped into the nearby decontamination unit.

The unit was more like an airlock—a transition between the exit room and the outside of the terminal—just like it was when someone got off a ship from Earth.

The decontamination unit here was gentle and noninvasive. It felt almost like taking one step out of a room, pausing in a corridor, as if he were about to make a grand entrance into the next room. The light was a little bright, the air a little warm, a slight breeze caressing his skin. But that was it.

Then he stepped out, stopped at a nearby washbasin, and scrubbed his face. Most people didn't even do that, but ever since his terrible major decontamination, he felt as if he could smell a chemical on his skin, something noxious and bitter.

He knew there was no chemical—they didn't use chemicals in the decontamination units—but he had also learned there was no arguing with his own mind.

How many oddities had he built up from traumatic moments in his career? How many tics?

Maybe he wasn't the person to interrogate Palmette after all. Maybe he should call in someone else.

But he knew better. He didn't make the offer to anyone because he knew as well or better than they did that he had an in with Palmette. No one else did.

Or no one else that he could find.

This room was also a locker type room, with clothing for someone who needed a change. He didn't. He did, however, look in a mirror to make sure his hair was smooth and his clothing wasn't out of place.

His eyes looked tired. His entire face seemed careworn—even to him. He looked older than he ever had before.

Maybe there was a way to skip this day every year. Maybe he could sleep through Anniversary Day, pretend it never happened, hope that nothing else would go wrong ever again in his entire life.

As if that would happen.

He sighed. Before he left this area and headed to the interrogation section of Space Traffic, he needed to do a few things, not the least of which was eat. He had a hunch he would be with Palmette most of the evening, if not into the night.

He wasn't sure if she would break—not after she had surrendered—and he wasn't sure if he would be able to get her to tell him anything. He wanted to have the longest possible session, and to do that, he had to be well fueled ahead of time.

And prepared.

But before he started the preparation, he needed to update DeRicci.

He checked around the room and made certain he was alone. Then he stepped into a privacy booth. Every police/government/security locker area had one. It allowed cameras in the locker area, but if someone felt they needed to change clothes in private, they could do so. If they needed to have a private discussion, they could do that as well.

But the monitors—people like Murray—would know that the person had taken a private moment. Sometimes that private moment was incriminating.

Sometimes it saved an entire investigation because it allowed the investigator to explore a few hunches.

The privacy room was more unsettling than decontamination. The privacy room had a musty sweat odor for one thing, making Nyquist wonder when it had last been cleaned.

Because of that odor, he didn't sit on the carpeted bench. Instead, he paced around the small area as his links pinged DeRicci on an encrypted channel.

She answered quickly. *Bartholomew. How did it go?*

No visuals, which meant she wasn't alone. And she didn't speak out loud for probably the same reason.

He saw no reason to talk either. *We found the source of the material that killed Soseki. Noelle, it was Ursula Palmette.*

She knew the name. She had given Palmette her special assistant job. Or at least had recommended her. And she had listened to Nyquist's story of that long ago rescue.

You're sure? she asked, displaying the same level of incredulousness that he had felt when he learned about Palmette.

Yes, unfortunately, he said. *She almost blew up Terminal 81.*

Then, as quickly as he could, he told DeRicci what had happened.

I'm going to interrogate her when she gets out of decontamination, he sent. *I have no idea if I'm going to get any information from her. But I figure I'm the one to try.*

Considering your history, you might be right, DeRicci sent. *Are you sure you're up for it?*

The question sent a wave of anger through him. How many times had she asked him that question since Bixian assassins' attack? Daily at first, weekly later, and now—

Then he realized she probably wasn't discussing his physical well-being, but his mental one. She had known that he had partnered with Palmette and saved her life during the bombing. But DeRicci didn't know how long the partnership had lasted—or, to be more accurate, how short the partnership had been.

She thought he had a relationship with Palmette, the kind DeRicci had with Flint, the kind that people who had once had each other's backs seemed to have for the rest of their lives.

If Flint had tried to blow up Terminal 81 and DeRicci had caught him, she would have been devastated. And she was one of the toughest women Nyquist knew.

Still, Nyquist did not like the question. It felt out of bounds to him, something that shouldn't be part of his relationship with DeRicci any longer.

I'll be fine, he sent.

If you need back-up, she started, but he interrupted before she could finish.

Then I'll send for it.

There was a momentary pause. She seemed to have caught his mood even though there were no visual or audio cues.

All right then, she sent. *Update me as soon as you have something.*

I will, he sent and ended the contact.

He stood still for a moment, letting that anger thread through him, willing it to go away. He had to stay calm when he talked to Palmette. He needed to remain in charge.

He also needed information.

It would take another hour, maybe more, for Palmette to go through all of the decontamination procedures. He needed to know as much of her history as he could before he went into that interrogation room. He couldn't rely on his own memory. He needed to research.

He let himself out of the privacy room, crossed the locker room and stepped into the corridor. There were half a dozen food carts between this section and Space Traffic Headquarters, not to mention the restaurants and cafes. He'd find a comfortable place to sit down, download as much information on Palmette as he could find, and study it before he met up with her again.

He wondered if he could get copies of her failed psychological exams. Those might help most of all.

They wouldn't come easily, however. Best to find a friendly judge and get a warrant, just in case.

Now he had to think like a detective as well as a man who had a limited amount of time to find some important answers. He had to both prepare a court case and get information on an existing threat.

He sent a message through his links to find out which judges were on duty.

He would do this part of the investigation by the book.

54

FOR WHAT SEEMED LIKE AN ETERNITY, FLINT SAT RIGIDLY, SILENTLY, uncertain what to say. He didn't want to look at his daughter, although he could feel her tension. He hoped DeRicci thought it was all about the severity of the news she had just imparted to them.

They were still standing in the middle of DeRicci's huge office, the images still frozen on the gigantic screen he hadn't even known existed. DeRicci had quickly told them a tangled tale of attempted assassinations all over the Moon, but all that Flint heard was "clones."

Clones. His mind jumped past the emergency, onto the aftermath. Clones were already hated in Armstrong—in most human communities, if truth be told. This would just make matters worse.

And he didn't dare look at Talia, who was biologically his daughter *and* a clone. A clone no one knew about except two lawyers, a very reliable cop in Valhalla Basin on Callisto, and Talia. Talia knew. That had been the devastating discovery for her in addition to the realization that her mother had either inadvertently or intentionally committed genocide. And Talia had learned all of that on the day Rhonda died.

Talia's clone mark was hidden, which wasn't legal. Most clone marks were on the back of the neck, obvious, even though the clones grew hair over them or covered them with turtlenecks and scarves. They were supposed to be obvious so that people knew they were dealing with someone who had been manufactured, someone who had been created from someone else, someone who—in theory—was the duplicate of the person whose DNA they shared.

Flint had soon realized that Talia wasn't anyone's duplicate. Yes, there were five other girls out there as brilliant and as beautiful as his daughter, adopted by people he did not know, but those girls had different families, different upbringings, and through the glory of cloning, they were 29 months older than she was, raised on different planets, in different cities, in completely different ways.

He once told Talia it was as if her genetic material—not her, but the DNA that composed her—got five other chances at life, five other ways to be.

Those girls had hidden clone marks as well.

But these men, these assassins, they wore their clone marks proudly. They were taking action as a unit, dressing the same, and on the same mission in different parts of Armstrong.

"Miles," DeRicci said, "I know this is a lot to absorb, but I need your help organizing information about these clones. We need to find out who made them."

Flint nodded, still speechless, worried, not quite certain what to say. For the first time, he regretted not telling DeRicci about Talia's origin. But at the same time, he was relieved no one knew. Because when this was over, clones would get persecuted throughout the Moon, maybe throughout the Earth Alliance, and he didn't want that to happen to his daughter.

Whom he was overly protective of.

Whom he loved with a ferocity he hadn't realized he was capable of.

"They were fast-grown?" Talia asked, and he could hear the hope in her voice. If the clones were fast-grown, they were nothing like her. They were created for one thing, and one thing only—to assassinate the leaders of the Moon.

"I don't think so," DeRicci said. "Fast-grow clones aren't capable of independent thought. Depending on how long they've been alive, they're little more than three-year-olds in adult bodies. These clones are too co-ordinated, too capable to be fast-grown. That's the other reason I need you. Because if they were fast-grown, I could put someone in the Arm-strong PD on the research and they could find these guys quickly. But these clones look like they're what—twenty-five, thirty? They could've been created anywhere, raised anywhere, trained anywhere. And to track that back, I need someone who knows how to go through more information than I want to contemplate in a very short period of time."

She was looking at Flint. She knew him well enough to understand that something was wrong, but she didn't know what. And he couldn't tell her, not now.

She really did need his help, and Talia's help as well. Talia had even more experience in this area than Flint did, because Talia had looked for her sisters, as she called the other clones of Flint's natural born child, Em-meline. Talia had spent months on that search before Flint had caught her and done his best to stop any damage she might have caused.

"Dad?" Talia asked. She sounded scared now. She hadn't made the mental leap that he had. She didn't know what was coming once this crisis was over.

He didn't want to tell her either.

He cleared his throat, and swallowed, feeling really uncomfortable. But he had to go forward. He couldn't change what had just happened. The best thing he could do was find these assassins and the person who had brought them to the Moon, and then he could worry about the future.

"Miles?" DeRicci said again.

"First of all," he said, sounding odd, even to himself, "let's not call them clones. They're assassins or wannabe assassins. There are a lot of law-abiding people on the Moon who happen to be clones. Let's not shove everyone into that category."

"Fine," DeRicci said impatiently. "I haven't let any word get out about them. What I want to know is can you help me?"

Talia was looking at Flint, her face pale. She had just realized what he was talking about.

"Yes," he said. "I can help. So can Talia. But we need a place to work. You're in a hurry, right?"

"I needed this done before these clon—men—attacked anyone," De-Ricci said. "Which would be yesterday. So yes, I'm in a hurry."

"Then you probably don't want us using your equipment. If someone backtraces our investigations—"

"Are you suggesting that you'll go to your office? Miles, we don't have time."

"We're not going to follow police procedure," he said. "What we do won't hold up in court."

"We'll reinvent that if we have to," DeRicci said, surprising him. She usually followed rules, even though she didn't like them. "I'm not worried about that. These clo—assassins are saying that this is just the beginning, but they won't say the beginning of what. We need to find out before they establish the ending, because I have a hunch we're not going to like it."

Expedience, not legalities. DeRicci was scared.

"All right then," Flint said. "Get us set up—and not inside your office. We'll keep this part as far from you as we can."

"I'll do it," she said. "I'm not sure I can trust Hänsel, and I really don't think Rudra is capable of doing this right."

Flint nodded. He didn't think so either. And this was much more important than DeRicci realized. At least for Talia and all the others like her.

Flint had to do this right.

55

When Nyquist arrived at Space Traffic's Interrogation Center, a computer informed his links that Palmette waited for him in interrogation room 65B. The number itself surprised him, even though he knew Space Traffic had more interrogation rooms than all of the other Armstrong authorities combined. Space Traffic handled everything from contraband materials to contraband humans. It was the first line of defense against alien governments trying to snatch someone without going through the proper procedures.

More red flags went through Space Traffic than anywhere else on the Moon. Not only did Space Traffic have a lot of interrogation rooms, it had a corresponding number of holding cells, ostensibly to hold anyone—or anything—until it/he/she/they got transported off the Moon again.

He hadn't been in the Interrogation Center before. He was surprised at how clean it looked, and then realized why. White walls, bright white lights, white floors, white tables, white ceilings. The Interrogation Center was designed to unnerve, and it did—even the interrogators.

Before he came in here, he had briefly spoken to Murray. Murray had explained how the Interrogation Center worked, and why it was better to keep Palmette here than it was to take her to Armstrong Police Headquarters.

Nyquist preferred familiar surroundings—he was already off-balance today—but he listened to Murray. Murray's argument, besides the basics (that she belonged here) was that she might need to be sent to the Earth Alliance for some stronger punishment than any Moon laws could dish out. So better to keep her here than subject her to transport.

What neither man was saying was that if the news got out that she was in any way responsible for the attacks on this day, there was no guarantee she would survive a transport. Not just because a mob might take her down, but also because the police themselves might not allow her to survive the journey.

It had taken nearly an hour longer for Palmette to go through decontamination than Nyquist expected. The Quarantine Squad had discovered a device attached to her body—although from what Nyquist understood, "attached" was not quite a strong enough word. The device had almost become part of her body, parts of it deeply embedded in the skin.

It took two high level medical avatars to remove the device. The squad leader wanted to send for an actual physician, but Murray had talked them out of it. He reminded them that Palmette had already tried to kill a bunch of people that day; there was no guarantee that the device wouldn't kill a living breathing person who touched it as well.

Nyquist was annoyed that he hadn't been consulted about this, although, in truth, he would have made the same decision. No one in Space Traffic had seen this kind of device before, nor could the avatars find it in any known database.

Palmette wouldn't tell anyone what it was. In fact, she refused to talk at all.

Nyquist hoped that wouldn't last. He needed to talk to her, and he had bet his part of the investigation on the idea that she would talk to him. Otherwise, he could be back at the Security Building helping DeRicci.

Before Nyquist went into the Interrogation Center, Murray told him where the nearest cafeteria was to Room 65B. Inside, Murray said, were sandwiches, sweets, and more coffee than the most dedicated investigator would ever need.

Since Nyquist had managed to choke down a lunch—not that he wanted food—he figured he wouldn't need anything else. Still, he was surprised that Space Traffic provided food to its interrogators. Armstrong PD certainly didn't.

The Interrogation Center had no direct openings into Space Traffic Headquarters or to any public part of the port. A prisoner had to go through heavily guarded, high security back corridors to get to an interrogation room.

So did the interrogator.

Nyquist used the walk through the white corridors to calm himself. He also had to review what he'd spent the last two hours learning about Palmette.

She had never married. No long-term relationships were on file with the City of Armstrong. No living children, which Nyquist found to be an interesting turn of phrase in her biographical material, one he sent an information bot to track down, wishing he had the time to sort through the public records himself.

He had to resort to police files, security department files, and the standard public records. The files from the various police psychiatrists hadn't arrived yet, although a judge had authorized their release. Nyquist would get pinged when they arrived. He planned to excuse himself from the interrogation to study them when (if) they got to his links.

She had been born in Armstrong, the only child of two engineers, now deceased. As far as Nyquist could tell, she had no living family. She lived alone, had no pets, and, according to her financials, seemed to spend no money in public places like bars or restaurants, suggesting that she didn't have much of a social life either.

This wasn't a change after the bombing. She hadn't done anything before it either, except tend to her career—a career that had gone off-track the moment she showed up, coffee in hand, outside Alvina's dilapidated house.

Nyquist didn't like what little he found. It gave him both too little and too much to go on. Enough so that he could speculate, but not enough for him to be confident of that speculation.

He had gone into a thousand interrogations with less, but somehow that felt wrong in this case. Perhaps because he knew Palmette. Or perhaps because he felt oddly guilty.

He'd been off his stride since she challenged him about law and justice.

Since he realized she wasn't the innocent victim he had hoped she would be.

Interrogation Room 65B looked the same as the other interrogation rooms near it. White with a one-way mirror, more ways to record and process information than any interrogation room in the Armstrong PD, and thick walls so that no creature could use its limbs to break through. Some of the other members of the Earth Alliance, aliens by Armstrong standards, had the strength to easily break standard human construction, but not here.

This place was designed for nonhumans. That it imprisoned humans easily was a bonus.

Nyquist stopped outside the one-way glass and looked in. Palmette sat at the table, her hands flat on the white surface. Restraints gave her some freedom of movement—she could move her arms to her side or back up the table—but not enough that she could attack her interrogator or try to break out of the room.

She was wearing some kind of beige jumpsuit, which was soothing to his eyes in all that white. He knew, from the materials that bombarded him as he went into the Interrogation Center, that he was supposed to change into pure white clothing as well, so that his clothing disturbed her eyes, but he wasn't going to do it.

He needed some psychological advantages, it was true, but not that kind. Besides, Palmette was too smart for the standard mind games. She'd been trained in them, just like the officers in Space Traffic.

Just like Nyquist himself.

She looked up as if she could see him behind the window. She couldn't, of course. Nor could she hear anything from outside the room.

She looked thinner than he remembered, thinner, even, than she had seemed inside Terminal 81. There he had seen her as a threat. Now he saw her as diminished woman, one who had nothing. Less than nothing really.

Logically, she had said, *it's better if I die.*

She had been right. It would have been much better for her if she had died.

Which begged the question—why hadn't she tried harder to get the squad to kill her? Why didn't she have her own failsafe, something she could have activated to facilitate her own death?

Maybe that device they had found on her would have done that, and maybe she hadn't activated it.

Did that mean she was willing to cooperate? Or was she regretting her decision in Terminal 81?

Somehow he needed to find out.

He put his palm on the door and waited for it to process his living flesh, his DNA, and his authorization. Before the door unlocked, it cautioned him that he might be dealing with a dangerous offender. Should there be any violence at all—from him or from her—other authorities would be summoned.

He had to indicate his formal—legal—understanding before the door allowed him inside.

He hadn't had to do that in police headquarters in more than thirty years. He had forgotten about all the strange legalities scattered through Armstrong as a matter of course.

The door opened inward. He stepped inside.

The air was much colder in here, uncomfortably so, and it smelled of cleaning fluid. He had the option of making the room hotter and having it smell of rotted flesh. The idea of that turned his stomach. He just left it as close to standard as possible.

"I didn't think they'd let you anywhere near me," she said before he could speak. "Don't you have a conflict of interest?"

He knew what she was trying to do; they had the same training. Whoever spoke first theoretically controlled the interview.

Provided, of course, that the other person didn't understand the mind game.

Nyquist had been playing that kind of mind game long before Palmette was out of school.

"What would that conflict of interest be?" he asked.

"I thought if you cared about...." She let her voice trail off.

He could actually read her expression for just a brief moment. She had believed him back in Terminal 81 when he said he cared about her. Now she was doubting that.

If she doubted it too long, she would not cooperate.

"For a standard investigation, you're right," he said as he sat across from her. "There's nothing standard about this."

She bit her lower lip, watching him.

"You're in a lot of trouble, Ursula," he said, deciding at that moment to go with her vulnerability. He was going to be the friend, the mentor, the person she could rely on.

"Is that why I'm still here?" she asked. "So that you can ship me off to some prison somewhere without sullying Armstrong any further?"

"No," he said, deciding to lie. "It's so that I can talk to you without Gumiela watching over this. She'd stop this interrogation from the start."

"That bitch," Palmette muttered.

He almost nodded, not because he agreed about Gumiela (although he'd had his run-ins with her) but because Palmette's reaction told him she was more comfortable with him than even she realized.

"Talk to me, Ursula," he said. "I'll see what I can do to help you."

Her gaze met his, then hardened. "And do what? Make sure I didn't get sent to some death hole? Make sure that people know how pitiful I am? You don't have any power, Nyquist. You can't help me."

She was right. But he didn't want her to think that.

"The whole day has been strange, Ursula," he said. "Soseki's murder, then you in Terminal 81. The fact that it's Anniversary Day. I looked at all of your behavior over the past few weeks. It's clear that you were trying to stay off the grid, and it's also clear that someone was helping you. At least, that's what the Quarantine Squad thinks. Me, I think someone was forcing you to act for them. What did they have on you? What were you afraid of?"

It was a gamble. He was giving her a defense. She could spin a web of lies here that would take days to unravel. But she was angry as well, and scared, and maybe even regretting her decision to let Nyquist bring her in.

"I'm capable," she snapped. "I'm smart, Nyquist."

"I never said you weren't," he said, sounding as defensive as possible. "But I don't have the computer skills to do the things you did. Not many people do. That's why I think you're in trouble. Because someone was forcing you into this stuff."

"I learned it," she said. "I learned a lot of things this last year."

He was about to answer her when his links pinged. Information had come in, but because of the nature of the Interrogation Room, he didn't know if it was the psychological evaluations or something else.

"I'm sorry," he said. "I need to step out for a minute."

"Yeah, of course you do," she said. "Is Gumiela out there? Does she want input? Is that why you have to leave?"

"No one's out there, Ursula," he said gently. "It's just you and me here. That's how I'm able to talk to you. Everyone else is dealing with the death of the mayor."

He didn't add anything about the governor-general or the other assassination attempts. He wanted her to tell him about them.

"It's a big deal today. Armstrong is in chaos."

He was laying it on thick, but he wanted her to think she had succeeded. She had disrupted the city as much as the bombing had four years before.

"Then why were you free to come after me?" she asked.

"I wasn't after you," he said truthfully. "I came to the port to talk to you about the quarantines. I found the zoodeh. I figured you could help me figure out how it got into the city. That's when I figured out you weren't at your desk. I had the guys in Space Traffic track you down. They think you're a threat, Ursula."

"They might not be wrong," she said, but he was heartened to hear the "might not." It meant she was thinking of cooperating.

He debated with himself for a moment, wondering if he should stay and press an advantage.

But he wasn't sure it was an advantage. He needed those psych reports. He wanted to make sure he didn't trigger something that would shut her down.

He needed her to talk.

"I'll be right back," he said, and let himself out of the room, closing the door behind him.

The hallway was blessedly warm. He hadn't realized how cold he had gotten inside that room. He stepped just a few meters away from the door, away from the window, not wanting to turn his back on her—even if she couldn't see him.

Then he examined the message that came through his links. It wasn't the psych report that he wanted. It was information he actually wished he hadn't had.

The device Palmette had attached to her body matched the one worn by Soseki's assassin in most ways. This one differed in strength. She wasn't going to use that lighter to set off the interior of the quarantined ship. The device would have magnified the laser blasts, making them even stronger, and sending them ricocheting outward, changing their frequency so that they would ignite the webs of protection, starting a chain reaction, not just with the webs of protection around that ship, but also around the nearby ship.

Murray's hunch had been right: she would have exploded Terminal 81, but the devastation was so much more than anyone could have imagined. It would have taken out the port and possibly an entire section of the city before it got contained. Thousands would have died.

Thousands.

Nyquist felt a surge of anger run through him. Sane people didn't do things like that. People with even a dollop of empathy wouldn't let something like that happen.

She could have told him about the device. Him or the others. But she wanted them to shoot her.

Or maybe she had chickened out at the last minute. Maybe Nyquist had done that with his little speech about saving her life for nothing.

The thing was, four years ago he hadn't saved her life for nothing. He had saved her life so that she could cause chaos throughout the Moon. So that she could help kill Soseki and maybe the governor-general and who knew how many others.

He put a hand to his face. If he hadn't saved her none of this would have happened.

Soseki would still be alive.

The day would have been just fine.

Or would it? Wouldn't whoever planned this have found someone else? Someone just as vulnerable as Palmette? Someone who wouldn't have backed down when confronted by the Quarantine Squad?

He let out a shaky breath.

He did have to switch the focus of this interrogation. He had to move away from *why* and move to *who*.

And she had given him a clue how to do it. She wanted him to believe she was capable of planning this, that she was smart enough, strong enough.

So he would pretend to believe she could do it. He would go along with that delusion until it fell apart. He would find out who the hell was behind all of this.

And then he would stop it once and for all.

56

Keptra rode with the would-be assassin in the ambulance. She wasn't going to let him out of her sight. The medical personnel had already searched him for more weapons—particularly the small kind, the kind he had planned to use to murder the mayor.

They had found that weapon and one other thing that might be something and it might not. But they were cautious. They took all of his clothing, then swabbed him down before putting him in the ambulance. They also checked all his body cavities, and they ran a scanner over him to see if he had swallowed bomb-making components.

The only thing they didn't do—they couldn't do, really—was see if he had ingested a fast-acting virus or if he had put some kind of compound on his skin, something that would interact with standard medical procedures.

Keptra wore a medical protection suit the ambulance attendees gave her. It felt bulky and awkward. She told them she didn't need it—she had already been close to him—but they insisted.

They were right.

The ambulance was boxy, roomier than she expected. It had flown to the Top of the Dome along with two others, preparing for casualties from the hostage situation.

She hadn't realized there were ambulances this size, the kind that could take half a dozen injured—and tend to them all—to the nearest hospital. The would-be assassin looked small in his bolted-down bed in the center of the ambulance.

The attendants had all focused on him, stabilizing his neck, splinting his broken arm, and immobilizing his shattered leg. He had a head injury, although they weren't certain how bad it was, and they had stopped the internal bleeding temporarily.

He would live, just like anyone else who dove out of a window in the Top of the Dome. He would live, but he would remember the pain.

The ambulance was returning to the hospital without its lights or sirens per her instructions. None of his injuries were life-threatening, so haste wasn't an issue. And she didn't want anyone to know he was alive.

Some of that was so that the hospital could work on him without problems from angry citizens. But part of it was so that his accomplices—if he had any—would think he was dead.

Keptra had made certain that she spoke to the press first; she told them that he had dived out of the restaurant at the Top of the Dome, and from the looks of him—she wasn't willing to touch him (that part was true)—it looked like he hadn't survived.

Only a few members of her team knew he had survived, and she had forbidden the ambulance attendants to talk to anyone outside of the hospital. They were usually good about that; the hospital could get sued for revealing a patient's condition. She watched them mentally file this into that same category of information.

But while they had cooperated on not releasing information, they weren't cooperating on one thing: She wanted them to wake this bastard up. She needed to talk to him before he got to the hospital and got threaded into the procedural maze.

The attendants claimed they didn't have the authority to wake him, so she made them contact someone in authority. She needed to talk to him, and she needed to talk to him now.

She was half tempted to wake the bastard herself. She was sitting on a bench near his bed, and she wanted nothing more than to slam her fist onto the visible bruising on his splinted arm.

She wondered what they could do to her for hitting him like that. Particularly since she wasn't strapped into her seat as the law required for anyone in a flying vehicle. She could claim that she lost her balance and put her hand out to protect herself.

Of course, there were probably cameras everywhere that would contradict her story.

She sighed as one of the attendants came over with a small syringe.

"You got your wish," he said. "Make it quick, though. They're taking him into the medical team the moment he arrives."

The attendant used his triple-gloved hands to swab an area on the bastard's good arm, then injected him with whatever the hell that was.

The bastard groaned and opened his eyes. Keptra was startled by their beautiful shade of blue.

It took them a moment to focus, then they settled on her.

"Oh, God," he said softly. He closed his eyes again, not in exhaustion, but in a realization that he hadn't died.

"The people that you work for," she said, guessing on the relationship, "don't know that you failed. They think you're dead. We can keep it that way, if you talk to us."

He opened his eyes again, a frown creasing his forehead. "They know that I failed," he said. "The mayor is still alive."

"So far as I can tell, you're not the only one who failed at that part of the mission. But you are the only one who survived your suicide attempt." She almost added, *which means that they will eventually kill you,* then stopped herself. If he was willing to die for the cause, then he would welcome someone trying to kill him.

He was watching her, beads of sweat on his forehead. The attendant sat slightly to the back, monitoring the bastard's vital signs.

"I don't know what you thought you would gain from the suicide attempt, whether it was a reward in heaven or whether it was some gift to protect a living person you love. I can't help you with your religious beliefs, but if what you receive is something tangible, a gift to the loved one or something, I can help with that. No one has to know you survived. Ever."

"What would happen?" he asked. "Would I Disappear?"

Many Disappearance Services did not work with clones, claiming they weren't human, and Disappearance Services only catered to humans.

"Yes," she lied. She really didn't care what happened to him after he talked.

He closed his eyes, but not before a tear formed in the corner of one and rolled down his cheek. It surprised her. She didn't want to see any emotions from him. She wanted him to remain a bastard.

"I can help you," she repeated.

He shook his head slightly, then opened his eyes. His lashes were wet.

"I don't know anything," he whispered, then glanced at the attendant.

"Give us some privacy," Keptra said.

The attendant frowned. He clearly couldn't leave the beds, but the ambulance was so big he moved far enough away that he wouldn't be able to hear anything.

"All right," Keptra said, leaning toward the bastard. "What do you know?"

He looked up at her. He was younger than she thought—in his early twenties, maybe even in his teens. "All I know are the rules."

"What are they?" she asked.

He glanced to one side, as if he expected someone to hurt him if he spoke. Then he took a deep, shaky breath. "Find the facilitator. Get to your location. Do the job. Wait until help arrives. Send the message. Die. Do not die alone."

She ran over those rules in her mind. He had tried to do everything except the last. He hadn't had the strength to take out others while he committed suicide. Which meant that there was something in him, some spark, that didn't completely believe in the job.

For all she knew, he had screwed up the assassination on purpose.

"Who follows these rules?" she asked, figuring she already knew the answer. He did. The clones did.

"Everyone," he said. "The rules are for everyone."

"Even the boss?" she asked, not knowing who the boss was.

He shrugged, then winced. His eyes lined with tears again, and she realized what she had taken for emotion might simply have been a reaction to pain.

"What about the facilitator?" she asked.

"Oh, yes," he said. "No one was to get caught. No one was to remain."

She felt chilled. That meant there was still someone else out there. "This facilitator," she said. "He looks like you?"

"No," he said. "She joined us later."

She. He knew her.

"What did your facilitator do?" Keptra asked, trying not to seem too eager. She didn't want to scare him off.

"She got me into the Top of the Dome, into the speech," he said.

"So she's important," Keptra said.

"I don't know," he said. "I don't know anything about Tycho Crater."

And he had tried to harm people inside of it. She felt that urge to slam her fist onto his broken arm again. But she didn't.

Instead, she asked softly, "Who is your facilitator?"

"I don't know her name," he said. "We don't do names."

"How did you meet her?" Keptra heard an edge in her voice.

He didn't answer that. He looked like he was starting to pass out.

She leaned closer. She would hit that damn arm if she had to. "How did you find her?"

"Oh," he said, as if he hadn't realized Keptra had been talking to him. "She has an office in the Top of the Dome. Eleventh floor, suite 8C."

"You're sure it's hers?" Keptra asked.

"Pictures of her," he said, his voice weaker. "And other people. Floating near the desk."

"Was she there this afternoon?" Keptra asked.

"She let me in," he said.

"Into the speech?" Keptra asked.

"The back of the restaurant," he said. "She let me into the maitre d's station."

After he had already escaped the authorities. Before Keptra arrived. She looked at him. He had passed out again.

"I'm not done," she said to the attendant. "Wake him up again."

"I can't," he said. "The law prevents me from doing anything that might harm him, and continually pumping him with drugs might do that."

259

In other words, she had gotten all she could. A facilitator. An address at the Top of the Dome.

And rules.

The last chilled her:

Do not die alone.

If the facilitator had to follow that rule as well, then the crisis wasn't over. It had just begun.

57

Nyquist paced for a few minutes, got himself some coffee, and forced himself to calm down. He was no good to this investigation if he made the interrogation of Palmette about him. As angry as he was at her, at himself, he couldn't let that taint the interrogation.

Not because of some future court case. He doubted there would be one. He had a hunch Palmette would plead, or be convinced to plead, and that would be the end of it all.

No. He had to protect the interrogation so he could get as much information from Palmette as possible.

Before he went back into that cold, stark room, he checked his links again to see if the psych reports had downloaded while he was dealing with the weapon Palmette had worn around her torso.

The reports still hadn't arrived. He sent a ping to the psych office, telling them this was of the utmost importance, and then he went back into the interrogation room.

Palmette watched him walk to his chair, her face drawn. She looked tired and defeated. She had hours to rethink her decision in Terminal 81, and it looked like she regretted it.

He wanted to scream at her about the weapon on her torso, about giving zoodeh to the assassins. But he couldn't. He needed to move the questioning away from that area until he calmed down.

"So, does Gumiela want someone else to conduct this investigation?" Palmette asked, her voice threaded with bitterness.

He shook his head. "I haven't spoken to her. That wasn't what had come in through my links."

He nearly mentioned the weapon. He was angrier than he thought. Maybe he should recuse himself from this. Maybe he should just walk away.

"So what did?" she asked. At the moment, she had control of this investigation. She had control of him—his emotions, and his thought processes.

But he was going to take it back. "I'm waiting on your psych evals from Armstrong P.D.," he said. "I was hoping to gain some insight. But they'll be delayed."

Her cheeks had grown red as he spoke. She was angry now. He almost smiled.

He could use that.

"Besides," he said, "I have a hunch they're not accurate. Remember, I had to go through the same thing when I came back from an attack that almost killed me. Those psychiatrists don't know a damn thing about the way the mind works."

"They cleared you." She nearly spat the words.

He smiled tiredly. He felt like two different people: the angry man inside and the weary, friendly investigator outside.

He said, "I have influential friends."

"I wanted you to use them for me," she said, so fast he knew she had anticipated his response.

He nodded. "I tried. That's how you got your job."

"I wanted to be on the force," she said.

"I know," he said. "But you'd have to sleep with the boss to do that."

He winced at the words. DeRicci would hate hearing that. Others would love to use that sentence against him. But it worked on Palmette.

Her eyes narrowed. "I knew it," she said. "They don't care about the work anyone does. It's just who you know and what you're willing to do to move forward."

"Everything in the Earth Alliance is like that," he said.

"I know," she said. "It's all rigged. That's why the Earth Alliance needs to be destroyed."

Such a dramatic statement, and yet she said it as if everyone believed it, as if it were an everyday thing to claim the governing body of half the known universe should disappear.

If he was conducting a standard investigation, he would jump on that phrase. But nothing about this was standard.

"I wish," he said with that tired tone. "But you can't go up against something that big, not by yourself. I mean, even the stuff you did on the Moon today isn't enough. It got people's attention, here, but you think the Disty care about it? The Rev? You'd have to hit them too, and that's almost impossible."

Her eyes lit up. She was leaning toward him. "What happened on the Moon today is just the beginning. It's the first volley in a long, long war. We're bringing down the Earth Alliance."

He noted the "we," but didn't focus on it. She was talking. He wanted that to continue, and if he suddenly switched into interrogation mode, it wouldn't.

"But your plan," he said, "you wouldn't have lived to see it."

She straightened. "When I nearly died," she said, "it was for nothing. I was in that house for a stupid reason. Really, who cares who murdered that guy? And the woman was insane. So put her away. It doesn't matter. Nothing mattered, not then. If you're going to die, you should die in the service of something. When you nearly died, didn't you feel that way? I mean, you were trying to save the life of a criminal."

"He was already dead," Nyquist said. "I was in the wrong place at the wrong time."

"Exactly!" She pounded her fist for emphasis. "That's the wrong reason to die. Better to control it, to plan it, to go out for something good."

"But you decided not to do that," he said sounding as regretful as he could. "Was that because of me?"

She made a face. "I can't kill you, Bartholomew."

He started. That was the first time she had ever used his given name. She did it with such casual intimacy that it meant she thought of him by his first name. She cared for him. Because of that bond that people often had with their rescuers? Or did she imagine more in her twisted little brain?

He didn't want to contemplate it. But he had to. He had to think about her so that he could learn as much as possible.

"I owe you," she was saying. "I'll always owe you. And I can't repay that by causing your death."

"You might have done so anyway," he said. "You had no idea where I was."

She looked at him, seemingly calm. He couldn't quite read her anymore. "It wouldn't have been deliberate then," she said. "Killing you in front of that ship, letting you die with me, that would have been deliberate, and that would have been wrong."

Killing innocents wouldn't have been wrong. Killing him would have been. He almost shook his head, but caught himself in time.

"I'm confused," he said, amazed that the anger threatening to overwhelm him wasn't evident in his voice. "I thought you said you were going to die in service of something. Wouldn't my death have been in service of that same thing?"

She frowned. Maybe he was making her brain hurt just like she was hurting his. "I didn't know what you believed," she said. "I couldn't ask you, not with all that squad nearby. They would have killed me."

"And then we all would have died as well."

She raised her head in surprise.

"We found the weapon you wore around your torso," he said. "It would have made the laser shots so much worse. Did you know that?"

His tone was accusatory. He could tell because she recoiled. He rested his palm on his thigh, willing himself to breathe. He couldn't antagonize her now.

"Of course you knew that," he said, gently this time. "That's why you stepped away. Because you knew that even one shot could have killed us all. And you didn't want to do that because of me."

She nodded. "That's right."

He was regaining control of himself, and of this interview.

"So do you regret it? It was your mission, right? You should have died."

"I'll get another chance," she said.

Not if you're in prison. He barely bit back the words. "Today?"

She shook her head.

"But I thought today was special," he said.

"It is," she said. "But what I do doesn't matter. I was just a cog. We're all cogs. Even without me, even though I failed, others won't. They'll succeed. And that's all that matters."

"Others," Nyquist said, trying to figure out a way to ask the question without turning into a true interrogator. "The assassins going after the mayors."

"Oh, no," she said. "Those attacks should be done by now. The others. The destruction. That should have started. I was supposed to start it, but I clearly didn't. So someone else will."

"Someone else? In Armstrong?"

She watched him, and her gaze had turned cold. He had finally turned into the interrogator he had been trying to avoid.

"I don't know exactly," she said. She was matter of fact, no longer a co-conspirator, but a criminal, who knew she was in grave trouble.

"Other people like you," he said.

"Facilitators," she said with pride. "We distract, and then we destroy."

He didn't quite understand that, and was about to ask for a clarification, when it became clear. The assassinations and the assassination attempts, they were the distractions. Had Palmette pulled off her attack, she would have hurt the city and killed hundreds, maybe thousands, of innocents. *That was the real attack.* That was the destruction she was talking about.

"And you gave all of that up for me," he said, unable to withhold the sarcasm any longer.

"I didn't give it up, Bartholomew." And from her tone, he could tell she hadn't heard the sarcasm at all. "I just elected not to participate. I'm sure that as we're sitting in here, others are getting the job done."

And then she smiled.

The smile chilled him more than her words ever could.

"Let me check," he said and fled the room.

58

SOMETHING WAS BOTHERING FLINT. DERICCI DIDN'T KNOW WHAT IT WAS, exactly, but it was serious enough to make his entire face go blank. After he had asked DeRicci not to call the assassins clones, she noted that Talia looked worried as well.

Did they know these men? Had DeRicci compromised the investigation somehow?

She hurried down the hall, away from the small room where she had set up Flint and Talia, giving them desks to work on, non-networked screens to get information. Popova had found two computers that hadn't yet been assigned and put them into the room. One computer was a tablet, which Flint gave to Talia. The other was built into a desk, which Flint seemed to prefer.

Popova managed to get them some food and two comfortable chairs as well. If it weren't for her puffy face and swollen eyes, Popova would have seemed her normal, efficient self.

But, DeRicci knew, Popova would seem efficient for a little while, and then the efficiency would fade. Popova must have really loved Soseki. And DeRicci had missed it all.

She was back in her office, coordinating information. Hänsel was getting the information she requested cobbled together. He still looked panicked. DeRicci wasn't even certain he had noticed Flint and Talia, or if he had cared.

DeRicci wanted the old Popova back. She wanted the day to stop and to be as calm and orderly as yesterday.

She wanted her biggest problem to be the Anniversary Day itself, and the reminders that the ceremony usually brought her.

Not this.

She had to check in on all of the investigations. She wasn't sure if she should move Romey to the governor-general's case or if she should leave those uncombined. She needed people in all of the other cities as well. It would take time for her people to get there, and to get up to speed.

Flint hadn't been the solution to all of her problems. DeRicci herself still had to coordinate these investigations, and she didn't have the authority to do so.

She had promised herself after the Disty crisis to get more authority, and she had worked with some of the councilors for the United Domes, but that effort had gone by the wayside with some new political crisis she hadn't entirely understood.

Then she had talked to the governor-general who had promised to try something.

But remember, Noelle, the governor-general had said. *We're fighting an uphill battle. The mayors don't want to give up their fiefdoms, not even in the name of security.*

The governor-general, who was dying by inches, a handful of kilometers from here. Or, for all DeRicci knew, might already be dead.

She sank into her chair. She always ended up being the default person in charge. And she hadn't signed on for that.

When this crisis was over, she was going to quit, take a long vacation somewhere, maybe even ask Flint if he needed some kind of assistant. Anything to take this pressure off.

Her emergency links pinged. When she was a detective, she would occasionally ignore messages like that.

She couldn't now.

She answered, scrambling the connection and putting it in the very center of that damn screen.

Nyquist's head filled the box assigned to this message. Behind him, she saw white corridors and a white ceiling. Nothing and no one else.

"It's worse than any of us thought, Noelle," he said.

Her stomach clenched. How could it be worse? He had no idea what she had been going through today.

But she wasn't going to contradict him. "Where are you?"

"I'm still in the port," he said. "I have been interrogating Ursula Palmette."

He told DeRicci exactly what happened—from the attack and how severe it could have been, to the vest Palmette had worn.

Another hole in the dome, this one in the ideal spot to create the most damage.

DeRicci shuddered.

"But that's not the worst of it, Noelle," he said. His voice was shaking. She had never heard his voice shake, not even when he was bleeding out from that Bixian attack. "She told me that she was the primary actor, not those clones. She called herself a facilitator, and she is, if you think about it. She got the zoodeh, she gave them the way into the city—"

"What's she planning?" DeRicci asked. She could hear the analysis later.

"It's not her anymore," Nyquist said. "I got her to divert her attack on Armstrong, but she tells me it doesn't matter. Each clone, each one, had someone like her to facilitate the meeting with the mayor or the governor-general. And those facilitators are the ones who are going to cause the most damage."

"How?" DeRicci asked.

"If I knew, I'd tell you," Nyquist said. "But she said the assassinations were supposed to be a diversion from the real destruction. And she said the attacks are going to start now."

What had Soseki's assassin said? *These killings today. They're just the beginning.*

And she had gotten similar reports from other domes. *Just the beginning.* Diversion to destruction.

DeRicci felt lightheaded. Then she remembered: she needed to breathe. And she did. She took in a deep breath, and let it out slowly.

"She didn't give you any idea what the other attacks would be, did she?" DeRicci asked.

"No, Noelle," Nyquist said. "But if she had succeeded, she would have made that bombing four years ago seem small. The destruction, not just with the bomb, but with the chemicals, and the quarantined material—I have no idea how many people would have died."

And these attacks were being planned in every single dome, maybe even being carried out.

The governor-general was incapacitated. Some of the mayors were dead, some injured, the rest incommunicado.

DeRicci was on her own.

And this time, she had absolutely no idea what to do.

59

THE ASSASSINS HAD ALL ARRIVED THROUGH THE PORT OF ARMSTRONG two weeks ago. They arrived in a group—twenty of them—and they didn't even try to hide the fact that they were clones, or that they were traveling together. They did dress differently, but they carried similar bags, and their clothing seemed to have the same manufacture.

They ate lunch when they got off the transport, in the same restaurant, talking and laughing like members of the same family. Then they peeled off as they headed to different destinations on the Moon.

Watching them through old security footage, tracking them, made Flint uneasy. They had been so visible. With the benefit of hindsight, they looked sinister. But he had seen clumps like that before, humans who looked alike. Some were clones, some were siblings—twins or triplets or quadruplets—and he had never thought anything of it.

He glanced at Talia. She was sitting sideways in her chair, knees hung over one arm of the chair, her back against the other. The pad she was working on was braced against her thighs. Her eyebrows curved down toward her nose in a slight frown, and her lips were pursed in concentration.

She was tracking the transport. She already had its origin, which was some starbase just outside the solar system. It was clear the assassins didn't begin their journey at that base. So she was tracking the passenger manifest and comparing it to the security identification provided through the vids.

As soon as she had the names of the twenty assassins, she would give it to Flint. He would see if he could find them, and see if they were using their real names.

He suspected they were: they weren't about hiding. They wanted to be seen, noticed, and eventually caught. They wanted everyone to know what they had done.

Which chilled him.

He had just switched his screen to a list of long-term cloning companies—companies that had existed for more than twenty years and had no trouble with human cloning—when DeRicci contacted him on his link.

Miles, can you come to my office? I need to pick your brain.

He glanced at Talia. She was biting her lower lip. Then he sighed.

"Bring your pad, kiddo," he said. "We have to talk with Noelle."

"What's wrong now?" Talia asked, her body instantly tense.

What isn't wrong? Flint wanted to say, but didn't. "I think she just needs to toss some ideas around."

He hoped. Because he didn't want to believe that things had gotten worse.

60

Keptra hadn't brought her own vehicle. She had flown down to the hospital in the stupid ambulance, thinking that was the best way to handle this crisis.

And it had been. She had to remember that. If she hadn't ridden with that bastard, she wouldn't now know that they were still in trouble.

Someone—a woman, a *facilitator*—was going to do something, something worse than the assassination attempt on the mayor.

And she was going to do it in the Top of the Dome.

Keptra commandeered an emergency vehicle in the parking lot outside the hospital. She was flying it back up to the Top of the Dome, avoiding other emergency vehicles transporting hostages and staff and God knew who else.

She told Strom to take a team to the eleventh floor, suite 8C. Not that she expected them to find anyone there, but at least they'd know who they were looking for. Not just who—they could get the name from the building directory—but a bit about her as well.

Strom hadn't gotten back to Keptra yet. And that worried her.

She had been complaining about the Top of the Dome for years, and no one had listened to her. No one cared.

But someone who worked in the Top of the Dome would know about its strengths and weaknesses. Particularly someone who knew the back ways into the restaurant.

As Keptra drove, she sent messages along her links. She needed her team to remain. She needed more officers. She needed—God forbid—a bomb squad. She needed sniffer bots and robotic equipment. She needed full-fledged emergency gear.

And she needed someone on the ground, investigating other venues, just in case the damn bastard had been lying to her.

Oddly enough, she didn't think he was lying about another attack. But she wasn't sure it would happen today. She wasn't sure when it would happen. She just needed to be prepared.

She was nearly to the parking structure at the side of the Top of the Dome when Strom reached her.

"First," he said, appearing as a small hologram on her dashboard. He was still wearing all his gear, and he looked tired. "Her name is Gronberg. Eugenia P. Gronberg. She's a mid-level bureaucrat who has worked here for about ten years. And I think she's been doing something to the computers."

Keptra was driving the vehicle herself, not using the automatic controls. She didn't want to switch over to the automated system, not when the driving was so tricky, when she was speeding, and when there were so many other emergency vehicles in the small airspace around the Top of the Dome.

So she switched off the holographic projection, leaving only the audio on.

"What do you mean, doing something?" she asked.

"Well, the in-house locator says she's in this office, and if she is, then she's invisible," he said. "Plus, when I tracked her actions for the earliest part of the day, and tried to see how she helped that would-be assassin, I still got information that she was at her desk all day. But when I looked at the video, the room was empty. She hasn't been here at all."

"Crap," Keptra said, narrowly avoiding an edge of the building. "If she was going to do some damage, what could she do? What are her skill sets?"

"I don't trust any information I have on her," Strom said. "Everything looks like it's been tampered with."

Keptra steered the vehicle into the parking garage and headed for premium parking. Not that she had to worry; the parking structure was nearly empty. Everyone who could leave the Top of the Dome had already done so.

"Then we need old information, something she wouldn't have thought to change," Keptra said. "Get her image out to everyone in the Top of the Dome, and send it to me as well."

"Already done," he said.

"Good. I'll join you in less than fifteen."

She hoped she had fifteen minutes. She was really worried about this. She had always known something bad would happen on her watch. This morning, she had thought it was the attack on the mayor.

Now she knew that whatever it was, it was going to be a lot worse.

She stopped for half a second, called up the image of Eugenia P. Gronberg. The woman looked harmless, like most of the human bureaucrats throughout the Moon. She had short brown hair in some kind of weird puffy do that didn't accent the rather plain features of her face. She was matronly, poorly dressed, and she had frown lines near her mouth. The frown lines were shiny, which meant she had already had enhancements to make the lines go away, but they had returned, taking over her face again.

A deeply unhappy woman.

Or so Keptra wanted to imagine. Because she didn't think a happy woman would "facilitate" an attack on the mayor.

Keptra sent the image, flagged emergency, to everyone in authority on Tycho Crater, as well as to every single dome operator and public transportation supervisor in the entire city. Someone had to have seen that woman today. Someone would give Keptra insight.

She only hoped she would get it in time.

61

DERICCI STOOD IN FRONT OF HER GIGANTIC SCREEN, LOOKING AT THE HOLE
where Nyquist's image had been. Her stomach clenched. This new bombing
would have been worse than four years ago, but Nyquist had prevented it.

Nyquist, who couldn't help her now.

And if DeRicci went to Popova, she had no idea if Popova could
help. DeRicci would waste precious time. Hänsel was useless. None of
the leaders of the Moon could talk to her. Getting someone in authority
in the Earth Alliance up to speed would take forever. Flint was working
on the bigger picture—whoever was behind the clones—and she needed
him there. He didn't know what she could do as Security Chief. Hell, she
didn't know what she could do sometimes.

Flint came into the room unannounced, followed by Talia. DeRicci
wished she could talk to Flint without his daughter, but she also knew
that Flint didn't want to let Talia out of his sight.

"Have you got anything?" DeRicci asked.

"I thought you wanted to pick my brain," he said.

"I do," she said, "but I'm half-hoping there's more information."

He shrugged. "The only new information I have is strange."

She felt more irritated at him than she should have been. He wasn't with-
holding information from her, but she hated the way he dragged this out.

"And it is…?"

275

"Nineteen others arrived with our assassin," Flint said.

DeRicci frowned. "Twenty clones?"

"Yeah," Flint said, "and they weren't hiding."

"Twenty." She swallowed hard. "Twenty."

Then she looked at him. His gaze met hers. He seemed to be waiting. But Talia wasn't. "Have there been twenty assassinations today?" Her question seemed breathless.

"No," DeRicci said, "but several have failed."

But what if a few quit? Or didn't make it to their target? Failures she didn't even know about.

And Nyquist had told her that the attacks were diversions, that each assassin had a facilitator, an insider. At least one of those insiders—Palmette—had a secondary assignment.

Flint was still watching her. "What?" he asked.

"Each one of these assassins had a facilitator," DeRicci said. "Someone connected who got him near his target. The Armstrong facilitator was supposed to blow up the port."

Talia started, but DeRicci ignored it. Flint glanced at his daughter, his mouth in a grim line.

"We caught her," DeRicci said. "We got this information from her."

"Do you think she was unusual?" Flint asked.

"I don't know," DeRicci said.

"You have to assume she isn't. That these other facilitators have a secondary job."

"I know," DeRicci said. "But what can I do? It doesn't feel like Anniversary Day. It feels like the day of the damn bombing…."

That last bomb, four years ago, it had been a nightmare. She had been in her office at the Armstrong Police Department, and then everything fell apart, lights out, building shaking, environmental controls off. And things got worse when the dome sectioned. Its protective walls came down and…

Her breath caught. She knew now. She knew there would be an attack. She didn't know where the attacks would be, but she knew they would be bad, and they would be in every single dome on the Moon.

"Noelle?" Flint asked.

She held up a single finger, silencing him. Then she sent a highly coded *Extreme Emergency* message through her links to every single authority in every single dome: *Section your dome. Now! We have a credible threat that your dome will explode within minutes. Section your dome.*

She set the message on repeat. Then she hurried across her office, pulled open the door, and pointed at Hänsel. "I'm sending you a message now. Send it to the Earth Alliance on my authority, and keep sending it until you get a response."

That message—simple: *All domes on the Moon under attack. Warn domed communities throughout the Alliance. We have no overt threat to them, but just in case, they need to be on alert.*

Then she turned to Popova. Popova's hair was a mess, but her eyes were bright, as if this new emergency had reawakened her.

"Make sure our dome sections. *Now!*" DeRicci said. "Then monitor the other domes here on the Moon. They need to be sectioning. I need to know what's going on. Got that?"

"Yes, sir," Popova said, sounding like her old self. Her cheeks filled with color as she started to work.

Flint stood near the door. "You're sectioning the domes?"

"It's the only thing we can do," DeRicci said. "Brace yourself. This won't be fun."

She stepped past him, and went back into her office. She sent the messages again, then made sure the message went to everyone who worked for the governor-general. DeRicci had no idea if the same woman that Nyquist had been working with had facilitated the governor-general's attack, but just in case that attack had a different facilitator, DeRicci made sure they were warned.

"What can we do, Dad?" Talia asked.

"Sit down," he said, pointing her to one of the chairs. Talia sat. So did Flint. But DeRicci didn't.

Then a loud bang echoed throughout the building, and it shook, hard. DeRicci grabbed onto her desk, but it slid across the floor. Flint and Talia's chairs slid too. Neither said anything, but Talia looked terrified. Flint seemed grimly determined.

The dome was sectioning, just like DeRicci had ordered.

It wouldn't stop an attack, but it would minimize the damage. Not counting, of course, the damage to the ground because of the sectioning. There hadn't been a lot of warning. She hoped no one got hurt.

Then she didn't think about it any more. She watched feeds from the other domes. Some were sectioning. Others hadn't yet.

She checked her message, re-sent it, added as much urgency as she could.

If Nyquist was right, and the attack on Armstrong was going to be first, and he'd been working on this woman for a few hours, then the other attacks were imminent.

"Hurry, hurry, hurry," DeRicci muttered. She felt completely out of control. She stared at the images. Then she had a terrible thought: How many domes could section? They had all been built to section, but they had balked at the order from the governor-general shortly after DeRicci's hire to check the sectioning mechanism. Too costly. Too difficult.

She clenched her fists and sent a prayer—or maybe a command—out into the universe.

Please let it work. Please let it work. It has to work. It has to work now.

62

Keptra sprinted for the stairs in the parking garage. It made no difference if she used the elevator—if the power went out here, she was screwed no matter what—but she hated being caught in small spaces. The garage was open to parts of the dome, one of the design features she hated about the entire Top of the Dome structure, something she had complained about for years.

It would be so easy to access the exterior of the structure from here. There were a dozen other places just as easy to access.

Maybe that bastard had been wrong. Maybe it wasn't just the facilitator working on something destructive inside Tycho Crater. Maybe an entire team of people worked—

Something shot past her vision, whistling as it went by. Then the entire structure rocked, and she nearly lost her footing.

She grabbed onto the wall and steadied herself, sending a message to Strom: *What was that?*

The dome is sectioning, he sent back. *The mayor's orders.*

What did the mayor know that she didn't know? How come that order hadn't come to her as well?

She was about to ask when a loud boom echoed through the parking garage, followed by another, and then another. Fire at one end, suppression systems working to put it out. Then another boom and another, and suddenly she was sliding, falling downward, grabbing onto whatever she could.

A final boom resounded and she had nothing to hang onto. The world was burning, collapsing, cratering around her. Cars were sliding toward her, sliding downward, and she couldn't reach them either.

She wrapped herself into a little ball, and felt herself bounce.

63

SOMEHOW THE CORONER MANAGED TO GET THE BODY OUT OF THE BOHEMIAN Theater. Lillian Miyaki watched as a group of bots with tops that combined to make a kind of tray lifted the body into the coroner's van. That body wasn't really a body. It was something other, something she really didn't want to think about.

Just like she didn't want to think about the other message that had just come through from Security Chief DeRicci. Somehow her team was supposed to find a "facilitator," the person or persons who had gotten the wannabe assassin into the Bohemian Theater or into Glenn Station—no one was clear on that point—and stop this person or persons from doing something nefarious.

No one was clear on that point either.

Miyaki's team was still inside the theater. DeRicci's people seemed to think there might be a bomb or some kind of improvised explosive. The mayor's office (really Adriana Clief) wanted security teams all over the city to look for something out of the ordinary.

And then Clief had given only a few minutes warning before sectioning the dome. That had happened not five minutes ago, nearly making the bots drop that icky, gory body. Miyaki wasn't afraid of many things, but she was afraid of dying like that—horribly and graphically, in a way that would leave her not quite human.

The coroner told Miyaki that the would-be assassin had died quickly, but after questions, Miyaki realized the assassin hadn't died quickly enough. The coroner estimated it had taken about thirty seconds for the stuff—this *zoodeh*—to work. Any cop knew that thirty seconds was a very long time.

One of the dome sections had fallen between the Bohemian Theater and the downtown train station. The dome sections hadn't been used in Miyaki's lifetime, not even on a practice drill. She was, frankly, a bit surprised that they had worked at all. Since they landed with a lot of force, shaking the ground beneath them, she suspected many things had gotten broken throughout Glenn Station.

If that was the worst of the day's events—that and the death of the wannabe assassin—then the day wouldn't be as bad as it had started out to be.

Still, she stared at the dome section. It was supposed to be clear, but it had aged into a yellow-gold color that made it seem brittle. The station, just beyond, looked like it had faded as well. The long building, which matched the Bohemian Theater in its old Earth design, seemed farther away than usual, probably a trick of the warped dome section.

Miyaki sighed deeply and headed back into the Bohemian Theater.

Suddenly, the dome section bowed in toward her, material hitting it, followed by a loud *whomp!* and then splattering sounds as the material kept hitting the section itself.

The dome section moved inward, then straightened.

Miyaki realized she was sitting on the ground. She had fallen and not even noticed. People were pouring out of the Bohemian Theater and other nearby buildings, talking and yelling.

She didn't pay any attention to them. She got up, then walked toward the dome section. It was scratched and charred and covered with bits of building. Stuff was dripping down the interior.

Stuff. Red and gray and black stuff. Ichor from some of the aliens in the station. Human blood. Human brains.

She was shaking. She couldn't see the train station any longer and it took her a moment to figure out why.

It was gone. It had exploded, and it had taken part of the dome with it.

If the mayor's office (Adriana Clief, bless her) hadn't ordered the dome to section, Miyaki would be dead now. The environment would be gone. The oxygen would be gone.

Not that it mattered.

Miyaki wouldn't have survived an explosion that large.

The dome section had barely held it in.

"My God," someone said beside her. "We have to go in and help."

"No," she said. "Not until we get some environmental suits."

"But people are dying in there."

She glanced over. The speaker was a thin man she didn't recognize. He was wearing civilian clothing, probably someone who had come for Mayor Tsepen's speech.

"No one's dying," she said, suddenly feeling very tired.

"Yes, they are." He waved his hand at the debris on the dome section. It wasn't sliding down now. Some of it was moving upwards. The gravity was gone, along with the rest of the environmental systems.

"No," she said. "No one's dying. I'm sorry to tell you, but they're already dead."

64

NELIA BYLER ARRIVED IN LITTROW AT EXACTLY THE TIME SHE AND THE governor-general and their entourage had been slated to return. Back when everything was just fine. When no one knew what this day would bring.

She managed to get out of the bullet train and find her way to the taxi stand. She supposed she should have sent for a car to bring her back to the governor's mansion, but she didn't want to talk to anyone.

She had cringed in her seat on the train from Armstrong to Littrow. It was only a thirty-five minute trip, but it seemed so much longer. How the citizens of Armstrong had complained when Littrow became the seat of the Moon-based government. But everyone had thought it so sensible.

If they didn't establish the Moon-based government in the Moon's largest city, then outsiders wouldn't find it so easy to attack the governor-general or the council.

But the governor-general had made her Anniversary Day speech in Armstrong, and they had gotten her. Those clones. Targeting everyone.

They had gotten the governor-general.

And she had died.

Nelia wiped her eyes. She should have told someone. The surgeons had left it to her. She was the only one in the waiting area.

I suppose you'll want to break the news yourself, the main surgeon had said. She was a blunt woman with an angular face, and eyes so intelligent they looked right through Byler. The surgeon had no real compassion, nor did she have any understanding of what she was telling Byler.

Or how much it hurt.

Byler had lived for Celia Alfreda. Celia wasn't just the governor-general. She had been a friend, a colleague, someone Byler had *believed* in.

And because of the medical protocols they'd installed, they'd prevented a quick death.

Byler spent the entire train ride wondering if Celia had been conscious. If she had known what was happening to her.

If it had hurt.

Byler shuddered.

"May I help you?" The taxi at the front of the taxi cab line spoke to her. She hated automated cars.

But she needed this one.

She opened the back door. "Governor's mansion, please."

She had to get there, to talk to the staff, to figure out what, exactly, to do now that the governor-general was dead. Attacks on mayors, some successful, and then this against the governor-general.

Everything was collapsing around her.

Then she realized the cab hadn't moved.

"I said I need to go to the governor's mansion," she said tiredly. Or maybe she sounded irritated. She didn't know and didn't care. She was just talking to a damn machine, after all.

"I cannot take you there," the cab said. "The dome has sectioned and I can only take you places within this section."

Her brain wasn't working quite right. She didn't understand what the cab meant. "I need to go to the Governor's mansion," she said.

"I cannot take you there," the cab repeated. "The dome has sectioned..."

Damn machine. She got out of the cab and moved to the next. She told it her destination and it said the same thing.

She blinked, forced herself to concentrate, and finally realized what they meant. The dome's sections had come down, probably in response to the governor-general's death. Someone had already heard and believed there was some kind of threat against Littrow.

Of course there wasn't. This town was the safest town on the Moon. That's why the Moon-based government settled here. No one ever attacked Littrow. No one would. No one outside of the Moon had ever heard of it.

Half the people on the Moon hadn't heard of it either.

She wiped at her eyes again and looked up at the governor's mansion, rising above all of the other buildings in the center of the city. It was a lovely building, precisely built with materials from each important section of the Moon. Large and imposing, and almost black because it had been made from the materials made of the regolith taken from the Taurus Mountains. She loved that building, and wondered if she'd still be able to work there, now that the governor-general was dead.

She had to find a cab with a human driver. Or one that would let her operate it. Surely she could get from here to—

The governor's mansion turned white, then red, and then vanished altogether. The dome fell inward, and then she couldn't see the center of the city any more. The buildings between here and there looked just fine, but the center of the city had vanished behind some kind of blackness.

"What the hell?" she muttered.

People were running forward, heading toward the city center. Then they all stopped at the edge of the street, and stared.

She was running with them before she realized what she was doing. She was running and muttering and wondering what else had happened.

Her brain wasn't working. Grief, dammit. She'd heard that grief did that. It made people stupid.

And she felt stupid when she realized why she had stopped. The dome had *sectioned*. The sections were down, just like they had practiced a few years ago, after the bombing in Armstrong. The governor's mansion was two sections away. Everything looked fine between this section and the next. But beyond that, on the mansion side, she couldn't see anything.

It had turned black. It was gone.

Something had happened.

What had happened?

She looked at the people next to her.

"What the hell?" she asked again.

But no one answered her. No one even looked at her. They were all staring at the center of the city, because there wasn't anything else that they could do.

65

IT WAS LIKE THEY WERE ON A TIMER, THESE EXPLOSIONS, AS IF A GIGANTIC, invisible hand was pushing button after button, making sure that each place fell one moment after the last one.

DeRicci stood in front of that screen—which she would have torn down when this was over, she promised herself, she never wanted to look at this thing again—arms crossed, hugging herself, and making herself watch.

Flint stood beside her, arm around his daughter. Talia had her head on his shoulder, her arms around his waist. Sometimes she buried her face in his neck.

DeRicci wanted to do the same thing. She wanted to hide, but she made herself watch.

Explosion after explosion. Sometimes the images she got went dark as the links between cities shut down. Sometimes she saw the whole thing: the governor's mansion, the pyramid in the center of Little Egypt, the public transportation hub in Second Mumbai.

Collapsed dome after collapsed dome—only a section, but each section represented hundreds, maybe thousands of lives.

People, others, she couldn't have evacuated. She had no idea where any of these attacks were going to strike and she wouldn't have known where to evacuate to.

She had been helpless. And she still was.

Talia had stopped watching, her face permanently buried in her father's neck. Flint held her, but stared at the carnage like DeRicci did. His expression was flat, as if this didn't bother him at all.

But it had to be bothering him. It bothered DeRicci.

All she could do was watch, her throat constricted, her mouth dry.

The world was ending. *Her* world was ending. And she couldn't do anything about it.

Five explosions. Ten.

Fifteen.

Sixteen.

Seventeen, eighteen, nineteen.

And then they stopped. She stood for what seemed like forever before she thought to check the time.

Nineteen explosions in less than ten minutes.

There would have been twenty, if Nyquist hadn't stopped that woman. The first would have come two hours ago.

Damn, whoever had planned this was good. Excellent in fact. First the mayors died. Then a big explosion in Armstrong. Everyone would react to that, all the emergency services personnel all over the Moon would respond, people would think that it was over, and then this cascade of attacks, panicking them further, making them wonder what exactly was going on.

People were dying, that was what was going on.

She activated one of her links before she even realized what she had done. She contacted Nyquist, maybe because she needed him. She wanted him here.

He answered. He wasn't interrogating that woman any more. He answered.

"You need to find out who the hell caused this," she said to him. "I need to know how many more attacks there will be. I need to know what we're facing here."

"I think twenty's it," Flint said beside her, even as Nyquist started to answer. Nyquist was saying he didn't know. He couldn't know. He wasn't sure if Palmette knew.

DeRicci glanced at Flint. Flint was looking at the screen, his light skin even paler than usual. Talia still hadn't lifted her head.

"You're sure?" DeRicci asked.

Nyquist was silent on the other end of her links. She had no idea if he could hear this.

Flint shrugged. "I can't be sure of anything," he said. "But it seems a logical guess."

Logical guess. As if this had any logic at all.

She nodded, then made herself take a deep breath. "Find out all you can," she said, and she wasn't sure if she was talking to Flint or Nyquist or both.

Then she shut off her connection to Nyquist, turned her back on Flint, and contacted first responders, to make sure that every attacked city, every attacked *dome*, had the supplies it needed.

First, she'd see how many lives they could save. Then she'd worry about who was in charge. Finally, she would deal with the press and the fear and the fallout.

But that was last.

Lives were first.

If there were any lives in those sections left to save.

66

HE HEARD EVERYTHING. STANDING ALONE IN A DAMN HALLWAY, WHITE on white, nothing here, except him and an insane woman in the next room.

Who helped plan the attacks that were killing people all over the Moon.

Nyquist brought a hand up to his ear, even though he knew that DeRicci had severed their connection. She sounded angry, terrified, *shaken*, and he had rarely heard DeRicci shaken.

The day he nearly died. She'd been shaken then.

You need to find out who the hell caused this, she had snapped at him. She hadn't even said hello, hadn't asked where he was, hadn't asked if he had learned any more, not that he had. She had just demanded he help her. And he wished he could.

Flint was there. Oddly enough, as uncomfortable as Flint occasionally made him, that comforted Nyquist. DeRicci trusted Flint and she needed someone like him right now.

Apparently he already had some answers.

Nyquist hoped they were enough.

He leaned against the cold white wall, and peered at the one-way window into the interrogation room. The port had locked down. He already heard the announcements, felt the shudders as the dome sectioned around the port.

The port was its own island, designed that way because everyone believed if anything bad happened in Armstrong, it would happen at the port.

And this nearly had. The destruction he was hearing about through his links, that had nearly happened here. But Palmette didn't do it, not just because of him, but because she trusted others to do it for her.

And they did.

He slammed his fist into a wall. The shuddering pain didn't do anything. It didn't make him feel better, it didn't soothe him. All over the Moon, people were going through what he had gone through during the first bombing—unstable buildings collapsing from the vibrations set off by the dome sectioning, injuries, attacks.

Deaths.

How many people had died because others got the job done, as Palmette had said. How many died? Hundreds? Thousands? Tens of thousands?

And once again, in a moment of great crisis, he was stuck with Palmette. He was dealing with Palmette. He had to figure out what to do with Palmette.

Besides kill her. Because that was what he wanted to do. He should have left her to die in that squalid kitchen, on the floor of that squalid house. No one would have known. No one would have cared.

Only back then, he had thought her worth saving. Hell, he had even thought Alvina Ingelow was worth saving. And she had cost him months in court time and in headaches.

In comparison, though, Alvina had been worth saving.

Palmette had not.

He clenched his fist and nearly sent it into the wall again, but the soreness on the side of his hand stopped him. Hurting himself wouldn't help. Punching a wall wouldn't help.

He couldn't go into those destroyed domes and save lives. He couldn't be a first responder. So far, everything in Armstrong was fine.

Everything here would rest on the investigation.

Because the assassins had said that the assassinations had only been the beginning. Maybe they were referring to these attacks. Or maybe they'd been referring to something more.

Why attack every major city on the Moon if it wasn't the prelude to something bigger?

Only what? He didn't know.

Maybe Palmette did.

It was time to find out.

67

FLINT WOULD NEVER GET THE IMAGES OUT OF HIS MIND, PLAYING AND replaying on DeRicci's gigantic screen. Worse, Talia had seen them too. Just after she had found the passenger manifests. Those twenty would-be assassins had been in each of the cities that had been attacked. Or the nineteen cities, since somehow Armstrong had been spared this time.

Was this how everyone else had felt four years ago, when the bomb had exploded here in Armstrong? He had been involved in his own crisis on Earth, and hadn't realized what had happened for days. And by then, the impact was a bit blunted.

So he hadn't experienced this shock to the system, this *I can't believe what's happening* feeling, as if he were watching an entertainment instead of seeing a crisis develop in front of his eyes.

A crisis that had DeRicci looking like a wild woman, even though she was trying to keep herself under control.

That request, *Find out all you can,* was spot-on. Because what else could he do? He wasn't anywhere near the explosions. He couldn't help rescue survivors or help with the first responders. He could send money—he had a lot of money—but at the moment, there was too much confusion. He didn't even know where to send it, what to do.

He took Talia's arm and led her from DeRicci's office. Popova was moving quickly, hands flying, as she worked on her screen and talked to someone through her links. Hänsel looked panicked, but he worked quickly as well. Hänsel nodded as Flint went past, as if they shared a secret.

Maybe they did. They both knew how tenuous everything was, how—in truth—no one was in charge.

It wasn't until Flint got back to his work area that he realized Talia was shaking. His daughter, who hadn't had anything easy since her mother died.

Talia's face was gray, and her eyes red-rimmed. But she wasn't crying—not yet.

"What do we do, Dad?" she asked. "They're going to bomb this place next, right?"

He didn't know the answer to that. He had made it a policy from the beginning not to lie to her, even if the truth was painful.

"I don't know what their plans are," he said. "I don't even know who 'they' are or what they want from this. We have to trust that the building's security will take care of any threat."

"But security didn't solve the threats to all those cities. Dad, those people, they're dying." Her voice rose and wobbled.

He put a hand on her back, and she stiffened. She didn't want him to touch her. She didn't want a hug or casual comfort. She had moved beyond that.

Now she wanted *answers*.

They all wanted answers.

"Yes," he said, surprised at how calm he sounded. "People are dying right now. But a lot more would have died if the domes hadn't sectioned. We'd be looking at casualties in the millions."

Talia stared at him, her eyes narrowing. He recognized the look. She was getting angry.

"And that makes it okay?" she asked. "Thousands dying instead of millions?"

"No," he said. "It's not okay. It's just not as bad…."

He realized how lame his argument was and quit talking. He ran a hand over his forehead. His fingers were trembling. He was more shaken up than he wanted to admit.

"We can watch this all day," he said. "We can follow the coverage, keep track of how many people survive, what happens to the various cities, or we can contribute."

"No, we can't," Talia said. "They shut down the trains. Didn't you hear that? No one is traveling right now."

"We're not going to travel," he said. "We're not going to leave this building. You and I have skills other people don't have, Talia. We can find things. We know how to get information. And that's what Noelle needs right now. The more information we have on these people, the faster we can solve this."

"So what?" Talia said. "They already killed people."

"And they might kill more," he said. "We don't know. If we find out who they are and what they're doing, we might be able to get to them first."

"Don't you think they're ready for that?" she asked.

He studied her. His brilliant daughter. She understood how people worked as well.

"Yes," he said. "I think they're ready for the authorities to search for them. They wanted the assassins to be traced. I don't think they expected anyone to discover who set off the bombs. We caught a break there. So we trace and track."

"Just like the police are doing," Talia said.

"The police aren't doing anything right now except dealing with a crisis," he said. Except in Armstrong. In Armstrong, the secondary crisis had been averted.

Talia crossed her arms.

"Besides," Flint said, "these attackers expect the police to follow the rules. Noelle brought *us* in here because she knows we won't. We'll follow the information wherever it leads us."

Talia tilted her head. Her eyes had brightened. He had her interest for the first time since she saw all the images of destruction. "So I don't have to do things the way I would if I was in school."

"That's right," Flint said. "Do it any way you can. The faster we find out what's going on, the better off we'll be."

She picked up the pad and tapped it on. "Do you think the assassins are the place to start?"

"I'll follow them," Flint said. "I'm used to tracing a lot of people at once. I want you to look into the communication files for that woman Nyquist captured. Someone had to put her up to this. Let's figure out who it was."

"That sounds important, Dad," Talia said. "I think you should do it."

He put a hand on her arm. "It *is* important. And you'll do much better than I ever would."

She stared at him for a moment. Then she took a deep breath and started to work.

He watched her for a moment, the frown of concentration on her face, the way she bit her lower lip. He had calmed her down. He wished he could calm himself.

But he had learned long ago that the best way for him to deal with a crisis was through a computer screen. He needed to focus on detail, on being busy, on solving things.

And he would.

He would solve this.

If it was the last thing he ever did.

68

Not every dome had been destroyed. DeRicci took that as good news. She was looking for good news wherever she could find it.

She had turned her back on that gigantic screen, but she had kept it on, the images filtering in from all major cities. She was standing in front of the floor-to-ceiling windows, looking at her city. Intact, glimmering in the mid-afternoon dome light. Light that someone had programmed, light that came through the very thing that protected them all.

Below, cars moved. People were still walking on the streets, even though they were monitoring what was going on.

Hundreds of other towns on the Moon had not been hit with an attack, and life went on there too.

She had a hunch those citizens were as shell-shocked as she was. But they didn't have to cope, moment by moment, struggling to wrap their brains around the magnitude of this crisis, not just because it had happened, but because they had to solve it.

She had to solve it.

So far as she could tell, she was the only one left alive who had the ability to do so. She could try to gather the Moon Council members, but she didn't know how many of them had been in Littrow near the governor's mansion. Or attending some Anniversary Day speech in some important venue that might have been in a section of some dome that got obliterated.

Nineteen explosions. Twelve domes had holes blown through them. If she hadn't ordered those domes sectioned, twelve cities would have been completely destroyed.

She had to take comfort in that. Just like she had to take comfort in the fact that seven of the explosions hadn't been severe enough to crack or destroy a dome.

Although the situation in Tycho Crater was bad. If the Top of the Dome fell, it would flatten the city center below.

She'd already received reports on the evacuation effort, but the authorities there were afraid they might not get people out of that area. The dome was still sectioned, and they weren't sure if raising the sections would dislodge the resort.

Who the hell built something like that against a dome?

She supposed she shouldn't rail at their stupidity. There were high rises here attached to the dome as well. Nyquist had nearly died in one.

Nyquist. She hadn't heard from him.

Even though she had heard from nearly thirty different authorities in the Earth Alliance. They were sending emergency personnel, aid, money, medical supplies and avatars, hospital ships, dome engineers, anything she could want.

She just didn't know what she wanted.

Except a guarantee that this attack was over.

Although this wasn't really an attack.

This was something more. An act of war?

She didn't know. No one had owned up to it. No one had claimed it.

Just like no one had claimed the bombing four years ago.

This was so devastating, someone had to take responsibility. She needed them to.

Why weren't they?

She asked the Earth Alliance to send ships and military personnel and all the help they could give. And they were.

But it would take time to get here.

Time she wasn't sure she had.

69

THE PSYCH REPORTS HIT NYQUIST'S LINKS JUST AS HE TOUCHED THE DOOR to the interrogation room. He paused, scanned them, and got even angrier.

Palmette had been an iffy hire in the first place. Parents dead in a murder-suicide when she was young, caused—or so it seemed—by an inability to hire a Disappearance Service. Palmette had moved in with relatives, always been the outsider, unhappy, unwanted.

But she had a fascination with crime and she'd scored better than any other candidate for the police academy on investigative techniques. She was also exceptionally brilliant, very driven, and extremely teachable.

She was also unable to connect with others, unable to form a close bond, and unwilling to go into therapy to work through the problems. She got an enhancement so that she could handle social situations, but even that was a stop-gap measure, one designed to help her in the field, not to improve her life.

Her entry psych report stated: *This woman is a marginal candidate emotionally, but so brilliant and talented that we would be remiss not giving her a shot at the work. If she suffers serious trauma, she must receive a greater and more thorough examination afterwards than more stable candidates. But many officers go through their careers without serious problems; we trust Ursula Palmette will be one of them.*

They trusted wrong. Nyquist wanted to let them know that they had gambled and lost big. But that wasn't his place at the moment. At the moment, he needed to deal with Palmette herself.

At least he understood what went wrong now. It had gone wrong when her father had killed her mother, and then killed himself. Something twisted in Ursula Palmette's brain. That twist had been evident from the beginning, but not something that the people in charge worried about.

They did what they were programmed to do—they didn't rehire her after she had nearly died in the line of duty. Maybe if they had rehired her, Arek Soseki would be alive.

Nyquist slammed the door open. Palmette looked up, startled.

As he stepped inside, letting the door close behind him, he realized he didn't know how to play this.

Then he decided he didn't want to play it at all.

"I need to know who your contact is, Ursula," Nyquist said.

She shook her head. "I don't even know."

"You do, and you'll tell me."

She frowned at him. "I don't."

Hundreds, maybe thousands of people died because of her, and he knew if he threw that in her face, she wouldn't care. She had stopped caring about dead people when her parents died. Dead people had become a puzzle to her.

He splayed his hands on the table. "What the hell were you thinking?" he asked. "You didn't just want to blow up Armstrong. You wanted to destroy the Moon."

She smiled—that cold, chilling smile. "Have I done so?"

"You haven't, no," he said. He sat down. He wasn't going to give her the satisfaction of knowing that the other bombs had gone off.

She tilted her head. "Then why are you so angry?"

"Because you of all people should know better," he said. "You know how it feels to be abandoned because someone got murdered."

She flinched.

"You know how it feels to suffer in an attack that wasn't aimed at you."

"You forget," she said. "I wasn't injured in the bombing. Alvina Ingelow nearly killed me."

"And you wouldn't have been vulnerable if the bombing hadn't happened," he snapped. "I saved your life. I thought you would amount to something."

"I *did*," she said.

He stared at her.

"People will remember me," she said.

His heart was pounding. He was alone here. Everyone in Armstrong was dealing with a different crisis. No one was observing him. He could probably even convince Murray Atherton to get rid of any footage from this interrogation.

He could do what he should have done before: He should have left her to die. He could make sure she died now.

But he wasn't like her. He wasn't a killer—except in self-defense. And this had moved beyond self-defense long ago.

"No one will remember you," he said coldly. "I'll see to it. They'll have no idea that you even existed."

She blanched.

"I'll wipe you from the records," he said. "I'll make sure you're not in any reports. You know how this chaos works. You know no one will double-check. Ursula Palmette disappeared on Anniversary Day, and no one knows why. Worse, no one will care."

"You said you cared," she whispered.

He nodded. "I did, until I found out what you were."

She raised her chin, but it was trembling. "I'm a good person."

"You're a mass murderer, Ursula. You're worse than Alvina Ingelow. You've killed many more people. You're worse than your father."

Palmette straightened. "I am not."

"You are," Nyquist said. "You did to countless people exactly what your father did to you. You destroyed their lives. You *purposely* destroyed their lives."

"I did not," she said.

"No one remembers him except you. No one thinks about him, no one cares about him. And that will happen to you."

"No," she said.

"I'll make sure of it." He sat down, crossed his arms, and glared at her. She shook her head. "You wouldn't."

"I will," he said. "In fact, I'll enjoy it. I'll happily destroy you, Ursula. And what's ironic is that I can."

She blinked, holding back tears. He watched her, knowing what was going through her mind. She knew he was manipulating her, but she couldn't stop the emotions. Emotions had always been her problem, and if she had been able to control them, she would still be on the force. She'd be a productive member of society, not one who had nearly destroyed it.

"All right," she said quietly. "What can I do?"

70

As Flint and Talia worked, neither of them spoke. The room wasn't exactly quiet—people ran down the hall outside. Occasionally some-one yelled. Talia didn't look up. Instead, she seemed to go deeper into her work, her teeth pressing on her lower lip. Every once in a while, she'd make a little grunt of acknowledgement or acceptance or discovery.

Flint would look up when she did that. He couldn't help himself. He had to keep an eye on her as well. Not that he expected anything to happen to her, not here at least. But he worried about the effect this event was having on her, whether it would bring up the trauma from the day her mother got kidnapped.

But his worry for her didn't stop him from focusing on his own work. He was doing a few things by rote. He had systems that he'd established when he became a Retrieval Artist, and he followed them now.

Retrieval Artists found people who had vanished on purpose, escaping prosecution from any one of fifty different alien cultures. Because of agreements the Earth Alliance had made, humans and aliens alike were subject to the laws of whatever place he found himself. That meant that sometimes humans received terrible punishments for things that they never believed to be crimes.

Corporations, in order to do business in truly different cultures, founded Disappearance Services, to help any worker (generally an executive) who inadvertently broke a law to escape punishment.

When Flint quit the police department because he had been unable to enforce some of those laws, he became a Retrieval Artist. Retrieval Artists found people who had Disappeared, but not for any alien government or even any human government. Retrieval Artists worked independently, finding someone whose sentence had been commuted or who had received a large inheritance.

Unlike Trackers, who did work for various governments, Retrieval Artists never found someone and turned them in to serve out their sentence. Retrieval Artists delivered a message or the inheritance, and let the Disappeared go back to their old lives.

Which meant that Flint had learned to cover his tracks. He didn't want some Tracker or police department to piggy-back on his work, finding someone who didn't want to be found.

Flint's search methods were different from other Retrieval Artists' methods. He often used techniques he'd learned as a detective as a place to start.

The legitimate routes added speed to his work, especially at times when he didn't have to worry about anyone tracking his preliminary searches.

Like right now. The moment he had decided to track the assassins, he ran a modified version of Armstrong PD's image search. He also ran one that DeRicci had here in the Security Office.

The Security Office program followed the assassins as they moved from Armstrong's port to their final destinations. If he wanted to, Flint could watch the assassins' comings and goings before Anniversary Day.

But he didn't want to. Let the prosecutors do that. He knew what they'd end up doing.

He wanted to find out where they came from.

Talia sighed heavily. She had moved in her chair so that she was sitting up again. Sometimes she sprawled, sometimes she sat up, but mostly she'd been leaning forward.

"Trouble?" Flint asked.

"Everything's encrypted. For the past year," Talia said. "I can't trace anything easily. I have to fight for each piece of information, and most of it's worthless."

"But the worthless stuff is hiding something important," Flint said.

"I hope so." Talia shifted in the chair again, sitting cross-legged, resting the pad on the chair's left arm. She kept pounding her finger onto the screen as if the pad itself had offended her.

Normally he would tell her to treat the equipment with a bit more respect. But he understood her frustration, so he didn't say anything.

One of his systems pinged. He glanced at the screen on the desk and froze. The computer identified the face "to ninety-nine percent" certainty. He touched the screen gently, unlike Talia had been doing, to see what caused the ninety-nine percent instead of the usual one hundred percent on this program.

Face reappears in several locations at the same time, the program said. *Even though features are the same, probability that faces belong to the same person in all locations low.*

In spite of himself, Flint smiled. Computers were so literal, and programs like this couldn't make the leap that these images could have been caused by something other than the same person. The program hadn't been designed to make that distinction.

He tapped the screen again, moving away from the explanation, to the image of the face itself. It was a 3-D image on a 2-D screen. He tapped it, and a holographic image of the head rotated on the desk.

"Creepy," Talia said. "Which one is that? The one that killed the mayor?"

Several of the assassins killed mayors, but Flint knew what she meant. She was asking if this was the man who killed Soseki.

"I don't think so," Flint said. "The hairstyle is different from what we've seen, and that high neck collar hasn't been in style on the Moon in generations."

"So who is it?" Talia asked.

PierLuigi Frémont, Ruler For Life of Abbondiado, committed suicide fifty-five years ago the night before his trial for genocide began, the computer said. Apparently Talia had asked a question the program thought it could answer. *Evidence suggests Frémont's crimes extended beyond those he was accused of. He killed indiscriminately—*

"Enough," Flint said to the computer. He was familiar with Frémont. Every school child learned about him—or at least, every school child had learned about him when Flint was in school. Frémont was a cautionary tale: a supposedly good-hearted man who left the confines of the Earth Alliance, was forced to take over an area at the outer regions of the known universe, only to lose control of the people who settled the area. Rather than work with them, he killed them and started a new colony; an act he repeated twice before the founding of Abbondiado which, surprisingly enough, managed to overthrow him with the help of the Earth Alliance. The Alliance charged Frémont with genocide, but the night before the trial was to begin, Frémont found a way to end his life.

Chillingly, he did not die alone. He took his guards and an entire wing of the prison with him.

These clones of Frémont, which were in their twenties, had been made thirty years after his death.

"This is some kind of message," Flint said, mostly to himself.

"We'd know what it is if you let the computer finish," Talia said.

He shook his head. "You didn't study Frémont?" he asked.

"I've heard of him, but that unit happened before I came to Armstrong," Talia said. "One more thing I'm supposed to catch up on."

The differences in the education system between Armstrong and Valhalla Basin struck him again. But he didn't have time to dwell on it.

Whoever had created these assassins and sent them to the Moon knew what kind of impact they would have, even after their deaths. Flint shuddered. The discussions of whether or not murderous behavior was innate would become important, along with the tendency toward suicide.

Even if the other attacks hadn't happened—

But they had. The other attacks had happened as well.

Everything was deliberate, from the choices of targets to the choice of assassins. Flint stood up.

"Where're you going?" Talia asked.

"I need to talk to DeRicci."

"Again?" Talia asked. "Can't you just send the information to her?"

Flint glanced at his daughter. She hadn't complained before about going to DeRicci's office.

But before, Talia hadn't known that the images would be playing and replaying on that gigantic screen.

"You can stay here," Flint said.

Talia immediately shook her head. She clearly didn't want him out of her sight—and he couldn't blame her.

Together they left the room to tell DeRicci more confounding news.

71

DOMES ALL OVER THE EARTH ALLIANCE ON HIGH ALERT. STARBASES USING security so high that many ships were unable to dock. Many spaceports refusing access to humans.

And reports from dozens of places of more clones, just like the ones that had attacked the Moon. Blond men in their twenties were getting scrutinized and, in some places, put in detention.

Not that DeRicci cared. She cared only about the Moon, which was devastated. Rescues happening all over the domes, the body count rising, different alien species demanding to know how many of their people had died, and whether or not the Moon's governments were responsible. The days ahead loomed, filled with crisis after crisis, and DeRicci didn't even know if this one had ended yet.

The door to her office opened. Flint and Talia came in. Apparently, Popova and Hänsel had dropped protocol and forgot to inform DeRicci that she was going to get visitors. Which was the second time in less than an hour.

Not that it mattered. Flint could come and go as he pleased.

"We found out who the original was," Flint said.

It took DeRicci a moment to understand him. Original—the source of all the clones. She wondered why he was being so cautious with his language, and then decided it didn't matter.

Nothing mattered except resolving this crisis.

"You ever hear of PierLuigi Frémont?" he asked.

DeRicci's mouth opened slightly. Who hadn't heard of Frémont? He was one of the worst killers of his time.

"You've got to be kidding," she said.

Flint shook his head. "The question is, have these attacks been planned for decades or were these people hired? And if so, how many of them can be hired out and by whom?"

"You're going to find that out, right?" DeRicci asked.

"It's going to take time, Noelle," he said. "I'm not sure we have time."

She glanced at the screen. She preferred not to look at it, but she had to. And every time she did, the images had changed. The immediate problems—the fires, the smoke, the destruction—had stopped now. The lack of atmosphere had put out fires, the debris had stopped falling into the broken domes. Only a few places still had events going on, like Tycho Crater with its stupid Top of the Dome resort, but the rest of the domes were in search-and-rescue mode.

"I have the sense that this is all designed so that we chase our tails," he said.

"I know," she said.

Designed to have them search and search and find nothing. Designed to terrify and demoralize them.

No one had ever attacked the Moon like this. The Earth was the center of the Earth Alliance, and the Moon was the Earth's gateway. Someone had just shown that they could get close to the heart of the human communities.

Not that this was her worry. Her worry was to protect the Moon.

"What do you think this means?" she asked Flint. Talia stood beside him, hands folded in front of her, not saying a word. DeRicci appreciated that.

"I think it means this attack was planned for a long time."

"We had two waves," DeRicci said. "The assassins, and then the bombings. Do you think there's a third?"

"There are no ships, right?" he asked. "Nothing surrounding us or trying to invade the Earth Alliance?"

"Not that I know of," she said. She knew what was going on in the space around the Moon. She didn't know about the entire Earth Alliance, but she assumed someone would tell her.

"So I'm guessing there isn't a third wave, or if there is, it won't happen here," he said. "We expect it now. They're doing things we don't expect."

"Distract and destroy," DeRicci said. Then she cursed. She raised a finger to keep Flint quiet, and as she did, she whirled away from him, sending a message to all her contacts in the Earth Alliance.

The survivors among the attackers have told us that the plans they followed had this rule, she sent. *Distract and destroy. These attacks on the Moon will distract the Earth Alliance. I know you're protecting the domes and the human communities, but expect something else, something that might be even larger, while your attention is focused on the Moon itself.*

Instantly, she got a message back from one of the leaders, asking her what she thought that attack might be. She had no idea.

It's not my job to figure out what's happening, she said. *I'm the only one remaining here who can handle the crisis on the Moon. I leave it to you. Figure this out. Figure out who caused this.*

And then she signed off.

She turned back around. Flint was watching her with that alert look he sometimes got, the one that made her feel as if he could see through her.

"Do you think the attack on Armstrong four years ago was a dry run?" Talia asked.

That caught DeRicci's attention. The girl asked a very savvy question.

"I don't know. We don't know any of this. But we didn't solve that case, and we're going to solve these."

"How do you know that?" Talia asked, and DeRicci heard something in her voice. A neediness, maybe, a willingness to believe in resolution, as if resolution made everything better.

DeRicci glanced at Flint. How did you tell a kid that sometimes there were no answers? Sometimes you simply had to live through something and get to the next day. And the next. And the day after that.

"Because whoever's behind these attacks expected the attackers to die," DeRicci said. "And not all of them did. We'll find out what we need to know soon enough."

If the attackers knew. DeRicci wasn't sure they did.

She wasn't sure of anything—except one thing.

Nothing would ever be the same again.

THE AFTERMATH
(TWO WEEKS LATER)

72

THE GROUNDS OF ARISTOTLE ACADEMY WERE QUIET—OR AS QUIET AS THEY could be, given all of the armed guards everywhere. The stepped-up security was mostly visible; the Academy had had top-of-the-line hard-to-see security since Flint helped to upgrade their systems after the Deshin incident.

He didn't like the armed guards, especially around children, but he had lost that fight with Selah Rutledge. She didn't want any "bad guys"— her words—to get into the Academy and blow it up.

Everyone had been on edge since the Anniversary Day attacks, some more than others. Armstrong, which was relatively untouched—if you could count an assassination of the mayor untouched—slipped into business-as-usual sooner than every place else. But the human residents still walked around like they'd been hit with a hammer. Many of the permanent alien residents seemed shell-shocked as well, although it was harder for Flint to see the obvious signs.

All he knew was that everyone, everyone, was tense and irritable and, underneath it all, frightened.

Especially Talia.

She walked beside him now, her shoulder brushing his. She had dressed carefully this morning, a sign of nerves for her. He'd learned that early in their relationship. When Talia was frightened or nervous or angry, she wore clothes like armor, as if they could shield her from anything bad that might head her way.

The stone path curved across the well-manicured lawn. Flint had come in through this particular side door because he found the walk to the entrance soothing.

So in some ways, he used things to calm himself, just like his daughter did.

"I still think this is a bad idea," Talia said.

"I know," Flint said. He kept his gaze straight ahead. He didn't want to see her expression or he might give in. "You've made that clear for the past three days."

"And you haven't listened." Her voice rose. "You need me on this research, Dad. You're the one who said it: We're the only ones who can do this."

He hated it when she hurled his own words out at him. He sighed and stopped walking. He put his hands on her shoulders and turned her toward him, not because she was going to look away, but because he knew the movement annoyed her.

She needed to separate from him for a while. Just like everyone else, she needed to get back to a normal routine. And she needed to remember that she could stand up for herself, that she could be independent and alone.

She couldn't be beside him all the time, even if her fears made her want to stay at his side.

But he couldn't tell her that. Not again. The first time he had said it, she had gotten so angry that she shouted for ten minutes. But she didn't storm out of the room, and he knew that was a bad sign. She had to be away from him, even for a short period of time.

So talking to her didn't work. Instead, he had to convince her that leaving was her idea. And that wasn't working either. So he did what he could to annoy her.

Even though he wanted her to remain at his side. In fact, he never wanted to lose sight of her again.

Which told him just how panicked he was, deep down inside.

"Yeah," he said to her, his voice down. "I said that about the research. We are two of the only people who can do it, and we're ahead on it. We've done a lot in the past two weeks."

Her eyes narrowed. She knew he was going to add "but..." "So that's why we should continue," she said before he could say anything else.

He sighed. "It took years to set this up," he said, then corrected himself. "Actually, it took decades. Which means that we're looking at something really big here."

"I know," she said. "That's why we have to hurry."

"We are hurrying," he said. "And we're not the only ones working on it now."

He glanced at the school. The doors were still open. The school day hadn't begun yet. And, more importantly, no one was around them, listening to the conversation.

"I think that discussion we had on Anniversary Day was accurate," he said softly. "I think the assassinations were the first wave, and the explosions were the second. I think there will be a third—"

"Which is why I can't waste my time learning Moon history," Talia said.

"That's exactly why you need to be here," Flint said. "I don't think, and Noelle doesn't think, and others don't think, that the third wave will happen on the Moon. I think Noelle was right when she said this is war. I think these attacks are on the Earth Alliance, not just the Moon, and I think the next will be just as devastating as Anniversary Day. I also think that attack was planned when this attack was—twenty or more years ago."

"So the research—"

"Is what these guys expect," Flint said. "They've set up trails and tracks that we have to follow, but they're going to lead us astray. If we hurry, which is also what they expect, we'll make huge mistakes."

She frowned. He realized he hadn't said this to her before.

He lowered his voice even more. "If I were planning these attacks, I'd do the next one a year or more from now, after we've relaxed our guard, after we've gotten used to daily life again, after our new security measures become routine. And then I'd attack some place unexpected, some place that would send a different message, and I'd make that attack just as devastating and inexplicable."

She stared at him for a long moment, looking wan and terrified. Then she smiled. But the smile didn't reach her eyes, so he knew it was forced.

"It's a good thing you're not planning these," she said.

"I'm worried that whoever is planning them is smarter than I am, Talia," he said. "This person is certainly more patient than I am. I couldn't wait twenty or more years to launch an attack, no matter how effective I'd believe it would be."

She hadn't moved from his grip. Her frown deepened. "I want to find out what's going on," she said.

"Me, too," Flint said. "But we have to go back to living, Talia. If we don't go back to our lives, then this person or these people really have destroyed the Moon."

Her eyes filled with tears. Then she blinked them away. She raised her chin. "I'm going to be bored," she said.

"I doubt that," he said.

"I'm going to hate every minute that I can't figure out what's going on," she said.

"I doubt that too," he said.

"I'm never going to think things are normal again," she said.

He nodded. "That I believe."

She shook herself out of his grip, then she leaned forward and, to his surprise, she kissed him on the cheek.

"Be here on time, Dad," she said. He had promised her that he would pick her up when school got out. "I'm going to want a progress report. And there better be progress."

He grinned. He wondered if that was his first real grin since Anniversary Day.

"Yes, ma'am," he said.

"Good." She nodded at him, and then she sprinted to the front door, leaving him behind.

He stood for a moment in the manicured lawn of the most elite school in Armstrong, his heart twisting. He didn't want to leave her either. He didn't want to do anything except bunker into his house and never come out.

But he was taking his own advice. He was returning to his daily routine. As were so many other people all over the Moon. Others didn't have that luxury yet. Others were still cleaning up the collapsed domes, mourning friends and family, and trying to rebuild ruined buildings.

He knew that DeRicci hadn't had more than a few hours of sleep per day since the attacks happened. And he knew that she hadn't seen much of Nyquist either, who was leading the interrogations of that facilitator, Palmette.

For everyone, life would never be exactly the same. But for a lot of people, daily life would never return.

Flint and Talia had been lucky this time.

He was going to make sure they remained lucky.

He was going to figure out what the hell happened, and make sure that the third wave never, ever, arrived.

He wasn't going to do it for himself or for the Moon or for the Earth Alliance.

He was doing it for Talia. She deserved a normal life. She deserved a bright future.

He was going to make sure she would get it.

73

NYQUIST CARRIED THE TWO TO-GO CUPS OF COFFEE INTO SPACE TRAFFIC'S
Interrogation Center. He couldn't remember the last time he had slept.
He wasn't really sure how many days had passed since the bombings.
Time ran together, the hours blurry and unimportant.

The white walls no longer distracted him. The silence of the place
made it seem almost like a sanctuary.

Maybe he would feel that way if Ursula Palmette wasn't in room 65B.
He had started to think of it as "her" room. It wasn't, of course. The rules
of interrogation and police procedure had kicked in. She had a cell.

So did he. He hadn't gone home in days. Gumiela had given him a
choice: a day off or a one-day suspension.

He chose the day off and slept. Then he grabbed half a dozen changes
of clothing, and essentially moved into the prison wing of Space Traffic.

He wasn't leaving until he knew everything about Ursula Palmette.
Every little detail, from the name of her teacher when she was seven to
the thought she had in her brain the day she decided to destroy the Moon.

He felt like he was partway there. He'd gotten names from her, names
that he passed on to others. People were watching the interrogation now,
or if they weren't watching, they would eventually watch in a few days.

He was part of a large investigation. Every single police officer, every single person with any kind of law enforcement authority all over

the Moon, had been mobilized to catch the sons of bitches who had done this.

DeRicci had also told him that the Earth Alliance was now involved. Law enforcement organizations all over the Alliance were investigating every single detail. There was more manpower devoted to this than any other investigation in Earth Alliance history.

If, indeed, manpower was the right word. The alien governments were involved as well, feeding information, seeking the killers, tracking the clones.

Nyquist couldn't hold it all in his head. He knew that DeRicci was trying. She hadn't slept much either, and he doubted she had left her office. Right now, she was the only real authority on the Moon. Several mayors were dead or incapacitated, and the ones that weren't were dealing with crises caused by all the dome explosions.

Even the mayors of the smaller cities were too busy to concern themselves with Moon government. So DeRicci had taken over. Or had slid into the role anyway, because *someone* had to be in charge, and she was acting like the person in charge, so people came to her with their problems.

Better her than him.

He was dealing with Palmette.

Without a partner.

Gumiela hadn't even insulted him by suggesting one. In fact, the day she had ordered him to take some time off, she had sideways apologized to him.

I'd partner you with someone, Bartholomew, she had said, *but you'd spend more time getting that person up to speed and then, I suspect, that person would hurt more than help.*

His long-time complaint. He had always done better alone.

He wondered what would have happened if Dispatch hadn't assigned Palmette to that crime scene four years ago. She'd probably still be on the force, and maybe, just maybe, this crisis never would have happened.

Or Armstrong would have been destroyed too, and no one would have had a lead.

He had to think that it made a difference, what he had done. He had to believe it. Because there were too many turning points otherwise.

What if Palmette hadn't come to the crime scene? What if he hadn't saved her life? What if he had stepped in after the trials to help her get her job back?

What if he had really cared about her instead of pretending that he did?

He shook his head. That was the tiredness talking. The tiredness and the frustration and the anger. He was furious at her, but he couldn't do anything about it—not directly. So some of that anger went inward.

He was doing his best to prevent that inward anger from becoming toxic.

So he was probing, every day, going deeper and deeper into Palmette's past, deeper into her psyche. He would know the color of her underwear on the day she graduated from the police academy by the time he was done.

Whenever he would get done.

Because they were all in it for the long haul now—him, the other detectives, DeRicci, the Earth Alliance. They had to find these people and whoever was running them around before another attack.

DeRicci believed there wouldn't be another attack, not soon. She had gotten the idea from Flint, and she said it was persuasive.

Nyquist hadn't listened to the rationale. He didn't want to know. He wanted to focus on Palmette only. He saw her as a pathway to the future, her knowledge as the key to the next part of this puzzle.

He also believed she didn't realize exactly how much she knew.

So he would pull it out of her one bit at a time, and he would pray there wouldn't be another attack in the meantime.

He reached the door to 65B. He paused. He was carrying two cups of coffee. One was plain, hot, and strong, for him. The other was filled with cinnamon and milk, masking the coffee taste.

Partners brought each other coffee in the morning as they got ready to face their day. It was a simple act, one he had never performed for any of his real partners.

He was pretending that Palmette was his partner now to get her to talk. He was aware of the irony.

He also knew that in the future, this simple action—carrying coffee to Palmette every single morning—would preclude him from ever doing it for a real partner, no matter how much he liked that person.

If Gumiela ever tried to partner him with anyone again.

He had strong arguments against it. And the rules had been destroyed along with nineteen domes across the Moon.

The old systems were gone, the new ones not developed yet.

And he wasn't the person who would develop them. He was the person who would make sure those new systems would remain in place for decades, centuries even. He would see to it that the bad guys, as DeRicci had taken to calling them, wouldn't win.

He balanced the coffees in the fingers of one hand, and used the other to open the door to room 65B. He didn't look at Palmette, not right away.

Instead he braced himself for another day of details, a daily grind that would eventually bring him to the answers he—and the Moon—so desperately needed.

The thrilling adventure continues with the second book
in the Anniversary Day Saga, *Blowback*.

The Moon, shaken by the Anniversary Day tragedies, deals with devastation. The Earth Alliance believes another attack imminent, but no one knows where or when it will strike. Just like no one knows who ordered the attacks in the first place.

The Moon's chief security office, Noelle DeRicci, does her best to hold the United Domes government together. But Retrieval Artist Miles Flint, dissatisfied with the investigation into the Anniversary Day events, begins an investigation of his own. He builds a coalition of shady operatives, off-the-books detectives, and his own daughter, Talia, in a race against time. A race, he quickly learns, that implicates organizations he trusts—and people he loves.

Turn the page for the first chapter of *Blowback*.

THREE YEARS AGO

1

DETECTIVE INIKO ZAGRANDO HURRIED THROUGH THE PORT IN VALHALLA Basin. He had his right hand up to show the bright gold badge on his palm. The badge blared *Police business! Move out of the way!* in that official genderless voice that seemed ubiquitous on Callisto. He dodged chairs outside of restaurants, passengers pausing to read menus, and the occasional alien, looking lost. A clump of passengers huddled near the ever-changing Departures sign—a sight unusual anywhere else, but common here. New non-sanctioned arrivals on Callisto often had their links automatically severed. Not only did it keep them in the dark, it made them feel helpless.

Aleyd Corporation, which ran and owned Valhalla Basin—all of Callisto, really—liked making people feel helpless.

Zagrando ran to the Earth Alliance departure wing, his breath coming harder than he expected. He was out of shape, despite the mandatory exercise requirements of the Valhalla Police Department. Apparently the damn requirements weren't as stringent as the idiots in charge of VPD seemed to think.

He wasn't dressed for this kind of run, either. He was wearing a suit coat, which had the benefit of hiding his laser pistol but was otherwise too hot and constricting, and brand-new shoes whose little nanoparticles had actually attached to his links and warned him to slow down or else the shoes would be ruined by incorrect use.

If he could shut off the shoe cacophony, he would. His links were giving him enough trouble without that.

Instructions had come from all sides: *Emergency at the port. Requesting street patrol backup and Detective Iniko Zagrando.* In all his years at the VPD—and that was more than he wanted to contemplate—he had never received a call like this, and certainly not at the port itself.

He was a *detective.* He investigated *after* the crime, not during the crime. And he certainly didn't get his hands dirty with an in-process emergency unless he happened to stumble on the scene.

Two security guards came out of nowhere to flank him and push away other passengers. The passengers emerging from the various departure wings stopped when they saw him, blinking in surprise and a bit of panic.

Welcome to Valhalla Basin, he thought. *It only goes downhill from here.*

But of course he didn't say anything. He couldn't even if he wanted to, he was breathing so damn hard. How had he let himself go like this? Of course, he knew the answer—misery caused a lot of problems. And because he didn't want to think about that, and because things *would* only go downhill from here for him as well, he commanded his VPD bio link to send him a surge of extra energy, something Aleyd happily provided all its public servants—in limited quantities, of course. No sense in having them overuse the energy and collapse in a heap that required massive hospitalization and weeks of recovery.

He had never used his before. Suddenly he felt like he could fly. He left the security guards in the dust.

Oh, man, would he pay for this.

Then he didn't think about it. He hit the Earth Alliance departure wing, and some port staff members used their arms to point the way as two more security guards found him.

With the staff members there, he realized that someone should have uploaded an illuminated map straight to his links. He should have seen his path outlined in red (for emergency, of course) over his vision, and he should have been able to follow it blindly. And he did mean *blindly.*

He should have been able to close his eyes and follow the backup voice instructions telling him how many steps to take and how far he had to go before turning a corner.

He didn't have an automated map and the port employees knew it. That was why they had shown up. Something was going very wrong.

Although he didn't know what that something could be. Emergency services links were always the last to shut down. Especially on Valhalla Basin, where Aleyd controlled everything and hated relinquishing that control.

Two more security guards joined him, faster guards, who managed to move passengers aside so that he didn't have to weave around them. He didn't have to weave around most of them now anyway.

Either the word had gotten out that he was running through the Earth Alliance wing or that there was some crisis here or maybe, just maybe, someone had actually augmented his emergency beacon so that the obnoxious genderless voice his badge was producing was blaring all over this part of the port.

Police business! Move out of the way!

Why the hell did the crisis have to happen in the middle of the biggest wing of the port, farthest from parking and the main entrance? Why the hell wasn't this thing built for easy access *behind* the scenes, where it was important?

He'd been in the back areas of this port, and it was a twisted maze of passages, tunnels, and viewing rooms that allowed him to spy on arrivals. It just didn't allow him— or anyone in port security—to get to those arrivals quickly.

Finally, he reached the part of the wing that his private message had directed him to. The arrivals area for Earth. This part of the port was festive, with blues, greens, and whites just like the Mother Planet herself. No sense surprising new arrivals from Earth with Callisto's odd coloring, courtesy of Jupiter, which loomed large over this—the second largest of her moons. No matter how much Valhalla Basin itself tried to look like an Earth city, it didn't even come close. It was too brown, too red, too uniform. No Earth city had a gigantic red ball looming over it.

Plus, the dome itself—with all its regulated light periods and dark periods—was too uniform, too predictable. Earth had winds and storms and blazing hot sunshine. Earth was about beauty and discomfort.

Valhalla Basin was about sameness.

Except today.

Just a few meters to go. Two more turns, if he remembered this section right, and he'd be in the holding area for suspect arrivals. He whipped around the first corner, and someone grabbed him around the waist.

He twisted, but someone else caught his right hand and pulled it down, pinning it to the arm holding him. Then a third someone put a hand over his mouth.

All three of the someones pulled him into a room he hadn't even known existed and slammed the door shut.

Then they let go of him.

"What the hell?!" he said as he turned around.

And stopped.

Three men stood behind him. He recognized only one of them, but that was the important one: Ike Jarvis, Zagrando's handler for the Earth Alliance Intelligence Service. Zagrando had been undercover with the Valhalla Basin Police for more than a decade.

"What's going on?" he asked, more calmly than he had a moment ago.

Jarvis took a step forward. He was smaller than the other two men he had brought with him, but not by much. They were brawny guys, probably enhanced for strength and muscle, but they were naturally tall.

Zagrando had been a good street fighter once upon a time, but he suspected those skills were as dormant as his running skills. No wonder these guys had taken him so easily.

"We have to get you out of here," Jarvis said. His gravelly voice had no hint of urgency, unlike his words.

"Am I blown?" Zagrando had no idea how it could have happened. He'd told very few people about his work with Earth Alliance Intelligence, and none recently.

The last person he had told had been a lawyer from Armstrong, on Earth's Moon. She represented a young girl whose mother had been kidnapped and who died as a result. The girl—Talia Shindo—had impressed Zagrando so much with her smarts and ability to operate under pressure that he had almost blown his cover with VPD to help her.

But he hadn't. Her mother's kidnappers had provided the best lead in his investigation of Aleyd. As he had told the attorney, his work came first.

Still, this moment caught him by surprise.

"No," Jarvis said.

"If I'm not blown, then what's going on?" he asked.

"We need you elsewhere," Jarvis said.

Zagrando shook his head. "I'm finally making progress after a decade in this sterile place, and you want to yank me out?"

"Your progress is why we're yanking you out. We can't do any more here—*you* can't do any more here—without letting Aleyd know that we're onto them." Jarvis had a little half-smile, almost a sneer, that he used when he was trying to smooth over something.

"Listen," Zagrando said, letting the urgency into his voice. "If I leave here for good, Aleyd will know that I was the one investigating them. People don't leave Valhalla Basin permanently without Aleyd's permission."

Jarvis's weird half-smile faded. He nodded his head, just once, in acknowledgement. "Believe it or not, I have always read your reports. I know how Aleyd works."

"Then you know that I can't leave," Zagrando said.

"You'll leave." Jarvis turned toward the back wall. One of the two men who had come with him touched the side wall, and a panel appeared. Zagrando had seen those before. They were tied to the security personnel at the port.

The man touched the panel and the back wall became grayish, but clear. The port's version of one-way glass. Whoever was in the next room couldn't see anyone in this room, but Zagrando, Jarvis, and the other two could see what was going on next to them.

And what was going on was a hell of a fight. A vicious fight, with lasers and knives of all things, and nearly a dozen people, many of them Black Fleet from their appearance.

In the middle of it all was Zagrando himself.

Zagrando's breath caught. The clothing was slightly off, and so was the body. It was a younger version of him, without the added weight and the gone-to-seed muscles. The other Zagrando fought like a demon, but he was outnumbered and alone.

Zagrando had no idea who these people were. Jarvis's assistant touched the panel again, and the side wall turned gray. Outside it, several street police officers mixed with security guards from the port and a couple of panicked administrators. They were all trying to get into that room, but something blocked them.

"They don't know we're here?" he asked Jarvis.

"They don't even know the room is here," Jarvis said. "Earth Alliance ports have extra rooms just for top secret Earth Alliance business. Without the rooms, the Earth Alliance doesn't sanction the port."

"Even with Aleyd?" Zagrando asked. He'd been around that corporation too long. Like everyone else on Valhalla Basin, he thought of Aleyd as unconquerable.

"Aleyd started as a small company in the Earth Alliance. They were nothing when they built this port. The rooms have been here twice as long as anyone has been on Callisto, and there is no record of them outside of the Alliance hierarchy. They don't know about us," Jarvis said. He hadn't taken his gaze off the fight.

"So those people are ours?" Zagrando asked, nodding toward the fight. He wasn't quite looking at it. It felt odd to watch that younger version of him somehow managing to stay on his feet, despite the cuts, slashes, and burns.

"Oh, no." Jarvis crossed his arms. "The only one in there who is ours is that fast-grow clone of yours."

Bile rose in Zagrando's throat. He had forgotten about all the DNA he had donated when he signed on with the Intelligence service. They were allowed to use it to heal him or to fast-grow a clone to get him out of a tight spot.

He swallowed hard, more shaken than he expected to be. "You're going to let him die."

"Yes." Jarvis watched as if he were seeing a flat vid and not an actual fight.

"Good God," Zagrando said, moving toward the window, actually looking at his clone. Strong, still surviving, fighting as hard as he could to live another few minutes. He was outnumbered, and his only weapon—a laser pistol that was a twin to Zagrando's—was on the floor by the door.

Outside the other door, the police and guards still struggled to get in. Zagrando knew they wouldn't, that the men in this room controlled that doorway, controlled that fight.

"We can't let this continue," Zagrando said.

Jarvis gave him a sideways look. "This is what he was designed for. Let him fulfill his mission."

"He has the brain of a three-year-old," Zagrando said. "He doesn't understand *mission*."

"He doesn't understand anything except fighting," Jarvis said. "That's what he was grown for, that's what he does. If you don't die today, then Aleyd will look for you forever."

"Let them look." Zagrando hurried the door, then stopped, and doubled back to the control panel. He peered at it. "How do I get in that room?"

"You don't," Jarvis said.

Zagrando shoved the assistant aside and hit the controls on the panel. Nothing happened. He used both his VPD clearance and his Earth Alliance clearance and still nothing happened.

"You can't do this," Zagrando said. "This is murder."

"I know how hard it is to see a replica of yourself go through this," Jarvis said in a tone that implied he didn't know, "but I have to beg to differ on the murder charge. Fast-grow clones are not human under the law, and if they are designed to die in an experiment or a mission, then their death is sanctioned. We filed all the necessary documents. His death is legal."

"Son of a bitch," Zagrando said, and launched himself at the door. But he couldn't get out. He tugged, pressed his identification against the door, gave the door some instructions through his links, and still he couldn't get out. Then he went to the window and pounded, thinking maybe he could get the attention of the police officers or the guards. But he couldn't. They continued their battle against their own door.

He realized at that moment that his links to the outside world were down. He hadn't heard any emergency notices nor could he send a message to them via his links. Plus the constant noise that Valhalla's government called "necessary maintenance" was gone.

"You can stop now," Jarvis said. "It no longer matters."

Zagrando whirled. His clone was in a fetal position on the floor, blood pooling around him. There was arterial spray on the far wall and on several of the fighters.

"You didn't give him any way to heal himself," Zagrando said.

"On the contrary," Jarvis said. "He has all the links you have except for the Earth Alliance identification and security clearances. He just doesn't know how to use them."

"Didn't know," the assistant said in a conversational tone.

Zagrando slammed the assistant against the control panel. "This is not something you should be discussing so easily."

The assistant didn't fight him. He let Zagrando hold him against the wall. Zagrando put his arms down and backed away. He had wanted that fight; they had known he had wanted that fight, and they hadn't given it to him.

"We have to leave now, Iniko," Jarvis said, his use of Zagrando's first name his only acknowledgement of Zagrando's distress. "We have to get out before they close down this part of the port."

"Oh, you don't have a secret room for that?" Zagrando snapped.

"Actually, we do have our own way out," Jarvis said. "And you're coming with us."

"And if I don't?" Zagrando asked.

Jarvis turned toward him, his expression flat. "You're already dead, Iniko. Which body those people out there find is your choice."

"I thought we worked together," Zagrando said.

"So did I," Jarvis said with that weird half-smile. "So did I."

The thrilling adventure continues with the second book
in the Anniversary Day Saga, *Blowback*,
available now from your favorite bookseller.

ABOUT THE AUTHOR

USA Today bestselling author Kristine Kathryn Rusch writes in almost every genre. Generally, she uses her real name (Rusch) for most of her writing. Under that name, she publishes bestselling science fiction and fantasy, award-winning mysteries, acclaimed mainstream fiction, controversial nonfiction, and the occasional romance. Her novels have made bestseller lists around the world and her short fiction has appeared in eighteen best of the year collections. She has won more than twenty-five awards for her fiction, including the Hugo, *Le Prix Imaginales,* the *Asimov's* Readers Choice award, and the *Ellery Queen Mystery Magazine* Readers Choice Award.

To keep up with everything she does, go to kriswrites.com. To track her many pen names and series, see their individual websites (krisnelscott.com, kristinegrayson.com, krisdelake.com, retrievalartist.com, divingintothewreck. com, fictionriver.com). She lives and occasionally sleeps in Oregon.